A PALE LIGHT IN THE **BLACK**

ALSO BY K. B. WAGERS

THE INDRANAN WAR TRILOGY
Behind the Throne
After the Crown
Beyond the Empire

THE FARIAN WAR TRILOGY
There Before the Chaos
Down Among the Dead

A PALE LIGHT IN THE BLACK

A NeoG NOVEL

K. B. WAGERS

HARPER Voyager

An Imprint of HarperCollins*Publishers*

A PALE LIGHT IN THE BLACK. Copyright © 2020 by Katy B. Wagers. All rights reserved. Printed in the United States of America. No part of this book may be used or reproduced in any manner whatsoever without written permission except in the case of brief quotations embodied in critical articles and reviews. For information, address HarperCollins Publishers, 195 Broadway, New York, NY 10007.

HarperCollins books may be purchased for educational, business, or sales promotional use. For information, please email the Special Markets Department at SPsales@harpercollins.com.

Harper Voyager and design are trademarks of HarperCollins Publishers LLC.

FIRST EDITION

Designed by Paula Russell Szafranski

Library of Congress Cataloging-in-Publication Data has been applied for.

ISBN 978-0-06-288778-8

20 21 22 23 24   LSC   10 9 8 7 6 5 4 3 2 1

For my nerds.

Thanks for always having my back.

It is the mission of the Near-Earth Orbital Guard to ensure the safety and security of the Sol system and the space around any additional planets that human beings call home.

The hardest part was the smiling.

Commander Rosa Martín Rivas pasted another smile onto her face as she wove through the crowds and headed for her ship at the far end of the hangar. She and the rest of the members of *Zuma's Ghost* had weathered the post-Games interviews with as much grace as a losing team could, answering question after question about how it felt to come within three points of beating Commander Carmichael's SEAL team without ever breaking expression.

That wasn't entirely true. Jenks had slipped once, muttering a curse and giving the reporter a flat look. Nika had smoothly stepped in and covered for his adopted sister, giving the volatile petty officer a chance to compose herself.

"Hey, Rosa?"

She stopped, letting Commander Stephan Yevchenko—leader of the NeoG headquarters' team *Honorable Intent*—catch up to her, ignoring the snide smiles from the naval personnel who passed by her. Yevchenko's people had made up the other half of their group for these Games. And though the Neos had all performed admirably, it had been Rosa who'd let everyone down.

The slender, brown-haired Neo stuck out a hand. "Next year, right?"

"We'll see." It was the best response she could come up with, and something of her mask must have slipped because Stephan didn't let go.

"It wasn't your fault," he said in a low voice. "Don't spend a year convincing yourself it was."

"Too late for that." The reply was out before she could stop it. Rosa muffled a curse when he smiled. Stephan was always good at getting people to say too much. "It's all good. See you at the prelims next year."

"Likely sooner," he said. "We've got a case building. I might need your help with it."

Rosa nodded, but didn't press. Stephan's work in Intel meant he'd tell her when he could and not a moment sooner. Instead she once again forced the smile she was really starting to hate and headed for the Interceptor ahead of her. The interior of *Zuma's Ghost* was dead quiet when she boarded, a far cry from the laughter and conversation that usually dominated the ship. Rosa pulled the hatch shut behind her.

"Take us home, Ma," she called up to the bridge.

"Roger that, Commander."

Rosa headed for the common area, taking in the downcast eyes and tight mouths of her crew. "All right, people." She spoke with a firmness she didn't quite feel, but if there was one thing she was good at, it was putting on a brave face for everyone else. "You've got the ride back to Jupiter to get it out of your systems. It's just the Games."

"We lost, Commander." Jenks's mismatched eyes weren't quite filled with tears, but there was a sheen to them and her jaw was set in a determined pout.

"I know. We don't lose out there, though, right? What are we?"

"The NeoG." The automatic reply echoed back from everyone, and this time Rosa's smile was genuine.

"That's right. Don't forget it."

T-MINUS FOUR MONTHS UNTIL PRELIM BOARDING GAMES

The battered ship drifted in perfect synchronicity with the asteroid as it passed across the face of Sol, for just a moment blotting out the G-type yellow dwarf almost five hundred million kilometers away.

Upon visual inspection, the ship appeared as dead as the asteroid, its gray surface pitted and dulled by years in the black. It was, or at least appeared to be, a shitty early-days system jumper made for long-haul flights from Earth to the Trappist-1 system.

The SJs had been made well before the days of wormhole tech and instantaneous travel. Their names were painfully incorrect, as they didn't jump anywhere but instead took the long, slow path thirty-nine light-years across the galaxy. Their inhabitants trusting that they'd go to sleep before launch and wake up a long way away from Earth on a brand-new planet.

Lieutenant Commander Nika Vagin watched as his little sister, Petty Officer First Class Altandai Khan of the Near-Earth Orbital Guard, put her hands on her hips and stared up at the ship from the asteroid's surface. "That's it. Ship 645v, aka *An Ordinary Star*. Launched on June 17, 2330. Carrying three hundred and fifty-three popsicles—"

"Jenks." He let the threat in her nickname carry over the coms.

"Sorry," she said with a grin, clearly unrepentant even through the dim glare of the star on her helmet. "Three hundred and fifty-three *people*."

She wasn't wrong about them being popsicles, though. These poor bastards froze themselves for nothing. The Voyager Company developed wormhole tech just before the last wave of transport ships left Earth. When they were sure it was going to work, Off-Earth sent in larger freighters via wormhole to scoop up the SJs and take them on to the Trappist system.

Correction: they picked up the ones they could find. Nika shuddered a little at the thought.

Some were destroyed by system failure or space debris and nothing was left but rubble floating in the black. And some had simply vanished into the great nothing—no signal, no trace. All told, there were still a few dozen registered vessels missing, and a double handful more unregistered ships carrying a few desperate families who hadn't realized or hadn't cared that there was one—and only one—company with the legal ability to ship humans off-world.

"I'm getting no life-sign readings at all," Nika said, staring up at the ship. "There had better be someone on that jumper. If there isn't and I hiked my ass halfway across this surface when we could have just called the station and had an Earth Security Cutter tow them in, I'm going to chew out someone's ass."

"Relax, Nik." Commander Rosa Martín's voice was crisp over the com. "There are people. Though the ones on ice are probably freezer burned and the ones who aren't have everything locked down so tight we can't see a single thing from out here."

"I still don't see why we couldn't have just used the EMUs straight from *Zuma's Ghost*."

"Because she's noisy on the radar," Jenks said, "and then I wouldn't get to do this." She took off running with that low-gravity bounce, did a handspring over an outcropping, and launched herself into the starlit blackness beyond.

Nika cursed, his ears ringing from Jenks's whoop and the laughter of the rest of the team as he followed her. His helmet display gave him the necessary trajectory, although he was sure his little sister had done it on nothing but faith.

He launched himself off the asteroid's surface, flying through the vacuum toward the mysterious ship. Jenks soared through space ahead of him, kicking in the thrusters on her EMU to slow her approach at the last second so that she made less noise than a piece of space debris when she hit the hull of the ship. The name was faded and pockmarked from dust impact but still read clearly AN ORDINARY STAR next to the door.

"This is an older model of SJ, Jenks." Ensign Nell Zika's cool voice came over the coms as the readings from Jenks's scan scrolled across her terminal back on their ship. "One of the last waves from 2330. It's registered, though, legal and everything. Huh—that's weird."

"What's weird, Sapphi?" Rosa asked the ensign. "Tamago and I just connected with the back end of this beast."

"We see you, Commander. Did you know that there were twenty-seven missing ships in total? And twenty of them were from the last wave?" Sapphi asked.

"I did *not* know that," Jenks replied. She didn't look up as Nika made contact with the ship next to her. "How many were in the last wave?"

"Only thirty," Sapphi replied. "The wormholes were the big news story and people wanted to wait and see what would happen with them."

"Yeah, I get that, but a sixty-seven percent loss for a single wave seems like a really high failure rate for Off-Earth Enterprises, and it was never in the news?"

"How do you know that?" Nika asked.

"I read the briefing."

Nika reached out and tapped the side of his sister's helmet once, hard enough to push her into the ship.

"Okay, maybe I read more than the briefing," she said. "It was interesting. People were flipping their sh—"

"Focus, Jenks, you had your fun. Time to work," Rosa ordered.

"That's on Sapphi, Commander. We're just hanging out in the middle of a deadly vacuum, waiting. Gotta do something to distract Nika here, or you know his noodle gets in a twist." She grinned at Nika's glare. She knew he hated space work and teased him about it mercilessly every chance she got.

But, in a way, she had a point—what fool pursued a career with an Interceptor crew when they were terrified of being out in space?

You. You're the fool, he thought.

"Give me two hundred seconds and you'll be in." Sapphi's voice was soothing on the com.

The timer in the corner of Nika's vision started ticking down as the ensign turned her brilliance toward the lock on the outside of the ship.

"Nika, if things go sideways in there you grab Jenks and get the fuck out, copy?" Rosa's order came straight to him rather than broadcast on the team channel.

"You expecting trouble?" He turned in toward the ship so Jenks couldn't spot his lips moving. His little sister had an amazing ability to read lips that she exploited mercilessly.

"Something feels off. I know Off-Earth wants any SJs recovered intact and there may be live passengers on board—though you and I know the odds that anyone on ice for as long as these folks have been not having freezer burn is atom small—but why would someone be hanging out in the belt with a derelict ship? I don't like it, and regardless of what Off-Earth wants, I'll blow that ship to pieces before I risk living, breathing people on a piece of space junk."

"I thought you wanted to space Jenks yesterday." He couldn't resist the tease, and Rosa chuckled.

"That's a daily occurrence, but I know you'd miss her, so I let her keep breathing."

"Eh, today you're right." Nika smiled as Jenks continued to worry over the problem of the ratios on a sixty-seven percent failure rate for a launch. "Intel said one, maybe two pirates and no more than five for a boat this size. I think they may actually be right—the ship's not big enough to handle a crew of more than five, and I doubt they'd expend that much personnel on something like this. Jenks and I will handle the front end. But yes, if things go wrong we'll double-time it out. Hand to Saint Ivan."

"From your lips to God's ears. Be careful in there."

"Same to you, Commander."

"Will do."

The airlock opened. Jenks looked at Nika with a smile. "You got my back?" she asked, thumping her chest twice with a gloved fist.

He grinned, swinging his own arm out, tapping the back of his fist against hers before grabbing her forearm and leaning in to bump their helmets together. "You've got mine."

"Let's do this."

The pair slipped into the airlock and pulled it shut behind them. As he watched the numbers cycle, Nika debated whether they should take their helmets off. If they did, leaving them here in the airlock would be safest, but it also meant they'd have to get back to this spot in order to get off the ship.

"We've got air. This can's been refilled," Jenks said. "There's definitely someone walking around in here. Helmets off, Nik?"

The fact that she even asked him meant Jenks was already

in battle mode—focused, unassailable. She'd keep with the jokes, but she'd do what he told her without question.

"Yeah, take it off. We'll stash them here." He hit the release on his own and pulled the dome loose. He shoved it into a spot behind the old suits hanging in the airlock, surprised they didn't crumble to dust when he touched them.

"I wish Off-Earth would hurry it up with those new prototypes. I'm tired of lugging this thing around." Jenks set her helmet next to his and tugged her skullcap off, revealing the bright shock of orange hair running down the center of her head.

"I'm as excited about a helmet that folds into our suits as you are, but I saw those failure tests," Nik replied. "I'd rather they take their time and make sure they figure out what the heck happened with the seals so we don't die out there. Speaking of not dying . . ." He jabbed a finger at the door behind them.

"Come on, Nik, live a little." She winked her blue eye at him and reached over her shoulder. The magnetic clamps released the moment Jenks's palm touched the sensor, the microsheath flowing away from the tip and down into the hilt.

Guns on spaceships were bad news, and no one yet had the lock on a reliable handheld laser weapon, a fact that Jenks regularly bemoaned even though she was more likely to settle something with fists than with her sword anyway.

The matte black blades of the NeoG weapons were ten centimeters at the widest point and thirty-five centimeters long, with the handle making it an even fifty. A wicked-looking hook curved back toward the hilt a handful of centimeters from the end point.

Nika's favorite trick with that during the competition fights was to hook his opponent's sword and send it flying. In real combat, though, it was equally effective in making folks more concerned about keeping their guts in than fighting him.

Jenks preferred to slap people with the flat of her blade,

which Nika felt was an accurate representation of how each of them approached the world. Jenks would kill if there was a need, but she didn't like it and avoided it right up to the line of endangering her own life.

He hoped neither one of them had to put their philosophies to the test today.

"Tamago and I are on board," Rosa said.

"Copy that, we are proceeding forward," Nika replied, and then turned off his com with a thought. "Jenks?"

She paused at his call, hand hovering over the entrance panel. "What's up?"

"Be careful in there."

"You think it's going to turn into a muck?"

Nika shrugged and reached back to pull his own sword. "It might."

"Can do, then." She blinked twice. "Readings inside are showing three life signs in the front section, two more in the back end by the commander." She highlighted their locations on the shared map. "Front two are just off the engine room and one up on the bridge. The ones in the back are with the pop—uh—people."

"I see them, Jenks," Rosa said. "We'll deal with these two, you and Nika take the trio."

Jenks looked at Nika, one eyebrow raised. The question—*How do you want to do this?*—was floating unsaid on the air. Nika gestured at the door and Jenks opened it.

It was a risk either way, because the commander would kill him if they split up. He'd put either of them in a two-on-one fight, but he also knew it was dangerous odds. Anything could go wrong. But if he and Jenks stayed together and went for engineering first, the one on the bridge could vent the ship if they heard a commotion.

Or engineering could blow the ship if they thought something was up.

He hated this. Snap decisions weren't his forte. Too many things to sort through, too many things that could go wrong. It paralyzed him every damn time, no matter how hard he worked on it. *You are a hell of an officer, Vagin,* he thought bitterly.

"You want an opinion?" There was no sympathy in Jenks's question, something he was always grateful for from her. She continued at his nod. "Let's do the bridge first. We'll take whoever it is out, and I can convince them to call one or both up from engineering. We'll just ambush them on the way. The odds that engineering will blow the ship are only slightly greater than zero. Survival instinct is strong no matter what is going on here."

"You really should have gone to the academy, Jenks."

"Pfft." She rolled her eyes. "I'd be trash as an officer and we both know it. You're the smarter one. I just know how to sneak up on people." Jenks tapped the panel and slipped through the door as it opened.

Nika knew it was more than that, but Jenks was right about the sneaking up on people.

That's how he'd met his adopted sister, when he'd been twenty-three, home on leave to deal with the remnants of his grandmother's life. Jenks had been a fifteen-year-old street dweller his dear grandmother had taken in and neglected to tell him about. Which meant their first meeting had been her thinking he'd broken into his late grandmother's house and trying to brain him with a frying pan.

She'd survived the streets of Krasnodar for eight years, and according to the letter written in his grandmother's shaky hand, she'd been living with her for close to three months.

That day, standing in his *baba's* kitchen staring down into the girl's wide eyes—one blue, one brown—Nika could hear his grandmother's voice. *"We take in the strays, Nika, and there's nothing wrong with it as long as you open your heart to the hurt that will come. Because you can't save them all—but some is better than none. Just don't lose yourself in the process like your mother did, you understand?"*

And that was how a brand-new ensign in the Near-Earth Orbital Guard had offered a fifteen-year-old girl a permanent place in his family and somehow managed to raise her through his first years in the NeoG without killing both of them.

He'd done something right in the end. Jenks could have split at any point, but not only had she decided to stay, she also fell in love with NeoG and enlisted the morning of her seventeenth birthday.

"Hey."

Nika jumped when Jenks tapped him on the chest, blinking dry eyes and swearing under his breath. "Sorry, took a trip."

"And Commander tells me to focus." She grinned at him. "Let's move."

The interior of the ship was as dingy as the outside and looked like it had been out in space for a hundred years without anyone tending to it. But there were a few signs of recent repairs, opened panels and up-to-date wiring Nika had to prod Jenks past so she didn't stop to inspect it.

"Sapphi, can we get some schematics?" Nika asked. He could practically hear Jenks roll her eyes from in front of him.

"The bridge is this way, I could see it as we came in," she protested.

"Here you go, Nika," Sapphi replied, and the layout of the tiny ship came to life in front of his eyes. The HUD in their helmets was excellent tech, but there was still that image-on-screen bit that couldn't quite beat how the DD chip displayed the images directly onto your retinas, making everything meld seamlessly with the world around you.

Dànǎo Dynamics, the consolidation of the shattered tech companies of the east and west, had developed the DD chip as a way to circumvent the wastefulness of their predecessors. The unprecedented organic cybernetics were the first of their kind post-Collapse and still unmatched in their simplicity hundreds of years later.

Nika had a hard time imagining life without it.

"One time. I take one wrong turn and you all never let me hear the end of it," Jenks was muttering to herself as she crept down the hallway. "Besides, we were on solid ground. Have I ever gotten lost on a ship?"

"You have not." Master Chief Ma Léi's deadpan voice came over the coms. "However, that one time on ground you nearly killed us all so, yes, you'll keep hearing about it."

Jenks said something under her breath too fast for the translation software to catch, but Nika had put enough effort into learning her native Khalkha Mongolian to be sure it didn't need to be repeated for the master chief's benefit.

"Jenks, up and to the left," he said, before anyone else could ask.

They followed the corridor to the open bridge door. Jenks peeked in, looked back at Nika, and held up a single finger that she pointed to the left before pointing at herself.

One man. On the left. I'll take him.

Nika nodded and Jenks slipped in through the door. He shifted his grip on his sword and scanned the corridor as a voice echoed from inside, then he followed her in.

"Boson, are you and Hobbs about done with the engine? The longer we hang out here the better the odds get that the cops are going to show."

"Those odds just went through the roof," Jenks said. She had her sword up and under the man's chin before he could even twitch toward the console. "Hi. I wouldn't. Prison's not great, but it's better than being dead."

The man swallowed.

Nika leaned in on his other side. "What's your name?"

"Shaw."

"Listen up, Shaw. I want you to get on the com and have Boson and Hobbs come on up to the bridge. If you so much as hint there's something going on, you're going to have one last bad day. Understand?"

"Yes."

"Do it."

The man's hand shook as he reached slowly for the console, his eyes locked on Jenks's down the length of her sword. "Hey, guys? Will you come up here for a minute?"

"What happened to 'get this shit done now'?"

"Don't argue. You need to see this."

There was an exasperated sigh from the other end of the com and then silence.

Nika tapped Shaw's hand away from the console and the man put it back in his lap. "Was that a yes?"

"Hobbs is short-tempered, but he'll be up."

Jenks leaned and frisked Shaw, raising an eyebrow at the gun she pulled free. "On a spaceship? You trying to kill yourself?"

Shaw swallowed. "It's necessary insurance."

"Right." She shared a look with Nika before turning her back on Shaw and poking at the console. "Your routing computer says you came from Trappist-1e? But the records say this boat never made it there. Now you're back here. That's a long way off target for this jumper, Shaw, and too far for you to fly on your own. What were you doing out there? Where are you headed? Why come all the way back here first?"

Nika kept an eye on the door as Jenks continued to poke through the ship's systems and peppered Shaw with questions, the man getting more and more anxious as the seconds ticked away.

Then her tone changed. "There's no people. Commander, the computer says there are no people on this ship."

"I'm seeing that, Jenks," Rosa replied over the com. "Our targets are secure. Tamago is questioning them."

Shaw froze when Jenks turned her gaze toward him. "Where are the people who are supposed to be on this ship?"

"I don't know what you're talking about, we just salvaged this."

"Oh fuck off."

"Jenks," Nika said.

Shaw cleared his throat. "Look. You've stumbled into trouble beyond recall. You can't run far enough away from this. I could give the lot of you more money to just walk away right now—more than you'll see in your entire military career. You don't know what you're messing with, our employers are—"

Jenks moved like a snake, flipping her sword over and bashing the guy in the temple hard enough to make him slump over, unconscious.

"What?" she said at Nika's look. "He was being annoying. Let's get him cuffed and go wait for the other two." She glanced back at the computer. "There's some other stuff here but it's coded. Hey, Sapphi, I'm uploading this to my DD chip."

"Got it," Sapphi replied. "My uncle always says double backups are best."

"All right—let's get the rest of these guys in custody and call it a day."

"Jenks . . ."

"What?"

"He had a gun," Nika said, grabbing his little sister by the back of the neck and tapping his forehead to hers. "The others might also. Be careful."

"Always." Her smile was quick. "Either side of the door. I'll let the first one through for you to deal with and take the second."

He could hear the footsteps and voices echoing up the corridor and released Jenks with a nod. "Deal." He backed up to the other side of the door and took a deep breath, holding it.

The first man stepped through. He was half the size of the hulking bear of a man behind him, but there wasn't time to change the plan. Nika muttered a curse under his breath as Jenks grinned.

"Near-Earth Orbital Guard! Stop right there and put your hands behind your head," he ordered.

The one in front put his hands up. He was a short, nervous-looking man with pale features, and Nika grabbed him by the collar of his dirty jumpsuit.

Jenks didn't have the same luck.

He heard her swear as the big guy spun on his heel and ran. Tamping down the desire to follow, Nika cuffed the first man, reciting his rights as he did. "What's your name? You going to give me any trouble?"

"Boson, and no." He shook his head. "Dead men don't give trouble."

For some odd reason, that made Nika think of his father and he laughed. "You'd be surprised. My old man caused us trouble long after he drank himself to death." He put Boson against the wall. "You sit here and don't move."

He grabbed his sword and sprinted into the hallway, just in time to see Jenks shoulder-check the other salvager in the back. The man flew forward, landing hard on the grated floor of the corridor.

"Stay down." She stepped on the man's back and put her sword against his neck. "I am Petty Officer Altandai Khan of the Near-Earth Orbital Guard and you are in violation of the Earth Space Treaty of 2195. The charges are human smuggling, illegal salvage, and resisting arrest." She smiled down at him. "Have a nice day."

"PACK IT UP AND STOW IT. NICE RUN, PEOPLE." ROSA TAPPED A fist on the concentric circle shield of the NeoG that was painted on the interior of the ship. "We'll debrief at zero seven hundred tomorrow, but I want your reports ready before the meeting. Before, as in prior to my ass standing in front of you at zero seven hundred. I'm looking at you, Jenks."

"Commander." Jenks spread her hands wide with a grin. "Why you always gotta call me out?"

"Because you sent me a file last time with nothing but 'That mission sucked' written in it four hundred times and some ancient-ass memes," Rosa countered. Jenks was an excellent Neo, but her obsession with the twenty-first century didn't always translate well into official reports. "Get yourselves some dinner."

"It did suck," Jenks muttered, dodging Nika's swing and racing for the door. She'd somehow timed it so the pressure lock released just as she hit it and jumped down onto the deck of the Jupiter Station docking bay with her robotic dog, Doge, trundling along at her heels.

Rosa kept from sighing, instead nodding to Sapphi and Tamago as the pair exited the ship, and glanced back into the cockpit. "You good, Ma?"

"I've got it. I'll do a pass on my way out, don't wait for me." Ma waved a hand without looking away from the readouts scrolling in front of his eyes.

"Don't stay too long," Rosa ordered, and the master chief grunted an assent that was the closest to an agreement she'd get. She shouldered her bag and swung out of the side door of *Zuma's Ghost*, patting the sleek white ship as her boots hit the deck. "Thanks for bringing us home, girl."

Rosa switched off her Babel as she crossed the massive expanse of the NeoG's docking bay. The shouting around her devolved into a mix of languages without the benefit of the translation tech embedded alongside her cochlear nerve. She preferred the somewhat scattered nature of the talking. The bulk of it was Mandarin; she'd never quite picked up the language despite repeated efforts to learn, but the rhythm of it was soothing and the lack of knowledge on her part meant her brain didn't attempt to do any work to understand it.

She could hear bits of her native Spanish as well as English peppered among the conversations. It was a wonder how such a simple thing as the Babel had brought humanity closer together in the aftermath of near extinction. The Collapse was a distant memory lost to over three hundred years of history, although kept alive by scholars and people like Jenks, who was mostly fascinated by the beginning of the twenty-first century rather than the bloodier end of it.

They'd survived it, somehow. Whenever Coalition politicians were feeling particularly nostalgic they'd go on about how humanity put aside their differences, pulled together, and saved not only themselves but the planet before stepping out into the blackness of space.

She was sure the reality was vastly different from the story they spun.

Rosa automatically reached for the pendant tucked beneath her thermal undershirt, fingers rubbing the worn disc as she murmured the litany of her childhood. "We are protectors of the Earth, and it is our duty to keep her and stay upon her always." The irony of it wasn't lost on her, but Rosa was willing to carry the shame that her family meant more to her than her faith and she would do her duty for them.

Even if it meant going off-world.

The pinging of incoming messages echoed in her head as her DD chip connected with the station's network. They'd been on patrol for nine days on *Zuma*, waiting for a sign of that ship in the asteroid belt, and the connection was too spotty filtered through the Interceptor ship to waste on personal messages. Now that she was back, the accumulated news started pouring in.

Rosa quickened her pace, weaving in and out of the crowd and slipping into the low-g corridor that led to the Interceptor team quarters. Her team's common room was predictably empty, and equally predictably a disaster of hastily tossed gear, as the others had dumped their stuff and headed for the bar.

She stepped over Jenks's duffel with a laugh. She didn't blame her crew in the least and would make her way to join them as soon as her call was done.

Tossing her bag onto the narrow bed in her room, Rosa

grabbed the tablet from the docking station and tapped in her code, checking the time sync with Earth.

"Coms, Sullivan here—hey, Commander, welcome back."

"Hey, Sully, put me through to home, will you?"

"Can do." Ernie Sullivan grinned at her. "You made it back under the wire, didn't you?"

"Just. But I had to—you know Gloria wouldn't forgive me if I was late calling on her birthday." Rosa shook her head. "Anyway, thanks for holding a line open for me."

"You know I'd do anything for Gloria, but it's been quiet and there's not a lot of outgoing coms right now, so it was no trouble. Tell her happy birthday for me," they replied. "Vidcom is live and ringing on the other end. Have a good night, Commander."

"Thanks, Sully, you too." Rosa blinked away the surprising tears that had crept into her eyes as the screen flickered and her wife's face appeared. "Hey, baby."

Angela Martín's dimples were peeking out from her round cheeks as she attempted to keep from smiling. "You were cutting that close."

"We just got back, but it was never in doubt. How's the birthday girl?"

"Bouncing around the house. Mama is trying to keep her out of the pile of presents. Here, talk to your mother for a moment." The camera Earth-side fuzzed a little as Angela moved through the sunlit house and handed the tablet off. "Gloria, your mama is calling all the way from Jupiter!" she called from off-screen.

"Rosa." Inez Martín's face appeared, smiling brightly at her daughter. "You're not getting enough sleep."

"I sleep fine, Mama. How are you?"

"Missing you every day you are not on God's green earth."

Rosa suppressed a smile and a sigh. "I'll be back soon for the prelims."

"It will have to be enough." Inez glanced over her shoulder.

"I have been taking Gloria to church as I promised. I keep hoping Angela and Isobelle will join us, but they do not."

"I hope you're not pushing. We talked about this."

"A mother's hope springs." Inez smiled as the noise level grew. "God watch over you in the black, my darling daughter. I love you."

"I love you, too."

"Mama!" A whirlwind of dark curls launched herself into the picture.

"My baby girl, how are you?"

"I am eight. Finally!"

Rosa laughed. "Yes, yes you are. Happy birthday, my darling."

"Did you send me a moon rock for my birthday?"

"I haven't been anywhere near the moon, but I did send you a present. Go ask Grandma Sia for the box with the gold stars."

"I miss you," Angela murmured as Gloria ran off shouting at the top of her lungs. "Iso said to tell you hi, but she had work so she had to run."

"Tell her I love her and I got her email the other day." Their oldest daughter was better at writing than these face-to-face talks, so Rosa didn't push her too much. "I miss you, too." She reached a hand out, tracing her wife's face with a fingertip. "We'll be home in a few months for the prelims."

"I know . . . it's just hard."

"It is. But we agreed it was worth it. There's not much longer. I do the full forty and it's permanent benefits. That means LifeEx treatments, not just for me and you but for Isobelle and Gloria."

"I know." Angela forced a smile, though her brown eyes were heavy with sadness. "Doesn't make the nights any easier."

"It doesn't, but it's only temporary."

"Don't mind me, I'm just being maudlin."

"I love you."

"I love you, too," Angela whispered.

"Mama!" Gloria came back into the room holding a package almost bigger than her. Her mothers hastily wiped away their tears, then Angela bent over to help her rip the paper away.

Her daughter's squeals of excitement were all Rosa needed. For that sound she would move the universe itself.

T-MINUS FIFTEEN WEEKS UNTIL
PRELIM BOARDING GAMES

"Max, just call them."

Lieutenant Maxine Carmichael gave her oldest sister a flat look over the vid-com. "No, Ri, not this time. I've spent my whole life apologizing. For not being good enough. For not being Carmichael enough. I'm not the one in the wrong here. I just didn't do what Mom and Dad wanted." There was a weight in her chest that wouldn't go away even in the face of her defiance, and Max wondered if this was what she would be stuck fighting her whole life. Caught between what she wanted and her family's endless dynasty.

It wasn't her. She wanted more than a life trapped on Earth, or freezing in the shadow of her parents' influence, never quite sure if her promotion had been because of her accomplishments or because of her family. She'd wanted the NeoG since she was a child, and nothing—not her brother's abandonment, not begging or bribery or even threats from her parents—had changed that.

"Max—"

"Last thing Dad said was pretty clear on that front. 'Bad enough you refused the Navy, Maxine—which I'm sure you did just to get back at me for some unknown insult of your childhood. But if you take this Interceptor course, don't bother calling again.'" The imitation of her father's voice was dripping with bitterness and Max spread her hands wide. "So here I am, headed for Jupiter to join my Interceptor crew, and that's that. I won't bother calling them again."

Ria Carmichael, newest president and CEO of LifeEx Industries, sighed. Her youngest sister was as stubborn as their mother, a fact Ria was sure drove both Rear Admiral Dr. Josiah Carmichael and Admiral Susanna Carmichael completely crazy. What Max didn't realize was that all of the admirals Carmichaels' ultimatums came from trying to keep their baby safe.

Not that Ria agreed with them.

Youngest child though she might be, Max was twenty-three years old and newly graduated from the NeoG's Interceptor course. She was an adult, and their parents' issues notwithstanding, she would be good at her new job. Ria had investigated and found that *Zuma's Ghost* was the best crew out there. So she'd pulled some strings—without telling her sister, of course; she didn't want that ire targeted at her—and gotten her assigned to *Zuma*. Rosa Martín was a solid, no-nonsense commander and got the job done. Max would be in good hands.

Even better than that, something told Ria that Max would find a home with the Interceptors. Her baby sister had always been different—quiet, serious to a fault, uninterested in the military trappings of the Navy that were their family's history or the hustling pressure of the family business. She'd done well at NeoG headquarters, but she didn't want to be stuck on Earth.

Ria knew that was part of the issue. Max hadn't joined the Coalition of Human Nations Navy because she wanted a chance to stand out on her own. And she hadn't gone into the business because life behind a desk at LifeEx wasn't for her.

Max had always wanted something more, so she'd joined

the NeoG instead. Of course, she'd mysteriously ended up with a desk job anyway despite her excellent record at the academy. Ria couldn't prove it, but she knew that their parents had been involved somehow—she'd been front and center for enough of their manipulations to know what they looked like.

Instead, their parents' attempt to keep their youngest child safe had backfired—*and how*—when Max had left her cushy job at headquarters and signed up for the Interceptor course. Because she was a Carmichael, or perhaps in this case despite it, she'd earned her right to fly with the best the NeoG had to offer.

Ria could sympathize with their parents, again without ever breathing a word of it to Max. They were shit at showing it, but they did love their children. At least as much as possible for two people who lived for their jobs and very little else. Interceptor crews frequently went into dangerous situations, and she'd be lying if that didn't make her worry about her baby sister.

Ria sighed. "I know. They do love you. Don't forget that. They messed up. They'll come around and admit it. Congrats again on your graduation and your posting. Stay safe for me, okay?" She put her hand up on the lens.

Max smiled, touching her hand to the same spot as her sister's, pretending she could feel the warmth of Ria's hand even though they were almost six hundred million kilometers apart. "You too. I'll send a message once I get settled. Love you."

"Love you, too."

Max sank back in her seat and tried to ignore both the jumping of her stomach as Jupiter grew larger in her window and the moisture gathering in her eyes. "Damn it." She swiped away the tear that slipped free and pushed to her feet to pace the private room the ship's captain had insisted she take. "Suck it up, Carmichael."

She'd busted her ass for this. Defied her parents not once but twice—first by going to the Near-Earth Orbital Guard

Academy and a second time by applying for the Interceptor program. Max wanted to be in space, saving lives, making a difference.

Of course, her mother's response to that had been "What, do you think we don't make a difference here? We're explorers, Maxine. We keep humanity safe."

Max sighed. It was always so damned difficult with her parents. It was always you were either with the family or against it, and so many times Max had found herself on the against side.

Ria and Pax were the only two siblings she still spoke to, and they were both so busy with their jobs it was hard to find the time. Maggie was old enough that she'd graduated from the academy shortly after Max was born, and all she had were vague memories of her older sister at the rare holiday gathering when everyone was in the same solar system.

In fact, the last time she'd seen Maggie had been that extremely public family blowout in a restaurant on Earth. Max had thought the public setting would protect her when she announced her intention to go to the NeoG Academy.

It hadn't.

Instead her siblings had sided with her parents and her parents in turn had abandoned Max on Earth. "If you want to be an adult so badly, Maxine, you can start now." Her father's calm announcement had happened after everyone else had left.

Max felt a tiny, familiar pang of hurt at the thought of Scott. Once upon a time she'd been close to her brother, idolized him despite the ten-year difference in their ages. But then he'd gone to the Naval Academy just after her eighth birthday and she hadn't heard from him again except for his occasional visits when their ships happened to be in the same area. And those had been stilted and formal, a hurt she couldn't untangle from all the other sharp wires of her childhood.

"Suck it up, Carmichael," she ordered a second time, shaking her head and blinking away the remaining tears. "You wanted this, you're going to do it, and damn them for trying to stop you. You're going to be on *Zuma's Ghost*, the best Interceptor team there is. For once, they can apologize for being wrong."

The door chimed and Max scrubbed at her face before saying, "Come in."

The young woman who came through had wide eyes so pale a blue they were almost clear and a frame of silver hair haloing her heart-shaped face. "Lieutenant Carmichael, we're coming up on Jupiter Station and Captain Banner thought you'd like to see the approach from the bridge."

"I would, thank you." Max grabbed one bag and slung it over her shoulder, hefting the other with her left hand. "We ate dinner together the other night—it was Ada, right?"

"Yes," The woman grinned. "Don't often see officers hitching rides with us, and the ones that do stay in their cabins rather than eat with us dirty space haulers. You'll be talked about for a while, Lieutenant."

"Max."

Ada shook her head. "The captain would space my ass, excuse the expression. You're a lieutenant with the Near-Earth Orbital Guard, I'll give you the respect you're due." She dropped one eyelid down in an exaggerated wink. "Besides, we like you NeoG a lot better than those naval types. They're a bit full of themselves. Flying around in their fancy ships doing nothing at all. Not like they've got aliens to fight, eh?"

Max fought to keep a straight face. On the one hand, she supposed she should defend the CHNN out of a sense of professional solidarity. On the other, the thought of how scandalized her mother would be made her want to laugh out loud.

It wasn't that space exploration wasn't important and that task had fallen to the Navy out of tradition more than anything.

Max was just reasonably sure sometimes Navy personnel took themselves and their mission to "protect humanity and explore the stars" more seriously than necessary.

This was why she'd taken a room on this freighter headed for Jupiter Station instead of waiting two days for the regular naval transit. There was less fuss, fewer people fawning over her name. She could just be herself here.

Plus, no one makes fun of the NeoG on a freighter when they all know who would come running to save their asses if something happened—which, in space, wasn't out of the realm of possibility.

Max chatted with Ada as they headed through the dimly lit but well-kept corridors of the freighter *G's Panic*. Captain Evie Banner didn't tolerate grime on her ship, of either the material *or* the personnel sort, and so the white walls gleamed under the cool white lights.

Maybe I'll do this next. Me piloting a freighter, Max thought. *Wouldn't that burn Dad's thrusters?*

She stifled another laugh as the door to the bridge slid open, and Max followed Ada through. "Lieutenant Carmichael as requested, Captain!"

"Thank you, Ada." Captain Banner looked up from the console she was bent over and smiled. The crow's feet at her eyes and the corners of her mouth were only starting to make an appearance, even though she was well into her eighty-second Sol year, thanks to LifeEx.

Max knew it was Banner's prior NeoG service that had afforded the woman the life-extending gene hack and telomere protection that made space travel possible, as well as the necessary follow-up treatments that were required every ten Sol years to keep the hack from shutting down. Max had technically been X'd because of her parents' military service, but the Carmichael family could have easily afforded the expensive treatment without the benefit of signing a portion of that extended life away to the military or some other form of service to the Coalition government.

Of course, her great-grandfather had developed the damn serum in the first place. Though she thought it was particularly inspired of him to make family members choose service to either the company or the government as a requirement for getting any part of their inheritance, even if it had been born of guilt over the decision to charge for the serum. Duty was paramount for the Carmichaels.

It was just supposed to be the *right* kind of duty.

"I'll leave you in the captain's capable hands."

Max smiled at Ada. "Thank you so much. I hope to see you again."

"Count on it." Ada nodded to Max and then at Captain Banner before she sauntered out of the bridge.

"Part of me thinks I should apologize for my crew," Evie said, giving Max a look. "But another part says you don't seem to mind the familiarity at all."

"I had enough formality growing up," Max replied, her eyes glued to the front of the bridge as Jupiter grew steadily larger on the massive curved screen.

The station was a speck comparatively, settled at the Lagrange point between Jupiter and its largest moon, Ganymede. The station was pulled along in Ganymede's wake as the moon made its seven-day orbit around the massive gas giant. As they closed the distance, the gleaming gray of the station was visible against Jupiter's rusty backdrop. It was a paradoxical visual. The station itself was massive, a giant structure with a pair of mushroom-shaped towers attached to a long central column with the hangar bays on the opposite end. The smaller tower was for H3nergy personnel and civilians; the other for CHN military members.

Max had seen the station only once before, when her mother's ship had stopped on a circuit while doing a border loop. Max had been ten and restricted to quarters with Pax rather than allowed to explore ("slum it," as her mother put it).

"There are only H3 miners and Orbital Guard," her mother had said in the same tone of voice she'd used for talking about dirty socks and unruly children.

"I'm right where I belong," she murmured, and then flashed an embarrassed grin at Evie when she realized she'd said it out loud.

"You'll do well with the NeoG, then, Max. They're not big on formality." Evie chuckled. "Headquarters skews closer to the other forces, but out here in the belt? It's a whole other world."

As if to prove her point, the chime signaling an incoming com sounded.

"Docking control, Captain."

"Put it on-screen."

"Freighter *G's Panic,* you are two days early."

Max's DD chip gave a little ping as it tagged the handshake from the woman who appeared on the screen in front of her with the helpful details of her public profile: rank or title/name/pronouns.

Jupiter Station's director of orbital traffic, Farah Totah, she/her, had hair as black as the liquid sloshing over the rim of the mug she was waving in the air. Unlike the liquid, her hair stuck up in wild abandon around her head.

"Nice to see you, too, Farah. We had an engine tune-up and I wanted to test her out. I've got a load of perishables for the station. You're welcome." Evie jerked a thumb in Max's direction. "Also, a passenger—Lieutenant Maxine Carmichael—for Admiral Hoboins."

Farah raised an eyebrow. "New Interceptor?"

Max gave a quick nod. "Yes."

"Farah Totah, director of orbital traffic for Jupiter, like it says on the tag." Farah smiled. "It's nice to meet you, Lieutenant. We've been expecting you, though not via freighter, I'll admit. Welcome to the station. I'll have someone let Vice Admiral Hoboins know; since you're early he'll want to send a person down to collect you." Her gaze flicked back to the captain before Max could think of a response. "Park that beast of yours in bay seventy-six, Evie—you owe me dinner and forty feds."

Evie grinned. "I was hoping you hadn't heard the news all the way out here."

"Are you kidding me? We watched it. Granted it was two days after, but I sat right in this chair and saw the slaughter. Company HQ even cleared us for booze as long as the admiral approved it, which he did." Farah pointed at Evie. "I'll see you later, Captain."

The screen blacked out.

"I will space the first person who laughs." Evie's warning did absolutely nothing to stem the tide of laughter that filled the bridge. She turned to Max, who was looking at her quizzically. Evie shrugged. "I have a notoriously bad streak of betting on the Zero-G fútbol games, but I really thought the Belize Hippos were going to win the championship this year." She sighed and threw a mock glare around the bridge. "Oh well, if it's only feds and dinner with Farah, that's more than enough to make up for the loss. Take us in, Boots."

"Docking bay seventy-six, Captain."

"GLORIA LOVED HER PRESENT, HUH?"

Rosa laughed as she swung out into the tube and pushed off. "She was ecstatic. A 'real' jet pack just like Mommy's. Angela messaged me at some point in the night with a photo of her passed out in her bed still wearing it." She caught the rung and easily landed in the corridor opening. "So it was worth every extra vacation day Jenks conned out of me."

"Ma and I triple-checked all the wiring to make sure it wasn't going to do anything more than light up." Nika's boots made a solid thud on the landing and he adjusted his shirt before nodding at Rosa. They started down the corridor.

"Angela would have flown out here to kick my ass herself if that had been fully functional." Rosa shook her head. "Which we all know Jenks probably could make happen given enough time and materials."

"True story." Nika paused outside the door to Vice Admiral Hoboins's offices. "Speaking of time, I wanted to ask before I leave if you're going to follow that thread of Jenks's about the jumpers?"

Rosa smiled at him. She was going to miss Nika. She'd trained a good number of junior officers, and saying goodbye never got any easier. Nika was good at his job and would only get better with this transfer to Trappist-1e. But the reminder of Jenks made her apprehensive about their team meeting tonight, where they would break the news to the others.

"I don't know. It's likely Lee," she said, nodding at the vice admiral's door, "will just pass it up the chain." Rosa tapped a hand on her leg in thought. She'd learned a long time ago that trying to keep Jenks out of things she was interested in meant fighting a losing battle. Much better to put her on the track with clear instructions. "It's not going to hurt anything to let her follow her instincts, though. Tell her if she comes up with something new to pass it along to Ma."

"Can do." Nika pressed his palm to the panel on the side of the doorway and gestured for Rosa to precede him.

"Morning, Commander." Hoboins's chief of staff looked up from her desk.

"Morning, Lou."

The petite woman waved a hand at the open door behind her as she got to her feet. "Go on in, he's expecting you. I have to go collect someone, I'll be right back."

Rosa crossed over into the spartan office dominated by a wide curved window with an impressive view of the planet below them. Lee Hoboins, vice admiral in charge of Jupiter

Station, was well into his ninth Sol decade, though LifeEx had him looking at least twenty years younger. He'd come into the program later than most, right at the edge of the NeoG Academy's cutoff of thirty-five years, the result being more visible aging than someone like Rosa, whose civilian parents had secured the treatment for themselves and their newborn daughter through their work as CHN employees.

Rosa thought it made him look distinguished, but she knew that people still thought looking older was a bad thing. Some stigmas never changed.

"Come in, shut the door." Lee waved away the screens hanging in front of his deeply lined face. "Take a seat." The gravelly order was accompanied by a quick smile.

"Morning."

"Somewhere," Lee replied. "Welcome home, Commander. I was just reading the reports. You did good out there."

That was high praise from the taciturn vice admiral, and Rosa felt a little glow of pleasure in her chest. "Appreciate it. We enjoy what we do."

Hoboins chuckled. "So tell me about this system jumper you found that the whole base is buzzing about."

Rosa settled back in her chair and gave her report, Nika occasionally interjecting and Hoboins stopping them both to ask questions.

"Odd that it was empty," Lee said as Rosa's report wound down. "Not unheard of, though. There was a system jumper found just last year in the same state. Salvagers probably ejected the bodies into deep space after they commandeered the ship."

"Really?" Rosa blinked. "Do you have access to the report on it?"

"It was a naval op, I think—let me pull it. Pure bad luck on the salvagers' part." Hoboins laughed as he tapped on his desk. "They were hiding out on an asteroid in the Kuiper Belt the *Bastille* was doing bombardment tests on. Here it is."

Rosa nodded as the file pinged its arrival in her DD chip. "I'll take a closer look at this, see if there's anything that matches what we found."

"I'm sure the techs will be able to retrieve the information that PO Khan downloaded off the ship on their own, but have her hang on to it for now. Never hurts to have multiple copies." Hoboins leaned back in his chair and scrubbed a hand over his short, salt-and-pepper hair. "What's your take on it?"

"I just gave you my report, Admiral."

"So you did. I also read Khan's as you were talking. She thinks there's something 'not right' about those disappeared system jumpers." Hoboins's expression was amused. "Master Chief Ma edited her report again, didn't he?"

"You know he did. He won't let her send out any formal communications without approval after that last incident." Rosa laughed and shook her head.

"I might agree with her," Lee said, suddenly serious. "Between that and the fact that one of them tried to bribe you, it makes me uneasy. But we don't have anything to go on and you know how HQ is about gut instincts and the budget."

Rosa sighed. "Do I ever."

"Anyway, I've sent you a list of the missing jumpers and their ID codes. I want you to keep an eye out on patrol, Commander. Just in case." Lee shrugged. "And for anything else that seems—not right."

"Will do, Admiral."

"Off-Earth is sending a hauler in to pick up that ship, so anything Master Chief Ma wants to look at is going to need to happen in the next few days."

"I'll let him know," Rosa said with a nod.

"Good. We've already sent the five people you picked up back with a Navy destroyer that was headed for Earth. I'm going to let HQ deal with them from there." He sighed. "Given there were no passengers and moreover no sign of people on the jumper, I doubt the human trafficking charge will stick, but we've got them on the others. We'll leave the case open for the moment, but I suspect it'll get shuffled out of our hands when they get to Earth."

It wasn't perfect, but Rosa would take it. She didn't want to think about what had happened to those colonists—best-case scenario they'd been dead already when the smugglers found them and their bodies ejected from the ship. Worst case—well, there were too many of those to go into.

"Works for me. I'll let Jenks know she can keep poking at it but to keep me updated."

"Okay. Now for the topic we're all avoiding." Hoboins steepled his fingers and looked between them. "Have you told the rest of the team about Nika's impending transfer?"

"Tonight," Rosa said. "Why?"

"Probably going to have to revise that timetable, Commander." He gave her that grin he so loved when delivering unexpected news. "Your new lieutenant is two days early."

Max stood on the deck of the docking bay and looked around with a wild mixture of excitement and awe rolling around in her chest. Lime-vested deckhands scrambled back and forth, running past where she'd pressed herself as far out of the traffic flow as possible.

Oh, Maxine, what have you done? You are out in the middle of nowhere. That familiar worried voice was whispering in her ear.

"I am right where I'm supposed to be." She only wished her declaration weren't so shaky.

"Watch yourself!" A woman in a CHNN uniform shouldered past her with an aggravated snarl. "Goddamned space cops, nothing better to do than stand around and stare."

"Lieutenant Carmichael, trouble here?"

Max froze and pasted a smile on her face for the tiny NeoG commander who'd just stepped into the Navy lieutenant's path. The woman wasn't looking at Max but glaring up at the Navy woman with a look that could have melted steel.

"Tell your newbie to stop standing in the middle of traffic, Commander."

"Little more respect there, Diesov, unless you want me to write you up a recommendation for a long-haul tour out of the system? I know Admiral Christin doesn't want another conversation with Vice Admiral Hoboins about how shit his spacers' manners are. On top of that, Lieutenant Carmichael has been in a year longer than you and is with *Zuma's Ghost,* so probably best to behave yourself."

Max watched the woman's eyes widen and there was a second of silence before she looked in Max's direction. "Sorry about running into you, Lieutenant."

"It's all right." Max felt like she was missing something big here, but before she could sort it out in her head, the Navy lieutenant gave them both a nod and stalked off.

"Sorry about that, Max. I'm Commander Lou Seve, Vice Admiral Hoboins's chief of staff for Jupiter Station." She stuck her hand out with a smile and Max took it. "Orbital Control rang and said you were in a bit early, and I was trying to get here as quick as I could to avoid just that kind of incident."

"I probably should have been watching where I was standing."

Lou snorted. "Look, maybe things are more polite at HQ, but out here the rivalry between branches is in full force and it often involves a lot of punches thrown. You'll want to watch yourself while you get the feel of things. And stick close to your teammates for a few days. The admiral is in a meeting, coincidentally with Commander Martín and Lieutenant Commander Vagin of your new team, or he'd have come down to see you himself."

"I appreciate it, but it wasn't necessary."

Lou waved her off. "Someone needed to do it, as you just saw, plus you'd have gotten lost without being connected to the station net. Which, speaking of, here's your log-in." She passed over the fist-sized glowing disc and Max blinked at the old tech but didn't comment.

"I highly suggest using the map function for the first few weeks unless you have a ridiculously good sense of direction. Do you?"

Max shook her head, thinking about how she'd gotten turned around at HQ on her very last day there and ended up in the basement. "I do not."

"Use your map." Lou stuck a finger in her face, though her smile was warm. "There's no shame in it."

"Thanks." Max reached down for her bags, looking up at Lou when she put a foot on one.

"Don't bother with them." She smiled even as she flagged down a passing deckhand in a lime-green vest. "These are Lieutenant Carmichael's bags; take them to Interceptor Five's quarters." She pointed across the docking bay. "Straight there, got me? I will come looking for you."

"Sure thing, Lou."

"That wouldn't have been necessary," Max said. "I could have carried them."

"Not up to the admiral's office. Besides, first-timers on the station end are supposed to have their luggage take a little joyride." Lou grinned. "Now, normally I'd have gone with it, but the fact that you flew in on a freighter with no fanfare and only have two bags says a lot about you. So I'll pay you in kind with clean laundry from the get-go." She patted Max on the arm. "Come on."

Max followed Commander Seve through the winding corridors of the station and up through a low-g section to the vice admiral's offices, where the sound of voices drifted through the door at the far end of the room.

Lou smiled and pointed at a cluster of chairs against the wall. "Sit."

Max sat.

I am right where I'm supposed to be.

"I KNOW THE PROMOTION DOESN'T KICK IN QUITE YET, BUT I get to call you by your new rank first because I'm in charge. I'm going to miss you, Commander," Hoboins said as he got up from his desk and held out his hand to Nika. "But since we know Rosa here won't go—"

"*Can't* go, Admiral, I'm pushing the bounds of my faith's patience as it is," Rosa said with a smile.

Nika muffled a smile of his own. This back-and-forth between Hoboins and Rosa had been happening for as long as he'd known the both of them.

The Earth-Bound Church, an offshoot of evangelical Christianity, had sprung into existence almost instantaneously with the first moon habitat.

God made the Earth and on it we should stay.

We are the shepherds and the keepers of her and it is our duty to protect her.

He'd heard the commander whisper those words often enough to know them by heart, even if they weren't part of his own, more lax, New Tech faith.

Rosa had a dispensation from her pastor that allowed her off-planet in the service of NeoG, as a concession to the Coalition government's recognition of the church as a legitimate faith at the beginning of reconstruction.

However, the boundary lines had been drawn at the solar system's edge, and that meant no postings in Trappist and no long-haul flights out of the Sol system for any faithful members of the Earth-Bound.

"Won't, can't, whatever. I'm still stuck with you while Nika gets to run away to Trappist-1e." He tapped on his desk console. "Lou, bring her in."

The door opened, and the vice admiral's chief of staff escorted in Lieutenant Maxine Carmichael. No, Lieutenant Maxine freaking *LifeEx* Carmichael. And now she was a member of the Interceptors. Nika could scarcely believe it. She was a decent handful of centimeters taller than him, with a riot of brown curls bound into a collection of knots whose neatness probably would have impressed a naval inspector, but out here in NeoG territory just made her look painfully straitlaced.

Nika muffled a groan as he thought about the terror that his sister could be with someone who wanted to do things by the book.

He was going to have to have a long talk with Jenks before he left, and now he wished he'd done it sooner. The reality of his departure settled into his bones and Nika shook off the sudden sadness as he crossed the room with a hand extended.

But Carmichael had snapped into a salute that had all three NeoG officers exchanging amused glances.

"At ease, Lieutenant," Hoboins said, returning her salute halfheartedly. "Welcome to Jupiter Station. This is Commander Rosa Martín, head of the Interceptor team you'll be joining, *Zuma's Ghost*. Commander Nika Vagin is headed for Trappist-1e, but he'll show you around the team and station before he leaves us. You two, this is Maxine Carmichael."

She has pretty brown eyes. The stray thought caught Nika by surprise. Thankfully the lieutenant was too lost in her own confusion to notice, and Nika stuck his hand out a second time when she dropped her salute. "Maxine."

"Max, please. It's very nice to meet you."

He had ten million questions, but they were all going to have to wait until he could get Tamago alone. He was pretty sure Max wouldn't want to answer them, but Petty Officer Third Class Uchida Tamashini was an expert on celebrity gossip and they'd be able to fill him in on pretty much anything.

For the moment, though, he should probably mind his manners before his *baba* rose up from the grave and slapped him about the head and shoulders. "Commander, unless you want to talk with Max here, I can show her to quarters and introduce her around?"

"Go on," Rosa said with a wave of her hand. "Get settled in. I'll talk with you later, Max."

"Yes, Commander."

Nika saw her hand twitch with the urge to salute and couldn't stop himself from chuckling as he took hold of her upper arm and directed her back out of the vice admiral's office.

"Did you have a good flight?" he asked, waving at Lou as they passed her desk.

"Very much so. Thank you. I took a freighter out from Earth a few days ago. The view coming in was stunning." She slipped out of his grasp, a mask of impressive politeness dropping into place.

A freighter. Nik's curiosity grew. He'd have assumed that a Carmichael would have a private transport or take a naval flight rather than schlep four days in a freighter. As distantly polite as the answer had been, he caught the hint of warmth in her eyes. She was telling the truth about the view, and unless he missed his guess she'd really enjoyed flying in on a freighter.

This one was a puzzle. It was a shame he wasn't going to get to stick around to solve it.

"Where were you stationed before, Max?"

"HQ," she replied. "I was Admiral Chen's aide."

"You mean *head of NeoG* Admiral Chen?" He frowned. "You were the admiral's aide."

She looked at him in confusion. "Yes, that's what I said. I applied for Interceptor training last year and just graduated. Pretty normal process."

Somehow he managed not to trip over his own feet, but Nika came to a stop and stared at Max. "You left a post at HQ to join the Interceptors?"

"I graduated first in my class, Commander," she replied, shoulders stiff, and Nika knew he'd put his foot in it.

"Sorry, that wasn't—" He held a hand up and smiled. "I wasn't calling into question your abilities. Just maybe your sanity."

"I was wasting my life behind a desk, and as much as I enjoyed working for Admiral Chen, I joined NeoG to be out here."

It was the note of longing that did him in, buried beneath the stiffness. He knew exactly how it felt to be wholly unsuited for planet-bound work. "That I can understand. Welcome to Jupiter Station, Max, and to the Interceptors."

MAX TRIED TO LISTEN TO COMMANDER VAGIN AS HE LED HER through the corridors of Jupiter Station, but at least a third of her brain insisted on detailing her failures from the moment she'd met him.

Wrong greeting. Check.

Too formal. Check.

Defensive and standoffish about your place here. Check.

". . . there's bound to be some interest in who you are, of course, but if it gets to be too much just tell Ma and he'll put a stop to it."

"Ma?"

"Master Chief Ma Léi. We all just call him Ma because someone has to mother this bunch when Rosa and I aren't around." Nika's smile was sympathetic. "I'm sure this seems odd to you. Things are a lot less formal out here than they are at HQ, Max. But don't worry, you'll get used to it."

She forced a smile, knowing it didn't do quite a good enough job hiding her nerves, and not quite sure how to tell Nika that growing up, Ma Léi had been a fixture in her household. He was an old friend of her father's who'd retired from the Navy and, rather than enjoying himself or starting a lucrative career as a private pilot, had enlisted in the NeoG not six months after his retirement.

Unsurprisingly, her father had disapproved.

Max, of course, had been ecstatic.

They went down what felt like kilometers of rounded halls, through two low-g sections where Nika bounced easily from one entrance to another and caught her without commentary when Max fumbled the first landing. She learned quickly and nailed the second transit, trying to tell herself the spark of approval in his blue eyes shouldn't mean as much as it did.

You don't need approval from every damn person you come across, Max. She'd worked so hard to break herself of the ingrained response, but the unfamiliar situation and nerves threw her right back into old habits.

"Interceptor quarters," Nika said, gesturing at the hallway with a smile. "There are twenty-three teams stationed here, though we're rarely all on base at the same time. We just got back from a nine-day haul in the belt yesterday. Asteroid, not Kuiper," he clarified as he tapped the panel near the door marked with a number five. It slid open, allowing a wave of sound out. Nika winced. "We're here. Sorry about the music."

"That's music?" She followed Nika into the room and blinked. Two people were dancing in the middle—one with black hair that hung in a straight braid, the other with bright orange spikes sticking up in a row across the middle of a shaved scalp. They were both dressed in what she was reasonably sure was their underwear and nothing else, while a third person sat on a nearby bunk with a mess of holo-display screens hanging in the air like ghosts.

"So, welcome to the Interceptors," Nika said again, nearly yelling in order to be heard over the din and sounding a hell of a lot more rueful about it than the first time.

"Jenks! Turn it off, we've got a visitor," Nika yelled, and Max jumped.

"Doge, music off."

The music stopped and silence filled the room, broken only by Nika's sighed question: "You two want to at least put some pants on to meet your new lieutenant?" There was a yelp of dismay from the black-haired person, whom Max recognized from the files she'd been given access to on the way to Jupiter even as her DD chip tagged Petty Officer Third Class Uchida Tamashini, they/them.

The others just laughed.

"Is that a ROVER?" The question was whispered, slipping out before Max could stop herself.

Petty Officer First Class Altandai Khan, she/her, skidded to a halt near a bunk. "Doge, say hi!" she ordered as she flopped onto the bed and pulled on a pair of sweats.

The Robotic Optics Vehicular and Extravehicular Reconnaissance AI unfolded itself from what looked to Max like a dog bed in the corner of the room and tapped over to her, sitting its long body down, looking disturbingly similar to her grandmother's pit bull mix, Shady.

She crouched, instantly fascinated. "I've never seen one running before. I thought they were all decommissioned."

"They were, I saved him. He'll say hi."

"The AI's still active?"

"She's not hooked in yet, Jenks," Nika said.

"Ah, right—sorry, he only talks on the channel. In that case: Doge, shake."

The robot lifted a paw, which Max took with a delighted grin and shook up and down twice. Then her father's disapproving voice slammed into her.

You're their lieutenant, Maxine. Excellent first impression, rolling around on the floor with the dog.

She scrambled to her feet, wiping her palms off on her uniform pants and pasting a smile on her face. Everyone was staring, but Max had learned how not to fidget under the watchful eyes of her parents and stood still, waiting for someone to say something.

No one said anything.

"Nika, what did the admiral have to say about that jumper? Is he going to let me take a look—" The tank of a man who came in from a side door broke through the tension and his face split into a friendly smile. "Max!" He crossed the room, his arms outstretched.

"Master Chief, it's very good to see you again," she said in passable Chinese. The Babel implant would have translated her words from English to the man's native Mandarin, but she saw the delight in his brown eyes even if her greeting was extremely rusty.

"How did you know she was coming?" Nika asked.

"I may have heard something on the stars." Ma shrugged. "You should have heard the message your father sent me last year after you went into the Interceptor course." He whistled at Max. "He wasn't happy."

"I'm so sorry. It's really not your fault." The squeak of surprise was undignified and she knew everyone was staring again when Ma swept her up into a hug, but she hugged him back as tightly as she could.

"You let me worry about your father," he whispered in her ear. "We've been friends a long time and he'll forgive me. He'll forgive you, too."

Max doubted it, but she didn't protest out loud.

"So, Ma neglected to tell me you two know each other." Nika's voice dripped with amusement and Max cleared her throat as she straightened her uniform jacket. "In order, you've got Ensign Nell Zika. She's our tech expert and navigator." He pointed to the woman with wavy brown hair who'd been flipping through holo-displays.

"Call me Sapphi, LT," she said with a wave.

"Sapphi does the computer side of things. You need anything on that front or electronics fixed, she'll be the one to see." Nika pointed to Khan, who was whispering fiercely with Petty Officer Uchida. "Petty Officer First Class Altandai Khan. She's our enforcer and mechanic."

"Jenks, Lieutenant. I can piece 'em together; Sapphi makes the software run." She nodded once, abruptly formal, and Max resisted the urge to sigh.

"Don't ask about the name," Nika said. "Jenks and Ma keep our shit running. You know the budget keeps getting slashed so we often have to make do."

"I thought Jupiter was a priority." She'd seen the budget figures come through the admiral's office, but hadn't thought much about them at the time.

"It is." Nika grinned. "This is what happens when we get priority."

"Heat and air. They feed us when they're feeling generous," the others echoed in unison, laughter in their reply.

"Petty Officer Third Class Uchida Tamashini. Also known as Tamago. They're our medic, also our negotiator. You need help getting things, they're the person to talk to."

Tamago waved a hand and smiled. "Nice to meet you, Lieutenant."

"We'll get you round with the boat crews later, but this is *Zuma's Ghost*." Nika gestured around. "Ma just came out of the team office. Commander's room is at the far end. There's a communal room for personal time, and a second one that's supposed to be the other officer's quarters. I sleep out here. If you want your own room you're welcome to it or you can take my bunk." He pointed off to the end of the row.

"Why would she take your bunk?" Jenks asked.

Max watched as Nika winced and flicked his gaze skyward, mumbling what could have been a prayer under his breath before he looked back down and forced a smile.

"Commander wanted to make a big deal of it at dinner tonight, but we all know how plans go. I have been promoted to commander," he announced, and the room exploded into noise once more.

Max stepped back so the others could congratulate their teammate, but rather than rush forward with the others, Jenks hung back. "Promotion means he's being transferred," she murmured. "You're his replacement." The look she shot Max was indecipherable.

She wasn't sure if a response was expected, but the manners hammered into her from childhood won out and Max extended her hand. "Max Carmichael. It's nice to meet you."

Jenks eyed her hand as if it were something unpleasant, then turned and headed out the door without another word, Doge on her heels.

"Ah, hell. Sorry, Max, she didn't mean anything by that," Nika said. "Ma, finish showing Max around, will you? I'd better go talk to Jenks before she punches someone in the face and gets demoted again."

I WILL NOT CRY. CRYING IS FOR BABIES. I AM NOT A BABY.

The mantra from the orphanage rolled on a loop in her head as Jenks strode down the corridor at a pace just short of a run.

She'd known this day was coming. They'd been so lucky to be together at all when it came right down to it, and she should be grateful for that.

"I never was good at being grateful," she muttered.

"Jenks!"

She ignored Nika's call and kept going. He'd catch up with her, that was just as much a fact as his leaving her. There was no getting around his long-ass legs. But she didn't have to make it easy for him.

Jenks snagged a rung and swung out into the zero-g tube that would take her to the top of the station. Doge took the leap, his momentum carrying him upward with her, though she reached back and locked her fingers in his blue collar. She heard Nika curse behind her, the words lost as she soared out of earshot.

She hit the upper observation deck, relief flooding her when she saw it was empty, and headed around the massive ring that encircled the top of the tower toward her usual spot. The heavy green scent of one of Jupiter Station's two bio-recyclers filled her nose, easing some of her anxiety.

"Jenks, come on."

She kept going.

"Petty Officer Altandai Khan, stop your ass right now." That was a tone she hadn't heard from her brother in a very long time, and it was enough to make her legs refuse to follow any orders from her brain to keep moving forward. Doge also came to a halt, looking between them with a whimper.

"Petty Officer, look at me." He always knew how to make her behave. Jenks would pull a lot of stupid shit, but throw an order into the mix and it was like flipping a switch.

She turned to him, her eyes wet with tears she refused to let fall.

"Everything is going to be okay," he said, bending down so he could look her in the eye. "I swear."

"It's fine." She mustered up a smile along with the mental bricks to wall off the pain.

"Don't do that." Nika shook his head, grabbing her by the back of her head and pressing their foreheads together. "I know you, Jenks, don't try to pretend with me. I know you're upset."

She pulled away, taking the six quick steps required to put her at the wide, curving windows that looked out onto Jupiter. She pushed aside a wide bioengineered leaf and wiped the condensation from the window with her fingers.

There'd once been a storm down there that humans had named the Great Red Spot. She'd read about it in one of her twenty-first-century-history binges. But it had burned itself out long before humans made it this far.

Nothing lasts, Jenks—live in the moment.

"I won't be far." Nika attempted a smile as he came up beside her, and Jenks leaned into him with a sigh.

"Light-years," she countered. "I know how far Trappist is, Nik. You'll be thirty-nine point six light-years away from me, and that's officially the farthest we've ever been apart."

"Okay, you got me there, but we'll talk. I promise. You'll always be my sister, you know that. No matter how many light-years are between us."

"Who's going to have your back?"

He tapped his fist to his heart, waiting patiently for her to echo it. Jenks blew out a breath and finally did, hitting the back of his fist with hers. Nika caught her arm on the return swing and pulled her in, touching his forehead to hers again. "You will. Forever."

"Find someone you can trust," she ordered as she wrapped her arms around his neck. "I love you. Go be awesome."

"I'm not leaving quite yet."

"You're staying until the Games?" She couldn't keep the

hope from her voice, but the brief flash disappeared when Nika shook his head.

"No, Max just got here early. I've got a few days yet before I need to ship out. The commander said you'd all manage. Trust her."

"She's not as good with the sword as you are. We need those points."

"Maybe Max is better."

"Who?" She said it because she could and to see the exasperated look from him one more time. "I'm kidding. Maybe. I don't think we're quite that lucky, though."

"You never know. Either way I have a feeling this is going to be the big one for *Zuma*." He pulled her into a hug. "So kick some ass, and you be nice to the lieutenant."

"I won't make any promises."

Nika cursed and cuffed her on the back of the head. "Be nice. Max seems like a decent sort. She's also lonely and could use someone to watch her back. That's what this team is about, right?"

Jenks heaved a sigh that was more dramatic than necessary. "I guess."

"ADMISSION TIME, COMMANDER."

Rosa gave her commanding officer a smile. "I caught that 'not my idea' comment when you first told us about the orders. What's going on?"

"As I said, this whole promotion thing came down from on high. I could have fought it, of course, but I'm hoping that Admiral Chen knows what she's doing." Hoboins rubbed at his cheek. "Carmichael doesn't seem like much on paper, but she's still shiny and new and the admiral seems to have a plan she doesn't want to share. My gut says Max will make up for what you're losing in Nika, just maybe not in a way we'd all expect. What's your plan for the Games?"

Rosa knew the question was coming, but she sighed anyway. "I'm sure Ensign Zika has her projections laid out, or rather she's furiously redoing them while cursing us both. Do you want me to send them to you?"

Hoboins pinned her with the steely-eyed look he was so famous for. "I want to know *your* thoughts, Rosa. Nika can do good work in Trappist, since you keep refusing my suggestions we send you instead. Meanwhile, Command is understandably hot about the Games this year, but for some reason they pushed this transfer through anyway. We came so damn close to winning, do you think they just blew this year's chances out of space with this promotion? Should I fight them on it? I can find another crew to put Carmichael in and Trappist can wait nine fucking months."

"No, it'll be fine," Rosa replied. She'd have said the words regardless and was reasonably sure the admiral felt the same way. Whatever the spirit of the Games was, it didn't override their mission and she wouldn't let it stand in the way of someone with Nika's skills getting the recognition he deserved. Plus, as he'd said, maybe there was more to Maxine Carmichael than met the eye.

But the pressure was on. They *had* come so fucking close to winning it last year. A century of the Boarding Games, and the NeoG had yet to win the overall competition. They'd won individual events multiple times, but never the whole thing. It was yet another reason the NeoG was looked down on by the other branches.

And when you added the team's loss last year by three points—three fucking points—it had been a humiliation at the much-publicized centennial event.

Rosa had only herself to blame. If she'd been a minute faster figuring out the puzzles in the Big Game, they'd have won. If she'd gotten just one more hit on her opponent in the sword fight, they'd have won.

No one on the team blamed her, of course—they were

all too busy asking themselves what *they* could have done better. But the three points were definitely there for the taking, and she was the commander, so she knew it was her fault.

And now the admiral's question still stood, and while her own swordsmanship was nothing to sneeze at, no one was as good as Nika.

"I don't recall seeing a note of her comp in her file," she said. The unspoken *Please tell me she's an amazing sword fighter* hung in the air between them like a lead balloon.

"She hasn't competed at all." Lee had the grace to look at least a little abashed as he shrugged his broad shoulders at her level stare. "Headquarters' team is compiled differently from ours, Commander."

"I know," Rosa murmured. *Honorable Intent* was a good team, for one that was mostly composed of Earth-bound Neos from HQ. "Admiral, can I ask what the story is there?" Rosa picked her words carefully. "Granted, what I know about the family is mostly from the news or—" She fumbled, changed track. "It seems a little strange to have the admirals Carmichaels' youngest daughter join the NeoG. Let alone go for an Interceptor slot."

"You're not wrong. She was ensconced safely at HQ until a year ago and likely would have spent her whole career there. I'd suggest asking her about it, though, or maybe the master chief."

"Why would Ma know?"

"He's friends with her father from way back. Rumor has it he's the one who influenced Max to join NeoG instead of the Navy." Hoboins grinned. "But you didn't hear that from me."

Rosa shot her superior officer a look. "The Carmichaels are big-time. Am I about to land in the middle of a political mess, Admiral? Because you know Jenks, she'll—"

"It's fine, Commander. Don't worry about it."

"I worry about everything," she said as she got to her feet. "It's my job."

"I know. It's one of the reasons I like you," Hoboins said, and waved a hand at her. "Dismissed, Commander. Go get your newbie settled in."

No one else seemed bothered by what had just happened, so Max tried to take a surreptitious deep breath.

"Since Nika will probably be with us for a few days, we'll put you in this room. You can move back out after he's gone if you want." Ma pointed at the room on the left. "But if you want to stay in it you're more than welcome." Ma smiled. "Privileges of rank and all that. Nika preferred to sleep in—"

"Ah, shit," Sapphi burst out. "Ma, the Games. *The Games!* I have to redo the whole strategy. Lieutenant, please tell me you're an amazing sword fighter?"

"I, uh, I've been trained. In basic." Judging by the wide-eyed look she got from the ensign, that wasn't at all helpful.

"You've never competed in the Games?"

"Sapphi, watch the tone."

"Sorry, Ma." Sapphi winced, worrying at her lower lip with her teeth. "I'll figure something out. We'll have to do a test round with her, see what needs to be shuffled. It's fine, we've got fifteen weeks before the prelims, we'll be fine. It's fine."

Ma chuckled in amusement as Sapphi wandered off muttering "fine" to herself. "Don't worry about it, Lieutenant. Tamago there, they didn't know much about the Games when they joined us, either."

Petty Officer Uchida smiled. "I knew about it, just hadn't participated. I suppose I'm going to have to get serious about my sword fighting, Chief?"

"Most likely." He pointed across the room. "Go keep Sapphi's head from exploding while I show Max around."

"The Games are a big deal out here?" Max asked after Tamago had crossed back over and plopped onto the ensign's bunk.

"You worked at HQ, Max," he said, the implications clear.

"I know." She lifted a hand. "But it wasn't—I remember conversations about it, but to be honest, I tried to tune them out."

"You are not much of a competitor, are you?" He laughed.

Max sighed. Growing up in a family of competitors had meant a childhood of endless, exhausting fighting to be on top. The minute she'd gotten out from under that had been a relief of unspeakable measure. She'd spent the next several years of her life convincing herself that she didn't need to be competitive. Her first-place ranking in her Interceptor class proved how difficult that lesson was to unlearn.

And here she was, back in the thick of it with an Interceptor team that was—had been—part of the second-place finishers at last year's Games. "Sorry, Ma. I know it probably bothers you."

"Don't be." Ma shrugged his massive shoulders. "We were hoping for revenge this year, but without Nika, I'm not sure it's possible."

Max felt the competitive streak she'd gone to such great lengths to tamp down surge to life once again. "Hopefully I'll prove to be good at something," she said before she could stop herself.

Ma smiled. "We'll get it sorted out. Head and showers are over there. We have an unlimited supply of recycled water thanks to the gardens, though if for some reason we run short we could always get it from Europa." Ma pointed across the room back toward the main door. "Team office is over there, like Nika said. Commander has a secure link in her room also.

"Nika can give you a tour of the station itself when he gets back, though the Commander might want to. Did you get a log-in?"

"Yes." Max patted her pocket. "Commander Seve gave me one."

"Let's get you hooked in, then. Over here."

She followed, whistling at the sight of the terminal. "Wow, I haven't seen one of these for a decade."

"Welcome to Jupiter Station," Ma said wryly. "The fancy equipment doesn't make it this far out unless H3nergy pays for it or the admiral really kicks up a fuss."

Max knew that meant almost nothing got replaced on the station unless absolutely necessary. Despite their altruistic tagline of *Helping Humanity with Helium-3*, H3nergy would watch its bottom line first. And Vice Admiral Hoboins would only rattle the trees for something really important.

"No worries, I know how to use one." The false brightness in her voice didn't fool Ma, but Max fished the log-in disc out of her pocket and inserted it into the slot under the palm scanner.

Nothing happened.

"You have to kick it, Ma!" Sapphi hollered from across the room, her instructions followed by a gale of laughter from Tamago.

"Good rule for most stuff around here," he muttered, giving the computer a thump with his palm. The screen flickered and came on.

"Welcome, Lieutenant Maxine Carmichael. Please place your right hand, palm down, onto the scanner and line up your right eye with the circle on the screen. Don't blink."

Max complied with the computer's instructions, her eye watering as the green light of the retinal scan took its sweet time.

"Identity confirmed. Maxine Theodosia Carmichael, Near-Earth Orbital Guard lieutenant, clearance level alpha-nine, logged to Interceptor team Zz5—*Zuma's Ghost*. You are now connected to the Jupiter Station Network. Please download the station map and all assorted orders as they come in. Welcome to Jupiter Station and have a nice day."

Max's internals pinged at her as the connection to the network was established and dutifully started the downloads. She blinked twice to clear the notification from her vision.

"You can send and receive messages off-station with your internals," Ma said. "But the connection is usually more stable if you use a tablet and go through the main coms. Any face-to-face video will have to go through coms, obviously."

"Makes sense." The microscopic wormholes that the communications office could open up would allow for instantaneous coms between here and pretty much anywhere with an equivalent system. Max's DD chip was good enough for a quick conversation as far away as Earth, but it was dangerous and would give her a headache like no other.

"Hey, I've got some bags for Lieutenant Carmichael. Where should I put them?"

Max turned away from Ma toward the door. "I'll take them, thanks."

"No problem." The deckhand dropped the bags and took off with a wave.

"How did you manage that?" Tamago was staring at her with awe as Sapphi scrambled off her bunk and over to the doorway.

"I didn't," Max replied. "Commander Seve took care of it."

Ma chuckled. "Sapphi, help her get those to her room. Tamago, let's go down and get dinner for everyone. I'm reasonably sure Rosa will want to eat in here rather than down in the mess."

"My bags were missing for a week," Sapphi said as the pair left the room. She patted her hips with a grin. "Jenks and I are a size match this direction, but on me, all her pants looked like someone had taken a laser cutter to them at the shins."

"Sorry." Max wasn't sure what else she could say. The part of her that wanted to fit in whispered that she should have told the commander to let her bags do their usual route, but a larger part was glad she could sleep in her own things tonight.

"Eh, perks of the name," the woman replied with a grin and a shrug. "I don't blame you for it." She grabbed a bag and headed for Max's room before Max could protest. Max grabbed the other and followed. "Jenks might, but we'll just pretend like they didn't show up."

"Seems like she has plenty of reasons not to like me already." It was hard not to make that sentence sound self-pitying, but Max ignored the voice in her head that tried to shout at her about it.

"Jenks is naturally suspicious," Sapphi said as she set Max's bag down on the bed. "Don't take it personally, LT. She'll come around. Get yourself settled. The commander should be back soon and Ma will have sweet-talked someone in the mess for extra dessert. We'll do a proper team dinner to welcome you. Rosa's big on those."

Max was glad that Sapphi was already headed for the door and didn't see her wince. Family dinners at the Carmichael level usually entailed an hour-long torture session of listening to her siblings get praised for whatever successes they'd had that day. As they'd left one by one, she'd been the only one to face the brunt of her parents' expectations.

The door slid closed with an odd sort of finality and Max sank down onto her new bed with a sigh.

Hopefully this is different.

It's gotta *be different.*

"WHY DON'T YOU JUST ASK HER?"

Nika raised an eyebrow at Tamago's question. "I didn't want to pepper her with questions."

"Sapphi is," they said.

"Tamago."

"Fine. What do you want to know that you can't look up on your own? There's this neat thing called the 'net. It's been around for a while, even survived the Collapse."

"Your sarcasm is improving. I think you need to stop hanging out with Jenks," he said with a smile. They grinned at him in response. "What's the deal with her family?"

"You mean as far as LifeEx or as far as her immediate family—who are all mostly naval officers?"

"Immediate family."

"Her oldest sister took over LifeEx this year. As of March 14, 2435, Earth date, she became the president and CEO. Two other siblings, Maggie and Scott, and her parents are CHN Navy. Her sister Patricia, who's a year older than Max, is a CHN senator. Elected last year."

"I heard the rumor they weren't particularly happy about her decision to join the NeoG?" Nika glanced across the room.

"Yeah. The family is normally pretty good about quashing rumors, but there was a hell of a row in a public restaurant," Tamago replied. "There's video, if you feel like looking it up. I'm not going to share it, though." They made a face. "You know me, I like the feel-good gossip, and that was definitely not. Seriously, Commander, this is all stuff you could ask her."

"I don't want to pry." He knew he was going to catch hell for that the second the words left his mouth. Tamago grinned, understanding washing over their face.

"Oh, I see." They held up their hands. "You're on your own here, Nik. Celebrity gossip is one thing. I'm not standing in this puddle while you put a live wire in it."

"You are the worst." He wrapped an arm around their shoulders and hugged them to his side. "I'm going to miss you."

"Same as, Nik." They hugged him back. "Same as."

"YOU SETTLED IN?"

"Yes, Commander."

"Good." Rosa studied the nervous woman sitting across from her before nodding her head. "Max, I'm sure you feel a little out of your depth, but I've read the exit reports from your instructors in London. They all had very nice things to say about you." She leaned forward, bracing her forearms on her thighs. "None of that matters out here in the real world, yeah? We do the jobs or people get hurt. There's little room for error and even less for hesitation."

"Yes, Commander."

Rosa chuckled. "Automatic answer. I know it'll take a while to wear that headquarters shine off you. I don't expect things to be easy here, Max. This crew has been together for a while. Nika's departure will leave a void. Look at me." She waited for Max to meet her eyes. "You're not expected to fill it. You're expected to be yourself and the team will find a new way to work with you. Is that clear?"

"Yes."

"That doesn't mean you're not going to work to find a new way, either. Not if what I read about you is correct, and I expect that as much as I expect the rest of the team to do their work. What's your biggest worry?"

Max blinked, the words already forming in her mouth, and she only just held them in. Rosa shook her head with a smile.

"Don't second-guess it, Carmichael, you had an immediate answer. I won't feed you some bull about it always being the right one, but don't ever second-guess yourself and not tell me the first thing that comes to mind when I ask you."

"I'm afraid of failing," Max said. "Of letting people, my team, down."

"Well," Rosa said. *Her* team, *she said, not her parents or her family. I wonder why that is?* "One of the things you'll learn about me, Max, is that I don't coddle and I don't lie. You're going to fail. You're going to let people down. It's an inevitable part of living in God's universe." She smiled, hoping it tempered some of the harshness of her words. "What you do after, that's the important moment. Remember that."

Max nodded. "Yes, Commander."

"Rosa works fine. Save the 'Commander' thing for when we're in deep shit or I'm yelling at you." She grinned. "Shadow Nika for the rest of the time he's here, see what you can pick up. It'd be a wasted opportunity otherwise. We're headed back out in just a few days, so don't get too comfortable." She stuck out her hand. "Welcome to the Interceptors, Carmichael. It's nice to have you on board."

T-MINUS FOURTEEN WEEKS UNTIL PRELIM BOARDING GAMES

Nika was gone and a pall had settled over the team almost without pause. Max lay on her bed, flipping the still sealed paper envelope over in her hands.

"Old-fashioned, I know, but it's tradition," he'd said with a smile as he handed it off. "I hope *Zuma's Ghost* treats you well, Maxine Carmichael."

The calendar alert in her DD went off and Max stood with a sigh, setting the letter back onto her neatly made bed and straightening the sheets one more time before she left the room. The rest of the team was likely down in the training area already, so she cued up her map and headed out the door.

The station had a pleasant background hum. The sound of fully functional air and water recyclers, of electricity singing in the wires, of humanity just going about their lives.

It wasn't fair to say that HQ had felt dead by comparison. For starters, the buildings had been on Earth and so the hum was vastly different with HVAC and concrete to muffle the sounds of people.

But Jupiter Station had a heart. Max could feel it beating under her feet. The gardens up top that Nika had taken her to see after dinner the first night were the station's lungs. And awkwardness with people aside, she felt like she belonged here.

"Now I just have to prove it," she whispered when the anxiety started twisting in her gut. "You knew you were getting into the Games when you came out here, so stop trying to avoid it."

She'd diligently read the files on her teammates, but hadn't looked at the Games folder Sapphi had so helpfully provided to her at all. Her normal determination to learn anything and everything she could was buried under a fear about the Games she couldn't quite put words to.

Like it or not, Max, here you are. Probably time to stop dodging it and ask Sapphi directly.

Max swung out into the low-g chute that ran through the center of the military section and started down the ladder with smooth, controlled jumps.

She hit the bottom and headed through the wide entrance to Jupiter Station's training area. The space gave one the true size of the mushroom stalk of the station and by extension the size of the station as a whole. An area as long as a fútbol pitch stretched beyond the doors. People were lifting weights and running on treadmills near the entrance, but Max could see all the way to the back, where the sparring areas were located.

She spied Ma and Jenks tangled together on a mat and headed in their direction. Sapphi watched from a nearby bench, shouting encouragement.

Or heckling, it was hard to tell.

"My third grandma hits harder! Kick her ass, Ma! Hey, LT." Sapphi patted the bench next to her. "Have a seat. Unless you want to go watch Tamago and Rosa, they're in the corner over there."

Max sat and watched as Jenks deftly avoided Ma's punch. "So, the Boarding Games?"

"What about them?"

"Can you tell me . . ."

"What?" Sapphi raised an eyebrow and waited.

"Well . . . everything."

"Space oddity, please tell me you're pulling a long joke on us?" Sapphi pleaded.

Max shook her head. "I'm afraid not."

"Even though *Honorable Intent* competed last year?"

"Even though. I really don't know much about the Games. The HQ team is mostly Intel folks, and they're all in a different building. I didn't interact with them very much." Max thought of Commander Yevchenko, who used to stop by to see Admiral Chen on occasion. She was fairly sure he was on the team, but she couldn't have picked the others out of a lineup.

Sapphi rubbed her hands over her eyes. "Okay," she said, and then unleashed a bright smile. "We'll be fine. Basics. So—there are six competitions, okay? Some are individual events, others are team based. Each competition has a total available point score of thirty, plus another five for the winner. If you want a detailed explanation of points and scoring and you have five hours to kill, I can tell you how it works, but most people don't care enough."

"Maybe later?"

Sapphi's laugh was clear and bounced around her like an unattended child at a candy store. "It's okay—you won't hurt my feelings if you say it sounds boring, LT. It is . . . to most people."

"So maybe not."

Sapphi laughed again, then continued. "The comps are hand-to-hand, a piloting obstacle course, hacking, sword fighting, the Boarding Action, and the Big Game."

"The Big Game?"

"The final puzzle," Sapphi replied with a nod. "That one's a team activity. It's timed. You're given a mission simulation and have to figure it out before the clock runs out. Faster you figure it out, more points you get, plus you're racing against the times of all the other teams. The points teams have earned from the previous year's Big Game help set the order for this year's. Obviously going last is preferable. And the order of all the competitions isn't fixed, it's drawn randomly at the start of each Boarding Games."

"Makes sense. So where do I fit in?"

"Don't know yet," Sapphi replied, and at first, it was a bit of a gut punch. *No one ever seems to know where I fit in.* And yet Sapphi hadn't said it with malice—she was just stating a fact in a way that made it clear that Max *was* going to have a place. As Sapphi continued, the trepidation Max was feeling at being here at all was tempered by the ensign's casual acceptance.

"Nika was our best sword fighter," Sapphi said. "More accurately, he was *the* best sword fighter across all the branches. But he's obviously gone now. So that leaves Rosa and Tamago, who both have experience where you don't. You've got a longer reach than I do, which would be helpful in the hand-to-hand. Three members from each competing team face off in a single-elimination bracket there. Standard competition rules. Cage match. Obviously no deadly strikes allowed, but broken bones happen. Right now the three are Ma, Jenks, and me. I'm decent in a fight, but it's not a lie to say Ma and Jenks carry the points in that comp. Are you a fighter, Max?"

"I—" A thousand worries flooded her mouth, choking off her answer. Max realized she wasn't even sure how to answer that question. She'd fought for this, but it was the first thing in her life she'd really ever gone for. "She's good," Max murmured instead as Jenks knocked Ma to the mat with enough force to rattle his teeth. He rolled to the side, narrowly escaping her descending elbow.

"Oh yeah." Sapphi grinned. "Jenks is one of the best I've ever seen, if not the best. She's currently sixty-three and zero. The undisputed champion for six years running now."

"She's never lost a fight?"

"Officially, no." Sapphi shrugged. "A few practice rounds here and there have been called as draws, but she's won every competition round she's been in. And this past year she's been performing at a whole other level. Which is good, because there are a lot of people gunning for her." She looked at the sparring pair with narrowed eyes and yelled, "Jenks, if you let him get a hold of you and choke you out, you'll never hear the end of it!"

Max thought about her sparring at the academy. She'd treated it like everything else, an obstacle to overcome, and while she knew the running joke had been that she only ever hit someone as a means of avoiding a fight, she also knew that she was very good at figuring out where people were going to be and how they were going to move.

I can do this, if they let me.

JENKS HEARD SAPPHI'S TAUNT AND TWISTED, SLIDING OUT of Ma's grip before he could complete the hold. She dropped down and used her lower center of gravity to flip him over her shoulder. He hit the mat with a thud and his laughter bubbled up into the air.

"I swear one of these days I'm going to get that hold on you."

"Not anytime soon, Grandpa," she replied, reaching down and helping him to his feet. "But keep trying."

"You are a brat," Ma said, accompanying his words with a slap to the back of her head. "I'd think you'd have more intelligent insults than the ones the Navy boys use."

"Oh, ouch. If only your punches hurt as much as your words," Jenks said, skipping out of the way before he could smack her harder. "Triumphant once more," Jenks crowed, grabbing the towel Sapphi threw at her. "You and I should go, Lieutenant."

Rosa laughed from behind her. "I don't think so, Jenks. We'll work her up to you."

"What? I wouldn't hurt her!"

"You gave me a black eye your first day here," Rosa reminded her with a grin that had the others—minus the lieutenant—laughing. "Come on, Max, let's see how your hand-to-hand is."

Jenks dropped onto the bench next to Ma as the commander handed her practice sword off to Tamago, the microsheath sliding back up around the edge.

"I wouldn't have hurt her," she muttered.

"You would have," Sapphi said, lifting her hands and spreading files only she could see wide across her vision. "At least a little."

"Okay, maybe a little." She grinned. "Isn't that part of the fun, though?"

"For who?" Ma bumped her shoulder with his and laughed. "Commander's thinking ahead, this way you can watch her. You're a better judge of someone's skill set than any of us."

Jenks couldn't argue with that, so she crossed her arms over her chest and leaned back against the wall to watch the fight.

The commander was tall—well, honestly, everyone was tall to Jenks, but at 178 centimeters, Rosa was a pretty decent height. The new lieutenant was taller than Rosa and had a similar long-limbed build.

The difference was that Rosa moved like she was comfortable in her skin, while the lieutenant decidedly did not.

Still, she didn't square off directly across from the commander, turning her hips and torso away and making herself a smaller target as she lifted her fists.

Too low to protect her head.

"Commander's gonna smack her right in the eye," Jenks muttered, watching Rosa's hips move as she threw the expected punch.

What happened next was not expected, though.

Max shifted to the side, blocking the punch and hitting the commander with a spinning kick in the upper back hard enough to knock Rosa several feet across the mat.

Jenks sat upright with a whistle. Max didn't pursue but settled back into her stance, arms raised—still not high enough—and waited. "Going to have to teach her to attack when she's got her opponent stunned like that," she murmured under her breath, already calculating the ways she could coach Max into something unstoppable.

The grin on Rosa's face had Jenks whistling again as the commander lifted her own hands and gestured for Max to continue. There was a moment when Jenks wasn't sure if Max would comply, but the lieutenant moved forward and threw a punch of her own.

The fight was on.

"She's good." Jenks didn't bother to keep the surprise out of her voice. "Hasn't fought enough, but the instinct is there. If she'd commit to actually fighting."

"She doesn't like it," Ma said, and Jenks nodded.

"Nothing wrong with that. Does make you wonder why she joined the Interceptors, though." She glanced in Ma's direction when he didn't reply. "You know why."

"Maybe," he said. "It'll be good for you to figure it out on your own, though."

Jenks shrugged with a noncommittal grunt, but then she winced as Rosa hit Max in the stomach with a particularly solid kick and the lieutenant folded in half. "Oof. Call that one a win for the commander." She got up and crossed the mat, grabbing the wheezing Max by an arm and stretching her out as the lieutenant struggled to suck air into her lungs. "Give it a minute, Lieutenant, you'll be okay." She patted Max on the shoulder and then left her with Ma.

"Thoughts?" Rosa asked, catching the towel Jenks threw in her direction and mopping at her face.

Jenks rubbed at the back of her head. "She's better than Sapphi, or rather, she could be better. There's something there."

"She moved like a ghost sometimes, but she wasn't invested in the fight."

"Could have been nervous about fighting a superior officer."

"*You* weren't."

"Not everyone's me." Jenks shrugged.

"Thank God." Rosa grinned down at her. "Get her trained up. Take it easy on her, but not too much. We're on a timetable now, plus I want to know she'll be up for anything that comes at us in the field. We'll have Sapphi put all her focus on the hack competition and everyone trains for the Boarding Action, but I want you and Ma and Max on the hand-to-hand."

"Can do, Commander." Whatever her misgivings about Max, Jenks trusted Rosa's decision on the matter and she'd do what she could to get the woman trained up. "How's Tamago going to handle the sword fighting?"

"Should be fine." Rosa frowned as she dried off the back of her neck with the towel. "They've got a natural grace that lends itself well to it, if—"

When Rosa paused Jenks waited a beat before finishing the sentence. "We can get them to commit to the fight. Same problem as Max." She shrugged and grinned at her commander's surprised look. "I know it doesn't seem like it, but I do pay attention."

Rosa chuckled and flicked her with the towel before going back to join Ma and Max. Jenks watched her go, her smile fading somewhat. For all their closeness, she knew the one thing Rosa hadn't confided in her. The commander wasn't just worried about Tamago's fighting ability with the sword, she was worried about her own, and shouldering an already heavy burden of trying to win these damn Games.

But it wasn't Jenks's place to be there for the commander to confide in. She knew how this worked.

She only hoped that Max was up to the job.

THE NEOG PREFERRED FOR ITS INTERCEPTOR TEAMS TO STAY together for long periods. It led to better team cohesion, lower stress levels, and better performance overall. But promotions also had to happen, and there was no denying that Nika's departure had left a giant hole in the heart of *Zuma's Ghost*.

The question was, was it one that Lieutenant Maxine Carmichael could fill?

Rosa pondered the problem as she sat at the table in her office, pretending to read the daily reports in her inbox. They were going back out today, and despite her own reluctance about the new lieutenant, she was looking forward to seeing how Max handled herself in the field.

The instructors at Interceptor training all spoke highly of Maxine Carmichael, and not because of her last name. She was, by all accounts, bright and dedicated. She was preternaturally good at predicting other people's choices—which explained her ghostlike moves in the fighting ring—but seemed to have trouble relating to her fellow Neos—which explained why she was shut in her room so often. Sapphi seemed at ease with Max, as did Ma. But those two were the easy pair. They got on well with everyone.

Tamago was more reserved, but would be fine. Jenks . . .

Rosa sighed and shook her head.

Jenks, while not hostile, displayed a formality that was completely out of character for her. The petty officer persisted in calling Max lieutenant while everyone else had fallen easily into using her name, or, in Sapphi's case, the more genial LT.

Rosa knew Jenks was still smarting from her brother's departure in addition to adjusting to a new lieutenant. Hopefully she would come around; if not, they were going to have to have a talk.

You miss Nik, too, Rosa.

She did, but she also didn't regret pushing him out the door. Nika deserved a team of his own and a chance to show HQ just how good he was at his job. He deserved the chance to show himself just how good he was. She laughed softly. "God help me but I could take some of my own advice."

"You keep sitting there laughing to yourself and people are going to get worried." Ma sat down in the chair opposite her.

"Among this bunch? I doubt it." Rosa scrubbed a hand through her brown curls and smiled in Ma's direction. "We ready to go?"

"Prechecks all checked out," he replied. "What's bothering you?"

"I'm fine."

Ma hummed. "I know you well enough to know that's bullshit. Max isn't settled in and until she's able to ask you what's on your mind, it's my job for the moment."

"It's just as well she isn't." Rosa mustered a smile.

"You worried about your new lieutenant?"

Rosa didn't answer. She knew Ma would keep everything in confidence but something about admitting her misgivings to anyone but Max seemed unfair. "You know her," she said instead, and Ma nodded.

"Watched her grow up."

"Tell me about her parents." Rosa glanced at the door as she leaned back in her chair. "The files don't say much beyond the basics."

"They're complicated. Her mother is an excellent officer. Her father is a brilliant doctor. They are both very good at their jobs," Ma said, rubbing at his chin, and Rosa didn't miss the incredibly diplomatic answer that held a wealth of information just out of reach. "Maybe not quite as great at being parents. They pushed their kids hard, and still do. Carmichaels are expected to uphold a certain image, and Max—" He shook his head. "She never quite did. It made things rough for her."

Rosa raised an eyebrow in his direction, holding in a snort of amusement. Ma lifted up a hand with a laugh.

"You won't hear the 'poor little rich girl' thing from her, Commander. That's why I'm telling you—without the specifics; you'll have to get those from her. Max is good people, dedicated and determined. She's sharp and has great instincts. But she's awkward as fuck and doesn't trust herself enough to take action sometimes. I just don't want you to take that hesitance as poor leadership skills."

"Admiral Chen's recommendation for Interceptor training was positively glowing. She talked about how much potential Max has and how with a good commanding officer she could—" Rosa broke off as the realization hit her like an asteroid. "Oh. Ma, you sneaky bastard."

He held his hands up. "What? I'm just a master chief. I don't have any pull around here."

Rosa gave him a flat look. "You are full of shit."

Ma tilted his head with a chuckle. "Seriously, I wasn't the one who suggested it, but I may have put in a good word on both sides of the aisle here. And I did get an early message she was headed this way after everything was said and done, but I figured you and Nika had your reasons for waiting to tell the team, so I kept my mouth shut. You know I wouldn't have broken up the team this close to the Games. I suspect someone else out there had your name at the top of a very short list of people they thought could watch out for her, Commander."

"I'm not a babysitter, Ma." She waved a hand in the air, but Ma shook his head at her dismissal.

"Don't argue with me, Rosa. You're good at what you do. You've trained, what, half a dozen officers in your time with the NeoG? All of who've gone on to have stellar careers. You and I both know you would have been a rear admiral by now if you could leave the system."

"I made peace with my choices, Ma." She couldn't stop her hand from reaching up to the medallion around her neck.

"I know. I may not get the God thing, but I get sticking to a decision." He smiled at her. "What I'm saying is you're doing good work here and you'll continue to do it with Max."

"You're not half-bad yourself there, you know."

Ma shrugged. "I'm old and grumpy, but it serves me well." He clapped his hands on his legs and stood. "Anyway, I'll get people rounded up and *Zuma* is ready to go. Your lieutenant just came out of her room and is headed this way."

Rosa stuck a hand out, smiling when Ma clasped it and squeezed. "Thanks, Ma. I don't know what I'd do without you."

"Hopefully neither of us will ever have to figure that out." He let go of her hand and left the room.

MAX EXCHANGED A SMILE WITH MA AS HE CAME OUT OF THE commander's office and then knocked on the doorjamb. "You have a minute, Commander?"

Rosa waved her in. "Ma's gone to get everyone rounded up. They'll head down to the boat. Something about the briefing?"

"No, it was about your mission with the system jumper." She watched Rosa's eyebrows lift and swallowed down her trepidation. "I know I wasn't involved, but I took a look at the reports and cross-matched the launch lists. Both *An Ordinary Star* and *Journey's Folly* were from the same launch day."

"Go on, Lieutenant."

"I'm not inclined to go so far as some of Jenks's suggestions." Max smiled sheepishly. "Aliens are pretty much out of the equation at this point, according to everyone who studies astrobiology. Natural wormhole sucking them off course is possible but also highly unlikely and doesn't explain how the ships ended up back in our solar system."

"You read her unedited report?"

"It was unfiled on the team server," Max replied. "I didn't think it would be an issue—"

"It's not." Rosa waved a hand. "If anything I'm impressed you took the time to see if there was anything unfiled on there." She smiled. "So not aliens or natural wormholes. Then what?"

"Salvagers coming across the derelict vessels and just ejecting the bodies makes the most sense, but—something's not right about that, either. I just can't understand why they would go to that kind of risk for such outdated components. I don't have an answer for you." Max hated to admit it, but the commander didn't seem the least bit bothered by it.

"Keep digging, then." Rosa got to her feet and grabbed her bag off her bed, pausing with her head cocked to the side. "You seem surprised. Were you expecting me to tell you to leave it?"

"I just—" Max stammered. "I suppose I was. Why don't you?"

"Get your bag, we'll walk and talk."

Max practically skidded across the floor toward her own room and caught up with Rosa at the entrance to their quarters. The door slid shut behind her, and red lights pulsed twice around the perimeter as Rosa pressed a hand to the panel to lock it.

"What made you look into this in the first place?"

"Nika mentioned it before he left. I thought it was strange." Max shrugged. "Jenks is right about one thing, the odds are ridiculous. That's far too high a failure rate for it to never have been talked about in the press. I went back and looked. Not only was there nothing in the news, Commander. There were no protests."

Rosa stopped midstride. "From the families?"

"Right—because there were no families," Max said. "All the people who were on that last wave were solo cruisers, or all the family they had in the world was on board with them."

"Jenks would have said something about that."

"She doesn't know. She doesn't have access to the manifest lists."

"*I* don't have access to those lists," Rosa replied.

"I do." Max looked at her hands and then back up at her commander. "They were all on the trial list for a newer version of LifeEx. *All* the travelers were. I messaged my sister yesterday and asked her for a favor."

It was hard to tell if Rosa's smile was amused or annoyed as she started walking again and then swung into the zero-g tube that led to the docking bay. Max was hoping it was the former and scrambled after her.

"So is that what you've been doing in your room?" Rosa asked, spinning gracefully around to look at Max.

"Partially." Max took a deep breath, blew it out, and took a chance. "I was also hiding. Trying to get my bearings. New places are hard for me."

"We're a team for a reason."

It was less a rebuke and more a gentle reminder, which somehow made it ten times worse, and Max felt her cheeks heat in response. "Yes, Commander."

"We're under orders from Admiral Hoboins to keep an eye out for any more salvaged jumpers. I suppose that would also include any information we happen to find about said jumpers, wouldn't it?"

"I guess so."

"Here's why I didn't tell you to leave it. This job? It's not all about what's up here, Carmichael," Rosa said, tapping at her temple. "You have to learn to trust this." She reached out and poked Max lightly in the stomach. Rosa fixed her with serious brown eyes. "I suspect you're very good at the former, so we'll work on the latter."

Max nodded once, grateful when Rosa turned away to catch the bar by the corridor that led to the Interceptor bay. It gave her a moment to blink away the tears that had sprung out of nowhere.

The easy acceptance in Rosa's tone would have been shocking in itself, but coupled with words that cut straight through her? It shook Max to the core. No one had treated her with that much respect since Ma, not even Admiral Chen, who'd been the most supportive person in Max's life for the last year. But the head of the NeoG stood on the other side of a yawning gulf of rank and Rosa, despite her position, already seemed far more approachable.

"Ma is already keeping an eye on Jenks and her interest in this," Rosa said as Max's boots hit the floor behind her, "so you won't need to. But despite Jenks's somewhat unorthodox temperament, she's good crew and she knows her shit, so feel free to bring her in on your investigation." She looked over her shoulder. "And once she unsticks her head from her ass about you taking Nika's place, I suspect you'll get along just fine."

"You noticed, huh?"

Rosa laughed. "I notice everything, Carmichael, get used to it." She pointed to her left. "We're going this way."

The Interceptor bay gave a sense of just how massive the station was, Max thought as she followed Rosa through the wide bulkhead doors. It stretched away from her until the curve vanished from her sight. The seventy-three-point-three-meter ships were lined up with military precision, following that same curve until they, too, disappeared in the distance.

From the doorway the ships looked resplendent, each glowing white with the NeoG logo emblazoned on its rounded side and a distinct green-and-blue hash marking at the tail end. As they got closer, though, Max could see the grime and space dust coating the ships, the residue of which wouldn't come off even with constant scrubbing. All of it evidence of a service hard-pressed for replacements.

But the deckhands waved and greeted them—or Rosa, rather—as they walked through the busy area, and competing music blared from several stations as well as ships.

"Rosa." A big man lounging in what Max was sure was

a beach chair tossed them a lazy salute from underneath a ship marked with a skull decorated with flowers. "You headed out?"

"Couple of days." Rosa waved a hand. "Commander D'Arcy Montaglione, this is our new lieutenant, Max Carmichael. Max, the commander is in charge of Interceptor team Ay13, *Dread Treasure*."

Commander Montaglione stuck a hand out but didn't get up, and Max shouldered her bag so she could shake it. "Pleasure." He grinned, white teeth flashing bright against his dark skin. His grip was firm, callused fingers squeezing for a moment before he released her. "What's your comp?"

"My comp?"

"For the Games."

"Oh, I don't know. Hand-to-hand, I guess?"

Dark brown eyes flicked from her to Rosa and the grin widened. "Oh, Rosa, did they saddle you with a total newbie just a few months before the prelims?"

"You think it matters? We're still going to kick your ass."

"We'll see, I guess. Nice to meet you, Max." D'Arcy winked at her. Rosa grabbed Max by the arm, kicked D'Arcy's boot with a decent amount of force, and walked away muttering curses in Spanish that were either too fast or too complicated for Max's Babel to translate.

"Ignore him," Rosa said, finally seeming to have run out of words.

"He's not wrong."

"Yes, he is. You'll do fine. We all will. And D'Arcy is just as invested in us doing well as the rest of NeoG will be. His team is good, but they haven't even broken the top three in the preliminary rankings for the Games the last two years running. If he does make it into the top two with us we'll be competing together against the other branches."

"What event does he—" Max stopped herself and tried again. "What's his comp?"

Rosa smiled. "Picking up the lingo is a good sign. He's a sword fighter, and a good one. Hell in the Boarding Action, too." She pinned Max with a look. "In more ways than one."

"Oh?"

"He likes to sweet-talk his way into people's beds, so stay away from him. Smooth as overpriced tequila, but will leave you with a shitty taste in your mouth the next morning all the same."

"Oh." Max blinked and raised her hand. "I don't, no, you don't have to worry about me."

"Ah, that's right." Rosa nodded. "I saw the ace designation on your file. Thank God above for that. I have enough trouble with Jenks." Rosa pointed behind her. "Just tell him you're asexual if he comes sniffing around. He's an ass about a great many things, but he'll respect a no." She smiled and gestured at the ship looming ahead of them. "Here she is."

Max dragged in a breath, grateful when Rosa ducked under the ship and headed for the other side, giving her a moment alone.

The Long-Range Interceptor *Zuma's Ghost* was the same as her sisters in the bay, and yet not. With five narrow stripes on her tail section—three blue, two green—and a front panel that had been dented and pounded back out so that only a shadow remained, she was a thing of beauty. Narrow and sleek, but rising up almost thirty meters in the air, she was built for space, atmo, and underwater. Once upon a time the hull panels had been white, but the years had reduced her shine to a dingier finish despite obvious attempts to keep her clean.

The Interceptors were long-range craft, designed to hold a crew of six but with capacity for a hundred additional temporary passengers should it be required. They had a pair of rail guns that fired Magsten rounds, seventeen-centimeter-long projectiles that could punch a hole in any unshielded hull.

Max ducked under the ship, trailing a hand along the plating until she came out on the other side. By the outer door, the painting of a grinning man with a half-rotted face stared down at her, somehow managing to look both pleased and disappointed.

Max gave him a pat as she stopped just outside. "Permission to come aboard, Commander?"

"Granted, welcome aboard." Rosa stuck her hand out with a smile. "Sleeping quarters are upstairs, your room is on the starboard side. Careful with the door, someone likely pranked it."

Max chuckled and shifted her bag as she grabbed for the rail by the stairs. "Thanks for the warning."

T-MINUS THIRTEEN WEEKS UNTIL
PRELIM BOARDING GAMES

"Did you expect it to be more exciting?"

Max shifted in her seat to look at Ma. They were eight hours into their twelve-hour shift. Rosa, Sapphi, and Jenks would be waking up in an hour or two. For right now it was quiet. Tamago was in the back watching sword-fighting videos.

Max liked the quiet. With only three people awake, the ship seemed impossibly huge. The overlap hours were the hardest, when everyone was up and the space was loud and filled with noise.

Like with so many things, though, she was getting used to it and had stopped jumping at the laughter and the good-natured shouting that seemed to be a hallmark of this close-knit team.

It was amazing how quickly she'd settled into life on board *Zuma's Ghost*. This first week had passed in the blink of an eye as they'd done training runs and patrolled the area between Jupiter and the asteroid belt.

"Not really?" She smiled and shrugged. "I knew there would be long stretches of waiting, that's the way of it." It was giving her time to study up on the mission specs and the Games, anyway. "Going to the Navy probably would have been safer."

Ma chuckled. "That's your parents talking." He shook his head. "Safe is relative, you know that."

"Why'd you join the NeoG, Ma? Why didn't you retire?"

"The girls asked me the same thing," he replied with a smile. His daughters, Julissa and Anabelle, were grown with families of their own. "I told them I wasn't the kind of man who could sit still and do nothing for whatever time I had left. Which was mostly true. But . . ." He let out a soft sigh. "Ai loved being out in the black and I couldn't stand the thought of being in a house on Earth all by myself. As long as I'm out here, it feels like she's still here with me." He tapped his hand to his heart.

Max reached out and touched his hand with a smile. "I miss her, too." She remembered Ma's wife. Ai had been full of laughter and always moving. She'd welcomed Max into their home with a kindness that had been lacking in the Carmichael family, and the young Max had clung to it like a lifeline.

"She'd be making fun of me for being so sentimental." He smiled. "She loved you, Max. She'd be proud of where you are now."

They lapsed into silence, and Max put her attention back on their course. The asteroid belt didn't ever look like people expected it to, with a bunch of massive rocks spinning together through space and crashing into each other.

Instead, the asteroids were spread thin, even though they numbered in the millions; and there were massive stretches of space without any asteroids in the belt at all, thanks to Jupiter's gravity.

It was easy to say space was big, but you never got the actual sense of just how much black nothing stretched out in front of you until you were there. Max tapped at her console, sliding her finger along the course line. At the moment, *Zuma's Ghost* was at the outer edge of one of the Kirkwood gaps and she could see two asteroids ahead of them.

"Hey, Ma? Do you mind if I adjust our course?"

"You realize you're in charge, right, Max?"

She felt her cheeks heat and was glad they were the only two people on the bridge. "Yes, but *Zuma's* more your ship than mine. You're the pilot."

"She's not my ship, Max, she's ours. I appreciate your consideration, just remember who's in charge. What do you see?" He leaned over to look at her console display.

"That asteroid will intersect with our route in about seventy-two hours." She pointed at the closer of the two. "It's not a big deal, the asteroid is less than a kilometer across, but it'll come close enough to us that we'd probably end up doing a correction to make sure we avoid it."

"Best to do it now, then," Ma said.

Max made the correction and looked up to find him studying her. "What?"

"Did you figure that out just from looking at it?"

Max shifted uncomfortably. "Yeah? Asteroids are easy, they don't change orbit unless something makes them change."

"You mean unlike people?"

"Most people are still pretty predictable," she replied.

Ma nodded. "You know for the piloting competition there has to be an officer and an enlisted person in the cockpit, right? One pilot and one navigator. Rosa and I have worked together well, but I'm thinking that maybe she should give up the seat to you."

Max stared at him suspiciously. "Why?"

"Because of that." He laughed and thumped a hand down on the console. "Listen. I'm good at what I do; the navigation helps, but I can usually see what's coming, and despite my old-man status I've got reflexes." His exaggerated expression had Max laughing despite her nerves. "But I'm thinking that you and me might make an unstoppable duo. I'll talk to Rosa about it and we'll run a simulator when we get back to Jupiter, see how it goes."

"Okay, I'll—"

The coms lit up, cutting her off. "Mayday. Mayday. Mayday. This is mining vessel *Viridian Hold* requesting assistance from any ship in the vicinity of six-seven-seven, niner-niner-four, one-zero-seven point eight."

"*Viridian Hold,* this is Near-Earth Orbital Guard Interceptor *Zuma's Ghost.* What is your status?" Max replied.

"Electrical short in our drilling equipment started a fire, *Zuma.* We got it taken care of but the short fried our nav system and our long-range coms. We've been stuck on this rock for three hours and I don't mind saying it's really good to hear your voice."

"No problem, *Viridian.* Looks like we're about twenty minutes away. How's your life support?" Max glanced up when someone put their hand on her shoulder. Rosa gave her a nod and then finished tying back her brown curls.

"It's good for now, *Zuma,* doesn't look like the short affected those systems or our power. We've got our suits should we need them, but we were working when the fire happened so the suits are already at half-full."

"Roger that, *Viridian,* we're on our way. Hold fast."

"See you in twenty, *Zuma.*"

Max hung up the com and looked back at Rosa. "Good morning," she said, and the commander laughed.

"Just enough time to pump some caffeine into Jenks. Got that called into Control, Ma?"

Ma nodded. "They're sending a tow our way. Should be a few hours, but *Viridian* only has a crew of eight."

"We've got the room. Let's bring them on board and siphon off the O_2 from their recyclers rather than wait to see if something else goes wrong with their system." Rosa tipped her head toward the stairs. "You ready, Max?"

"Commander?"

"You took the call, Lieutenant, so you get to go over and say hi." Rosa waved at the door. "Don't worry, Ma and Jenks will be with you. It'll be fine."

Max nodded and headed for her cabin, sliding a hand down to the pocket on her right leg as she climbed the stairs to the second level. She still hadn't read the letter from Nika, but had started carrying it around like a talisman. For some stupid reason just the presence of the thing gave her assurance.

Likely would help even more if you actually read it.

"I will, after this, I promise."

The twenty minutes sped by in a rush of prep, nerves, and more jokes from Jenks than Max had expected. But moments after they'd landed on the asteroid next to the drill rig, all the joking slid away and she watched Jenks efficiently check over Ma's gear and then perform the complicated handshake she'd seen everyone do. No one had taught it to her and Max couldn't find her way past her uncertainty to ask.

"Lieutenant." Jenks performed the same check on her, minus the handshake.

Tamago passed their swords over with a nod.

Max blinked. "We expecting trouble?"

Ma handed Max her sword and then slapped his own to his back, the magnetic clasps catching with a click. "SAH."

"Shit always happens," Jenks supplied with a brief smile, Tamago nodding from behind her.

"Everything seems on the level," Rosa said. "But it's wild space out here, Carmichael. For all we know, pirates could have taken the rig and called in a fake problem to try to get their hands on an Interceptor."

"That seems like a lot of work for a lot of trouble that would follow."

"Possibly." Rosa smiled. "But you stay alive longer if you're suspicious. This is a different world from HQ, best to learn that now."

"Understood, Commander." Max kept her sword in her hand as Tamago reached for the airlock.

"IT WASN'T THE FLASHIEST OF RESCUES, BUT NOT BAD FOR A first." Jenks patted Doge on the head and stretched her legs out under the corner table at Corbin's. "Plus it bought us a freebie day back on station, so what's to complain about?"

"Nothing I can see," Tamago replied with a shrug, lifting their own beer in answering salute. They scanned the bar and then made a face. "Ugh, naval annoyance alert."

"Where? Aw shit," she muttered when she spotted the pair of naval officers and watched as they cornered Max the moment she walked into the bar.

"Jenks, you know Rosa said if you start another bar fight she'll have to write you up."

"I'm not going to start a fight, promise." She got to her feet and wove through the few patrons dotting the bar. It was a weeknight and the place was mostly empty. "Might finish one, but I won't start it."

Nika would be laughing at her, but just because she didn't fully trust her new lieutenant didn't mean she was going to leave Max to fend for herself.

"What's a Carmichael doing slumming it in the space cops?" the taller of the pair of officers asked. He didn't see Jenks approaching, which gave her the perfect opening to jam an elbow into his ribs and step on the foot of the other lieutenant blocking Max against the bar.

"Shit, sorry!" Her smile was bright as the sun. "It's so crowded in here tonight. Someone must have shoved me. We've got a table over here, Lieutenant." Grabbing Max by the wrist, Jenks made her escape before the pair could react. "You wanna watch out," she said, even as she listened to see if either of those fools was going to follow. "Navy doesn't come over to this bar all that often, but sometimes they do. When that happens it's only to start shit."

"Thanks."

Jenks knew Max was hurting from the jerk's comment. Her expression didn't change from the same placid one she always wore, but her shoulders slumped as she curled inward, trying to escape the feeling. "Hey, Lieutenant, it sucks. We get it a lot, you just have to learn to ignore it."

Jenks slid a hand up Max's back, pressing between her shoulder blades until she was standing straight again. "We're motherfucking NeoG," she murmured, pleased when Max smiled.

"*You* don't ignore it."

"I do when the commander gets too much flak over me starting bar fights."

That got a laugh out of her new lieutenant, but it faded just as quickly and Max gestured over her shoulder. "I'll go get a table. You don't have to pretend like you want me to sit with you."

Jenks almost let her go, but then her brother's voice echoed in her head.

"She's also lonely and could use someone to watch her back."

He knew. Nika knew that was the one thing that could get Jenks's sympathy. She'd known lonely before she met the Vagins, and it was a feeling she wouldn't wish on anyone.

"Nope," she said out loud, tightening her grip on Max's wrist. "You're part of the team, you sit with us."

Lieutenant Maxine Carmichael/Max—

Lieutenant Commander Saynor left me a handwritten note like this when I took his place, though I'll tell you the same thing she did, which is that you don't have to try to find some real paper to write me back on. You know how to get a hold of me and please, if you need anything—advice, a friendly ear—anything at all, just email me.

Here is what I want you to remember:

You earned the right to be here. It was not given to you. You claimed it. You paid for it in blood and sweat and tears.

You are smarter than you realize and you will still make mistakes. We all do.

You are part of a team now. That means you don't have to go it alone. Relying on others doesn't make you weak, it makes you stronger.

Sometimes you can do everything right and death will still come for people. Learn what you can and then let it go into the black. Don't carry it around with you. The weight of it will drown you.

Good luck, Max, and take care of them for me.

Commander Nika Vagin/Nik

T-MINUS TWELVE WEEKS UNTIL
PRELIM BOARDING GAMES

"*Zuma's Ghost*, we're getting a request for help from the Enceladus Research Station. Their power went down and they're running on emergency backup. The company has techs on the way with replacement couplings, but their arrival time is cutting it pretty close to when their air runs out. You're the closest ship to the station—seemed to me like Jenks could rewire those into some semblance of power, or should we get one of the boats here to bring them a few spares?"

"We can do it, Control," Rosa replied, sitting up in her seat. "Send us the coordinates."

While Rosa was talking, Max pulled the specs on the research station and scanned through the information. "There are only eleven people at the station. Worst-case situation, Commander, we could bring them aboard until the repair techs get there."

"We'll keep it on the list, though they don't seem to be in nearly as bad straits as those miners were." Rosa nodded and turned in her seat. "Hey, Jenks?" she called out over the coms. "Come to the bridge."

"Can do, Commander." Moments later the clatter of her

boots echoed from behind them. "What's up?" Jenks asked, skidding to a halt.

"You know anything about rewiring power couplings?"

"From scratch?"

"Possibly," Rosa replied, and Jenks made a face.

"Here," Max said, sliding the schematics across the display. They'd settled into an almost friendly rhythm since Jenks had saved her butt in the bar, but Max still couldn't get a read on the woman like she had with the rest of the team.

Jenks scratched at her head, disrupting the now purple strands of her hair as she studied it. "Yeah, shouldn't be a problem, depending on what I have to work with, but we can get it done. We going that direction?"

Rosa nodded. Jenks gave a sloppy salute in reply and headed for the back of the ship, shouting for Tamago.

"She'll get the gear together," Rosa said. "We've got a decent complement of spare parts. Never know when you'll have to make a repair on the fly."

"Every other week," Ma muttered, shooting a grin at Rosa over his shoulder.

Max listened to the banter with half an ear as she studied the specs for the research station. The power core was in the center spike, slightly below the ring. She expanded the view, zooming in on the interior.

"Know anything about power couplings, Carmichael?" Rosa asked over her shoulder.

"I don't," she admitted. "But I figured it was better to take a look and at least know where the core is than show up there and be totally lost."

"Fair enough." It could have been approval in Rosa's voice, but Max wasn't sure. "Go with Jenks when we get on board. You'll learn something."

"Yes, Commander."

For the next ten minutes, Rosa walked her through the schematics, patiently explaining the basics. "The CHN mandated that all major components going into space had to be interchangeable no matter the original producer. So a power coupling from the Hudson Company will still work within a system designed by Voyager."

"It's smart," Max replied with a nod. "That way you don't have someone dying out here just because of a brand war."

"We had enough of that in the Collapse."

Max watched in silence as Rosa reached up for the medallion at her throat. The Collapse was so far in humanity's past and yet had affected everything moving forward. It seemed sometimes that it had been only yesterday that the world fell into chaos and ruin thanks to the indifference and greed of humanity.

"Hey, Max, have you seen Saturn up close?" Ma asked, looking over his shoulder with a smile.

"No." Max's eyes were locked on the view rapidly filling the main window and the word came out in a breathless gasp.

Saturn loomed ahead, a yellow-brown oblate sphere ringed with innumerable particles. This close they no longer looked like rings, but a kilometer-thick carpet of ice and debris stretching between the ship and the planet.

"She's beautiful." Max couldn't take her eyes off it.

The rings moved, undulating in waves at spots and shifting like the ebb and flow of a river.

"It's Ma's favorite planet. Jenks's is Pluto." Sapphi grinned from her spot on the bridge opposite Max. "Despite the fact that it's not a planet."

"I can hear you! It is a damned planet, Saph, reinstated and everything in 2240," Jenks hollered as she clattered back up the stairs.

"Only because they felt sorry for it." Sapphi winked at Max.

"It's because Jenks feels a kinship with small things that don't fit in the solar system."

"I heard that, too, Ma!"

Laughter echoed through the ship.

"It's got a heart on it, for crying out loud," Jenks muttered a moment later from Max's side. "How can you not love it?"

"For what it's worth," Max whispered with a smile, "I like the heart, too."

Jenks eyed her for a moment, then a slow smile curved one side of her mouth and she bumped her shoulder into Max's arm.

They flew around the planet. And then, the bright white orb of Enceladus came into view, stunning against the black backdrop of space, hovering above the rings. And orbiting it, the research station.

It was shaped like a spindle with a rotating ring two-thirds of the way down the narrow, spiked center.

"Enceladus Research Station Control, this is Interceptor boat Zz5, *Zuma's Ghost*," Sapphi said.

"Roger that, *Zuma's Ghost*. This is Enceladus Control." A dry voice echoed back over the com.

"Commander Rosa Martín here, Enceladus. Heard you needed the power back on. We thought we'd swing by and see what we could do."

"We've got sweaters aplenty, but it would get hard to breathe after a while. We appreciate the assistance."

"Are we okay to dock? We can use the ship to power the sequence."

"You are cleared to dock, *Zuma's Ghost*, and thanks for the offer. Less of a chance of something going wrong if you use your power grid instead of ours."

"Sounds like a plan, Control," Sapphi replied after exchanging a nod with Ma. "Docking procedures initiated."

Max grabbed for the nearby bar as the ship angled in for the docking port and slipped easily into position.

"Docked and locked, Commander," Sapphi announced.

"Good job, Ensign. You and Ma hold the fort here. Lieutenant, you're with me."

Max followed Rosa down the stairs to the door, where Jenks

and Tamago waited, gear slung over their shoulders. They piled into the airlock and Max rested a hand on her sword.

The other door slid open, revealing three people just inside the station's airlock, and a message from Jenks scrolled across Max's vision.

Verified station staff. Visual matches files.

"Commander Martín Rivas of the NeoG," Rosa said. "This is Lieutenant Carmichael and Petty Officers Khan and Uchida."

The man in the front lifted his hand with a smile. "I'm Dr. Julien Apostas, head of Enceladus Research. This is Dr. Via Hugh, she's in charge of our biology department, and Svetlana Krupin, my assistant and our head repairwoman."

"He's being kind," Svetlana said. "Our repair tech went home a week ago because their wife is having a baby any day now. I got stuck with the duty. At which, I'm afraid, I haven't done all that well."

"Well enough, Svetlana," Julien replied, rubbing a hand over his short beard. "Now that we're all sure we are who we say we are, should we take this out of the airlock, Commander?"

Rosa's lips twitched. "Sounds like a plan, Doctor."

"Call me Julien." He stuck his hand out. "Thanks for coming to our rescue."

"Why didn't you just head for Jupiter until the techs could get here?" Rosa asked, shaking his hand.

"Rules for something like that are we all go or we all stay." Julien smiled. "And since we've got a few timed experiments, we weren't willing to leave." He shrugged. "Here we are. It wasn't much of an emergency as they go, and Jupiter Control said you could be right over."

"Jenks has a talent for putting things back in working order. She and Lieutenant Carmichael can go with Svetlana." Rosa pointed in their direction. "See what they can do to get you up and running again, at least until the company techs arrive. In the meantime, I suspect Petty Officer Uchida would love a tour. They've got a background in biology."

"University of Utopia." Tamago smiled. "I did my studies on the underground ice floes there."

"Excellent!" Dr. Hugh clapped her hands. "You'll find this fascinating, then, Petty Officer. We've been studying the development of microbes on Enceladus." She pointed off to the left. "If you want to follow me, I'll show you what we're working on right now."

Max took the bag Tamago was carrying and nodded once to Rosa in acknowledgment of the order scrolling across her vision.

Check in every half hour.

"So, you had couplings in storage, didn't you?" Jenks asked Svetlana as they followed the petite redhead down the corridor in the opposite direction.

"The couplings in storage were bad. Or at least I think they are? Nothing changed when I plugged them in. I know enough to put them in and hit the switch, but not enough to rewire from scratch." Svetlana lifted her hands helplessly.

Jenks grinned. "If you're up for a lesson, I'll teach you how. I'm going to teach our new lieutenant here anyway."

"Awesome! I left the couplings down in the core room. It's this way."

Max followed along behind as Jenks peppered Svetlana with questions about the power core and about the particulars of the power problems the station was having. It seemed random, but Max spotted the pattern and the way Jenks was able to coax information out of Svetlana without assuming the scientist knew the answer to the problem because of her own experience with the power core.

The stationary nature of the core meant it had different requirements from a ship's, but the core itself wasn't all that dissimilar from that of a ship a class or two larger than *Zuma's*

Ghost. Thankfully, what was bad was the couplings that fed power out from the core and not the core itself. They found themselves in front of three cylindrical nodes set into a nearby wall about half a meter off the floor.

Jenks tossed her bag down and dropped into a crouch by the pile of parts in the corner. "Hey, Lieutenant? Hand me the power tester in the outside pocket of the bag you're carrying."

Max set down her bag, fished around until she found what she was reasonably sure looked like a tester, and handed it over.

"Thanks." Jenks took it, turned it on, and slammed it against the deck a few times until it actually cooperated and powered up. "I swear to God, if I don't get that equipment requisition in soon I'm dumping this entire bag of junk onto Hoboins's desk and quitting."

"Jenks said you were new to the team?" Svetlana asked Max as Jenks continued to curse under her breath.

"Yes. I just transferred in a few weeks ago."

"I've been here for almost two Sol years. Two more months and I'll get my LifeEx bonus." She smiled brightly.

"Bonus?"

"If you do two years out past the belt on any of their research or mining facilities, Hamatachi Corp pays for the initial treatment and the re-ups for as long as you're with the company. It's incentive to get folks to be out here away from Earth for so long."

Max frowned. "They're required to provide the treatment if you're working out here, aren't they?"

"Oh sure, CHN regs for space work and all that. But if you flake on your contract you have to pay them back for every day you're short. After two years you can quit whenever and just lose the re-ups." Svetlana smiled. "If I stay with the company for a full twenty I'm set for life."

"The lieutenant wouldn't know about that, Svetlana," Jenks called. "She's minted."

Max sighed and shook her head. "I am not."

"Oh," Svetlana breathed, her blue eyes suddenly round in her heart-shaped face. "Carmichael—I didn't even think."

"It's fine." Max wondered what kind of scene it would make to kick Jenks, who'd dived back into her work, her shoulders shaking with suppressed laughter. "We have to earn our LifeEx same as anyone else."

"You could just buy it, though." Svetlana winced. "Ooh, I'm sorry. That was rude."

"I couldn't. Not really." Max smiled. "Our great-grandfather wrote several provisions into his will that are mandatory for all future generations. I do get an annual payment from my inheritance, but if I were to leave the military, that would stop unless I took a job with the company or with the Coalition government."

"That's all super-fascinating stuff, but *this* is really interesting. Come here you two," Jenks said, waving a hand over her head. "So, Svetlana, every single power coupling on this station is utterly fried. All three of the ones in use and all three of the ones in storage. The odds of that are really impressive. Again with the impressive failure ratios," Jenks muttered the last bit to herself. "Did you have a power surge or something recently?"

"Nothing I can think of." Svetlana frowned.

"Well." Jenks clapped her hands. "The good news is, all three are bad."

"How is that good?" Max asked, sharing a look with Svetlana.

"Teaching moment. They're bad, but fixable. I'm going to rewire this one. Watch close, and follow along." Jenks pointed on either side of her.

"What?"

"Time to get dirty, Lieutenant. You and Svetlana will do

the others while I'm working here." She took hold of her coupling and twisted until the cap came loose in her hand, trailing a mass of wires along with it.

Max swallowed and grabbed for her coupling.

AN HOUR LATER THE THREE OF THEM WERE GREASY WITH THE slippery green biolubricant that was used to help keep the conduits cool, and all three grinned in delight at the humming sound that now emanated from the power core of the station.

"Flip the emergency power off, Commander; let's see if she'll take the load," Jenks said over the coms.

"Emergency backup going off in three, two, one," Rosa replied.

There was barely a shimmy as the power swapped back over. Svetlana whistled her approval while Max stared at the whole thing with a kind of dazed amazement that broke only when Jenks punched her in the shoulder.

"Good job, Lieutenant."

Max seemed ridiculously stunned. It hadn't been a hard rewire job, but the look on her face made Jenks wonder if anyone had ever taken the time to show her how to do something so mundane. "I did it right?"

"Probably. We'll know in five minutes if the whole thing blows."

Max's eyes snapped wide.

"Kidding, I'm kidding." Jenks slung her arm over Svetlana's shoulders, pleased when the pretty research tech leaned into her. "I think this calls for a shower and a drink."

"I just might have something stashed away, and you're more than welcome to shower with me." Svetlana glanced in Max's direction. "I'm sure Dr. Apostas won't mind if we drop you off at his quarters, Lieutenant. He's got a private shower you can use. I'll message him and get permission."

Jenks tried not to chuckle at the look of relief on Max's face.

Jenks—

Settled in. Finally.

Mission requires us to be on the ground here as much as up in the black. Right now they have me on the dirt on Trappist-1e as a point of contact for the planetside dockyard. It feels weird being on solid ground, no lie. (And shut up, I know you're making some joke about how I finally found the perfect solution to my space problem.) The new team is great. They're not you all, but, well, you know what I mean.

There's so much traffic. I didn't realize how big the habitats had gotten. The news makes it sound like they're still super small. Spoiler alert: they are not.

I miss you. No, that's a lie. I really miss Doge, give him a hug for me.

—*Nika*

Nika—

You're going to turn into one of those Army dudes staying dirtside all the time. I think you should come home.

I'm being nice to the lieutenant. Taught her how to rewire a power conduit on a run out to Enceladus the other day. You'd have thought I taught her brain surgery, as impressed as she was.

Most of the time she moves like she doesn't know what to do with herself, but we put her in the ring and it's like watching a ghost fight. I had her spar D'Arcy yesterday and he couldn't put a hand on her. I can't figure out if she's letting me punch her or if I'm immune to her creepy powers. Ma's talked Rosa into putting her in the navigator seat, too, and the first simulation they did was a thing of beauty.

She's all right, I guess. I'm going to keep punching her in the face until she learns how to keep her damn hands up, though.

Doge misses you, but I don't.

    —J

T-MINUS TEN WEEKS UNTIL PRELIM BOARDING GAMES

"Hey, Jenks, you got a minute?"

Jenks hit send on the email to her brother and then looked up at Max. "Do now, Lieutenant. Whatcha need?"

"Rosa just passed on a report from Admiral Hoboins. Those five people you picked up with that system jumper out in the belt before I arrived are dead," Max said, sitting down at the table across from her.

"Dead?"

Max nodded at Jenks's incredulous look. "There was a malfunction in the fire suppression system in the brig of the naval transport. Four sailors had to be treated for oxygen deprivation and eight prisoners were beyond revival—our five were among them."

"Should I be the one to say that's extremely convenient?" Jenks asked.

"You can," Max replied. "You wouldn't be the only one thinking it, though."

"Why are we only hearing about this now?"

"Navy just sent the word to Hoboins." Max shrugged. "I guess they didn't think it was all that important."

"Figures. It was odd enough with the ratio thing and that all those people were on the trial list for the new version of LifeEx." Jenks rubbed a hand over the back of her neck. It still surprised her a little that Max had shared that information with her so easily, and that Rosa apparently was encouraging them both to look into this weirdness more than a month out from the mission.

"The problem is this means the case is officially closed," Max said. "Off-Earth has their property back, the criminals are dead. There's nothing for NeoG, or anyone else for that matter, to do."

"Did we get a report on that fire and anything on the autopsies of those criminals?" Jenks asked.

"I've got it. Also have a list of the passengers who were on the ship," Max replied, and the notification blinked to life in the corner of Jenks's vision at the same time. "For all the good it'll do. Short in the wiring, no sign of foul play. Open and shut."

Jenks muttered a curse. Max was sitting carefully still at her side, waiting. "Do you want me to drop it, Lieutenant?"

"No." Max blinked at her in surprise. "I was kind of hoping you'd have an idea of what we should do next because honestly I'm at a loss. Technically we can't do anything with a closed case unless we find a reason to reopen it."

"Oh . . . well, give me some time to look through the reports and I'll get back to you?"

Max nodded, then smiled as she got to her feet. "I'm going to go to bed. Let me know if you've thought of anything when I get up."

Jenks watched her head for the stairs. Nika would have pushed, wanted to know what she was thinking. But Carmichael just accepted that Jenks knew what she was doing for no reason beyond the fact that she trusted Jenks to do her job.

She wasn't sure if that was a good sign or not.

She spun in her chair, checked the time back on Earth,

and then tapped the com codes into the console behind her. A few moments later, the screen flashed as Chief Petty Officer Luis Armstrong answered.

"Morning. I wasn't expecting a call from you." *Honorable Intent*'s lone enlisted man wasn't just built like a brawler. The CPO *was* a brawler, slower than Jenks but dangerous enough that she knew not to let him get his hands on her—at least while they were in the cage.

Outside of it was another matter entirely.

Jenks eyed his bare torso and grinned. "Did I interrupt you?"

Luis's grin matched hers as he finished drying his blond hair. "Just getting ready for work. The boys left for school half an hour ago."

"How are they?"

Jenks saw his startled surprise before Luis's easy smile slipped back into place.

"They're good. Riz is already harassing me about the preliminaries. Elliot got busted sneaking out of class to read in the library. The usual."

The kids were supposed to be off-limits. When they'd met five years ago he'd been reeling from the death of his wife in a shuttle accident. A single father left with almost-two-year-old twin boys struggling to juggle the pieces of his broken life while he competed in the Games.

They'd fought in the cage. She'd won. And then . . . after. She still had to mentally fan herself whenever she remembered the overwhelming encounter in the gym showers.

They'd agreed to keep things casual, which was how she preferred her relationships. They weren't dating. They were just two people who had sex occasionally and that was it.

Except . . . it wasn't.

She'd been breaking the rules more often in the last year. Calling him for no reason other than to see his face and hear how his day was. Asking about his kids. Caring about his life.

It'd started without her even realizing it when she'd seen a poster of herself in the background of his home during one of their chats and teased him about it. Only to discover it belonged to one of his sons.

"Good."

"Sooooo." Luis dragged the word out. "Not that I mind seeing your face, but did you need something?"

Sometimes Jenks felt like they were doing that carefully choreographed dance that spelled the end of a relationship, where she stepped on the other person's feet just enough to convince them it was time to call it quits. Other times the thought of not having Luis in her life was a painful weight in her chest.

She cleared her throat, grateful that Rosa and Sapphi were on the bridge. "Yeah. Can you help me out with something?"

"You know I can. What?"

"Remember that system jumper we snagged a few weeks back? The criminals ended up dead in a very convenient accident on their way to Earth."

Luis's eyebrows took a trip upward. "You mean that accident with the fire suppression system? I didn't realize those were your guys."

"Of course you knew about it. We just got word. Fucking Navy." Jenks spread her hands. "I've got the accident report and the autopsies from the lieutenant, but I was hoping you might have more on it."

"It wasn't our jurisdiction." Luis shook his head. "Sorry, I would have told you sooner if I'd realized. I can do some digging for you, though—if I know what to look for."

"That's the problem," she replied. "I don't know. It was just weird. The one guy who tried to bribe us was freaked, like he knew he was dead. But the ship was clean. If they were smuggling something in it they hid it really well." Jenks reached down and patted Doge when he shifted. "This whole thing is making Doge anxious."

"Your cortisol levels have increased eleven percent in the last half hour," Doge replied over their link, and Jenks was glad that Luis couldn't hear the ROVER. Though judging from his amused look he could guess well enough what the AI had just said.

"I'd imagine so," he said instead. "Send me what you've got. I've gotta go, Dai, but I'll poke around some. See what I come up with."

"Thanks. I'll owe you one."

Luis flashed a wicked grin and then disconnected. Jenks blew out a breath and folded over, pressing her cheek to the top of her dog's head. "Oh, Doge, what the hell am I doing there?"

"I don't have a good answer for you."

"Yeah, me either."

"GOOD WORK OUT THERE, COMMANDER." HOBOINS LEANED back in his chair with a smile in Rosa's direction before he continued. "I've got you scheduled for two more two-week hauls around the belt before you head for Earth for the prelims. How goes the training?"

"Good." Rosa hoped the smile she offered didn't look forced. It wasn't entirely a lie, just didn't go into detail on the dismal results that Sapphi's program was coming up with for *Zuma* as the news of the other NeoG teams trickled in. *Honorable Intent* was pulling some strong numbers in the early projections and rumors. And there were at least three other teams who looked as though they could take the top spot—including *Dread Treasure*.

Rosa suppressed a sigh.

The whole point of the Boarding Games had been to test each branch's infiltration teams against the others, and as such the competition was supposed to be limited to already formed teams—like hers.

And yet, that hadn't stopped things from twisting and

evolving over the years. Now teams were formed with the express purpose of winning the Games, or at least making a political showing. Like the team from NeoG headquarters.

"We're good, Admiral," Max said, slipping easily into the silence with a reassuring smile. "There's still plenty of time for training, but Jenks thinks it's distinctly possible for us to take the top three spots in prelims for the hand-to-hand— depending on how the brackets fall." She laughed. "I get the feeling she's pulling for a championship match versus me."

"You'll have to fight Jenks for real then, Lieutenant. The judges frown on people throwing matches, team or no team. Not to mention the reaction you'll get from the crowd."

"Oh, I know, Admiral. I'll give it my best. If it comes down to me and Jenks, I'm still going to lose." Max pointed at the bruise that decorated her right cheek. "She's so far beyond me."

"How is it you can evade everyone else's strikes but she keeps nailing you?" Rosa asked.

"Most people are easy to predict." Max shrugged. "Jenks, she's almost impossible."

"That's because even Jenks doesn't know what she's going to do until she's done it," Hoboins said.

Rosa chuckled at the look of surprise on Max's face at the vice admiral's sarcasm and reached out to pat her on the shoulder. "Don't worry, you get used to it. Is there anything else, Admiral? Because speaking of training, we should be getting to the gym."

"We're good here." Hoboins pointed a hand at the door in dismissal. "I'll talk to you later."

Rosa followed Max from the room, waving a cursory goodbye to Lou on their way through the outer office, but she didn't say anything until they were alone in the corridor headed across the station toward the gym. "Out with it, Carmichael."

"Curious why you didn't tell the admiral about Sapphi's projections, Commander."

"Because it'll just stress him out and I've got enough on my plate without pissing Lou off."

Max frowned. "Why would it piss Commander Seve off?"

"Because Admiral Hoboins likes to mess with her carefully tended schedule when he's stressed." Rosa grabbed for the bar in the low-g tube, pulling herself out and angling her feet downward in one smooth motion. She watched as Max followed, and the lieutenant managed a similar maneuver with only a little bit of fumbling. "Anyway," she continued as they headed for the base of the stalk, "there's nothing he can do. It's not false optimism on my part."

"I didn't think it was. You're not the kind of person who does that."

"Blows smoke?" Rosa asked. "True." She stepped to the side as her boots hit the deck.

"Commander." Max folded her narrow hands together, long fingers rubbing against the skin on the back of her hand. "I know you're worried about me. That the rest of the team is worried. I just want you to know I—"

"I'm not worried about you, Carmichael." Now was as good a time as any to open herself up to her new lieutenant. Rosa smiled as the look of surprise crossed Max's face for the second time that morning. "You'll do fine. Either work your way through the competition with that uncanny ability you have and get your ass kicked by Jenks, or at least make it far enough up in the bracket to get us some decent points."

"If you're not worried about me, then what?"

"Have you even looked at those projections?" Rosa asked. "Nika was the best there is at sword fighting. I am a poor substitute for his ability. We lost last year because of me."

Max had this stare she did, where it felt like she was looking right through you, and it was pointed in her direction now. Rosa clamped down on the urge to keep talking to fill the silence.

"With respect, Commander, you sell yourself short," Max

finally said. "People always ask me how I can guess people's movements or their choices. I don't really have a good answer, beyond that when I stop thinking about it, it all seems very clear." She lifted a shoulder with a tiny smile. "Maybe I'm reaching, but when I watch you fight with the sword it seems like you're as much in a battle with the weapon in your hand as you are against your opponent."

"You sound like Ma," Rosa said, not unkindly.

"He may have given a gangly teenager similar advice when she was fighting with these." Max waved her long arms in the air in front of her. "It helped. The sword isn't your issue, Commander. What's in your head is. NeoG didn't lose last year because of you. I get why you're taking that burden on, but you need to let it go into the black."

Rosa stared at her for a moment. She sounded like Nika, insisting to let her failures go instead of hugging them tight. And Rosa had to admit they both had a point. She had been carrying this one for long enough. "You're pretty smart for a lieutenant."

"I'm going to pretend that was a compliment and say thank you." Max sniffed and headed toward the gym.

Rosa laughed and followed. It was good to see Max settling in, better still that she felt comfortable enough to give her commanding officer unasked-for advice. That wouldn't have happened a few short weeks ago.

To top it off, her suggestion had merit. Rosa was always too far in her head, with the exception of when she was out in space. Out there her brain was quiet—fully and completely quiet—and if that was her own private heretical shame, so be it.

The longer she spent out here, the more she questioned everything she'd been brought up to believe. Angela would support her, would so gladly pack the girls up and move them anywhere so they could all be together again. Iso would fuss, but probably also look forward to the adventure. But Rosa's mother and her family?

They would not understand, and neither would her church, and the loss of all that was too terrifying for her to contemplate.

She'd come so close to telling Admiral Hoboins to transfer her to Trappist when the discussion had first come up, but the words had stuck in her throat. And because of that she was stuck here in a dead-end spot with no promotions heading her way and the seemingly impossible challenge of winning these Games settled squarely on her shoulders.

"Hey, Commander, you going to stand there and stare off into space all day or come fight me?" Tamago's call broke through Rosa's circling thoughts and she blinked, forcing a smile as she stepped into the gym.

"I'm coming, keep your pants on."

Commander Vagin—

I wanted to thank you for the letter you left me and apologize for taking so long to do so. I feel like you won't judge me for admitting it was because it took me several weeks to read it in the first place and then even longer to figure out what to say in this email. (To be perfectly honest I still haven't figured that part out so bear with me.)

I am equally feeling like "I've got this" and "This is so much harder than I thought it would be." Training was hard, I mean, you know how training was, but—does this feeling like you're missing something ever go away?

Everyone is well. We had a mission to Saturn the other day. Helping out a research station who'd lost power. Jenks taught me how to rewire a coupling set on the fly. It was exciting.

I think she's warming up to me. At least . . . well, she's still punching me in the face but either I'm getting used to it or she's not hitting me as hard.

Hope you're well. How is Trappist? Thank you again for the letter, it has been helpful in ways I can't quite explain.

—*Max*

Max—

So good to hear from you, and please don't feel like you need to be so formal. Yes, the feeling goes away. Sadly it's often replaced by some other worry. *laughs* But you'll do fine.

Jenks told me about Saturn. She was impressed with how fast you picked up the rewiring, and she's had nice things to say (mostly) about your fighting skills. Keep your hands up, will you? I'd hate for her to break your nose, and she will if you don't start protecting your face.

Trappist is a different world. It's a bit strange being on the ground more than on a ship (or station) but I'm enjoying the work and learning more than I thought I would about how goods are transferred from Earth to our habitats. The people here are . . . interesting? Rougher, but more honest I think. It's a tough place to make a living and they do it almost effortlessly.

I doubt I'll make it for the preliminaries, they don't have a team out this far that's competition ready, but maybe by this time next year I'll whip mine into shape and come compete against you. So make sure you keep training.

Thanks for the email. It's . . . appreciated, more than you know.

—Nika

T-MINUS EIGHT WEEKS UNTIL
PRELIM BOARDING GAMES

Max eyed Jenks uncertainly. "Are you sure about this?"

"Well yeah, just don't break anything. Rosa knows we need to train some even while we're out here in the black." She pointed to a deep scratch high up on the wall of the common room. "Where do you think that came from? And why did she put me on your rotation this go-around and Tamago on hers?"

That made sense. "Okay." Max put her hands back up, lifting them a little higher when Jenks raised an eyebrow. Sparring in the common room seemed like a bad idea, but of all the places on *Zuma's Ghost* where they could get the slightest bit of a match in, it was better than the bridge.

"So here's the deal," Jenks said, putting her own wrapped hands up and moving forward. "You've got these things—" She reached out and took hold of Max's wrist, shaking her arm in the air. "And it gives you this incredible range. But they're also a liability."

"My arms are a liability?"

Jenks took another step forward until she was toe-to-toe with her lieutenant. "Definitely."

"How?"

"Because you don't know what to do if I get this close." She grinned up at Max, who was clearly so uncomfortable with her hands still up and her elbows pressed against her chest. "Now, you can punch me in the head, but what's it going to do with no power behind your swing?"

"Not much."

Jenks winked. "Right. Head butts are an option, but I advise against them. They make your head hurt almost as much as your target. So what do you do?"

Max looked up at the ceiling and then shook her head so quickly Jenks suppressed a sigh. One of these days she was going to get her lieutenant to have a little faith in her own brain. But that wasn't the point of the lesson. She backed up.

"What you do is don't let me inside your guard." She took a step forward. "Punch."

Max's fist came straight out and Jenks had to sidestep it. She moved in again. "Come on, Lieutenant, don't let me get close."

Max swung again, but this time she misjudged and drove her fist into the door of the pantry. Jenks grinned. "You have to be aware of what's around you. The cage limits your movement, not like the mats in the gym. You'll get pinned to the wall and demolished eventually. I can think of at least three people who'll only let you get away with your ghost routine for the first round. So hit me, Lieutenant, with enough power to keep me from moving forward."

Jenks tossed an easy uppercut with her left, knowing that Max would ghost out of the way, but she moved in as she threw the punch, aiming a jab at Max's midsection with her right as she did.

Max's answering punch wasn't the surprising part—what was surprising was that Jenks hadn't anticipated it actually happening. She couldn't move fast enough and the pain shot through her face.

"I AM SO SORRY." MAX DIDN'T KNOW WHAT TO DO, SO SHE just stood at the entrance of the galley area watching helplessly as Jenks reset her own nose—the nose Max had somehow just managed to break—over the sink and rinsed the blood off her face.

"I'm fine, Lieutenant. I'm never going to fucking live this down, but I'm fine. Hand me that." She waved a hand at the clotting agent Max was holding and held the tube under her nose, inhaling deeply. Then she chuckled. "You really are a goddamned ghost. I didn't see that punch until it was too late."

"I—you're not mad?"

"Why would I be mad?" Jenks demanded, clearly confused as she pulled off the tank top she was wearing and wiped the rest of the blood off her face. "You did exactly what I told you to do. Don't move, let me get another shirt. This one's toast."

Max sank down into a chair as Jenks bounded for the stairs.

I can't do this.

Her hands were shaking and she pressed them to her eyes as the scene replayed in her head. The punch, the realization she was going to make contact. The feeling of her fist impacting. The blood.

Why did I think I could do this?

"Lieutenant?" She heard Jenks's footsteps and then the sound of the chair sliding out. "Hey. Look at me."

Max dropped her hands into her lap and looked at Jenks, trying not to wince at the bluish-purple circles forming in the corners of her eyes.

"Did you see blood during Interceptor training?"

Max blinked up at her. "No, and before you ask, I have no idea how I managed that."

"Well, don't worry about it. Everyone freaks the first time," Jenks said after a quiet moment, and Max wondered what was going on in her head. "Now you've seen it. It's no commentary on your abilities to need a moment to process it. That's why it's infinitely better to do it in training."

Max debated the question, decided she wanted to know bad enough to risk the expected tease. "When was your first time?"

Jenks didn't disappoint and grinned at her for a moment, but then she sobered and looked down at her wrapped hands. "I was thirteen. Killed a guy because he was trying to kill me for my coat."

Max dragged in a breath, but Jenks looked up with a smile. "You expect me to feed you some bullshit about how I tossed his pockets and whistled as I walked away, right? Nah. I cried and threw up and cried some more. Then staggered off super fucking grateful I was the one alive."

There was silence for a moment. Then Max said, "We had very different teenage years," and Jenks laughed.

"We did, Lieutenant. But that's not the point—the point is I don't want you to work yourself into a knot over a perfectly valid reaction to seeing blood." She tapped her fist on the tabletop and then started unwinding her wraps. "And I know you will, because you second-guess the shit out of yourself on a constant basis. Anyway, I think you learned the lesson I was trying to teach you there, and it gave me time to check my messages: I got some interesting info just now about our system jumper mystery."

"Info?" Max straightened. "From who?"

"Friend of mine on Earth," Jenks replied with a shrug. "Here's a weird thing. London PeaceKeepers found a body in the Thames. DNA matched to one of the people on *An Ordinary Star*'s passenger list."

"*What?*"

Jenks lifted her hands briefly and then picked up her wraps to start rolling them. "That's what I said. But the match is certain. The body belongs to Sebastian Cane, who supposedly vanished with *An Ordinary Star*. His body wasn't in the water long—no more than a couple of days. He's still sort of recognizable."

"That doesn't make any sense. Who would bring a corpse all the way from wherever it ended up and toss it in the river?"

"That's the high-dollar answer, isn't it?" Jenks's smile was humorless.

Max tried to ignore the chill crawling its way up her spine and started unwinding her own wraps. "Do we have the autopsy report on that body?"

"Yeah, here." Jenks rubbed a hand over the back of her neck. "I've got my friend looking for more matches between the passenger lists and random bodies."

"I hate to say it, but I think they'll find more. We thought they wanted the ship, but what if they wanted the bodies? If someone . . ." Max trailed off as she opened the file that Jenks had just sent over and skimmed through the report. "Jenks, this puts the time of death at two weeks ago."

"I hadn't read it yet. That can't be right."

"Cause of death: drowning."

"How the fuck does a popsicle drown?"

"Popsicle? Oh." Max surprised herself by laughing. "That's super inappropriate, Jenks."

"So is reviving people who've been in a freezer for a hundred years only to drown them," Jenks replied. "That means he was alive, right, Lieutenant? Or breathing at the very least, if he had water in his lungs."

"Yeah." Max finished with her wraps and put them on the table. "Okay, what do we have so far? Two ships from the same wave headed for Trappist. Both found empty."

"No obvious signs of foul play on the ship—at least the one we were on—but they could have cleaned it," Jenks said. "And now we have the body of a man who was forty-one when he left Earth over a hundred years ago fished out of the Thames as though he's only been dead for two weeks."

"The freezing tech was only good for fifty years. All the system jumpers could travel at eighty percent the speed of light at the time they launched. It's one of the things that made Trappist so attractive a system." Max frowned, shaking her head. "We picked up a ship that had been lost back around the turn of the century, bodies still intact. They tried to revive them, no one survived the process. Even with the newer LifeEx version they weren't able to overcome that extra twenty years of suspension."

"So what are our options here? That either someone figured out how to revive those people on the lost jumpers despite the odds, or they've been awake all this time?"

"Neither of those things is possible." Max pointed at Jenks. "And if you say aliens, Petty Officer, I'll punch you in the nose again."

"Can I say sufficiently advanced tech?" Jenks grinned and held her hands up. "Seriously, though, Lieutenant, what if something went weird with that new LifeEx out in the black? It could have—"

"Max, I've got a call coming in," Ma said over the com.

"We'll be right there," Max said. "Hold on to that thought, Jenks. We'll tackle it when we're done here."

"LETTER OF THANKS FROM THE TOURIST COMPANY FOR OUR good work rescuing their stranded ship," Rosa said, looking at the pair sitting across from her. "I'll put a copy in both of your files since you two spearheaded that mission. Good work."

"Thanks," Max said.

Jenks just shrugged, but she smiled as she said, "All part of a day's work."

Rosa cleared her throat and tapped the tabletop. "About the other report. You know I still don't have enough to reopen the system jumper case, right?"

"Commander—" Jenks subsided when Rosa raised her hand.

"Hoboins will say the same thing and you know it. What we've got right now is a lot of weirdness, but no crime." She shook her head. "I need something more than what we've got here."

"A dead body isn't 'more'?"

"Not when the autopsy says he drowned but can't make a determination that he didn't just trip and fall drunk into the Thames. Don't waste my time again, Lieutenant."

There was a curious flash of fury in Jenks's mismatched eyes at Rosa's reprimand, but Max nodded. "Yes. Sorry, Commander."

"Dismissed."

Jenks got up without a word and left the office with only slightly harder than normal footfalls that made Rosa grin.

"Max," she called, and the lieutenant stopped at the doorway, turned back to her. "Any particular reason you didn't tell me Jenks pushed you into bringing this to my attention?"

"Because she didn't. It was my call. There's something there, we all know it. We just don't know what it is yet."

Rosa studied her for a moment. Max's back was straight, but her hands were in her pockets, her arms loose rather than tense. She and Jenks weren't quite at easy status yet, but the last few weeks had definitely had an impact on their relationship and on Max's own awkward separation from the team.

"You've got five dead bodies who were originally in our custody. If there's something there, Max," Rosa said, "find it on them."

"Yes, ma'am."

Rosa smiled again after Max left the room. She didn't stomp away, but that reply had been the most formal thing she'd seen from Carmichael since her first day in Hoboins's office.

"I'm going to take a guess that that smile has something to do with why Max looked extremely annoyed coming out of here, which for her is basically the same level as anyone else being really pissed off. I just hope you know she immediately went over to Jenks and now they've got their heads together."

"Good." Rosa waved Ma into her office. "They're working on that system jumper mystery."

"Ah." Ma chuckled. "The dead-body thing got them both pretty excited. You don't agree?"

"No foul play as far as the coroner is concerned. Which means we don't have anything to build a case on. Never mind it would be hard to connect it to our jurisdiction. Even if the man had been murdered, it would be the PeaceKeepers' case, not ours." She shook her head. "Max should have thought of that."

"Maybe," Ma replied with a shrug. "Or maybe she was hoping that the fact that a man who was a passenger on the ship we picked up was somehow alive before he died was just strange enough to get your attention."

"Hoping for miracles does jack shit if you don't do the work."

"Don't toss your parables at me." He grinned when he said it. "Even if it's just weirdness and nothing comes of it, they're working together and that's something good."

"True. But you and I both know we need something to tie it back to those five criminals and the ship we picked up or Hoboins will never be able to make the case that we should have jurisdiction."

"My plan is to let the kids figure that out. You want to grab a beer?"

Rosa laughed. "I suppose emailing Stephan back about how we haven't seen a single smuggler on the last three runs out can wait, huh?"

"Maybe he'll actually get out and find a hobby if you don't give him work to do."

Rosa shut down her tablet and got to her feet. "Not after all these years. He's married to his work, you know that." Commander Yevchenko was an amazing Intel specialist and an even better sword fighter, but the running joke about him being married to the NeoG had been going since their academy days. He spent his time at work or training, and his sword-fighting abilities were as good as Nika's. All their fights had been down to the wire during the prelims.

With Nika gone you have to figure out a way to beat him.

Rosa patted Ma on the shoulder as they headed for the door. "Besides, you're a fine one to talk."

"True enough. Though I'll admit I've been thinking about it a bit more than usual. Julissa keeps dropping hints that they'd love to have me whenever I feel like putting my boots back on the ground. She's expecting another baby, did I tell you that?"

"You did not!" Rosa gave him a quick hug before she swung out into the low-g tube and pushed off. "That's wonderful."

"Her husbands are beside themselves, of course. It'd be fun to watch this one grow up, up close rather than over the com links." He grabbed for the bar and pulled himself onto the landing, reaching a hand out for Rosa. "But it would also be nice to go out on a win," he said with a grin. "So maybe after the Games."

"Thank God, because I don't need more stress in my life."

"Plus, there's Jenks. We probably want to see if she can actually make it to chief—and *stay there*—before either of us do any serious talking about retirement." Ma laughed as they walked into Corbin's.

There were multiple bars on Jupiter Station, but Corbin's was the most popular one with the military folks. Most nights it was a mix of Neos and Navy spacers with only the odd scattering of the other branches.

"I'm proud of her, she hasn't been in a bar fight for almost two months." The words were no sooner out of Rosa's mouth than a young Navy ensign turned around and bumped shoulders with Ma.

He sneered. "Watch out, Grandpa."

Ma didn't bat an eyelash, but Rosa grabbed the kid by the upper arm, digging her fingers into his ulnar nerve until he gasped in pain.

"That's 'Master Chief' to you, Ensign." She shook him once, rattling whatever he'd been about to say back down his throat. "You're in the wrong place to be starting shit."

The bar had gotten quiet and everyone was looking at them. D'Arcy met Rosa's eyes across the room and raised his eyebrow in silent question. She shook her head and looked at the ensign again.

"Say good night," she said.

"But I haven't finished my drink."

"Say good night to the commander, kid," Tussin said from behind the bar. "You've drunk all you're going to tonight."

"Good night, Commander." His jaw was tight when he said it, or rather snarled it, but Rosa merely smiled and let him go with a little push toward the door.

"Learn some manners," she said to his retreating back.

There was a beat and then the bar returned to its normal noise level. Rosa smiled at Tussin and took the beers he slid in their direction with a nod, passing one to Ma as they made their way over to D'Arcy's table.

"I appreciate the irony of you nearly getting into a bar fight, but don't feel like you need to do that on my account," Ma said.

"That doesn't bother you at all?" she asked.

He shrugged. "Technically I am old enough to be his grandpa, but my kids were raised to be more respectful."

"I'll admit it was as much for me as it was for you. He wouldn't have done it if you were wearing a different uniform."

"That's his loss, not mine." Ma shook D'Arcy's hand and then took a seat. "How goes it?"

"Good," the commander replied, tipping his beer in Rosa's direction. "Thought for a moment my night was going to get exciting."

She rolled her eyes at him and lifted her own beer. "To children; may they grow up before they do something that gets them killed."

"I can't tell if you're talking about the ensign or me," D'Arcy said.

"Neither can I."

Max—

Thanks for your letter the other day. I hear from a little bird (named Sapphi) that you are responsible for the broken nose I saw on Jenks when I talked to her last. She refused to tell me how, or she was just too excited to tell me about the stranded tourists you all rescued to be bothered. With Jenks it's hard to tell, but that means you're going to have to spill the details.

My own lieutenant has decent skill with a sword. It's nice to have some focus there, and they're getting better every day, which is always good to see. I don't know if this team will ever be competition worthy, but they are good at their jobs and that's what matters.

Speaking of, we came across something I thought would be of interest to you. Jenks mentioned she and you were still poking at that system jumper case and that the people we arrested were killed in an accident?

Anyway, we busted some smugglers a few days ago and I just got the manifest lists back. Imagine my surprise when I saw there were ship parts with *An Ordinary Star*'s ID tag on them. I've flagged them and will send along if Rosa thinks it's important. Attached is the manifest in full, maybe you'll see something that I missed.

I hope you're doing well.

—*Nika*

Nika—

Did Jenks mention we have a sixth dead body? The London PeaceKeepers found a guy floating in the Thames whose DNA matched one of the original passengers on *An Ordinary Star*. If that isn't weird enough for you, the fact that he apparently drowned and didn't die of freezer burn should do it.

Despite it all, Rosa says we don't have enough to reopen the case and refuses to forward it to the vice admiral on the off chance that he'll say yes. I confess there's probably some political thing here I'm missing, isn't there? Otherwise I don't understand it.

Honestly the most frustrating part of that was she acted like I'd only brought it to her attention because of Jenks, as if I'm not able to make my own conclusions and decisions about the evidence right in front of me.

Part of me insists I'm overreacting. Part of me knows there's something going on and the commander told me to trust my gut.

Do you maybe have some time to talk on the coms about all this? I have a feeling something else is going to happen and I'd like to have everything lined up so that when it inevitably does we can use it to reopen this case and I'm prepared. I know you're busy, I just, I could use the help.

—Max

P.S. I'm sorry, what happened to Jenks's nose is con-fidential mission-critical information that I'm unable to share.

T-MINUS FIVE WEEKS UNTIL PRELIM BOARDING GAMES

"That's the last of them!" Max pushed the final refugee into the ship and slammed her palm down on the airlock panel. "We're sealed. Ma, get us out of here."

"Aye-aye, Lieutenant. Brace yourselves, all power to the aft shields, this explosion is going to rock the boat in about thirty seconds."

Max grabbed for the nearest bar as *Zuma's Ghost* sped away from the dying ship, counting down with the timer in her vision.

"Simulation end," Rosa said, and with her announcement the refugees clustered around Max vanished.

She blinked, shaking the last of the virtual reality away as the room came back into focus around her.

Rosa looked disappointed and Max scrubbed a hand over her face with a sigh.

The others were scattered around the room. Ma was in the chair next to her and Sapphi sat across from him with her feet tucked up underneath her. Jenks was sprawled on the floor, her head pillowed against Doge. And Tamago sat against the far wall, long legs delicately crossed at the ankles.

The competition for the Big Game would take place in a prefabbed room built specifically for whatever scenario the judges chose for the Games and would be integrated into their virtual reality simulators so the teams would move through the space and the crowd could watch it play out in real time.

All teams were given the basic layout and idea of the Big Game a week before the main Games, but each team would end up with a different objective, given just before the start of their event. So while they could watch the previous teams compete, their task would be unique to their team.

But there wasn't room on Jupiter Station for running a full-on practice, so they did the bulk of their training in virtual reality simulators while sitting around their quarters.

"Hey, the good news is you're not all dead," Rosa said.

"What's the bad news?" Max asked. Rosa had made her take point on this one under the excuse that there was always a chance she'd end up dead or injured in the Big Game, and while the result hadn't been a complete disaster, something had felt off.

"*Dread Treasure* did this run forty-five seconds faster and without any civilian casualties," Rosa replied.

"Where did I mess up?" Max slumped in her chair.

"Nowhere." Rosa shook her head. "Everyone did what they were supposed to."

"We were just as smooth as a broken gearshift," Jenks said, making a clicking noise with her tongue. "And that cost us a minute at least, plus three dead civvies."

Max blew out a breath. She vaguely remembered the mention of a gearshift in history class when they were talking about gasoline-powered vehicles, but other than that could only guess at the meaning of Jenks's comment. "I take it that's not good."

Ma wiggled a hand. "It's bad. Plus it means we're getting nowhere."

"You're hesitating, Max. You don't have this problem on our actual runs," Rosa said. "What's the deal?"

"You're in charge during real runs."

Max regretted the words instantly when Rosa's eyes narrowed. "And what happens if I'm suddenly not in charge in the middle of a real run, Carmichael? You just going to half-ass it and get everyone killed?"

Max opened her mouth and then snapped it shut again. "No, Commander," she said finally, straightening her shoulders. "Set it up, let's run another one."

Rosa nodded and Max closed her eyes, taking a deep breath as the room resolved itself around her, the others standing around a narrow white table.

"*Zuma's Ghost*, your task is to navigate your way through this facility to this room and retrieve the data stored there," Rosa said, and a map with a highlighted area appeared on the table. "You have to do it without being seen. No exceptions. You have twenty minutes."

Max stared at the map. "Computer, give me a layout of the hostiles."

The map lit up and Ma whistled. "That's a lot of hostiles to slip by without the time to watch for a pattern."

"Ideas, people. Toss them out." The timer was ticking in the corner of her vision as they burned through several suggestions. Max blew out a frustrated breath and looked at Jenks, but the petty officer wasn't saying anything; instead she was staring at the ceiling.

Max followed her gaze. "Jenks, what are you—oh." She tapped the tabletop. "Computer, give me a schematic of the HVAC."

The overlay appeared in green and Jenks leaned forward, tracing a path with her finger, then pointed above them. "This one. It'll take us all the way through."

"I'm not fitting through there," Ma said.

"You and Sapphi stay here. Tamago, Jenks, and I will go." Max rummaged in her pack and pulled out an electro-wrench. "If we stack a chair on the table you can reach the vent. You have two minutes to get those clamps loose. Figure something out." Max slapped the tool against Jenks's chest with a grin.

"TO OUR FEARLESS LIEUTENANT." THERE WASN'T A HINT OF sarcasm in Jenks's voice as she lifted her beer. "Nice job today."

Max leaned back in her seat and raised her own water. "Back at you. I'm impressed that you didn't get us lost."

There was a moment of stunned silence and then laughter erupted around the table. Jenks stared at her for a long moment, then chuckled into her beer before taking a drink. "Who told?"

Sapphi raised her hand and winked.

"Next time we spar, Zika." Jenks pointed a finger at her and then settled lower in her own chair with a happy sigh. "Whole day off tomorrow. I am camping in my bunk and binge-watching the new season of *The Unreal*."

"I need to catch up on that," Tamago said. "I'm a season behind you. Don't wait for me, though, I promised Burns I'd help him tackle the forbidden dungeon he keeps getting killed in." They waved their hands in the air with a snicker. "Poor *Yancy's Treasure Hunt* noobs."

"If you're lost, you're not the only one," Ma murmured to Max. "I can't keep up with the shows and the games and everything else."

"That's because you sleep through your days off and then spend the rest of your time off in the flight simulators."

Ma shrugged off the good-natured tease from Jenks. "Prelims are in five weeks, have to stay sharp."

"Pfft, I *am* sharp," Jenks replied with a grin. "We're going to whomp everyone in the prelims and we'll whomp everyone in the Games." She raised her glass again. "We're the motherfucking NeoG."

The others joined in, even Max, though Jenks noticed she

didn't curse. That couldn't be an officer thing, because Rosa said "fuck" plenty.

"Tell me something, Max: Why is it you don't drink?" Jenks wiggled her own glass. "No pressure, I'm just curious." She recognized the shrug Max gave, that uncomfortable roll of the shoulders. Jenks did the same thing when faced with a topic she'd rather avoid, and she suddenly regretted the question.

The alarm blared throughout the station and everyone snapped upright even before the message scrolled into Jenks's view: *All interceptor crews assemble at your ships.*

Jenks bolted from her seat, scrambling for the door with the others on her heels. "Tussin, put it on my tab!"

The owner tossed her a nod as they ran out the door.

"We'll meet you there, Commander," Max said out loud as she caught up with Jenks.

"What is it?" Jenks asked.

"Cargo freighter left here an hour ago with a load of liquid metallic hydrogen farmed off Jupiter. They suffered a massive engine failure and containment might also be failing."

"Shit," Jenks muttered as she launched herself into the low-g tube after Max.

"How many liters?" Ma asked.

"A hundred and forty-five thousand."

"We do not want that thing to blow with that much LMH on board." Jenks was already calculating the blast radius in her head. "Station shielding is good, but it will do serious damage."

"Admiral is ordering all civilians to their quarters. All military is to proceed to their ships," Max relayed the information as it scrolled across her feed. She grabbed for the bar and landed on solid ground, taking off running through the growing crowd.

The NeoG bay was organized chaos and Jenks dodged a group of CHN Marines double-timing it across the floor, pulling Sapphi out of the way. "Focus before you get run over."

Sapphi blinked twice. "Sorry, digging up specs. Ship in question is the H3nergy freighter *Poseidon's Fury.* She's an older model with the standard H3 fusion drive."

"What year?"

"Twenty-three seventy-eight," Sapphi replied.

Rosa stood by the door of *Zuma's Ghost,* and she stepped back as Max scrambled up the stairs. "Ma, ship's hot and ready to go," she said.

"Got it." He slipped toward the bridge, Sapphi on his heels.

Rosa looked at Jenks. "You sober?"

Jenks rolled her eyes. "Barely time to have a beer, Commander, but I'll take a spray if it'll make you feel better."

"Do it—we're getting on that freighter and I need you completely greenlined."

Jenks caught the tube Tamago tossed her way and took a hit off the anti-inebriator. "Sapphi already gave me details on the freighter. What happened to the engineering crew?"

"The engineering chief died in the initial leak, sounds like the coolant vented without warning straight into the core room. Captain Guru said the chief pushed his assistant out the door just before it closed. She's not injured beyond some bruised ribs, but obviously shaken up."

Jenks nodded. "Do we have schematics for this engine? I want to look at it before we get on board."

"Up here, Jenks!" Sapphi called.

Jenks took the stairs two at a time to the bridge, grabbing for the railing as the ship shook underneath her feet on takeoff.

They made it to *Poseidon's Fury* in record time, helmets under their arms as they disembarked through the linked airlocks. Jenks watched as a woman with light blond hair ran up to them.

"Commander Martín? Thank you for coming. I'm First Officer Raya Asgrin. The captain is overseeing the evacuation. She asked me to take you to med bay, where our engineering assistant is."

"I'm not in med, Raya, I'm right here." The woman who approached had one hand pressed to her ribs on the right side, and a freshly bandaged wound peeked out from beneath her white bangs.

"Tiga, you should be in med."

"I'm fine, just hit my head when Jim shoved me out the door."

Something passed between the women before the first officer finally nodded. "Tiga will take your people to engineering."

"It's this way." Tiga didn't wait for them to follow, just took off back down the corridor.

"Jenks." Rosa jerked her head toward the retreating woman. "Go. Carmichael, go with Jenks. We'll facilitate the evac onto the ships."

"Yes, Commander." Max nodded and exchanged a worried glance with Jenks as they caught up with the engineering assistant.

"A little farther," Tiga said after introductions had been made, never breaking stride. She winced, unable to hide her pain.

"You bullshitting your first officer back there?" Jenks asked. She'd had her share of bruised ribs and recognized that familiar attempt to move as gingerly as possible.

"I'm all right," Tiga replied, and Jenks let it go, but she made eye contact with Max and knew she had heard the conversation.

They reached the engineering section, the wide doors illuminated with the pulsing red of a failure warning.

"Helmets," Max said as she slipped her own on.

Tiga winced again and Jenks took her helmet from her. "Here, let me. You really should be lying down."

"I need to help," Tiga said. "Jim saved my life at the cost of his own."

"Maybe that means you should evac with the others," Max said.

"No." She smiled. "It means I'll be damned if I don't go down swinging just like he did. Come on. Time's wasting." She gestured.

Jenks lowered Tiga's helmet, sealed it, and put her own on. "Coms up. Everyone read me?"

Tiga nodded and Max gave her a quick thumbs-up.

"Here goes nothing." Tiga punched the access code into the panel by the door.

The trio crossed into engineering. The only sound in Jenks's ears was her own breathing until Tiga spoke.

"Over there," she said, tapping Jenks on the shoulder and pointing to the bank of consoles circling the massive cylindrical drive in the center of the room.

The coolant had been pulled into the recycling system, but wisps of it still hung in the air. Jenks spotted the body in the corner and gave Max a quick look, pointing in that direction before she spoke to Tiga. "Run me through what happened."

"We get weird spikes on occasion. It happens with these older ships. We didn't think anything of it when the containment field fluctuated. This old bitch liked to give us readings like that all the time." Tiga was tapping on the console as she spoke and a series of redlined warnings flashed across the screen. "Then out of nowhere the coolant vented and everything went to hell." Her breath caught for just a moment before she continued. "Jim pushed me through the door as it closed. I—he was a good guy."

Jenks glanced Max's way, meeting her solemn eyes where she knelt by Jim's body. The lieutenant shook her head to confirm the man was dead. They'd known it, but it sucked regardless.

"I'm going to take him to medical. I'll be right back," Max said on their private channel, and Jenks nodded. Max hefted Jim's body up onto her shoulder with an ease that startled the petty officer and headed for the door.

"Hey, Tiga, look at this." Jenks put a hand on the engineer's shoulder, directing her away from the body before she spotted it.

"THIS IS LIEUTENANT CARMICHAEL OF *ZUMA'S GHOST* TO ANYone in med bay. Can someone meet me outside with a transport for a body?"

"Roger that, Lieutenant. I'll meet you there," replied an unknown voice.

Max came around the corner a few minutes later and met a woman with a low-g stretcher. She lowered Jim's body down and looked up to the pair of brilliant green eyes watching her. They were coated with unshed tears, but the woman's smile was genuine as she reached out to brush a hand against the man's cheek.

"He would have joked about how you could have tossed him like a sack of potatoes. 'I'm not in it anymore, Lila, there's no cause for reverence.' I am grateful that you didn't. Dr. Lila Dani." She stuck her hand out. "Thank you, Lieutenant."

"You're welcome." Max shook her hand quickly. "I should get back to engineering. Are you almost done evacuating?"

"I'll need to get Jim's body loaded. It won't take more than a few minutes." She smiled again. "Though I'm obviously hoping we can come back."

"We'll do what we can. It was nice to meet you, Doc, circumstances being what they are."

"Good luck, Lieutenant."

Max jogged back to engineering and slipped through the doors, punching the panel nearby to close them again.

Jenks and Tiga had their helmets pressed together and the heated discussion burst to life as Max rejoined the com link.

"Ejecting it is not going to help. The damn thing will still blow too close to the ship and ignite the LMH." Jenks turned to look at Max, and she gave a little nod in reply to the petty officer's unasked question.

"I want to take a look at this from a different angle," Jenks said, abruptly dropping to the floor and pushing herself under the console with her heels. There was a banging sound and then the panel dropped down next to Max's feet. "If we're dealing with two separate failures here then maybe isolating one of them will help us fix the other."

"How can I help?" Max asked as Tiga crawled under the console.

"Keep an eye on that gauge right there," Jenks said, kicking up with a foot in the general direction of the console she was underneath. "Let me know if it starts moving—up or down. And talk to me about your favorite video game."

Max looked down at the flashing yellow bar showing the temperature of the core and the series of numbers flickering back and forth next to it. "That would be hard. I've never played a video game."

"You've *what*?"

"How does that happen?"

Max smiled at the twin responses of confused outrage from the women. "I don't know. It just does?"

"You'll want to go through there," Tiga said to Jenks. "If you can't—"

"Naw, I got it. It was really just a matter of getting past those power wires. But I don't think that's as much of an issue as the fact that Lieutenant Carmichael has never played a video game. In her whole life."

"Shouldn't you be focusing?" Max asked.

"I am focused; talking helps me focus, Lieutenant."

"Fine." Max leaned on the console. "I've never played a video game. My parents didn't approve. And then when I was fr—an adult—I just had other things to do."

"Sometimes I regret not having parents. This is not one of those times." Jenks chuckled when Max kicked her in the leg. "I cobbled together a system from scraps on the streets, used to charge kids to play *Swords and Shields*. For a while there I was eating good."

"What happened?"

"Korthan caught wind of it. Head of the local gang. Greedy bastard figured he should get a cut of my take because I was technically in his territory. I had a disagreement with the guys he sent to talk to me. They trashed my shit and I had to get out of town."

"I'm sorry."

"Eh, don't be," Jenks said. "It's over and done. Plus it led me to Gran and to Nik. No point in crying over the past. Just be here now. Which—fuck."

"What?"

"I can't fix this. The containment wires are all melted together." Jenks slid out from under the console and banged her head on the floor twice in frustration. "Fuck," she muttered again, and there was just enough worry in her voice to make Max straighten.

Well, that and the fact that the line had just crawled up into the red zone. "Gauge moved up. Do we need to get out of here?"

"*We* don't. You should, though, Lieutenant."

A smile flickered through the tension on Max's face as she looked down at Jenks. "Pretty sure you don't get to order me around. I'm not leaving without you."

"Pointless sacrifice," she muttered.

"We're not dying today, Petty Officer. I trust you to fix this."

"I can't! It's completely and utterly fucked. The damn wires are melted. Can't eject. Can't—" Jenks narrowly avoided slamming her helmet on the underside of the console as she sat up and grabbed Tiga by the arm. "You said the magnetic containment was fluctuating just before the coolant vented?"

"Yes, it spiked hard and then dropped back to the green zone. Computer started the normal coolant sequence and that's when engineering flooded."

"Is there still enough coolant to get this engine back into the green zone?"

Max took Jenks's outstretched hand and hauled her to her

feet. Tiga grabbed for the edge of the console and carefully got up. The engineer tapped a few keys.

"Barely. But if we turn the system back on, it's likely that it'll just flood engineering again instead of going to the core."

"It's locked. Damn it all to the bottom of the greasy Volga river. The core is locked down and I can't touch it." Jenks tapped her gloved fingers on the sides of her helmet. "The spike in the containment caused the coolant to respond, but the vent doors must have failed, which is why the compartment flooded!" She slapped herself in the head as Max stared at her.

"The coolant was shut down when we came in," Tiga said.

"Because Jim managed to shut it down and was trying to get the doors to close again. That's why he was over there." She pointed to where Jim's body had been and Max watched Tiga frown in confusion. "He couldn't get to them before the coolant flooded the room."

"Asshole, if he'd told me I could have helped."

"You'd both be dead, and I'd be clueless," Jenks replied, crossing the room. "Lieutenant, come here."

"What do you need?"

"Stand there. Hand here." Jenks pushed her hand toward the screen with a pair of square buttons lit up in blue and orange. "That orange one is going to start flashing. You press it only when I say so."

"On your mark," Max replied with a nod. "What are you going to do?"

"When in doubt, bypass the safety features," Jenks said, and flashed a grin. "Tiga and I are going to kick the vents closed. When that happens you're going to slam the button and coolant will go where it's supposed to. There's enough left to cool things down and—hey, Commander?"

"Yeah, Jenks?" Rosa replied over the team com.

"Get on the com with Control and tell them to send us an extra coolant rack ASAP."

"Will do. You all good there, Lieutenant?"

"Yes. Jenks has a fix for this. We're about to put it into play." Max glanced at Jenks, who lifted a shoulder at her silent question about whether this was going to work. "Recommend you finish the evac and move ships away, though, just to be on the safe side."

"Roger that, Lieutenant. We'll see you two when it's done."

Jenks and Tiga separated, moving to opposite ends of engineering and popping the access panels on either side. Max tore her gaze away and focused on the console in front of her. A warning started flashing at the top and the button in front of her picked up the pulse.

"Jenks, orange button is flashing. Temp is going up again."

"Yeah, it's going to keep doing that until it fails or we stop it."

"That's reassuring."

"Hey, no worries. It won't hurt. At least I'm assuming it won't. Found the vent—as expected it's jacked open. Tiga, how's yours?"

"Same. Can I start kicking?"

"Do it."

Max could hear the filtered impact sounds over the com and the grunts of the women as they bashed at the vents.

"Got mine!"

Jenks grunted. "Get out of there. I've almost got this one."

Max swallowed as the temp continued to rise and the warning flash grew a little more insistent. "Jenks?"

"Almost."

"We're almost out of almost, Jenks."

"I know. Would. You. Close!" Each word was punctuated with a thud. "Got it." The sounds of scrambling followed. "Punch it, Lieutenant!"

"Please let this work," Max begged as she jammed her finger into the button with more force than was probably necessary. For a heartrending moment nothing happened. Then there was a whooshing noise and she looked up to see the coolant flowing into the core to her right.

Tiga punched the air, her cheer breaking off into a swear as her ribs protested. Jenks smirked and polished her knuckles off on her suit. Max gave a shuddering laugh.

"No dying today?"

"We good, Tiga?" Jenks asked.

Tiga was furiously tapping away at the console. "Looks like. The coolant is burning out fast, but it'll hold temp until we get more here and can get it shut down fully. Since everyone else is off, I'm shutting down all the systems that I can."

"No dying today, Lieutenant," Jenks confirmed with a wink.

"Commander," Max said on the coms, "we're clear. Core is stable. Tiga says we'll need that coolant as fast as Jupiter can get it here and she's shutting down all the systems she can to help with the power strain in the meantime."

"That's good to hear. Captain Guru is with me, she'd like to speak to you."

"Thank you, Lieutenant." Captain Guru's voice was soothing, carrying a hint of the recognizable Martian-born inflection.

"Don't thank me." Max shook her head. "Petty Officer Khan is the one who fixed it. Along with Tiga's help."

"Pass my thanks along to them, then. To all of you. You saved a lot of lives today."

"I've got you on the main com, Captain, consider them thanked." Max saw Jenks wrap an arm around Tiga and pull her in for a gentle hug, surprised by the slight pinch of jealousy that twisted her gut.

She's not going to treat you like her brother, Max. I don't know why you keep hoping for it. Inwardly, she scowled.

The voice in her head was too hard, hitting with deadly precision.

"You should hear the stories swirling around about that freighter rescue last month." D'Arcy spun his sword in a frivolous gesture as he circled Rosa.

"Oh yeah, what are they saying?" She watched him, always envious of his grace. D'Arcy was a big guy who moved like a dancer, limbs and torso in perfect synchronicity.

"All manner of things. I did hear people are very impressed that your newbie stayed with Jenks the whole time she was trying to keep that core from blowing."

Swords rang out as she attacked, dull metal edges striking with discordant chimes.

"I told her to go with Jenks," Rosa said when their swords locked and she dug in, shoving D'Arcy back a half meter with effort.

"Sure you did, but you didn't order her to stay. She chose to do that. Jenks tried to get her to leave, you know?"

"Did she?" Neither Jenks nor Max had mentioned it to Rosa.

"Yup. Carmichael told her they weren't dying and she trusted Jenks to fix it. People are impressed. Hell, I'm impressed. Most people would have gone."

"*What* people are we talking about here?"

D'Arcy smiled as he pressed an attack of his own. "All sorts, but the ones who matter a little more up at command level are very interested."

"That's all we need, more scrutiny." Rosa ducked under D'Arcy's swing, bringing the pommel of her own practice sword down into his left kidney before she folded over into a forward roll, sword stuck out to the side to keep from impaling herself. She heard him wheeze with laughter as she bounced back up to her feet.

"God damn it. I miss that every damn time."

"You need a time-out, old man?"

D'Arcy snorted and gestured at her with his free hand. "Come on, Rosa. The day I have to take a break during a sword fight is the day I should probably think about retiring."

"Are you, then?" Rosa teased as she approached cautiously, switching her gaze from his eyes to his torso as he shifted.

D'Arcy lunged instead of answering, or maybe that was his answer, and for several minutes they fought silently. Swords slashing and locking together, rapid breaths, and the soft shuffling of their bare feet on the mats were the only sounds in their little corner.

Rosa saw the move. She knew it was going to disarm her, but she'd overbalanced and there was nothing she could do. D'Arcy blocked her sword with his, reaching up with his free hand and tipping the pommel of her sword up and away from her, tucking it behind him with a grin that made her want to punch him.

But the dull blade of his own sword was at her throat.

"If I had a delightful family like yours to go home to, I might think of retiring," he said, handing her sword back with a wink and a smile. "But I'm sadly alone and so here I'll stay."

"You love it here and you're only alone when you want to be."

D'Arcy shrugged a shoulder. "That's not the point, and also

we're not talking about me, are we?" He took a step closer. They were isolated from most of the others in the gym, but there were still people around and D'Arcy dropped his voice to keep from being overheard. "What's wrong, Rosa? You have shadows in your eyes."

All these years and he still managed to catch her off guard when he dropped the dashing pirate persona to truly be himself. Rosa knew more about him than most. His criminal past, his final chance with the NeoG. There was always more about the man she realized she didn't know. D'Arcy trusted so few people and she still wasn't sure how she'd made the list, but the first time he'd done this soul-seeking thing to her she'd been so stunned her jaw had hit the floor.

He'd laughed himself silly seeing the effect his question had on her then. Now he patiently waited for an answer. D'Arcy was good at patience. The man could sit for hours without moving if the occasion called for it.

"You know that feeling when you step off solid ground into the low-g chute and for just a second the primitive part of your brain wakes up and screams at you?" Rosa took a deep breath when D'Arcy nodded. "It doesn't care that you've done it a million times, it's convinced that you don't know, that you can't possibly know what's going to happen this time."

Suddenly needing to move, Rosa spun away and stalked to the benches. D'Arcy followed but stayed silent as she dropped her sword into her pile of things and braced both hands on the wall.

"I'm so tired of the disrespect. I knew what I was getting into when I joined the NeoG, but our people bust their asses day in and day out. You say the higher-ups are noticing, but does it matter? Will it translate into money to replace some of this antiquated equipment we have to deal with? Will Max be able to walk through the fucking hangar without getting shit from some self-important naval bastard about how she's slumming it?"

"You think it bothers her?"

"It bothers all of us, doesn't it? We pretend and smile and take it. We deal with shit equipment—we do our jobs with shit equipment." Rosa sighed and sank down on the bench. "These Games are important. I know in the grand scheme of things they're just games, but if we win? Maybe it'll finally change things around here."

D'Arcy sat next to her. "I know. It would do more than just give us bragging rights, though what rights they would be." His grin was sharp and quick. "I'm aware enough of the politics of all of this to know that if we won it would be a good bargaining chip for Admiral Chen. But that's not all on your shoulders, Rosa, so stop taking the weight."

"We were so close to winning last year. I was determined to find a way to bring that damn win home this year. Ever since Nik got promoted, I've felt like something is conspiring to keep us from this path. I don—" The words clogged her throat and Rosa tried to push past the fear. "I think if we don't win this Games I'm done."

"Rosa, you only have a little over a year left to retirement."

"You think that matters to the higher-ups? Someone should pay for the loss. We all know it'll be me." She looked up at him. He'd set his sword down and was leaning against the wall, arms crossed over his chest, a frown carved into his face. "Why would they keep me on after? What would be the point?"

"The same fucking reason they'd want to keep you on when you *do* win the Games. You said it yourself. They're fine entertainment, a bit of friendly—or not so friendly—rivalry between the branches. But it's what we do the rest of the time that matters, and you do that better than anyone."

"You sound like a recruitment poster."

D'Arcy snorted and waved a hand. "I'm serious, Martín. You're a damn good Neo and Command wouldn't be so stupid as to throw that away just because you didn't win." He reached out, stopped. "Do you need a hug? You look like you need a hug."

There wasn't any sarcasm in his offer, so Rosa nodded and leaned into D'Arcy's embrace. He was solid and just tall enough she could lean her head against his shoulder.

"Don't worry about it, Rosa. We're gonna win this thing anyway."

"What's this 'we' stuff? Did I black out and miss prelims?"

His rumbling laugh echoed against her ear. "Nope, they're still next week, but it's you and me going to the Games."

Rosa tipped her head back to smile up at him. "This new-found optimism is not a bad look on you, Commander."

D'Arcy squeezed her once before letting her go with a smile. "Your newbie is settled in well enough. And more than that, she's got something . . . undefinable about her. Command has to have an eye on her for something. And you are as good a sword fighter as Nika was. You just need to believe that."

"I feel like you're setting me up just to kick my ass in the prelims."

"I'm going to try," he replied. "The ass-kicking part, that is. I'm serious about the winning-this part, too." A smile pulled at his scarred cheek. "My team's been in this gym as much as out of it for the last eight months and there's no other team I'd rather go up against the rest of the branches with than you and yours."

She swallowed. "You're a good friend."

"You are, too."

Rosa looked down at her hands, surprised by the sheen of tears suddenly coating her vision. D'Arcy also wasn't the kind of man who'd admit that he cared about people. It meant something that he would say such things to her. "You mean it, don't you? About Command watching Max?" Rosa asked.

"She's a Carmichael." D'Arcy shrugged and grabbed his water. "Someone put her here for a reason, Rosa, you and I both know that. Which means they're watching. Could just be her parents, though from what I gather they're not on the best of terms. You know they were unhappy about her decision to go to the NeoG?"

"I did not." That was a failing on her part. In her push to get Jenks and Max to jell, she hadn't taken the time to get to know Max nearly as well as she should have.

"And even more unhappy about her joining the Interceptors," D'Arcy said. "I hear they didn't even show for her graduation."

Rosa stared at him in shock. "Seriously?" The idea of unsupportive parents was almost unfathomable for her. "Why wouldn't they—"

"Not all of us grew up with your kind of family, Rosa," he replied with a wry smile. "And money doesn't matter if the love is missing."

"When did you get so fucking profound?" she asked, tossing a towel at him. D'Arcy chuckled, batting it out of the air with one massive hand.

"I took a class last week. Don't tell anyone."

Max—

Just wanted to drop you a line to tell you good luck and kick some ass at the prelims. I know you're likely nervous, so remember to breathe. And keep your damned hands up.

Jenks said there hasn't been any more movement on that system jumper mystery but that she'd passed the smuggler information on to Luis at HQ. I know I'm technically not on your team any longer, but I appreciate you keeping me in the loop as much as you have.

I hope talking about it on the com the other week helped, even if we didn't seem to get anywhere on it. It was nice to see your face.

—N

Nika—

I'm hoping we'll have some time after the preliminaries to investigate further. I did appreciate that conversation and it at least gave me and Jenks some new ideas to kick around. Seems like everything for the last week has been wholly focused on the Games. I'm not complaining, the focus is welcome, I guess? It helps make this a little more real.

I am terrified.

You said recently that you wished you could have stayed here. I find myself wishing the same thing. It's selfish, though, isn't it? I only wish it because then all these eyes wouldn't be on me. All these people wouldn't be wondering if I'm going to mess up and ruin everything.

That sounds horrible reading it back to myself. I don't

only wish you were here because of the Games. I am no good at people. I never have been.

I'm going to send this and then go stick my head out the nearest airlock.

−M

P.S. It was nice to see your face, too.

Max−

I know what you meant. Don't worry about it. :) And please don't stick your head out the airlock, we need it.

−N

T-MINUS FORTY-SIX HOURS UNTIL
PRELIM BOARDING GAMES

"Mama!"

Jenks grinned as Gloria raced across the deck, easily dodging the mass of people until she was close enough to launch herself into Rosa's arms.

"Softie."

Jenks elbowed Ma. "Hush. You'll ruin my rep."

"Nothing wrong with liking to see people happy." He slung an arm over her shoulders. "You ready for this?"

"As ever," she replied, eyes straying to Max as the lieutenant climbed down from *Zuma*. "You think she's going to make it?" Max's hands were clutching her bag straps so tightly it made her knuckles pale against the rest of her skin. "Or is she going to fold before we even get in there?"

"She's tougher than she looks, Jenks. She'll be fine."

"There's tough and then there's competition. You know that." Jenks scanned the docks as she spoke. "Look—there's *Honorable Intent*. Stephan has put on some muscle." Luis had, too, but she wasn't going to comment on that. Their relationship wasn't exactly a secret, it was just . . . private.

Because you care about him more than you want to admit.

"Your heart rate is elevated. Is it because you saw CPO Armstrong?" Doge's comment was for her com link only and she tightened her fingers in his collar.

"Doge, I will reprogram you if you're not careful," she muttered, hoping that Ma didn't hear her over the noise of the hangar. The damned AI was starting to make her nervous with how well he was articulating her feelings back to her.

Or figuring them out before even she did.

"*Flux Capacitor* over there." Ma pointed to his left, apparently oblivious to the conversation. "Where the hell is that name from again?"

Jenks rolled her eyes with a chuckle. "I'm still mad they snagged such a great name. I wonder if they'll manage to do better than dead last this year." *Flux* was a hell of an Interceptor team, but their competition record was legendary for how utterly bad it was. Dead last four years running, and hadn't won a single individual competition yet. Jenks didn't see the point in showing if you weren't going to win, but they got something out of it, she supposed.

"Doubt it," Ma replied. "But they have fun. For some people that's enough."

"Not me. I'm in it to win it."

Ma grunted in agreement and tapped the fist she held out. "There's the family." He crossed the dock and was swarmed by grandchildren before he could wrap his daughters in his arms.

Sapphi was talking rapidly with some of her siblings. Tamago's parents had made the trip and their mother held their hand. Rosa stood off to one side, Gloria's head resting on her shoulder and Rosa's forehead pressed to her wife's. Their older daughter, Isobelle, had her arms wrapped around Rosa's waist, hugging her tightly from behind.

The sudden, sharp ache in Jenks's chest stole her breath away. Normally she'd be talking with Nika right now, all the family she'd ever needed in these rare moments when the team split back to their component parts with the lives they'd left behind.

"Hey."

Jenks glanced at Max. "Where's your family?"

"They won't come." She shrugged. "My older brother, Scott, has competed for a few years. He's a SEAL and the captain of a CHNN team. We didn't go to see him compete, either. My parents think it's gauche—um, beneath them."

"I know what 'gauche' means, Lieutenant. I grew up on the streets, not out in the wilds of Siberia raised by bears." The words were out before Jenks could stop them, and she swore when Max winced. "Sorry, that was a little much. I'm missing Nik."

"Me too."

This was far and away *not* the place for such a conversation, but once again Jenks couldn't stop the words from leaving her mouth. "You knew him for a handful of days, how can you possibly miss him?"

Max blinked. "We've been emailing. He didn't—"

"Never mind." Jenks held up a hand. "It's not my business." She walked away before she said something else that would get her in trouble, Doge trailing along behind her.

MAX WATCHED JENKS WALK AWAY, MOUTH HANGING OPEN until she snapped it shut with an audible click. Thankfully no one else was paying attention.

The words hadn't been hostile, but—had she crossed a line she wasn't supposed to? How could emails be a bad thing? They were just—

"Oh god. What did I do?" Max pressed a hand to her mouth. She always messed these things up, stumbled over her own feet and her own inability to just be around people without it turning into a massive—

"Maxine!"

She jerked as her name split the air, spotting the lanky form of Lieutenant Rachel Bingham weaving through the crowd toward her. "Rachel!" Dropping her bag just in time to catch the trans woman in a hug, Max let her sudden anxiety over Nika go with it. "It's so good to see you."

"Hey, famous girl." Green eyes sparkling, Rachel cupped Max's face and rubbed noses with her. "Sorry I'm late, my transfer took forever."

"I didn't even know you were coming."

"Of course! I wouldn't have missed this for the world. We need to talk about your letter-writing skills. I know, I know, awkward Maxine and all, but we're friends, remember? I said it was going to happen."

Rachel Bingham was outgoing, gregarious, all the things Max wasn't, and she had declared their friendship on the first day of the academy with the same energy that she tackled everything in her life. Max hadn't known quite how to respond to the whirlwind beyond a polite smile, however it had worked out because Rachel also oddly understood Max's need for quiet, for space.

And Rachel had a mean right hook she wasn't afraid of throwing at people whose teasing had taken a cruel turn a time or two.

Max squeezed her again before letting her go. "You did. Best thing that ever happened to me."

"Eh, second best. I don't mind taking a back seat to this, though. It's so exciting!" She waved a hand around the bay. The screens were lit up with notices about the prelims, and at least one was running a sports newscast. A clip of Jenks's championship fight last year appeared briefly before the camera cut back to the commentators.

Rachel bent and picked up her bag. "What's your schedule? Can I take you out to lunch? We'll go put this in your room and then eat."

Max glanced around. Rosa was still forehead to forehead

with her wife, a smile on her face and her daughters chattering away in her ear.

"Sure, we're supposed to get settled. Let me just stop and talk to Ma on our way to our quarters."

Max navigated through to where Ma was speaking with his daughters, a cluster of children around them, and managed the introductions without too much awkwardness. Ma insisted on taking her bag and then, with a wave and a promise to check in in an hour, Max followed Rachel out of the docking bay and onto the bustling streets of London.

The headquarters of the Near-Earth Orbital Guard had been established in 2281 on the outermost edge of what had remained of the English city after the Collapse. The underwater ruins from the rising water were used as training facilities to simulate zero gravity for the academy cadets.

Max had hated every second of it. The place was a graveyard. A several-centuries-old graveyard with only the extremely rare skeleton sighting, but a graveyard, nonetheless.

"Hey, focus there." Rachel looped her arm through Max's. "And start telling me everything that's been going on."

ROSA WATCHED MAX LEAVE WITH THE STATUESQUE BLONDE after speaking to Ma and turned her attention fully on her younger daughter. Angela's hand was warm in hers, Gloria's weight a comfortable pressure on her chest. Isobelle was looking around with wide brown eyes and bouncing with poorly concealed excitement.

"It's so good to have you here," Rosa murmured. "Thank you for coming."

"Where else would we rather be?" Angela asked with a smile that lit up her face.

"But right here in your arms." Rosa leaned in for a kiss that was interrupted by Gloria's squeal.

"No smooching, Mommies!"

"Yes, smooching," she replied, kissing her daughter until she squealed again. "I'm putting you down, my love. Do not wander off."

"Can I go see Ma?"

"I'll take her," Isobelle offered, and Rosa leaned in to press a kiss to her older daughter's cheek.

They watched the pair race across the deck to Ma and his family, who welcomed them with open arms.

"That's better." Rosa leaned in again, this time sinking into the kiss, pulling Angela against her. A selfish part of her wished for the ability to blow off everything—the prelims, the team, even her own daughters—just for a chance to drag her wife into a bedroom and show her how much she'd missed her.

The unwelcome sound of someone clearing their throat broke through the moment and Rosa turned with a snarl in her throat that abruptly got stuck there. As a result, her fumbled greeting was garbled and she coughed.

"I'm sorry."

"No, it's I who owe you an apology for the interruption, Commander Martín." Admiral Royko Chen smiled up at Rosa, her dark green eyes sparkling with amusement as she rolled her wheelchair back and forth in a little wiggle.

"No, it's fine, Admiral." Rosa snapped into a salute, but the petite head of NeoG waved her off. "What can I do for you?"

"First, please reintroduce me to your wife—it's been a while. That way she can forgive me for stealing you for a few minutes. I promise it won't take long."

"Angela, you remember Admiral Chen, head of the NeoG."

"It's very nice to see you again." Angela shook Chen's hand and then smiled at Rosa. "I'll go rescue Ma from Gloria."

Admiral Chen watched her go before turning her gaze back to Rosa. "That's a lovely family, Rosa. Though I remember when Isobelle—isn't it?"

"Yes, Admiral."

"I remember when Isobelle was the size of a loaf of bread."

Chen held her hands apart with a grin. "Where has the time gone?"

"It passes as God wills, Admiral."

"So it does." Chen nodded, then looked around. "Walk with me for a moment," she said, pushing her chair away from the crowd dominating the deck. Rosa followed, brain spinning as she tried to figure out just what the head of the NeoG would want from her. Her answer came with the admiral's question.

"How's Maxine settling in?" Chen slanted a sideways glance at Rosa, a smile pulling at her mouth. "And don't give me the bullshit 'fine' answer, either. How's she really doing?"

"She's an excellent officer, Admiral. That's not a formulaic response," she continued when the frown started. "She's got the talent for it. She's hesitant sometimes, but that's the newness more than anything. Max is very good at seeing things before they happen. One of these days she'll trust that in the field and not just in the cage."

"Good. I hate it when a gamble doesn't work out."

"I don't know that I'd celebrate this as a win just yet, Admiral."

"Ah." Chen smiled again. "I owe you an apology for that, too, I suppose. I know I threw some carefully laid plans into disarray with this transfer. It's a gamble for sure. But one I think is going to play out in ways none of us expect."

"I would have gone in Nika's place if I could have. At least then the team would have had a better chance at winning the Games."

"Oh, horseshit." Chen's laughing epithet startled Rosa. "Maxine isn't the only one who needs to trust in her abilities, Rosa."

"Admiral?"

Chen gave her a flat look. "You are an excellent swordswoman, Commander, with far more years of experience than most of the people you'll be fighting both here and in the Games themselves."

"I'm—"

"Thirty-eight-plus years with a sword in your hand. There are only two people I can think of with more who still compete in the Games, and neither of them is NeoG, which is an automatic downgrade as far as I'm concerned." She poked a finger in Rosa's direction. "Stop thinking of this as a sport, Commander, and start thinking of it as a boarding action. That's where your power is."

Rosa stared at her, brain scrambling to catch up, but before she could say anything in reply, Chen reached out and squeezed her hand with a smile.

"I've taken enough of your time, Commander. Go see your family, and good luck; I'm counting on you." With a final nod, Chen pushed away and headed across the deck, stopping to speak with nearly everyone she encountered on her way through.

"What was that about?" Ma's murmured question made her jump and Rosa shook her head.

"A pep talk? I think?" She knew her laugh was slightly hysterical, but she couldn't help herself. "I don't really know."

"Well, whatever it was, ruminate on it over food. If you four come with us, Julissa and Anabelle will keep Gloria occupied while you and Angela catch up."

"That's not fair to you—"

Ma waved off her protest. "It's fine—you know I wouldn't have offered if I didn't mean it. We're family and it's the quiet before the storm. Let's drop our gear and get some food. I'm starving."

Rosa knew this was one of those times she could do nothing but say "Yes, Ma." And follow along. She shoved the conversation with Admiral Chen into a box in the corner of her brain and left it there for later.

Quiet before the storm indeed.

PRELIMINARIES DAY ONE, T-MINUS ONE HOUR UNTIL OPENING CEREMONIES

Max swallowed and blew out what she hoped was a surreptitious breath as they descended into the chaos that dominated the academy's massive gymnasium. It felt like she'd just left here—the Interceptor facility was just next door and she'd practically gone from the academy to training when you got right down to it.

"This is nothing," Sapphi murmured as heads turned and the noise swelled to even more impossible levels. "Wait until we get to the Games themselves."

There were eyes on her and Max could hear the whispers of "Carmichael" on the air. But she took her cues from Jenks and Rosa at the head of their little pack and kept her eyes forward.

"Commander Martín. Welcome to NeoG Academy." The cadet skidded to a stop in front of them. "Senior Cadet Mendoza. Head of the academy sword-fighting team. I'm to show you to our changing room, Commander. It's yours for the duration."

"Lead the way then, Cadet," Rosa replied with a smile.

The cadet got them settled and then excused himself. Though Max noticed the quick selfie he took with Jenks before he left.

"All right people, gather in," Rosa said. "We've got an hour before openers, so use it wisely. Stretch, review our Boarding Action strategy, take a few deep breaths." She looked at Max on that last one. "I'm going to pick up schedules, our placement, and the Big Game scenario."

With that she left and the others slipped into their pregame rituals with ease while Max sat down on a bench in the corner with her bag between her feet and focused on breathing so she didn't have to run to the bathroom to throw up.

You are fine and you are going to continue to be fine. You're decent enough in a fight, Jenks said so, and if anyone knows it's her.

She inhaled, rubbing the heel of her hand against her sternum.

You are fine and you are going to continue to be fine. The Big Game and the Boarding Action are team comps; you're not alone in this.

"How are you doing?" Ma sat down next to her.

"I'm . . . fine."

"Really? Because you look—" He gestured at her.

"Like I'm gonna throw up?" Max finished with a rueful smile. "I was hoping it wasn't that obvious."

"You'll settle." Ma patted her hand.

"Can I go out onto the floor?" Max asked. "Take a look around?"

"Sure, just keep an eye out for Rosa and be back here with her."

Max nodded, smoothing a hand over her blue track pants as she stood. The green and white stripes down the sides matched the white shirt with green stripes around the sleeves.

Zuma's ID number covered the back, while the front was emblazoned with the ghost of Zuma himself.

Rosa had said the final Games would see them wearing something more representative of the NeoG as a whole, but for the prelims the teams stuck with their Interceptor logos.

Max spotted a few of those logos, recognizing them now only because she'd spent the past month familiarizing herself with all the teams. *Honorable Intent,* the team for HQ here on Earth, was in a corner along the far wall. They'd unsurprisingly claimed the NeoG logo for themselves. Across from them were the six cages where the forty-two hand-to-hand fights would take place over the next four days.

Next to those were the sword-fighting mats, the five larger areas dominating almost all the rest of the gymnasium. Despite Jenks's popularity, the sword fights commanded almost as much attention from the public.

On the far side of the arena was an ominous, low-slung black structure Max guessed was for the Boarding Action, since the Big Game was a three-story permanent building on the academy property that was modified each year to fit the specs of the course.

The facility for the hacking comp was in a nearby building as well, and of course the piloting competition took place out in space.

Max knew the permanent Boarding Games facility was similar to this one, though it was located on the outer western edge of the habitable zone of the former United States and was a city unto itself.

Movement caught her eye and Max turned her head, spying a man in the stands on her left. He had sandy-brown hair and a bright yellow press pass hanging from his neck.

"Carmichael?" said a voice from behind her.

Max turned and blinked at the bright blue gaze staring at her from a mass of silver and pink curls. "Yes? Sorry, caught me thinking."

"Commander Till, Vera Till." The woman stuck out her hand with a grin. *"Flux Capacitor."*

"Max. It's nice to meet you, Vera."

"Call me Till." She grinned again and shoved the curls out of her face. "Saw you were on the roster for the fights, thought I'd come over and say hi since we'll likely be tangling in one of those before the end of this." She gestured at the cages. "Most everyone's friendly around here, despite the competition, but given you're a Carmichael I suspect folks will be hesitant to approach. Anyhow, you had that look about you."

"Look?"

"The 'Holy God above, what have I gotten myself into' look." Till poked her tongue out between her teeth. "I've been around for a while. Seen it plenty just before the Games start. Don't worry about it. Once you get moving it whizzes on by you. Can hardly catch your breath."

Max spotted Rosa striding across the gym, a tablet in her hand and a grim look on her face.

"Ah, that doesn't look great," Till said, and patted her on the back. "Nice to meet you, Max. I'll see you later." Max was halfway back to Rosa when Till called out again. "Hey, Max?"

She turned. "Yes?"

"Do me a favor and tell Jenks I'll see her in the cage." Till blew a kiss and took off back across the mats with a laugh.

Max caught up with Rosa at the edge of the sword-fighting mats. "Commander, you okay?"

"Fine." But her smile was short. "We drew last place on the Big Game."

"But?"

Rosa dragged in a breath, closing her eyes for a moment before she opened them again and stared at Max. "I'm squared up against Commander Yevchenko in the second round of the sword."

"From *Honorable Intent*." Max nodded. She knew the lanky commander from headquarters from his visits to Admiral

Chen, and had seen a few fights when she'd helped Tamago review training videos. "He fought Nika in the finals last year and lost."

"Exactly. And I've beat him twice," Rosa said, her voice just above a whisper and her fingers tapping nervously on the tablet. "But one of those times was an exhibition match. He had the flu."

"You'll beat him again." Max put her hand over Rosa's, stilling the movement. "Healthy or not. We'll figure it out."

Rosa glanced past her. "Doors are open. Public's coming in. We should get in the changing rooms or we'll end up signing autographs right up until the bell sounds."

JENKS GLANCED AT THE DOOR AS ROSA AND MAX CAME INTO the changing room and rolled her shoulders as she turned off the music blaring in her ears. "What's the news?"

"We rolled the final spot for the Big Game."

"Nice." The algorithm for the slots of all the competitions took last year's ranking into account, but there was still a high degree of luck involved and scoring the coveted final run for the Big Game was something all the teams hoped for.

"Here's the schedules for everything else," Rosa said, and Jenks's DD chip pinged in response to the new file on the team servers. She pulled her comp first, eyes scanning over the names. Most were familiar and she cataloged opponents at lightning speed, tagging the unfamiliar names to investigate when she had the time.

So many people thought that she just threw herself into a fight and let luck sort it out, which wasn't entirely wrong. However, Jenks paid attention to her competition with a focus she applied to only a few other important things in her life. She had detailed files on all her previous fights and those would get shuffled into this year's fight profile as the bracket progressed.

She didn't sleep much during the prelims.

"Scored a bye on the first round, nice." She flicked a smile in Max's direction. "That means I can watch your first round, Lieutenant. Come here and we'll figure out how to beat Lieutenant Shay MacDonald from *Sol Rising*."

"It's going to have to wait," Rosa said, sticking an arm out to stop Max before she could cross the room. "We've only got ten minutes until the opening ceremonies and we need to go over the Big Game objective." She slid the tablet into the slot in the wall and cued up the video.

Admiral Chen's face appeared on the wall. "*Zuma's Ghost,* welcome to the preliminaries. We have cooked up something a little different as an experiment for this game." She smiled.

"Oh boy," Max muttered. "I know that look."

"I have been taken hostage by a group of approximately forty-five well-trained mercenaries and am being held on the top floor of a three-story building. Your objective is to rescue me. However, you will not be able to do it alone. There are essential pieces of information you will need to successfully complete your mission. All of which rely upon the success of your competitors. Your scores hinge on each other's performances. So watch them closely. Cheer them on. My life—your win—depends upon it."

The screen went dark and Jenks rubbed a hand over her face. "Well . . . shit."

"We have to get info from the other teams? How is that going to work?" Sapphi demanded.

"Better question is why would they give it to us? We go last, which used to be a good thing." Jenks shared a grim look with Rosa. "Now all the other teams will have their points, if they let us fail . . ."

"No." Max shook her head. "Admiral Chen is big on teamwork. She would make sure that translated into anything they're doing here. She said, 'Your scores depend on each other.'"

"Meaning everyone's scores depend on the operation being successful across the board." Rosa nodded.

"Let's hope you're right," Jenks replied with a sigh. "Otherwise there's a really good chance we're fucked here." She weathered Rosa's look, shrugging into her blue jacket and checking her hair one last time in the mirror before she headed for the door. She paused, waiting for Rosa before exiting the changing room into the narrow hallway that led to the staging area.

Most of the fifteen teams were already gathered in the large area just off the gymnasium, and the sounds of the excited crowd filtered in to mix with the conversations of the Neos.

"I almost forgot—Commander Till said to tell you she'd see you in the cage."

Jenks glanced at Max briefly and grinned. "I'm hoping so. She's over there with the rest of *Flux*." She pointed a finger to her right, raising her hand a little higher in greeting when she caught Till's eye. The commander lifted her chin in acknowledgment and blew her a kiss.

Jenks laughed, drawing more attention in their direction. She tapped D'Arcy's outstretched fist as they passed *Dread Treasure* and exchanged a look with Luis.

The wink that dropped over one of his amber eyes was so quick no one else saw it and Jenks was glad that shit-eating grin was her default. Luis was built, broad shoulders sliding down to a narrow waist and powerful thighs. He was twenty centimeters taller than her, not enough to make fights complicated, just enough to make things interesting.

She dragged herself out of that distraction just in time to catch Max frowning at her.

"What?"

"Did you—" Max shook her head. "Nothing, never mind."

"Multitasking, Lieutenant. It's a valuable skill." She patted Max on the back, feeling oddly cheerful as she followed Rosa toward the entrance.

The newest team to the prelims, *Sol Rising,* watched them as they passed, wearing identical looks of nervousness.

"You're up against Lieutenant MacDonald in the first round. She's right there," Jenks said to Max, pulling the file on the pale-skinned lieutenant and sending it to Max. "I'm not seeing a lot of—wait, member of the academy hand-to-hand team. Won a couple of tournaments. There will be video of it. I'll find it during the opening ceremonies."

"I appreciate it."

Jenks smiled and patted Max on the back again. "Teammates, Lieutenant. You enjoy your first opening ceremonies. I'll handle this bit."

Rosa glanced back. "Ready?"

"Let's do this," Jenks replied.

PRELIMINARIES—DAY ONE

"Did you hear about the Big Game?"

"Who hasn't? I don't understand the point of it, to be honest."

"Someone said Admiral Chen wanted a reminder that NeoG is in this together, even during the preliminaries."

"Making it so everyone fails the Big Game if she doesn't survive is one way to do it." The speaker paused. "Though what happens if *Zuma's Ghost* chokes on the final run? It's not announced, but you know they'll have to be the ones to rescue the admiral."

The first speaker laughed. "You haven't seen any of these, so I'll give you a break. *Zuma's Ghost* doesn't choke, Malcolm."

"They lost the Games last year."

"By three points. That's not choking."

"Yeah, well their best sword fighter got transferred."

"He did, but they'll still be fine. Come on, let's go get those beers before the next round of fights gets going."

Rosa watched the fans wander past the corner she was leaning against as they went in search of drinks.

"Eavesdropping again, Commander?" Stephan Yevchenko joined her, an easy smile on his handsome face.

"It relaxes me." She stuck her hand out and the man shook it. It would have been easy to hate the commander of *Honorable Intent* if he'd had a single jerkish bone in his body. But Stephan was as easygoing as he was kind, somehow untarnished by his position in NeoG's Intelligence division. "How are things?"

"Pretty quiet. You've had some excitement lately, though."

"What, the freighter?" Rosa shrugged. "Jenks had it well under control."

"Hell of a thing." He leaned against the wall.

Rosa studied him, something in his tone ringing the warning bells in her head. "Something I need to know about that?"

Stephan shook his head. "No. From everything I looked at, it was just a magnetic failure. Rare as can be, but not impossible. Heard your new lieutenant stayed the course."

"She's good at her job."

"We're lucky to have her in NeoG." A quick grin flashed across his face, lighting up his blue eyes. "I was about to beg Admiral Chen to let me lure her over to Intel when she announced she was taking the Interceptor course. She was wasting her talents as an aide, and I think Chen knew it."

"I'm glad she's with us."

Stephan grinned again. "You don't have to say it, I know you'd have been happier if they'd waited until after the Games, but I won't lie and say I'm not glad I don't have to face Nika in the ring."

"I am not surprised, mercenary."

"Word is she's decent in the cage, though," he said.

"She's got some skills." Rosa smiled. "I'm not giving you more than that, Luis and the others will just have to deal with not knowing until you see her fight. Why are you here, Stephan? We usually save these chats for the afterparty."

"Eh, Chen changed the rules up on us." Stephan shrugged.

"*Honorable* is tasked to find a security code for the Big Game, which I suspect you'll need to get into wherever the bad guys are holding the admiral. I'll pass it on as soon as we get through our round."

"I appreciate it, Stephan." Rosa stuck her hand out. "You're a good guy, I don't care what Jenks says about you."

Stephan laughed, shaking her hand. "Tell Jenks Luis is pretty sure he's going to win this year."

Rosa snorted. "Whatever."

Stephan started away, then stopped and looked over his shoulder. "Since we're changing things up here, let's have a drink after I kick your ass. I want to pick your brain about something."

"Loser's buying," Rosa replied, and Stephan laughed.

"Fair enough. See you in the ring, Rosa."

"Later, Stephan."

"MAX?"

"I am so sorry to wake you up, but I wanted to ask you about Commander Yevchenko."

"Stephan? Why? Wait, shit, you're at the prelims." Nika snapped awake, rubbing both hands over his face. "Sorry, we just got back from patrol two hours ago."

"Rosa drew Yevchenko for the second round. I'm on break. I thought it would help her if I could bring her some kind of information on how to fight him."

"You already had fights? How did they go?"

"Sailed through my first two rounds." Max couldn't stop the giddy grin from spreading across her face. "Jenks is fighting right now. Ma and I are set to tackle the second round of the pilot course in a little over an hour."

"But Rosa's fighting Stephan?"

"Yes, in ten minutes. I wish I'd thought of it earlier, but—"

"Don't worry about it." Nika waved her off. "Stephan is

good. I can't believe they got paired in the second round, that doesn't happen very often. He got a bye in the first, didn't he?"

Max nodded.

"Look, he's too nice a guy to be arrogant, but he'll be over-confident. Rosa can use that. When he gets excited he has a tendency to drop his guard on his left side. Tell Rosa to play up her insecurity about the fight, use it to her advantage." Nika laughed. "She'll give you this look and try to pretend like she has it together, but I know her, she's a wreck on the in-side right now and convinced she can't win this fight. Tell her this, exactly: 'You're the best sword fighter in the ring in this moment—act like it.'"

Max nodded.

"Don't look so skeptical," Nika said. "The only difference between me and Rosa is that she always thought I was better than her and she fought like it. She's got more experience than all of us put together."

"I'd better go."

Nika nodded and rubbed a hand over his face a second time. "I guess since I'm up I'll find the broadcast. Hey, Max?"

"Yeah?"

"Go kick some ass out there."

"I will." She was smiling when she terminated the com, though, and raced out of the changing room. She wove her way through the people on the gymnasium floor past the cage fights, where a sudden roar went up. Max glanced up at the massive screen hovering in the middle of the open in time to see the replay of Jenks bodily driving her opponent, a well-muscled warrant officer, into the mat.

"Careful." Hard hands caught her when she ran into someone and Max brought her own up reflexively. "Easy, Lieu-tenant, just didn't want you to land on your butt."

"Chief Petty Officer Armstrong." Max nodded to the *Hon-orable Intent* fighter with a calmness she wasn't feeling.

"Nice to meet the mysterious Carmichael at last." Luis's

smile was broad, dominating his round face. "I'm bummed we won't get to have a fight, Lieutenant, though maybe you'll surprise me and beat Jenks."

"Unlikely." She slipped free. "Thanks for the catch, I've got to run."

"You headed to the sword fights? I'll block for you." He held out a hand with a smile and Max found herself smiling back as she took it. Luis turned and cleared a path through the crowd. People parted almost unconsciously and within a few moments Luis had led Max over to Rosa and departed with a bright grin and an irreverent salute.

Rosa chuckled. "Met the chief, I see."

"He seems nice."

"He's seeing Jenks." Rosa laughed again at Max's surprised look. "They think they're sneaky about it, but it's been going on for years. Kinda hard not to notice."

Max wasn't entirely sure how to respond to that, so she changed the subject. "I just talked to Nika."

"Nika?" Rosa frowned.

"I thought he might have some pointers for you for the fight." Max gestured across the ring at where Stephan was laughing with Luis as she relayed what Nika had said. "He said to tell you that you're the best sword fighter in the ring in this moment, act like it," she finished.

"Asshole." Rosa laughed. "He would say that."

"He said, too, that you've got more experience than all of us combined."

"Admiral Chen said something very similar," Rosa replied with a frown. "She also told me I should stop treating this like a match and go into it like a boarding action."

Max practically felt the air contract around them and her next words felt weighty in her mouth. "I think you are the better of the two fighters about to step into the ring, Commander. You've got the combat experience Stephan will never have. It's time for you to give yourself the kind of recognition you're always giving those of us around you."

She watched Rosa's shoulders pull back, spine going straight, and her gloved hand tightened on the dulled sword. Max reached out, putting her hand over Rosa's. "You can do this. I have faith in you."

JENKS WIGGLED A LOOSE TOOTH AS SHE MADE HER WAY across the gymnasium floor. Nilsson's right hook was a thing of beauty, if only she didn't leave herself so open when she threw it. That had been the warrant officer's downfall in the end.

Jenks accepted the congratulations and paused to take selfies with a few fans who'd scored passes to be at ground level as she moved across the floor. The tooth would settle by tomorrow thanks to the accelerated heal that medical had shot her up with, and she was done fighting for today thanks to her bye in the first round.

No replacement tooth for me this year.

She spotted a man with a press pass and a camera taking photos of Max as the lieutenant watched Rosa's fight. "You got an admirer," she said, bumping her shoulder into Max's and tipping her head to the side.

Max glanced away from the fight and frowned. "I saw him before the Games started."

"Unsurprising. Get used to it. I've got a guy who's followed me around since I started. I send his kids Christmas presents." Jenks winced when Stephan hit Rosa right in her sword arm with a blow that knocked the weapon from her hand.

The ref blew the whistle to end the second round.

"I was about to say you were doing good," Jenks said, boosting herself up on the ropes and holding her hand out for the sword.

Rosa slapped it into her palm and looked down at her suit.

Eight pulsing red marks decorated the gray surface, the sensors buried within showing where Yevchenko had tagged her. She glanced over at him and sighed.

"Hey, you got him six times, you're still in this." Jenks grabbed a towel and rubbed down the sword as Max handed Rosa a water.

"Remember what Nika said about his left-side guard," Max said. "Play up your hesitation, act like those two points have you worried."

"They do have me worried." Rosa flexed her hand.

Jenks resisted the urge to ask Max when she'd spoken to Nik and instead handed the sword back to Rosa. "She's right, Nik's right. Yevchenko gets sloppy when he thinks he's about to win. Use that against him; you only need three hits to win." Jenks glanced over her shoulder to make sure no one was watching. "Hit him left side, thigh, torso, and spin to take the final shot in the back. I'd say hold him off for two and a half minutes and then strike in the last thirty seconds to keep him from being able to retaliate, but that's me."

"I actually agree with her," Max said when Rosa looked her way, and Jenks snorted, rolling her eyes with a smile.

"He'll get more and more certain of his victory. Make a few attempts to score on him, and if you do, bonus. I don't see him being worried until you actually catch up on points or take over."

"Time's up." The referee came over. "You ready, Commander?"

"She's ready," Jenks said. Rosa nodded. Jenks held out her fist. "Kick his ass, Commander."

Max leaned in, whispered something in Rosa's ear before stepping down off the ropes. Jenks jumped down, shoving her hands into the pockets of her pants, and worried at her loose tooth as the fighters squared up.

The referee blew his whistle to start the match. Rosa backed up a step in what Jenks really hoped was feigned caution.

"Saw you beat Ito," she said to Max as the two fighters circled. "Good job."

"Thanks to you." Max didn't look away as Rosa fended off an opening attack from Stephan and the crowd roared.

"Eh." Jenks waved a hand. "You fought the fight. I just pointed out some weaknesses."

"Are you ever going to accept that you're an integral part of this team?" Max asked. "Or do you just deflect it all in the hopes that it will keep you invisible?"

Jenks shot her a curious eyebrow, but Max's eyes were locked on Rosa.

"You're not, you know."

"Not what?"

"Invisible. Granted, it's only been four months since I got here, but I've watched you help everyone with their comps— including me, who you don't particularly care for—all the while holding things together like a champ whenever we go out into the black. I know you miss your brother a lot, but you've—"

"Careful, Lieutenant. That's a subject we probably shouldn't wander into in the middle of Rosa's match. If I punch you here it'll cause a commotion."

"Fair enough." Max sucked in a breath when Rosa narrowly missed another touch from Stephan and staggered backward. "All I'm saying is that you're important to this team."

"He dropped his guard," Jenks hissed, grabbing for Max's forearm without hesitation. "Come on, Rosa!"

"Yeah!" Max punched the air when a pulse of red blossomed on Stephan's suit right in the middle of his left shoulder. The crowd echoed their cheers and the referee raised a hand to indicate the score.

"Still a minute thirty left." Jenks glanced at the clock and at the score, which was now eight to seven in favor of Stephan. "You're wrong, you know."

"Jenks—"

"I do care for you. You're my teammate, yeah?" She flicked her eyes away from the ring as Rosa and Stephan lined back up and the ref blew the whistle to restart the match. "I don't trust people very well and it was hard for me when Nika left, but I never hated you. I knew it wasn't your fault."

"I'm glad." Max exhaled a long breath.

Jenks poked Max in the side. "Don't go getting all sappy on me, though, Lieutenant. We're trying to watch the commander kick some honorable ass!" She raised her voice as Stephan and Rosa circled in their direction, swords dancing together in a rhythmic beat.

Jenks glanced at the clock. "She's got to make her move here soon."

No sooner had the words left her mouth than Rosa stumbled. The crowd sucked in a united breath and Stephan smiled as he moved in—but the stumble was a feint. Rosa swung her sword up, leaning backward to avoid Stephan's strike, and lit up a spot on his thigh, then his stomach.

She spun, blocking him with her free arm and striking him in the back with the flat of her blade.

The referee's whistle blew. "Three points to Commander Martín!"

The crowd erupted.

Max gripped Jenks's arm so tightly it was painful, but she didn't say a word as the fighters reset, Stephan no longer smiling, Rosa with an intense look in her eyes Jenks knew all too well from every single mission they'd been on.

Thirty seconds lasts forever in a fight, Jenks knew that as well as anyone, but the last thirty seconds of Rosa's fight seemed to last an eternity as she defended herself against Stephan's attacks.

By the time the whistle blew again she'd scored two more hits and Jenks launched herself over the ropes to pick Rosa up in a bear hug.

PRELIMINARIES—DAY TWO

Max kept her eyes locked on the console in front of her, one hand pressed to her mouth, the pain of her split lip from her previous cage match forgotten as Ma swung the ship in a vicious turn, narrowly avoiding the markers. He'd had a bye for the first round, then had decimated his competition yesterday in the second with his stunning times and completion ranking.

Their completion ranking, he kept reminding her. But it was hard for her to take any credit here. All she was doing was laying a path for him—he was the one flying like a demon.

Of course, they'd spent months training together for this. Max was, as Ma kept saying, overprepared and underconfident about her skills for the piloting course; but now that they were out here flying it, she was moving on instinct and so was he.

There was an obvious path through the course, but pilots and navigators could shave seconds off their times with numerous little shortcuts and maneuvers—if they could figure them out. And with her intuition and his touch, there was a good chance they could do just that.

Max kept one eye on the flashing icon of *Honorable Intent*'s pilot, Lieutenant Alvar Mel, as he closed the gap on Ma.

She wasn't going to let Mel and Luis catch up, let alone win this. She scanned the course ahead of them, hunting for something, anything that would extend their lead. Then she spotted it, a tempting but dangerous path that went deliberately off the preferred course.

To take it was to risk losing.

To take it and win would mean bonus points for the technical difficulty.

"Cut starboard and down eighteen degrees," Max said, using their prearranged directions. "Now."

Ma obeyed without question.

"Three degrees up and starboard, Ma, now." She was sure the crowd was screaming at them, wondering what they were doing, but the shortcut would put them over the finish line with a full thirty-second lead.

If she didn't mess up and lead Ma astray.

"Hard forty-five to port and immediate two degrees up. Now. Watch the port side!"

"I see it." Ma grunted a little with the effort as they pushed the ship to the limits of its capabilities.

"Next mark is back onto the regular course. You cut through, Ma, over and down. Only a meter of clearance on the top buoy."

"I would not have picked this route, kiddo," he said, but he was grinning.

"I know, but you can do this." Still, she held her breath as he maneuvered the ship through the markers and they sailed over the finish line, with Sapphi's cheers echoing over the team com. Max grinned at Ma, taking the hand he held out and squeezing it for a long moment.

She sent out the notice on the team chat: Ma took round two!

And immediately received a series of replies from the other four members of *Zuma's Ghost*.

JENKS: *thumbs up*

ROSA: Well done, both of you!

TAMAGO: *cheers*

SAPPHI: You are both awesome!

SAPPHI WAS BOUNCING UP AND DOWN IN THE HANGAR WHEN they landed. She barely waited for Ma and Max to shake hands with *Honorable Intent*'s crew before she started cheering again.

"Done and dusted. Dusted!" Sapphi called out, pointing across the hangar at Captain Davi Kilini, who just laughed and shook her head. Ma scooped Max and Sapphi up into a hug.

"Come on, let's go get lunch," he said, putting them down.

Max looped her arm around Sapphi's neck and dragged her toward the door.

The spring air in London was cool and a light rain dripped on their heads as the trio made a run from the shelter of the walkway away from the hangar.

"Go *Zuma*!" A yell came from a passerby and Max stopped, eyes widening slightly as they were suddenly surrounded by a group of excited teens.

"Can we get a selfie?"

"We saw your fight, Lieutenant, you were amazing!"

"Rumors are swirling about the Big Game, are you ready for it?"

Max smiled for the photos, answering questions as best she could, and signed a program a young man thrust in her direction with a shy smile at her. Sapphi was signing a jacket as a nonbinary teen chattered excitedly at her about how they were taking hacking classes at the university. Ma smiled and answered questions about enlisting in the NeoG from the oldest of the group.

As Max hugged the last of them, she spotted the man with the press pass hanging back in the cover of the walkway and an uneasy feeling crawled up her spine. She tried to push it away—being followed was a fact of life for a Carmichael, this wasn't any different—and yet she couldn't shake the feeling something was off.

"Sorry, folks, we need to get going. Have fun!" Sapphi took Max's hand and pulled her down the walkway. The teens waved goodbye, heading in the other direction.

One of them stopped and called after them, "Commander Till just won her fight, Lieutenant Carmichael. Means you're facing her in the next round. Kick her ass!"

"Will do!" Max replied, and the teens cheered again.

"They'll keep you there all day if you let them. Best to get in and out with as much cheer as you can muster," Sapphi said as they hurried Max away from the crowds.

"Them I don't mind," Max said. "This press guy who keeps following me around but not saying anything is making me uneasy."

"Where?" Ma frowned.

"Our seven o'clock."

Sapphi snuck a look. "Huh. It happens. If it's really bothering you I can go tell him to piss off."

"No." Max shrugged. "Press I'm used to, part of growing up a Carmichael. They just usually talk to me—a lot more than that guy has." She pushed it to the back of her mind. "When's your next round?"

"Fourteen thirty. I'm gonna finish quick again so I can go see Jenks's fight at sixteen hundred."

"Sounds like a plan. Tamago's fight is the same time as your comp, so I think Rosa and I are splitting. One of us'll be there."

"Ah, go watch Tamago, they'll notice you. I don't see anyone once the timer starts." Sapphi grinned, brown eyes warm with amusement. "Nika used to say you could detonate a nuke next to me and I wouldn't even blink."

Sapphi liked to protest that she couldn't stand the pressure, but the reality was she did fine when the pressure was focused on her. She only tended toward falling apart when she watched everyone else. Max had seen the video of her wiping the floor with her competitors yesterday. Max hadn't quite understood *what* she was watching—coding was way beyond her. But she knew Sapphi had looked completely unfazed and—as she had just said about their piloting competition—dusted her opponent.

She wrapped her arm around Sapphi's shoulders again. "I believe it. One of these days I'd like you to teach me how to shut the world out like that."

JENKS STUDIED LUIS WITH A SMIRK. "MA AND MAX WHOOPED your ass this morning. That's another for me."

Luis's chuckle was this rumbling purr she always imagined was similar to the big cats lost to the Collapse. It did funny things to her breathing, that laugh, and for a moment she was very glad they were in the middle of a crowded café.

"Mel's great, but we all know he's got a long way to go before he's even close to Ma's level," he replied, rolling his glass between his palms. "And that shortcut Max took? I'd never have thought to look for it, let alone take it."

Lieutenant Mel was barely old enough to shave and the newest member of *Honorable Intent*. He had some piloting skills, but Luis was right about the gap in experience.

"True," Jenks replied, lifting a shoulder. "If you want him to learn anything, you're going to have to get his butt out of that chair."

Luis chuckled again but didn't rise to the bait. "Some of us have to be file monkeys, Dai, you know that."

That was the other thing that did her in. Luis was good about calling her Jenks whenever they were around others, but when it was just the two of them? She suppressed a shudder. The way he said her name was almost better than the sex.

Almost.

"Besides, I like being on Earth, and it gives the kids some stability."

"Fair enough."

"They're coming in tomorrow with MM. I think Riz is actually cheering against me if we end up fighting each other in the finals." He hesitated. "They might like to meet you. They've been asking lately."

"They know?"

Luis shrugged. "I haven't told them, but kids are smart. Either they heard us talking at some point or me with my moms—"

"You're talking about me to your moms?"

"Dai, look."

"It's fine." She waved a hand. "I can sign something for him?" she asked, slipping behind the mask she instinctively used as her public face. She couldn't stop herself from withdrawing, and saw the flicker of hurt Luis couldn't quite hide.

"Ouch, that stings." Luis held his hands up in surrender, the easy smile back. "I'm sorry, I know that's pushing the rules. I just thought you'd like to know. Can I have my Dai back?"

"I haven't gone anywhere."

"Yeah you have, you're backing away. I'd let you do it except you keep taking steps forward like you don't quite know what you want."

The warning bell went off in her head to let her know she had an hour before her fight. "I should go. I have a match." She was on her feet, paying her half of the bill with her DD chip before she finished talking.

"Damn it, Jenks, come on."

She didn't wait. Didn't expect him to actually follow her or grab her and spin her into a deserted access corridor. She'd never taken a swing at him outside the cage, but her fists balled up of their own accord.

"Don't." He caught her by the wrists, stepping in close until she was pressed with her back to the wall, and touched his forehead to hers. "I'm sorry. I just—I've missed you."

"You've what?"

Luis laughed, the sound pained. "It's this thing people do, Dai, when they don't get to see each other as often as they'd like."

"Why would you miss me?"

Sadness washed over his face. "I hurt for you, that you don't even think you're someone people miss—that you don't think I miss you. We don't have time for the list of ways, and I was going to pick a better time for this, but . . . I love you, Dai. I miss you when you're not around."

There was something sharp in her chest. Jenks imagined it was what being stabbed in the heart would feel like, but she was caught up in Luis's amber eyes and couldn't find the words she needed before he moved.

He let go of her wrists, cupped her face, and kissed her. His were lips soft on hers, missing the heat and speed that usually dug into her gut and pulled her forward. Still, something spiraled, unfurling in that painful spot in her chest as Luis deepened the kiss.

Then he was gone, backing up well out of range with his hands up and a strange, sad smile on his face. "Good luck with your fight, Dai. Watch out for Pashol's roundhouse kick—it's vicious."

Jenks stared at his retreating back, unmoving until she was alone in the corridor. "What the actual fuck was that?" she muttered, pressing her lips together with a frown.

"My Dai," he said, like I belonged to him.

Though that wasn't really what bothered her. It was the shift, the fucking unexpected shift in something she'd thought had been settled.

"He's not supposed to love me. This isn't love. It's just sex. It was settled. Five fucking years of settled. Good sex and nothing else. What is he doing?"

Nothing else, really? Is that the lie you're telling yourself? You started it, Jenks, this line-stepping and rule-breaking. Thinking it would make him back off. Instead it backfired on you and now you get to deal with the fallout.

Jenks got moving through sheer force of will back out into the foot traffic of the outdoor market up the road from the academy. Her hair was tied back in a ponytail at the crown of her head so she flipped up the hood on her jacket to avoid recognition as much as possible and cranked the music on her DD chip to something suitably angry.

People melted out of her way as she crossed the gymnasium and ducked into *Zuma's* changing room, which was, thankfully, empty. Jenks rubbed absently at her heart as she wandered through to the sinks. She flipped on the cold water and splashed it into her face, cursing at the shock of it.

"Jenks?"

"In here," she called. "Toss me a towel, will you?" She cracked an eye and caught the towel Sapphi pitched through the air to her.

"Everyone else is out there already. You okay?"

"I'm fine," Jenks lied, coiling around her confusion like a trapped snake. She dried her face, ignored Sapphi's raised eyebrow, and turned the music up. The savage beat of Busta Rhymes filled her head.

She headed for the gym floor, thoughts rolling. The energy of the crowd was already electric, and it sharpened when she came into view. Normally this would be the point where she played to the people in the stands, ramping them up even more.

But not today. Today she needed to be alone.

Jenks caught Rosa's eyes as she neared the cage and gave a single shake of her head. The commander nodded, putting a hand out and whispering something in Tamago's ear before the petty officer could start forward.

Jenks flipped her hood up again and started her prefight routine. The music blaring in her ears drowned out the noise, and before she knew it Sapphi was touching her on the arm and pointing to the cage.

Sapphi tapped her fist to her heart and Jenks echoed it, performing the handshake on autopilot and forcing herself to meet Sapphi's gaze when their foreheads touched. She could see the questions, but she didn't have answers for them, so she pulled away with a quick smile.

Everything always narrowed at this point for Jenks, but the world seemed painfully sharp as she turned the music off and let the sound of the crowd fill her instead. She shrugged out of her jacket, toed off her shoes, and peeled her socks away as she ran through what she knew about Commander An Pashol.

"I love you, Dai."

Luis's words intruded and Jenks snarled. Was this just a ploy to get her distracted? If it was, it was working.

A softer voice in her head tried to insist Luis would never do something like that. That they respected each other's fights as sacred. That the cage was separate from everything else between them. That had been the agreement.

But too many years of not trusting spoke louder, building the fury as she strode through the door of the cage, rolling her shoulders and giving Commander Pashol a perfunctory nod.

Jenks barely heard the ref's opening remarks, nodding in all the right places. She could recite the rules of the fight in her sleep anyway.

He doesn't really love you, Jenks. You're not the kind of person who gets that. Your own mother didn't love you enough to keep you.

"Ready?" The referee looked between them and at their nods—hers mechanical—blew his whistle. "Fight!"

Jenks dodged Pashol's opening attack, putting all her weight behind her answering punch. It connected with his jaw and he dropped faster than someone stepping onto a high-g asteroid.

"Hold!"

Jenks backed off at the referee's shout, falling into parade rest out of habit more than anything with her shaking hands clasped behind her back.

"He's out! That's match!"

The stunned silence that had swept through the crowd was just as quickly destroyed by the roar.

Jenks waved off the ref before he could raise her arm and headed for the cage door.

"Hey, Tai," she said, catching PO Majrashi by the arm as they passed her. "When he wakes up tell him I'm sorry. That was, um, a little harder than it should have been."

"No worries, Jenks." Tai flashed her a grin. "He's not going to live this one down for a while, though."

Her teammates made way for her as she left the cage, Rosa merely raising a curious eyebrow while the others wore looks ranging from concern to awe.

"What?" Jenks finally snapped, grabbing for her things.

"Nothing," Sapphi said, lifting her hands with a smile. "Whoever you're mad at, stay that way. Don't transfer it to me."

Jenks strode to the changing rooms, holding on to her confusing emotions until she was alone in the shower, where she finally let the tears fall.

Because she was starting to realize the person she was mad at was herself.

PRELIMINARIES—DAY THREE

The day dawned bright and early as the NeoG teams got under way for the grueling final forty-eight hours of the preliminaries. Legends were made or broken in this span as the first round of the Boarding Action started at an ungodly hour that only the most dedicated fans roused themselves from their beds for.

Rosa cupped her coffee between her hands and took a sip as she watched D'Arcy and his team demolish *Green Machine*.

"*Dread Treasure* is on a roll," Ma commented as he joined her. "They're nipping at *Honorable*'s heels in the overall points."

Rosa grunted, sipped again, and sighed at the heat of the coffee. "I'm really glad we got a bye on this. I would not want to be out there trying to fight this early."

"I don't know, dragging a grumpy Jenks out there probably would have meant the rest of us could sit back and watch."

Rosa chuckled, though her amusement faded quickly. "She open up about what got her so worked up yesterday?"

"No, and I'm not pushing it. I don't want to end up like Commander Pashol."

"He's okay, right?"

"Yeah, just a wicked headache and a shit-ton of embarrassment." Ma's grin was quick and sharp. "As for Jenks, she'll shake it off, she always does."

Rosa hummed. She wasn't so sure. Jenks was focused as a default and the Games only made her more so. But that punch she'd landed on the commander of *Nitro Horizon* had seemed to shock her, which meant she hadn't been in control—and that concerned Rosa. Because an out-of-control Jenks was something that she had only ever had to deal with once in the last six years. She didn't want to have to deal with it again.

"*Nitro* has to go up against *Keppler's Folly*. I suspect with Pashol not performing at top speed they're not going to win." Rosa continued to watch the screens.

"Highly likely and works for me. *Keppler's* team is predictable. We should be able to handle them."

"We'll fight them this afternoon," Rosa said. "I want to do a quick strategy session before that in the break."

"*Flux* is doing surprisingly well this year." Ma pointed at the screen where *Flux Capacitor* was fighting with *Impossible Star*. "Commander Till may have a team that places above last."

"Anything's possible. Max has to fight her today, I'm curious to see how that ends up."

"Even if she loses it won't affect our points all that much, though don't tell Max I said that." Ma chuckled. "She's done well so far. Her navigation is spot-on."

"She has," Rosa agreed. "Everyone's performances have been excellent. Everyone's making it to the semis, or close enough to give us points for the total. We're tight, but your and Sapphi's wins today will give us some breathing room. If Tamago can pull out a win against D'Arcy . . ."

"That's a tough fight. And Sapphi and I do still have to win our comps first, Commander."

"True. But I have faith, Ma."

"Whatever gets you through the day."

"What gets you through the day?"

"Breakfast. Tell anyone who wakes up I'll be at Sam's."

Rosa smiled at him, then went back to watching the Boarding Actions.

There were four fights going on and another three would start within the hour. One team was designated the "bad guys," but the objective was the same for both teams. Secure the ship against your opponents. It was, oddly enough, the most fun competition of the Games, with a great deal of hilarity amid the fights. Anything was legal, no matter how wild. The seriousness was saved for the Big Game and it was a balance that even Rosa enjoyed.

The structure in the corner of the gymnasium contained the competition while the fourth round of the sword fights and cage matches continued, not to mention the final rounds for the pilots and hackers. This was the point in the Games where Rosa didn't envy the organizers. The field shrank and they had to make sure that contestants' comps didn't overlap. Which was a huge part of the reason for the early-hour start. The sword and cage matches wouldn't begin for another two hours, giving everyone plenty of time to finish up here and prepare for what came next.

If Max were here she'd likely pick the winners out from these four matches after a couple of minutes of watching, but Rosa had ordered her to sleep in. Max's bout with Commander Till was gathering nearly as much attention as Jenks's fight later in the day with Ensign Vicks from *Keppler's Folly*.

Jenks's fight was almost a sure thing, especially if she hadn't calmed down from whatever was bothering her; but *Flux Capacitor*'s commander was a good fighter and Rosa wasn't sure even Max's spooky ability to predict people would garner her a win.

"Morning," Tamago said, drifting by with a cup of coffee in their hands.

"Anyone else up?"

"Max is stirring. Sapphi and Jenks were out late. They'll be up in an hour or so." Tamago yawned and leaned a hip on the table. "How goes it?"

"*Green Machine*'s last man just went down." Rosa pointed

at the screen in the middle. "And I don't think *Avenging Heroes* is going to be able to pull a win out of that early fiasco."

"I hope *Green* at least wore D'Arcy down a bit, give me an edge in our fight today," they replied, scanning the other two screens with sharp brown eyes.

"Anything's possible, but don't count on it. Keep your sword up and watch him when he comes in close." Rosa glanced Tamago's way. "Did Jenks say anything about yesterday?"

Tamago shrugged. "Armstrong." It was all they needed to say.

"She talked to you?"

"No, you know how she is. Easier to open up HQ's vaults than get her to talk about feelings. But he's the only thing that would get her in knots like this. Something's been going on— they've been messaging and calling so much more than normal these last few months—I'm surprised you didn't notice."

"To be fair, I try not to stick my nose into your private lives too much. Plus, we've all been pretending we didn't notice this thing between them for how many years now?"

They laughed. "True. Well, something happened. I don't know what and I'm not asking."

"You don't think he's doing it deliberately to try to get her off-balance, do you?"

Tamago blinked at the suggestion, but shook their head. "No. Anyone else, I'd maybe consider it, but not Luis. He doesn't operate like that. Honestly there's only one thing that would shake her up this bad. He—" Tamago broke off, tipping their chin at the door, and Rosa glanced behind her to see Jenks stumbling into the room.

"Later," Rosa said, pointing a finger at Tamago, who shook their head and pantomimed locking their lips.

"Coffee, Jenks," they said, crossing the room. "Meds too— open up." They tossed a couple of pain meds into Jenks's mouth and then handed over their coffee cup.

Jenks swallowed the pills with a hiss, handed the cup back, and scratched at her scalp. Doge sat patiently next to her and Jenks absently patted one side of his metal frame. "Morning, Commander. How go the Boarding Actions?"

"Good. You're up early."

"Eh, got three hours in." Jenks shrugged as she came to stand next to Rosa. "That's enough for me."

"You hungover?"

Jenks stuck her tongue out and grinned at Rosa. "A bit, but I'll be fine by this afternoon."

"You okay?"

A flicker of something passed over Jenks's face, washed away just as quickly by an impressively fake smile that was all Jenks. "I'm fine, Commander. Didn't even drink all that much when you get down to it. And dragged Sapphi out of there before she did, so you're welcome."

"Fine." Rosa knew it was a losing battle, so she let it go rather than press forward. "Make sure you're with Max for her fight with Till. I know she may not win, but if she does it's going to put us on solid footing going into tomorrow, and you might see something that can help her."

"Was planning on it." Jenks smiled. "I like watching Till fight anyway—she's always coming up with some new trick. Going to get breakfast. Do you want me to bring anything back?"

"No, I ate already." Rosa waved. "Ma went to Sam's Place if you want to join him."

"Mmm, pancakes." Jenks saluted as she headed for the door. "See you in a bit."

"INHALE," JENKS SAID, HOLDING THE TUBE JUST UNDER MAX'S bleeding nose. "Come on, Lieutenant, inhale for me."

Max finally managed to inhale, choking a little as she

sucked some blood the wrong direction along with the clotting agent. Within moments it had done its job and her gushing nose stopped.

"She all right?" Vera asked.

Jenks laughed as she looked over her shoulder at Till. "She'll be fine. You try that kick with me, though, and I'm going to pull your leg off and beat you with it."

"You always say the nicest things. Feel free to pull my leg anytime," Vera replied, and sauntered off.

Jenks watched her go with a little sigh. Normally she'd be following Vera back to the showers for a quick bang, but even if she didn't have to babysit the still woozy Max, she wasn't feeling it.

Damn you, Luis.

The med tech ran the last of her scans and nodded at Jenks with a thumbs-up. "Brain scans are fine. She's a little rattled, but no concussion. Sleep would be good." The tech pressed an injection gun to Max's forearm. "She'll be fine and ready for the next event this afternoon. Come find me if there's any problem."

"I did not even see that kick coming," Max said, her words slurring together as Jenks slid an arm around her waist and hauled her to her feet.

"Most people don't. Let's get you back to the changing rooms; you can lie down in there for a while until the world stops spinning."

"Sorry I lost."

"You're fine, Lieutenant. You held her till the end, which is what we were hoping for. That's good enough points to keep our lead solid. We're going to do some hard-core studying of the teams for the final Games, you and me."

"I'd like that. We should spend more time together."

Jenks rolled her eyes and laughed. "Ease up there, space ranger."

"I just mean we should be friends. I'm not like you, Jenks.

I don't know how to just be around people without it getting all awkward."

"I can see that." Jenks was starting to wonder if the med tech had missed a scan, but it appeared Till's kick had just knocked loose whatever filter Max usually employed that kept her silent and watchful. "Okay, on the cot, LT."

Max sighed as she lay back. "You just called me LT."

"Yeah, I did." Jenks raised an eyebrow. "That's what you are."

"Yeah. No. It's . . . it's just you've called me lieutenant pretty relentlessly since I got here. Which for someone not hot on formalities says a lot. Does this mean you trust me?"

"Not in the least. You've gotta save my life at least once for that," Jenks replied, but she smiled. "Go to sleep, LT—I'll check on you in an hour."

"Okay."

Jenks watched Max roll onto her side and shook her head as she grabbed for the blanket folded nearby and draped it out over the sleeping woman.

"She all right? That was a wicked kick."

Jenks froze at the sound of Luis's voice, forced herself to smooth the blanket over Max's shoulders, and then carefully turned around. "She'll be all right according to the doc. Besides, she's tough."

"She is at that."

Was that admiration in his voice? Jenks frowned. "You know her? You didn't say anything."

"No. Just of her. There was a lot of buzz when she applied at the academy and then came to HQ. Commander Yevchenko had been trying to get her for our Intel squad when she signed up for the Interceptor course instead."

"One more perk of being a Carmichael." Jenks forced a smile.

"I guess." Luis shrugged and leaned on the doorjamb. "Seems to me a pain in the ass to be from that family if you're not willing to toe the line. From what I've heard that's where Max has landed. But I didn't come to talk about her."

"Really, because you're doing a pretty good job of it." Jenks looked away, muttered a curse. "Sorry, that was uncalled for. What do you want?"

"To apologize. I did not want to get into that discussion with you right then and I shouldn't have pushed it. I also shouldn't have manhandled you the way I did. I'm sorry."

"If you'd crossed a line I would have laid you out."

"I know." His grin was quick, vanishing almost as fast as it appeared. "I saw the video from yesterday's fight. I feel like I need to send Commander Pashol a fruit basket."

"You might. Soft fruits, though."

"Are we good?"

"I accept your apology," she replied carefully.

Luis opened his mouth and then closed it again with a sigh. "Fair enough." He dragged a hand through his dark blond hair and then shoved it into his pants pocket. "We'll talk after, okay?"

She couldn't say yes, not knowing that she'd likely try to avoid a conversation with him about this at any cost. And the lack of answer wasn't lost on Luis—he knew her even better than Nika did.

"Right," he said with another sigh. "Jenks doesn't make promises she knows she can't keep."

"Luis—"

"No, it's fine. This is my own damn fault, top to bottom. Good luck out there today." He mustered up a smile, amber eyes filled with so much emotion Jenks had to look away.

"You too," she whispered, but when she looked back he was already gone.

PRELIMINARIES—DAY FOUR

"I'm in." Sapphi blew out a breath. "Tell Commander Till thanks for those passcodes. It would have taken me an hour to crack through those layers on my own."

Max looked away from the door. The voices of her teammates were muted in her ear as Rosa and the others cleared the floor room by room. Ma was in the hallway, sword out and watching for any sign of trouble, but so far things had been quiet.

We've kept things quiet.

As Sapphi sifted through the information she now had access to, Max marveled at just how well Admiral Chen's plan had come together. Commander Till's *Flux* and four other teams had broken previous passcodes wide open, passing them on from team to team. Without those codes the teams following almost certainly wouldn't be able to proceed in enough time to complete the mission.

"Max, you copy? I'm showing four hostiles incoming through the front door. Looks like the shift change is showing." Rosa's voice was calm over the com, but Max's heart jumped in response to the news.

"Ma, go down and help her." Max jerked her head and he

followed her back into the room. "Sapphi, get moving on that shutdown. I want this whole place to go dark before we go."

Intel gathered by *Burden of Proof* carried the warning that the facility was next door to a massive troop installation and any alarm would result in the team being overwhelmed before they could get to the admiral and get her out. Max and Rosa had built up their strategy piece by piece as the information filtered to them these past few days, and now it was flowing.

True to Max's guess, the other teams had done exactly what Admiral Chen wanted. Working together even as they competed for the top spot. Sharing vital information from team to team to allow everyone to succeed in their objectives.

It was a testament to the strength of the NeoG that not a single team held out.

According to Jenks, it wasn't something that would ever fly in the main Boarding Games. There was too much bad blood between the branches. But the preliminaries, especially for NeoG, were different. Max had felt the camaraderie already in a hundred different ways, and once more she felt she'd made the right choice in choosing the Neos over everything else.

The clock in the corner of her vision was ticking relentlessly. They were down to less than ten minutes in the Big Game, and the door at the end of the hallway upstairs was where their target was being kept.

Unless I got this totally wrong, Max thought. *Please don't let me have gotten this wrong.*

"Got it, LT. Let's move." Sapphi scrambled out of her seat and the pair headed for the door.

"Jenks, Tamago, we're coming around the corner. Form up, we're headed for upstairs."

"Roger that, Lieutenant. Where're the others?"

"Downstairs holding the door." Rosa's reply was breathy. "We're good, go ahead. Max has the door code."

"Clock's ticking," Jenks said as she and Tamago met them at the stairs.

"No radio chatter," Sapphi said quietly. "I'm showing two people in a room just off the stairs. More in a room at the end of the hall."

Jenks looked to Max, who nodded once. "You two up the stairs, clear the room. Quietly. We'll be right behind you."

"You got faith in me." Jenks winked and started up the stairs, Tamago on her heels. Max and Sapphi followed, swords out. They stopped at the top of the stairs, Jenks gesturing silently to Tamago, who nodded in understanding.

Max took a deep breath as the pair slipped in through the doorway and watched as Jenks bypassed the first guard, the distraction of her sudden appearance enough for Tamago to sneak up and deliver a killing blow to the back of his suit. Jenks locked the second guard up in a choke hold that in a real-life situation would have knocked him out in seconds, but the man tapped her arm in acknowledgment and then grinned at them as he sat down on the floor.

Max ignored the "dead" men. "Sapphi?"

"End of the hall," she replied. "Three standing, one sitting. Seated person is in the far corner. Others are opposite side of the room near the door. How do you want to proceed?"

"I've got the door code from Stephan," Max said. "I'm moving forward. Jenks, you and Tamago on my six. When I open the door I want you two through it. You take the bad guys. I go for the admiral. Rosa, how are we downstairs?"

"Good," she replied. "Clear and quiet."

"You, Sapphi, and Tamago keep your eyes peeled."

Max held her breath and crouched by the door. She entered the code, then flashed the countdown with her right hand before punching enter. The door hissed open.

It took the three men in the room several seconds to register what was happening, but by then Jenks and Tamago were on them. Max sprinted across the room, grabbing for Admiral Chen and pulling her out of her chair to the floor.

She felt the sting of a gunshot hit her in the back, her suit flaring with approximate pain, and muttered a curse.

"Targets are down," Jenks announced.

"I'm hit," Max said. "Admiral, are you all right?"

"A little bruised, Lieutenant, but otherwise unharmed. That was quick thinking."

"Where, Lieutenant?" Tamago asked, dropping to her knees next to them.

"Back. I'm assuming not fatal or I'd have lit up like a Christmas tree."

"It's not, but you're going to lose a kidney if we don't get you out of here."

"I've got a spare," Max replied, and heard Admiral Chen choke back a laugh.

"And that's time, *Zuma's Ghost*," the game runner's voice announced through the coms. "Excellent work achieving your target in twelve minutes and forty-two seconds. No friendlies dead, one teammate injured—" There was a pause and then the woman continued, humor lacing her next words. "But since Lieutenant Carmichael threw herself into harm's way to keep the admiral safe, I'm inclined to score you as no casualties at all. Nicely done."

ROSA KNEW TWO THINGS AS SHE WATCHED JENKS IN THE final cage match. The first was that Tamago was right and whatever was bothering her was connected to Armstrong. The second was that Jenks was going to win the fight regardless, just like she'd defeated Commander Till earlier in the day.

It was hard not to be bitter, at least in some corner of her mind. Jenks could win distracted as she was because she was just that good. Rosa could pour all her focus into the sword fight and still lose.

"You lost close, though; stop beating yourself up."

Ma's admonition just after her championship match with D'Arcy had ended echoed in her head. He was right: they were still ahead on points and had dominated every comp except the sword so far.

With only Jenks's fight to go, Rosa knew their spot in the main Games was assured, win or lose here. The only thing left to decide was who would take second place—*Honorable Intent* or *Dread Treasure*.

Rosa would gladly fight with either at her side. When this was all said and done it was NeoG against the rest of them, not two separate teams fighting for a win.

But if I don't get my *shit together and get better at this, we're not going to win*. It pissed her off that that thought was already circling her head, like water down a drain.

"Commander." Max slipped into the open spot at Rosa's side. The two black eyes she'd earned from Commander Till's well-placed kick were starting to fade to a greenish stain against her light brown skin, but they were still obvious.

Max seemed to be wearing them as a point of pride, and Rosa wasn't about to begrudge her the badge of honor.

"She's going to beat him," Max said after a moment. "She's better than he is anyway, but his heart's not in this fight."

Rosa blinked. "He wouldn't throw this—"

"No, not deliberately." Max glanced to Rosa and then back at the cage. "I don't think it's intentional. He loves her too much to do that to her. He's just tired of fighting."

"Tamago mentioned Armstrong was the problem," Rosa murmured as everything snapped into place on that particular puzzle, and it was Max's turn to blink. "Oh, he told her he loved her. That's what's got her all worked up."

"She's set to run." Max smiled sadly as Jenks kicked Luis's feet out from underneath him. He hit the mat hard and Jenks pounced. "She's very good at building walls to keep herself safe. He got inside somehow and it's terrifying for her. She doesn't think she deserves whatever he's willing to give. I like Luis, though, and according to Tamago he might be patient enough to—" Max broke off as the ref blew the whistle and separated the fighters.

"I'm torn between thinking you should have ended up with Intel and being sort of relieved you didn't, because that is a mind-blowing ability you have there," Rosa said as the ref blew the final whistle, raising Jenks's hand to declare her the winner on points, and the crowd went wild.

Max shrugged a shoulder, eyes still tracking the pair in the cage as Jenks offered Luis a hand to shake and he pulled her into a hug instead. "I'm right where I belong, Commander."

"I'm glad to hear it." Rosa hugged Max, feeling her jerk in surprise. "We just won the preliminaries, Lieutenant. It's time to celebrate."

THE AFTERPARTY WAS CHAOS OF THE BEST KIND. JENKS wandered through the darkened club, drink in hand, letting the music thumping through the air into her veins clear out the remnants of the tension from the Games.

They had twenty weeks now. Four and a half months to prepare, to train, to work with *Dread Treasure* on a game plan.

That was for tomorrow. Jenks resolutely pushed the thoughts out of her head as Tai grabbed her and spun her onto the dance floor in an exceptionally smooth move that didn't spill her drink.

"You are oddly single, Khan," they said, voice raised to be heard above the music.

"I'm always single," she replied, and watched their silver eyebrow lift.

"You know what I mean. I saw Armstrong in the back corner, also oddly single. Usually by this point in the festivities you two have dropped smoke bombs and vanished." Tai grinned.

God damn it, did everyone know?

"Are you fishing for gossip or a punch to the face?"

"You think I want to end up like Pashol? I'm just assessing my chances with you tonight."

Jenks hummed in the back of her throat, grinning at the lanky petty officer over the rim of her glass as they danced. "Tempting, but I'm on lieutenant babysitting duty," she lied. "Don't want her to get corrupted by all you wastrels her very first Games."

"You are such a spoilsport. Max is a doll and we'd never do a thing to hurt her." Tai leaned down and kissed her and for a moment Jenks was very tempted to fess up to her lie and drag Tai into a dark corner.

Instead she pulled away with a sigh of regret covered by the music. "Go find Tamago. I caught them eyeing your butt yesterday."

"Really?" Tai grinned. "You are an amazing human being, Jenks, don't let anyone ever tell you differently." With a dramatically blown kiss, they wandered off into the crowd.

Jenks spotted Max in an animated discussion with Commander Till, clearly not in need of babysitting if the glass of water in front of her was any indication.

Ma and Rosa were both off with their families. Sapphi was probably already back in her bunk asleep, this club being the furthest thing from her favorite place to be.

Which meant she *was* flying solo at the moment.

"Fuck," Jenks muttered, and against her better judgment she headed for the back of the club. It took her a while to work her way through the crowd, collecting hugs and kisses and congratulations along the way. Not to mention a healthy dose of people who actually were trying to get the latest gossip about her and Armstrong.

"I thought we were being discreet, but judging from how many people have asked me if I'm okay this evening, I'm guessing we weren't?" she said by way of greeting as she dropped down onto the couch next to Luis.

"You too, huh?" he asked, shooting her a sidelong glance and a halfhearted smile.

"Yeah." Jenks rubbed a hand over the back of her neck. "You wanna get out of here?"

"No, I'm good."

Jenks blinked, unable to stop her sharp inhale. "Oh, Luis, no. I meant, fuck." The panic welled up in her throat as she reached for his hand and he moved away. "To talk. You want to get out of here so we can talk?"

She'd hurt him. The surprised look on his face told her just how badly, and Jenks felt ten thousand times an asshole.

Luis pushed to his feet, leaving his untouched drink on the table, and for a moment she was certain he was just going to walk off without her. But some nonexistent god was watching out for her and he stopped, turned back to her, and held out his hand. "Come on."

No one stopped them on the way out, no one even said anything, but Jenks felt like the eyes of the entire place were on them as they slipped through the doors and out into the night.

She busied herself with tugging her hoodie over her head, protection against the springtime chill of London, and then tucked her hands into the pocket as they started down the street. She wasn't sure if Luis had a path in mind but was content to walk at his side in silence.

At least for a while. Twenty minutes in she got restless. "You know the Thames flooded this whole area when the Collapse happened? It's receded some, but not all the way back to twentieth-century levels."

"Jenks." Luis stopped and leaned his forearms on the guardrail overlooking the flowing waters of the new Thames. "What is this thing between us now?"

It hurt to have him use her nickname—she'd never realized just how much until it happened. She pulled her hands free of her hoodie and shrugged. "I don't know. I thought I did, Luis. If you'd asked me six months or a year ago? I'd have said we were friends. Competitors. People who occasionally had sex."

"And now?"

Jenks boosted herself up onto the railing, hooking her feet to secure herself as she tried to find the words. "I don't know. You sprang this on me at the worst possible time and I can't get my bearings. How can you love me?"

His eyes snapped open. "How can I not? Holy shit, Dai, how can I not love you after all these years? I cared about you in the beginning, you know I did or I'd never have slept with you."

"I'm not worth it."

Luis moved fast, clamping his hands down on the railing on either side of her, boxing her in, and Jenks fought against the immediate desire to run that started screaming in her brain.

"Tell me you don't love me. That's your right. But you don't get to tell me if I think you're worth it. I love *you*. Everything about you. I love your snarky commentary on the show recommendations you send me. I love how for years you somehow managed to ask about my kids without actually asking about them and that it was simply because you cared, Dai, you cared about me and you cared about them.

"I love how dedicated you are to your job, how fucking good you are at it. I love the way you dance around to the music in your head without a care in the universe. Jesus, I even love the way you punch me in the face because I am apparently a goddamned masochist."

Jenks stared up at him. The feelings rolling around in her chest were so overwhelming she couldn't think. She wanted to run and hide and pretend like this all hadn't happened. "I don't know what to say."

Luis cupped her face with one hand and pressed his forehead to hers. "Say you'll go back to Jupiter and think about it. Say you'll keep talking to me and you won't shut me out.

Because I know you and I know you want to run. Just promise me you won't, that you'll put some trust in me and in this. I'm okay with waiting.

"I'd wait forever for you."

"Luis, I'm not—" She leaned back, almost lost her balance, and grabbed for him before she fell into the Thames. "I'm not—" Words failed her and she swore, pulling his mouth down to hers.

He didn't resist, stepping closer and wrapping his arms around her as he kissed her back. This she could do, she thought, pouring all the feelings she couldn't find words for into the kiss.

Luis pulled away. "Open your eyes, Dai."

She did, and the look on his face ripped the breath from her lungs.

"You are the most amazing woman I've ever met. I need you to trust that. Trust me. And trust yourself. Okay?"

"I can't promise you forever," she said.

"You don't have to. Just promise me tomorrow."

T-MINUS TWENTY WEEKS UNTIL
THE BOARDING GAMES

"The look on D'Arcy's face when you knocked him on his ass!" Jenks was laughing so hard she could barely get the words out and Tamago was making a wheezing noise that had Max a little concerned. "How did you know he'd come around that corner?"

"He'd done it in the previous two actions," Max replied with a shrug. "It worked both times. So it made sense he'd try the same thing with us."

"It makes sense to you," Rosa said from her spot behind the counter as she prepped dinner. "The rest of us are still in awe of your ability to do shit like that."

Max grinned. The adrenaline of the ship was still running high even an hour after they'd taken off from the docking bay and headed away from Earth back to Jupiter. The shiny trophy for the preliminaries that got passed from winning team to winning team every year had returned to its place of honor on the dining table of the crew quarters on the upper deck and she'd noticed she wasn't the only one who would occasionally reach out and brush her fingers over it.

Her nerves had settled and she felt almost, if not quite, a

part of the team. Even Jenks had softened, though Max wondered if that had anything to do with the kiss she'd seen the petty officer share with Armstrong just before coming into the docking bay.

It seemed she'd been wrong about Jenks running. Though to be honest, that wasn't a surprise.

The world might end when I figure her out.

Jenks leaned back in her chair, hands hooked behind her head. "Fifteen out of ten, would totally fight again."

"Good," Rosa said with a snort. "Because you get to in four and a half months."

Max blinked when Jenks bared her teeth in what could only be called a savage grin. "I am so looking forward to it. We're going to take those Navy punks apart, piece by piece."

"Hey, LT?" Sapphi popped her head up through the stairwell. "You got a minute to look at something?"

"Sure." Max got up from her chair.

"Tell Ma dinner's ready in five minutes," Rosa called after her, and Max raised a hand in acknowledgment as she followed Sapphi down the stairs.

"Hey, Ma, Rosa said dinner in five," Max said as she pulled herself up the few steps to the bridge. "What's up?"

"Remember that press guy who was following you around at the Games?"

"Yeah, he up and vanished on the fourth day, which I thought was weird." Max trailed off at Sapphi's grim look. "What is it?"

"I thought I'd look for him, you know, just in case we did actually need to do something about it." Sapphi grabbed Max's hand and pulled her to the bridge. "I've been through every single press pass issued to every single person."

"And?"

"I can't find him anywhere."

"What? How?"

"He's not in the system. He's not in security. I don't know

how he got his pass to work throughout the whole event without leaving a trace, but he did." Sapphi tapped at the screen at the back of the bridge. "I did some additional searching and was able to pull up images of him on two public streams of your events. But they're quick, almost like he—"

"Was avoiding the cameras," Max finished grimly and sighed. "Okay. Send me everything you have. I'll talk to Rosa about it."

"You don't seem very concerned."

Max laughed. "To be honest, I'm not. Stalkers are kind of commonplace as far as my family's concerned. I had three before my fifteenth birthday. My oldest sister, Ria? She gets three a month."

"Really?" Sapphi made a face. "That sucks."

"It's life as a Carmichael. You get used to it. I had a bodyguard in kindergarten."

"It sucks." Sapphi drew the word out and then hugged her. "If I see him again I'm punching him in the nose."

Max froze and then hugged her back with a laugh. "I appreciate the support. We'll—"

"Rosa, Max, get down here," Ma said over the com.

The clattering of feet echoed down from behind them, Max pulling Sapphi out of the way as Rosa took the stairs in two strides.

"What is it?"

Ma hit the internal coms. "Commander is listening, Earth Control. Repeat again?"

"*Zuma's Ghost*, this is Earth Control, we're getting a distress call from the civilian vessel *Portsmith High*. Their power dropped to zero and engine died. Life support is fine, but there's a proton storm expected to sweep through the area in the next ten minutes and the tow won't be there in time."

"Control, Lieutenant Carmichael here. You're talking about the CME that happened yesterday?" Max pulled up the data on the screen behind her. The path of the proton storm from the coronal mass ejection cut a swath right through their flight path—she'd noted it on their way out, but they'd be well past it by the time it hit this area of space, so she hadn't been concerned. It was narrower than most, but the stranded ship in question was not going to clear the outer edge of the storm before it hit.

"Yes, Lieutenant. It wasn't a big one so we didn't completely shut down traffic in this area, especially with so many outgoing post-Games. But somebody is going to catch hell for approving that flight plan for a civilian vessel. It should have been outgoing military only. Granted, they'd have been well past it if their engines hadn't failed, but still . . ."

"Roger that, Control," Rosa said. "You want us to extract? Our shielding isn't good enough to withstand a storm this close to the sun."

"Yes, Commander. It's a Binary JetSol, but their shielding isn't good enough, either. Otherwise we'd have them just ride it out. But you were in the path on your way out of the system, so we thought we'd send you in."

Binary JetSols were expensive cruisers, not meant for long-haul trips, but they could easily handle something to Mars and back. However, proton storms were bad news. LifeEx's secondary protection against the dangers of radiation exposure in space had been a happy accident, but even it wouldn't protect an unshielded living creature from a proton storm. And only the bigger naval carriers had shields good enough to withstand that kind of radiation blast straight from Sol.

The saving grace of this situation was only in how slowly the storms moved, comparatively that is, given the sheer amount of space they had to cross to interact with traffic around Earth and Mars. It was easy to chart their paths and easier still to avoid them. As Control said, someone was about to catch hell for something that could have easily been prevented.

And the news was about to get worse.

"Can't hook up to that kind of ship and do a straight transfer, Commander," she said after a glance at the schematics of the JetSol. "We'll have to walk them out. Do they have gear?"

And training, she thought, *please let them have had at least a basic spacewalk course.* It was technically required for all who went out into the stars, but she also knew that people who had the kind of money to spend on a JetSol were the same subset of people who thought things like safety procedures weren't for them.

"Confirmed, *Zuma.* They have gear. No training beyond a basic course."

Max watched Rosa's lips press together as she suppressed a curse and then nodded. "Control, advise *Portsmith High* to put their suits on. How many people?"

"Will do, Commander. Two adults and a nine-year-old girl. Tosh Bhatt; his wife, Constance; and their daughter, Shala. Mr. Bhatt owns Portsmith Shipping, just for your information."

Max's breath caught, an audible inhale, and Rosa sent her a sharp look.

"Roger, Control. We're on it. ETA two minutes. *Zuma* out." Rosa turned. "Cough it up."

"I know them," she said. "I should have made the connection. Portsmith ships for LifeEx. Tosh is a friend of the family."

"Okay, that means you're going. It should help keep them calm. Remember, we're on a schedule and extended reunions are not part of the timetable. Jenks and Tamago, get suited up to go with her. Ma will drop you on the first pass, then get us as close as we can when he comes around, but you're still looking at a thirty-meter spacewalk with untrained adults and a child."

"And the clock is ticking," Max said, nodding. Getting blasted inside the ship would be bad enough, but if they got caught in that storm while they were outside in only suits? It wouldn't kill them immediately, maybe, but it was a one-way ticket to the dead zone for sure.

"So much for dinner," Jenks muttered, and Max laughed.

They scrambled for their gear and were outfitted and at the airlock when Ma had them in position.

"Com check," Max said.

"Loud and clear, Lieutenant," Jenks replied, echoed by Tamago.

"Helmet check." Max checked Tamago's, turned and did the same to Jenks, and then attempted a smile when the petty officer did the same for her in turn.

"These folks going to do what we tell them?" Jenks asked.

"I think so, but let me handle them if they don't."

"Right—you speak their language."

That stung, but Max didn't have time to respond before the airlock warning cycled and Ma's voice called the jump countdown.

Max took a deep, possibly unnecessary breath and followed Jenks out of the airlock, hitting the thrusters on her EMU as she stepped out and keeping her eyes fixed on the stranded ship ten meters in front of them.

"Nice drop, Ma!" Jenks said.

"Commander, drop successful, we're ten meters out and closing," Max said.

"Copy that, Lieutenant. *Portsmith High*, this is Commander Rosa Martín with the NeoG Interceptor team *Zuma's Ghost*. I have three Neos inbound for your ship if you will open your outer airlock."

The airlock opened, even though Max hadn't heard a reply. It didn't surprise her. Tosh was probably nervous enough he only replied to the ship and not the whole channel.

She floated through the opening, dropping the last few inches to the floor as the ship's internal gravity kicked in, shifting forward as Jenks and Tamago piled in behind her. The airlock cycled, the inner door panel blinking green and then sliding open. Max unclipped her helmet, pulling it off and grabbing the edge with her left hand as she extended her right. "Tosh, how are you?"

He blinked at her for a heartbeat before a wide smile creased his face and Constance gave a little cry of surprise. "Max!" Tosh folded her into a hug. "They'd said you went to the NeoG, but I had no idea it would be you here. What a coincidence."

"Timetable, Lieutenant," Jenks said in her ear, and Max nodded, disengaging herself from Tosh.

She gave her most calming smile when Constance squeezed her gloved hand. "These are Petty Officers Khan and Uchida, they're going to be right by Constance's and Shala's sides the whole time. Have you ever done any spacewalking?"

Tosh shook his head. "Only for the safety course, and that was more than ten years ago. I'm ashamed to admit we didn't retake the course when Shala got her certification last year."

"It's fine. You're all going to be attached and safe as can be. Jenks, you take Shala." She closed her hand around Tosh's upper arm and kept her voice low as she led him back into the airlock. "Tosh, we are expecting a solar proton event in this area in the next eight minutes. We are in a race against that storm here, so I'm going to need you to do exactly what I say when I say it, okay?"

"Yes, absolutely." Tosh was a businessman, the same rich set that her family had rubbed elbows with all her life; but he didn't seem the least bit bothered by her orders.

"Helmet on for me."

Tosh looked around for a moment, some desperation showing on his face. Max smiled again as she grabbed it off the rack and handed it over. She double-checked all his suit parameters, looking back over her shoulders as Tamago and Jenks started the same procedure with the others.

Jenks dropped to a knee in front of Tosh's daughter, a slender child with dark curls and wide brown eyes. "Hey, Shala. I'm Jenks."

"Hi."

"You ready for a little fun?" Jenks glanced up at the noise

that escaped from her mother and exchanged a look with Tamago, who led the woman to the airlock with an arm around her shoulders.

"Mom's scared."

"I'm not going to lie to you. This is a little scary," Jenks replied, taking the helmet Max handed her.

"We did our certification inside," Shala said. "I've never been in space for real."

"Space is kinda overwhelming the first time you get out there, but it's beautiful, too. We're going for a little walk in it. I'll be right with you the whole time and we will be fine. You'll be clipped to my suit right here, see?"

"How many times have you done this?"

"More than I can count, kiddo, so you do what I say and we'll be all golden. I'm going to put this on you. Here's the rules. Breathe easy. No crying. No puking. Just breathe." Jenks's smile was reassuring as she slipped the helmet over Shala's head. She snapped it down and checked the seals. "There, all cozy."

"You clip her on both sides," Max said over the team com and Jenks lifted a thumb in acknowledgment.

The airlock was big enough to fit them all, barely, and Max slid her own helmet on, spending a few precious seconds letting Jenks check the seals before she tapped the panel.

The airlock slid open and Tamago stepped out into the black, Constance glued to their side. Jenks followed her out.

"Wow." Shala's breathy exhale slid across the main channel and Max muffled a chuckle at the awe contained in that single word as she stepped through the airlock with Tosh slightly in front of her, the bright orange of the safety strap a reassuring spot of color in the darkness.

Zuma's Ghost glowed against the backdrop of black velvet, Earth on one side of her and the sun burning fiercely on the other. Max's helmet kicked the filter in automatically, but she still closed her eyes to the brightness for just a second.

She turned and pressed the button, watching as the door slid shut.

"Airlock is closed," she said. Max closed her hand around Tosh's arm again and hit the thruster on her EMU, the jets pushing them closer to *Zuma's Ghost*. The clock in the corner of her vision was steadily ticking down to the expected storm.

Tamago and Constance were within two meters of the ship with Max and Tosh ten behind them when she heard Jenks curse from the middle of their group and watched her smooth forward progress jerk slightly. "Jenks?"

"EMU's being pissy," she replied. "It's fine, though, I—"

The bright flame shooting from Jenks's EMU was stark against the emptiness, streaking out past Jenks's shoulder and into space. All Max could do was watch Jenks lock her arms around Shala as the unexpected thrust sent them both spinning away in a twisting arc.

"Close your eyes, kiddo. Squeeze 'em tight. No puking, remember." Jenks's voice was impressively calm over the com as her EMU sent them on an ugly carnival ride.

"Jenks!" Had she been alone, Max would have turned right then and gone after them, but the civilian on her arm reminded her of his presence when he pulled free with his daughter's name ringing across the main com. "Shit! Tosh, I need you to hold still. Commander, Jenks's EMU just went haywire."

"Copy that, Lieutenant." Rosa's voice was clipped and cut through the chaos.

"My daughter!"

"Yeah, I see it," Max muttered, finally getting a hold of him again and hitting the boost on her thrusters, propelling them away from Jenks and closer to the ship.

"Mr. Bhatt, I need you to remain calm," Rosa said. "Get him in the ship, Max," she continued on the team com. "That's an order."

"Yes, Commander." Max gritted her teeth as they sped toward *Zuma's Ghost*. "Jenks, hang in there."

"Not much else to do, Lieutenant," she replied. "EMU just stopped, but we're in spin. Going to try to stabilize us, or I'm going to throw up. Kid seems to be okay, though. She is professionally calm."

"I've got you on radar, Jenks," Sapphi replied, and the image appeared across Max's vision.

"Sapphi, overlay the expected proton storm for me," she ordered.

"Fuck, LT, they're still in the blast zone."

"I see it." Max was already doing the calculations at lightning speed in her head. It was insane, but it would maybe work. "Commander, I can—"

"Get your ass in the ship, Max." Rosa's voice was tight. "They might make it outside the range before the storm."

"Negative on that, Commander," Jenks said. "I'm dead in the water here, so to speak."

Max knew that already. There was less than a minute left and Jenks was floating aimlessly within the storm blast zone with a nine-year-old held to her chest. The only thing that would get them out was a hard enough hit to knock them clear.

Max landed on the side of the ship, turning her thrusters off at the very last second as Tosh's momentum carried him into the airlock, where Tamago caught him.

She unclipped Tosh from her belt as soon as Tamago gave her a thumbs-up, watching him stumble to his wife and embrace her. Constance was weeping, shoulders heaving with sobs, and Max could see her face wet with tears even past the glare of the helmet.

"Not on my goddamned watch," Max muttered. Bracing herself on the side of the ship, she took a deep breath. "I'm really sorry about this, Commander," she said over the team com, and pushed off the ship with all the strength in her legs, hitting her thrusters to maximum at the same time.

The shouted protests faded to nothing as Max soared through the black, her eyes fixed on Jenks and the girl.

"Everyone quiet!" Rosa snapped the order and silence fell.

Then Ma's calm voice was on the com. "Max, you've got fifteen seconds until the storm hits. I am bringing the ship around to catch you all on the backside. Counting down. Fourteen."

Max locked her elbows to her sides, hands ready to wrap around Jenks, who had managed to turn so that Max would hit her in the back rather than crushing Shala between them. Space seemed to well in an endless black wash between them and Max coaxed the last little bit out of her EMU's thrusters with a muttered plea to anything listening.

This was going to be close.

"Five. *Zuma* is clear of the storm zone."

She could see the ship coming in on her right side.

You did the math, it's solid. You're right on the edge of the storm's path. Just hit them square and it will knock all three of you into the safety zone. Throw the shield for extra protection, you'll all be fine.

"Four."

Max could hear Jenks on the com, talking calmly to Shala. "We are good to go, you and I, kiddo. I want you to keep your eyes on me. Right here. Squeeze tight if you need to, but I've got you, you're not going anywhere. You breathe in, breathe out, and you keep your eyes on me, okay?"

"Okay."

Max braced herself, but the shock of hitting Jenks's back still rocked through her. Jenks grunted, and Max could feel her arms tightening around the girl as they were all propelled forward.

"Three. Two."

"Come on, be enough, damn it," Max muttered, throwing the extra blast shield up across her back.

"One. Brace for storm. Brace for storm."

Max braced, as much good as that was going to do—

"Clear, they're fucking clear!" Sapphi called. "She did it!"

Jenks's whoop rang through the coms. "That's a hell of a ride. You okay, kiddo?"

"I'm fine," Shala replied. Her voice was trembling, but then she laughed. "Are we safe?"

"As can be," Max replied, surprised her own words were thick with emotion. "Storm has passed, radiation levels nominal on my end, Commander."

Cheers erupted across the com.

"Ma, let's pick up our crew." Rosa's clipped order cut through the celebration.

"You are in so much trouble," Jenks chuckled, patting Max's arm. "'I'm sorry about this, Commander.'" She mimicked Max's voice, laughter dancing on each word. "You fucking apologized before doing something reckless. Who does that?"

"Me, apparently." Max squeezed her tight before fumbling for the clip at her belt and attaching it to Jenks's loop. The adrenaline was draining, leaving her shaking, and she blinked twice at the smear of soot arcing across the back of Jenks's EMU before it registered. "You're lucky this thing didn't blow."

"What is it? Felt like a sledgehammer hit me in the back when it went haywire."

"Had a short or something. I saw the flame from all the way across."

"Impossible, we did maintenance on these a week ago."

"I know what I'm looking at," Max said. "But I want to pull it apart when we get on ship and take a closer look."

"Get your asses on board first, Lieutenant," Rosa ordered.

Jenks chuckled again. "You are in so much trouble."

Max swallowed as they closed the distance to *Zuma's Ghost*. The airlock was empty and she pushed Jenks through the opening first before stepping in and hitting the panel behind her. The cycle was mercilessly short and Shala's excited voice was the first thing to greet her ears when she pulled off her helmet.

Worth it, Max thought. *Whatever happens. She's alive. Jenks is alive.*

Rosa grabbed her by the collar of her suit before she even cleared the airlock and jerked her in so close their noses almost touched. "You ever pull a stunt like that again I will have you court-martialed so fast you'll be in storage before your parents hear so much as a whisper about it. Am I understood, Lieutenant?"

Max swallowed. "Perfectly, Commander."

Chuckling, Rosa tapped her forehead to Max's. "'I'm really sorry about this, Commander.' You are a piece of work, Carmichael. Thanks for saving lives."

"Just another day in the NeoG," she replied, blinking away the threatening tears.

Rosa laughed out loud and pushed Max toward the others, who swarmed around her, hugging and joking. Then the crowd parted to reveal Jenks. "I said something about saving my life, didn't I? Thanks, Max." She tapped her fist to her chest twice. "You got my back."

Max fought with the second round of tears as she tapped her own fist to her chest and swung it out to connect with the back of Jenks's. "You've got mine." The woman grabbed her forearm and yanked her down until Max's forehead touched hers.

"Welcome to the Interceptors," Jenks said with a wink.

"About damn time."

"We are never going into space again," Constance declared.

"Mom!" Shala squirmed out of her mother's grip and bounced in a circle. "It was the coolest! Like something out of a movie! How old do I have to be to join the NeoG?"

Rosa's lips twitched as she fought to maintain a neutral expression, and Max covered her mouth with a gloved hand to hold in her laughter.

The rescue had cost them half a day, but *Zuma's Ghost* was on her way back to Jupiter when Max laid Jenks's EMU on the floor of the common room and started peeling away the outer shell.

"That is fried," Sapphi murmured from over her shoulder. Jenks was on the opposite side and set aside the panel Max handed her without comment.

"It shouldn't be." Max frowned, staring down at the circuit board they'd just revealed inside Jenks's EMU pack. "This is—" She broke off, froze. "Fuck me."

Both women recoiled in surprise at her curse. "What?"

"Get Rosa."

Jenks, surprisingly, didn't argue, and instead scrambled to her feet and raced for the bridge.

"Ma, get my pack," Max said, taking the EMU when he handed it over. With quick, efficient movements she stripped it open and laid it next to Jenks's.

"What's going on?" Rosa asked as she crouched down.

"This was *supposed* to blow." Max looked up at Rosa, watched the color drain from her face. "This wasn't a random accident. Someone sabotaged Jenks's pack. Look at this." She pointed at the circuit board of her pack and then at the ruined one. A twisted piece of wire poked out from the middle of the board just to the left of the blackened mass in the middle. "That's not supposed to be there."

"Could the short have—"

"No." Max shook her head. "There's no way. That's not a shifted wire. It's a whole new set put in to cause it to overload when the thrusters had been burning for a long enough time."

Jenks nodded. "She's right, Commander. I know these packs inside and out. That wasn't there when we did maintenance on them before leaving for the prelims. It's not supposed to be there."

"Why the fuck would someone want to kill Jenks?" Sapphi asked.

The predictable jokes didn't come as Rosa shared a grim look with Max. "Photograph everything. I'm calling the admiral. Ma, take the stick from Tamago and push us as fast as you dare."

"Who could have gotten to them?" Sapphi said. "They were locked in the ship the whole time we were on Earth."

Max swore again and scrambled to her feet, sliding down the stairs and then stumbling to the bridge. "Ma, bring us to a full stop!"

Rosa spun. "Lieutenant, what are you—"

"If they got to the EMUs, what would have kept them from messing with the ship itself?"

ROSA FROZE AS MAX'S WORDS COLLIDED IN HER HEAD. IT lasted just a moment before she snapped back to the present. Ma had already reached over Tamago's shoulder and cut the engines and now he was on the com, sending out a distress call on the military channels. They'd shut down all the other systems, including long-range coms back to Earth, and the shorter-range coms were a bit like throwing a bottle out into the ocean and hoping someone found it.

"Any ships in the vicinity of two-three-eight, niner-niner-eight-three and one-zero-seven point seven. This is the NeoG Interceptor *Zuma's Ghost*. We are dead in the water. Requesting assistance." He clicked off the com. "Sapphi, run a full diagnostic."

"Do you really think someone would mess with the ship?" Rosa asked Max in a low voice.

"I don't know, but can we take the chance?" Max rubbed at her neck. "Right before we got the call about *Portsmith High*, Sapphi was telling me the press guy who was following me around all prelims wasn't actually with the press. His pass wasn't in the system anywhere and neither was he."

"Why is this the first I'm hearing of it?"

Max had the grace to look embarrassed. "I was going to tell you, I just didn't think it was a big deal. It's normal for me to be followed around by the press, Rosa. And with the prelims?" She lifted a shoulder. "Then the rescue, and—"

"Okay, fair enough." Rosa held up a hand to stop her explanation and then raised her voice. "I want everyone in suits, right now." She grabbed Max and dragged her off the bridge, talking as they dressed.

"Let me get this all straight. Someone was watching you during the prelims, someone we now know wasn't on the press roster. Someone snuck onto my fucking ship and fucked with the EMUs."

"Jenks's, at least. Mine was clean. We'll have to strip all the others and see."

"Why would someone do this?"

Max shook her head and grabbed for her helmet. "That I don't have an answer for, Commander."

"We're going to get one." Rosa put a hand over Max's. "Hold off on the helmet but keep it right next to you in case we need it."

Rosa's brain was combing through the problem as she headed back to the bridge, trying to make sense of the seemingly random pattern in front of her. She glanced around. Everyone was on the bridge and suited up, helmets at their sides. Tamago called out results of the diagnostics to Sapphi, who was scanning the software for any sign of tampering.

Max had crossed to Ma and was leaning over the console, doing a search for nearby ships as the master chief continued to repeat the distress call.

Her team. Rosa felt a swell of pride that overtook the fear. They'd jelled at the prelims and the rescue had been the final piece to pull Max completely into the fold.

The emotion vanished all too quickly. They were vulnerable out here. The military channels were encrypted, but there could be bandits or smugglers in the area with illegal tech, and the sight of a lone Interceptor might be enough to override the limited good sense any criminal would have not to mess with the NeoG.

Someone already lost that good sense, she thought. *Trying to kill my people.*

Rosa fisted her left hand, stepped back off the bridge into the quiet space below, and prepared a message to Stephan. They were already past Mars, and with the systems shut down the message would take a bit to reach him, but it would at least give him a sense of where to start looking if something happened.

"Stephan, Rosa here, obviously." She smiled at the camera. "We're in a spot of trouble. You probably already heard about Jenks's difficulty with her EMU and the rescue, but we're at two-three-eight, niner-niner-eight-three and one-zero-seven point seven. The ship is functional, but we're not sure if we can move without something going wrong. Max discovered the EMU had been tampered with, which means someone was in our hangar and our ship during the prelims. Recommend you pull all the video surveillance of the hangar for the last week. Might want to tell others to look into their own gear as well. And I'll . . . well, hopefully I'll talk to you soon." She nodded and disconnected, sending the message on the command channel.

"Rosa, I've got an incoming transmission."

She looked up at Ma and forced a smile. "Coming up." She pulled herself up the stairs and settled into the chair as Tamago vacated it.

"*Zuma's Ghost,* this is Captain Finnegan Vaughn with the CHNN carrier *Fury Road.* We got your distress call. We're half an hour out, but can push if needed." Vaughn was a pale man with carefully tamed copper-bright hair and dark brown eyes. But his smile was genuine and Rosa felt the tension in her gut unwind a little.

"Good to hear from you, Captain Vaughn. This is Commander Rosa Martín Rivas. All crew is fine for the moment. We have life support. It will be good to see you, but no need to push past safety measures." Rosa glanced sideways when Sapphi gave her two thumbs up to confirm the image and name matched their files for the Navy carrier.

"What's going on, Commander?"

"We'll talk once I'm on board," she replied, watching his eyebrow quirk in response.

He dipped his head. "Hang in there, Commander, we'll see you soon."

"JENKS."

Jenks stopped prowling the captain's ready room at Rosa's quiet call, settling against the wall and crossing her arms over her chest. She wasn't built for this cloak-and-dagger bullshit. She just wanted them to point her at a target and tell her to beat the shit out of it.

Captain Vaughn frowned and rubbed a hand over his smooth chin. "The ship should be fine, but we've got an extra field up and I've cleared the bay to be safe. If it blows or something goes wrong, though, we're still going to be in for a hell of a ride."

The door slid open and Vaughn's XO stuck her head in. "Sorry, Captain. I've got a Commander Yevchenko on the coms from NeoG Intel. He's wanting to know if we've got *Zuma*. I guessed Commander Martín might want to speak to him directly."

"Thanks, Bea, put him through here." Vaughn nodded.

The screen lit up in the center of the table, revealing Stephan. Jenks spotted Luis just behind him. Their eyes met and she forced a quick smile.

"Everyone okay, Rosa?"

"Intact. Ready for a nap, though."

Stephan's chuckle had zero humor in it. "Got your message. We're looking into it." His eyes flicked to Captain Vaughn. "Appreciate you picking up our folks, Captain, and I'd hate it to seem like we're kicking you out of your own ready room—"

"But you're kicking me out." Vaughn grinned and held up a hand. "No worries, Commander, I know how things go. I'm going to go make sure *Zuma's Ghost* has a place to sleep for the next day."

Jenks tracked the captain as he left the room. He seemed very nice, for a naval type, but her nerves were screaming and her already fragile trust in people had been blown out of the water in much the same way she should have been. Right now, she trusted the people in this room and the two men on the screen and that was it.

Full fucking day on a Navy ship. I am going to get demoted again.

"Dai?"

It took several seconds for Luis's voice to filter in and she blinked, realizing everyone was looking at her. "Sorry, what?"

"You okay?"

"I'm pissed and I need something to hit." She closed her eyes. "Sorry, Commander."

"Don't be," Rosa replied.

"We're going over the hangar footage, Rosa," Stephan said after a nod in Jenks's direction. "If someone got in there, we'll find them."

"What do you mean 'if'? We saw the tampering with our own eyes." Jenks knew the snap in her voice was earning her a look from Rosa, but she couldn't stop herself.

Stephan held up a hand before Rosa could say something. "Sorry, Jenks, just habit. It's not that I don't trust you. Did you take the EMUs out of the ship, or are they still on *Zuma*?"

"They're still on the ship," Rosa said. "I know there's a risk they could blow, Stephan, but Max took thorough photos. On our ship it's slightly more controlled access than on a ship where I don't know anyone. I'm not a complete newbie at this, you know."

"I know, just covering bases. I'm glad you're all safe. We'll check in again when you get to Jupiter. I've sent a message to Admiral Hoboins, so he'll probably be contacting you soon."

"I was planning on talking to him next. Let me know if you find anything, Stephan."

"Will do."

Jenks caught Luis's eyes again and held them until the screen vanished. She pushed away from the wall and started pacing again. This time Rosa didn't stop her.

"Start throwing out ideas, people," she said instead. "I don't know what's caused this sudden interest in having Jenks, and potentially the rest of us, dead; but I'd like to figure out who's doing it before they get another chance at it."

"I'll start," Max said. "The Games."

Jenks skidded to a halt and stared. "Really?"

Max shrugged. "Some people take things too seriously. It doesn't have to make sense to us. I don't think we should discount it."

"Agreed," Rosa said. "People have killed for far less important things. What else?"

"That guy you punched out eight months ago in the bar." Sapphi held up her hands when Jenks pinned her with a look. "He was in the wrong, but didn't he shout something about how you'd regret it when the MPs hauled him away?"

"Do we have a name on him?" Rosa asked, and Sapphi nodded.

"I'll have to dig a bit, but it's in the Jupiter Station records."

"We're going to be here awhile if we put everyone I've punched on the list," Jenks said, dropping into a chair, and Rosa chuckled.

"True, I think we'll limit it to the last year or so."

Jenks put her head on the table as her teammates tossed out every altercation she'd been involved in over the last year. As strange as it was, the list proved to be at least somewhat amusing and the knot of tension in her shoulders loosened.

Then, suddenly, the words of the man they'd arrested on that system jumper flooded into her brain.

"You've stumbled into trouble beyond recall. You can't run far enough away from this."

"Fuck." She lifted her head to stare across the table at Max. "The system jumper."

T-MINUS NINETEEN WEEKS UNTIL
THE BOARDING GAMES

"Ship's clean." Ma dropped into the seat between Max and Rosa in their quarters. "She'll be out of quarantine tomorrow. Whatever those bastards did, it looks like it was only to Jenks's EMU."

"Why not ours?" Rosa asked, shoving a hand into her hair. Her nerves were on high alert since they'd gotten back to the station. "Tamago and I were on the ship with Jenks and Nika. Why aren't they coming after us?"

"Maybe they were hoping to pick us off one at a time, make it look like more of an accident."

"An Interceptor going boom certainly would have drawn a lot of attention." Ma shook his head.

"We were doing a lot of digging on it before the prelims," Max said. "What if we kicked over a rock and made them twitchy?"

"I feel like I owe you an apology, Max," Rosa said.

"No you don't."

"How do you figure?"

Max smiled. "We still don't know if the system jumper is the answer—we're reaching, at this point. You were right that we didn't have enough to push for reopening the case and we still don't. But even if we had?" She shrugged. "It wouldn't have changed how things went down."

The younger woman's assurance effectively doused Rosa's guilt. "How do we find a link?" she asked.

"I feel like there's something staring me right in the face and I'm missing it," Max said. Her voice was quiet, her eyes unfocused. She'd been scanning records since they'd gotten back to Jupiter in an effort to find something that would indicate what Jenks's would-be killers could be after. "I keep coming back to the question of why did they hit us on Earth?" She blinked, refocusing on Rosa across the table. "Jupiter Station has security, but it's not foolproof. There're too many civilians in and out of here for that. The security at the prelims was supposed to be top-notch."

"Your stalker got in," Rosa said, and Max nodded.

"And whoever tried to kill Jenks got into the docking bay where the Interceptors were. Which tells us something, doesn't it?" Max crossed her arms when neither Rosa nor Ma responded.

"It means they've got some pull on Earth, but potentially not out this far. And something happened between when you picked up that system jumper and the prelims to make them feel like they needed to move."

"More chaos at the Games, too," Ma said. "Our people know who's supposed to be in the bay here, they would have stopped a strange face. But on Earth? They could have gone onto *Zuma's Ghost* dressed as anything."

"Right. Has Commander Yevchenko had any luck with the bay surveillance?" Max asked. Rosa shook her head.

"No, whoever did it was deliberately avoiding the cameras. Intel's trying to figure out if there was tech involved or if they were just doing it the old-fashioned way."

"How's Jenks handling this?" Ma asked.

Rosa chuckled. "Mostly annoyed that it's overshadowed our

win. You know how she is. She wanted a few days to celebrate before we got back to work." She rubbed at her medallion. "And I partially agree with her. I wanted to be able to come back here and get to work, but not like this. We've landed ourselves in the middle of some conspiracy. I know it sounds weird, but if we could at least figure out what they are so willing to kill us for I'd feel better about it."

"I suspect that's the dangerous bit," Max said with a ghost of a grin sliding over her face. "Smuggling seems the most likely scenario, since 'lost' system jumpers would be the perfect transports. Off the radar, low power, practically unknown."

Ma held up two fingers and started ticking them off. "What are they smuggling, and how did they find the system jumpers in the first place?"

"We figure out one and I suspect it will lead us to the other," Max replied. "The report said the system jumper you all picked up had Trappist-1e in its routing computer as the last destination."

"Yes." Rosa nodded.

"Two questions." Max mimicked Ma's upheld fingers. "What were they doing on Trappist-1e in the first place? And how did a ship without wormhole tech or even a decent engine by today's standards get from there to the belt?"

"They were waiting for something bigger to punch a hole for them," Rosa said. "It would have had to be farther out or Jupiter's sensor would have caught it."

"It still doesn't answer why they were in system." Ma shook his head. "If they'd been carrying whatever it is they're smuggling I'd be able to understand it better. But we went over that ship top to bottom and it was empty."

"Did you look in the pods?" Ma pinned Max with a look and she raised her hands in surrender. "Just checking. Ugh. I don't want to fly back to Earth, but I do kinda want to check out that ship." She rubbed both hands over her eyes.

"When was the last time you slept, Lieutenant?"

"I—am not sure," Max admitted, and then she yawned.

"You're no good to anyone half-awake, Max. Go get some sleep," Rosa ordered, pushing out of her chair. "I need to go catch Hoboins up on what's happening anyway."

MAX WOKE FROM THE NIGHTMARE WITH A GASP, EYES FLYING open in the pitch-black room. She blinked twice and muffled a groan as the 02:43 timestamp appeared in her vision.

There was no point in trying to get back to sleep. The dream would just pick up again as if she'd paused it. That was the annoying thing. Didn't matter the subject: for Max, once a nightmare started it was determined to see itself through the second she closed her eyes again.

"You've never even seen a real bear," she muttered as she slid out of bed and grabbed for the workout gear folded neatly on the end. Her shoes were by the door, and with the bundle cradled to her chest she tiptoed from her room.

"Where're you going, LT?"

Max stifled the scream, but a squeak escaped out into the darkness. It was followed by Jenks's low chuckle.

"I couldn't sleep, thought I would go down to the gym," Max whispered. "Why are you awake?"

"I don't sleep much. You want company?"

The offer was so surprising Max stood in the dark for several heartbeats before she recovered. "Of course. Sure."

There was a rustle as Jenks slid from her bed. "Doge, stay." What could only be described as an electronic whimper issued up out of a corner of the room and Jenks sighed. "Fine, you can come. Quietly."

Max patted Doge on his metal head after they'd slipped into the corridor. "Good dog."

"Clingy mutt," Jenks corrected, but she put a hand on Doge's back with a smile as she said it.

The gym was mostly deserted, but Max recognized a face

or two from her previous early-morning visits. Jenks seemed to know everyone, and exchanged fist bumps or one-armed hugs with several people as she passed.

"I was just going to run," Max said, glancing down at Jenks's bare feet.

"Knock yourself out. I'll be at the weights."

Max headed for the locker room, changing and slipping into her shoes. Then, with music playing on her Babel, she stepped onto the treadmill and started running.

Feet on the track, the steady rhythm of her breath and her footfalls syncing into an alternating pattern, Max let the movement and the music clear her head. Running had always been her haven, the way out from under her mother's eagle eyes in the vastness of whatever Navy ship or station they'd been on. All the Carmichael children were encouraged to be active and so long as she was keeping fit, her constant runs were unsupervised.

However, what had started as an escape became something she enjoyed, something she was truly good at.

Pity there's not a footrace in the Games, she thought, and laughed at herself. *Not a surprise, I guess. Where are you going to run in space?*

That stray thought hooked into her brain, echoes of Jenks's report about the people they'd captured on the system jumper. One of the men had said the Neos couldn't run far enough away from the trouble they'd stumbled into.

Figuring she could kill two birds with one stone, Max pulled the files from Admiral Hoboins on the accident in the brig and looked through them as she ran.

Malfunction of several key systems. Too complicated for her to look at in depth while running. Max dismissed them in favor of the forensic report, scanning through it until her eyes skidded to a halt—along with her feet—and she grabbed for the safety bar on the treadmill to keep herself from falling on her face.

"Shitshitshit."

The molecular structure hung in her vision as she bolted for the showers, hoping that they were empty. They were, and she barely spared a second checking the time on Earth before she put the call in to Coms.

"Coms here, Tobin Hudson." The man on the other end had a polite smile that vanished with Max's next words.

"Hi, Lieutenant Carmichael. I need to put a priority call in to Earth, please."

"Through your DD? The signal's going to be crap and it's going to give you a headache at best, or make your brains liquefy at worst."

"It's fine. My tech is good and I only need a minute." She tried not to bounce impatiently on her toes. Her DD tech was better than good—it was the best money could buy—but she didn't want to bother with that discussion.

"Okay, you've been warned. Putting the call through. Good luck."

Max dropped onto a bench as the vertigo washed over her. A moment later, Ria appeared in her vision, and Max had to blink several times to get her sister's face to resolve.

"Hey, Max, I'm about to head into a meeting, what's up?"

"I need a minute, that's all."

Ria frowned. "Your signal is shit and I can't see your face, what's going on?"

"I'm calling straight from my head." Max waved a hand. "Don't worry about it. I need you to look into something for me. I'm sending you a file on a guy who was picked up a while back with a stolen system jumper coming from Trappist. Can you tell me if he ever worked for LifeEx?"

"Ryback Hobbs?" Ria tilted her head at the photo that appeared on her side and then shook it a moment later. "No, I don't see any record of him. Why?"

Max muffled the curse that wanted to burst free. "He had traces of maishkin in his clothes. The naval forensics specialist obviously didn't know what it was, but I—" She rubbed at her eyes. Any Carmichael or someone who'd worked directly with the labs knew the distinctive molecular structure of LifeEx's essential component.

Ria's brown eyes narrowed. "Where was this? Is this why you wanted those trial lists a few months back? Never mind, send it to me via text. I'm hanging up before you burst a blood vessel."

"I'll call you later," Max said. She pushed to her feet and stumbled to the toilet, making it just before she threw up.

"I thought I was reckless," Jenks said, and Max glanced over her shoulder to find the petty officer leaning against the stall opening. "That would have been super messy if your chip had overheated."

"It was fine."

Jenks rolled her eyes at the protest and stuck her hand out, helping Max to her feet. "It was stupid, and I don't use that word lightly. What was so important that you rushed out of the gym and tried to have a convo with Earth through your DD?"

"I needed to talk to my sister. One of those men you arrested had traces of maishkin in his clothes," Max said, and received a blank look from Jenks in return. "The main compound in LifeEx."

"Huh. Is that bad?"

"He didn't work for the company. That's the only place he could have come into contact with it." Max made her way to the sink to rinse her mouth out. "It's highly controlled, Jenks. My family, the company, has kept the design of maishkin a secret for hundreds of years."

"Could he have come into contact with someone who does work for LifeEx?"

Max shook her head. "At the concentrations noted on the forensic report? No. Besides, the labs are locked-down clean rooms, no one would have tracked or brought it out with them. He would have had to be in the room with it."

Jenks stared at the wall for several minutes. "He wasn't anywhere near Earth when we picked him up, but that doesn't mean he couldn't have been there previously."

"There was—" Ignoring the pounding in her skull, Max scrolled through the report again. "There was also dirt in his boots, but not from Earth. From Trappist-1e—and other dirt they couldn't pinpoint."

"We should call Nika." Jenks grabbed for Max. "Actually, first I'm taking you to medical, Lieutenant. Then we'll call him like normal human beings do—with a tablet."

JENKS STOOD AT ATTENTION. THAT WAS RARE FOR HER, BUT so was the kind of shouting that Admiral Hoboins was engaging in right this moment. None of it was directed her way, thankfully, but holy shit did the lieutenant look like she was going to cry.

"Waking me up for emergencies is one thing, but when I get com calls at zero dark thirty just to have my ass chewed by a superior officer because she got her ass chewed by someone from the Navy protesting that Ria Carmichael came in and took all the evidence for a closed case—and *then* I get a call from Carmichael herself demanding all the files containing the information on LifeEx? It makes me a little grumpy."

"To be fair, Admiral, you said the case was closed. Why did the Navy get their shorts in a twist?"

Jenks bit the inside of her cheek and kept her eyes locked on the window behind Hoboins, even though she wanted to stare at Rosa in shock.

"Because it's the Navy, Commander. They get their shorts twisted over everything!" Hoboins stopped and dragged in a breath.

"With respect, Admiral—" Jenks cleared her throat as those fierce brown eyes turned her way and her interior voice screamed at her to keep her own damn mouth shut. "The lieutenant couldn't have known her sister would pull rank like that—she was just trying to solve the puzzle and that was the only place to go for answers."

"The point is, Lieutenant Carmichael *should* have come to Commander Martín first, not called her sister about it, and certainly not put her soft brain in danger doing so!"

"I agree with you, Admiral."

"Well, thank God for that, Petty Officer Khan." Hoboins looked back at Max. "Make a choice, Lieutenant: either the NeoG is your first and last or you find somewhere else to finish your stretch. I don't need split loyalties in my crews or on my station, am I clear?"

"Perfectly, Admiral."

"Fine, you're all dismissed. Get the hell out of my office."

Max walked out, Rosa and Jenks on her heels. Her head was down and Jenks watched her swipe at her face before she disappeared into the corridor. She caught Rosa's eye, and the commander jerked her head toward the door.

Jenks shook her head. *Not my job,* she mouthed.

Rosa's mouth tightened. *Mine?*

You're the commander, Commander.

Rosa gave Jenks a narrow-eyed glare and headed out the door.

"You're gonna pay for that one," Lou said, and Jenks grinned.

"Probably. You know me, I'm shit for comforting people, unless it's in bed."

"Get out of my office," Lou said, laughing and waving a hand. "Boss is going to be grumpy all day because of this. Hudson, get your ass in there for a chewing."

"I'll order him a fruit basket." Jenks bolted out the door before Lou could throw something at her, shooting a sympathetic smile toward the coms tech who'd put Max's call through.

Poor bastard.

"LIEUTENANT, HOLD UP."

Max stopped at the sound of Rosa's voice, and wiped the remainder of the tears off her face before she straightened her shoulders. "Commander, I know I screwed up, but—I don't want to go. NeoG is the best thing that's happened to me and I—" She broke off when Rosa lifted a hand.

"Hoboins makes big dramatic statements when he's mad because he doesn't get mad very often." The smile on Rosa's face was surprisingly kind. "You're not going anywhere, not unless you really want to."

"I don't." Max hated how small her voice sounded under the pounding of her head.

"It was a shit decision, but I agree with what Jenks said in there. I understand what you were after and you thought your sister—" Rosa stopped and smiled again. "You didn't think your sister would compartmentalize things like that, but that's her job and she knew it. You need to start thinking like that, too. That's what Hoboins's point was."

"I'm sorry, Commander."

"Don't apologize," Rosa said as Jenks came down the corridor toward them. "Get our files back."

Max smiled slowly. "I still have my copy."

Rosa grinned. "Excellent." Then she sobered. "Now, about the contacting Earth directly: I don't care how fancy your gear is, Lieutenant, don't ever do that again. That's an order. Am I understood?"

Max swallowed as Jenks mouthed *Told you so* from behind Rosa. "Perfectly, Commander."

Rosa nodded. "All right. I've got practice with D'Arcy in half an hour." She pointed at Max. "You go lie down like Dr. Blun told you. And you stay out of trouble."

"Kick his ass, Commander," Jenks said with a grin, taking Max by the elbow. "I'll make sure she gets back to quarters."

Max let her pull them in the opposite direction, waiting until Rosa was out of sight before she looked down at Jenks. "What are you doing?"

"Taking you back to quarters." She grinned again. "We've got a com scheduled with Nika and I want to make copies of those files before your sister orders you to give them up. Sapphi's got some, uh, secret storage where we can stash them. Just in case."

Max let Jenks lead her back to quarters and shove her onto Nika's still vacant bunk. It was probably just as well, she thought as she lay down. Her head was throbbing and she took several deep breaths to stave off the sudden wave of nausea.

"Hey, wake up. Doc said no sleeping for another five hours," Jenks said, kicking the bunk frame hard enough to make the whole thing rattle. Max opened an eye to glare at her.

"I was just resting my eyes. Sapphi."

Sapphi looked unhappy. "LT, don't tell the commander about my spot, please." She slanted a look at Jenks. "*She* wasn't supposed to be telling anyone."

"Hey, it's important." Jenks plopped onto the bunk, a tablet in hand. "Send her those files, Lieutenant."

"Done." Max looked up at Sapphi. "Don't worry, I won't say anything. Just promise me you won't go spreading that around?"

"It stays here." Sapphi tapped at her temple. "Promise."

"I trust you." Max mustered up a smile, then closed her eyes again, resulting in a poke from Jenks.

"Hey, Sully," Jenks said. "Can you put a call through to Trappist for me?"

"Yup, give me a second."

Max struggled back into a sitting position, her side pressed against Jenks's as the tablet screen blacked out and then Nika appeared.

His hair was disheveled, and he covered up a yawn with the back of a hand, revealing a line of text tattooed on his wrist that Max wasn't able to make out before he dropped his arm. "Sorry. Late night. Hey, Max."

"What am I? Chopped liver?"

Nika blew a kiss in his sister's direction. "What's so hopping important you're messaging me to actually schedule a call?"

"We found something," Max said. "After the thing with Jenks's EMU we started digging again. I just had a—"

"Wait, what happened to Jenks?"

"Did you not tell him?" Max leaned forward. "Someone sabotaged Jenks's EMU while we were on Earth and it went haywire during a rescue. We think it was whoever killed those salvagers you picked up."

"Jenks, what the fuck?" Nika sat up, all sleepiness vanishing at the news. "How are you just telling me this *now*?"

"In her defense, we've been a little busy around here. That's not the most interesting part of this," Max said, lifting a hand when Nik glared. "I just got around to looking at the forensics report for those deaths on board the Navy ship. The report noted several interesting compounds on the bodies and clothing. Namely dirt from Trappist-1e and maishkin."

"The LifeEx compound?" Nika's blue eyes went wide in surprise. "How did they even know they'd found it? I heard its makeup is a closely guarded secret."

"They didn't know what they had," Max replied. "I'd have heard about it a lot sooner if they did. I recognized the molecular breakdown in the report." She took a deep breath. "Then I called my sister to see if the man they found it on had been an employee at any point, but he hadn't. Then Ria went off the rails and may have pulled all the evidence from the Navy and from us."

"Oh." Nika whistled. "Oops."

"Little bit." Jenks grinned. "LT got her ass chewed just half an hour ago. Though a chunk of it was for making a direct call to Earth from her DD and nearly frying her brain."

"You did *what*?"

Max buried her face in her hand while Jenks chuckled beside her. "I'm fine. It was a quick call and as you can see I am still alive and coherent."

"She puked and I had to take her to med bay." Jenks's voice was gleeful. "Dr. Blun said off duty for at least fifteen hours and then come back to see them."

"Okay, hang on, we're getting off track," Nika said. Max lifted her head just in time to catch a stern look from him. "Don't do that again."

"Rosa already read me the riot act, thanks. So did Admiral Hoboins."

Nika leveled an impressive stare her direction and Max felt her cheeks heat. "I think it bears repeating, right?"

"Yes."

"Okay. So, we've got five dead smugglers, one stolen system jumper, three hundred and fifty-three missing bodies, links to LifeEx and to Trappist-1e. Did I sum that up right?"

"And the dead body in the Thames," Jenks chimed in.

Max nodded. "But no motive or idea of why."

"I'd say send me the reports on the dirt sample and I could follow up here to see if we can pinpoint the area, but if your sister took them all—"

Max pulled just the soil report and sent it off before Nika had finished his sentence and he raised an eyebrow at her.

"I still have a copy—at least at the moment."

"Ah." His eyes flicked to Jenks. "Did you give Jenks a copy?"

"She knows about Sapphi's storage," Jenks said. "It's taken care of."

"Okay, good. I'll poke around here and see what I can find.

The university isn't far from base and I'm sure there are some geologists who can help me."

"Sounds good." Max paused. "I'll let you two catch up. I need to talk to my sister again." She smiled and maneuvered herself off the bunk.

"Use a tablet," Nika said with a smile of his own.

"Yes, Commander." Max gave him a mock salute and then headed for her room.

JENKS WATCHED HER BROTHER WATCH MAX SLIP AWAY UNTIL she was off-screen and arched an eyebrow. He looked back at her, face impassive, and they stared at each other for several moments before Jenks finally relented and shook her head. "It's your heart that'll get broken, Nik, so I don't really care, but it's still a bad idea."

"I heard you call her LT, so don't even start. Anyway, you think I want your advice, O Queen of Keep My Heart Locked Away from Everyone? How's Luis?"

"Hush," Jenks said, smiling even though his words stung. She knew better than to open that particular box up with Nika. He was as likely to throw his heart gleefully into the shredder as she was to keep hers under lock and key. She hadn't talked to him about what happened with Luis at the prelims and now didn't quite seem like the time.

Nika had never shamed her for her choices, but he'd seen straight through to why she only chose sex and never the risk of a relationship that would lead to heartbreak.

"I do like her, it's just—"

"How are things?" Ever the diplomatic one, Nika changed the subject with only a smile and a nod. "Besides the strange mystery people trying to kill you, that is. Don't think I'm going to forget you neglected to tell me about that. The prelims went well?"

"They did. Would have been better if our lieutenant there

had some sword-fighting skills, but she's good enough with predicting people's movements. She did amazingly with Ma in the navigation seat of his races. Her hand-to-hand skills aren't bad, either." Jenks shrugged a shoulder and looked up at the ceiling. "They're not tournament quality, though. I don't know if we're going to swing this, and I still really want to punch whoever in Command thought this was a good idea."

Nika smiled. "Have a little faith, Jenks. I have a feeling everything will come together, and you've still got a decent amount of time to get to the Games."

"Maybe. Nothing else we can do about it besides bust our asses and hope that every competitor has a bad morning on the big day."

"True." Nika stretched. "I'm up now, so I guess I should find someone to take a look at that sample you sent me before the day starts."

"I can see your ribs. Eat more," Jenks said.

"I love you, too, sis. Talk to you later."

MAX CLOSED THE DOOR OF HER ROOM, SHUTTING OUT THE sounds of Jenks and Nika, and sank down onto the bed with a sigh of relief. "He's not wrong. That probably was not the brightest thing you've done, Maxine Theodosia."

But she shoved the dizziness to the side and reached for her own tablet. Within moments she was connected with Ria's private line again.

"You look awful."

"Thanks, I just spent an hour getting my ass chewed by the commander of the station."

"What for?" Max gave her sister a flat look and Ria pursed her lips together for a moment. "Oh."

"You could have told me what you were going to do!" Max threw her hands up in the air. "I could have made the request, then it would have been one branch to another instead of LifeEx coming in and throwing their weight around."

"I did no such thing."

"You served the Navy with a cease and desist order, Ria, and told the coroner if he didn't hand over the samples and the documents you'd sue him for property theft. Then you called Admiral Hoboins and basically demanded the same thing."

"Max, you know as well as I do that the breakdown of maishkin can't be available to the public. You know what could happen if it was. Do you really want that?"

"Might be a good idea for this family to be knocked down a peg," Max muttered, earning a sharp look from her sister.

"While I don't necessarily disagree with you on that point, that's not for some criminal to do. You know how dangerous the risk of knockoffs is, what it could do to people. How dangerous and unstable this whole process was. It took Great-Granddaddy years to get it sorted, and you and I both know there was blood on his hands from it."

"Hence the reason for the will." Max sighed. They'd all been told this from childhood. The sacrifices and salvation of Great-Grandfather Alexander as he grew up with nothing in the aftermath of the Collapse. Humanity struggled and clawed its way out from under the debris of the shattered world to save itself from extinction.

And through it all their great-grandfather dreamed of longer lives for the survivors, a way for humanity to recover the numbers that had been lost in a more sustainable fashion.

Max remembered the agonizing two weeks at school during the history lessons covering her family, the horror of her classmates and the sympathy from the teacher. Her great-grandfather had charged for his discovery.

Unlike Pierrette Rouseaux, the pre-Collapse tech giant who'd saved millions of lives with her terraforming technology and then preserved the tech by crowdsourcing it out around the globe so that the CHN government had been able to use the information to terraform first Mars and then three of the worlds in Trappist-1.

It made Max sick. Yet another thing to separate her from the rest of the family, who were all apparently fine with the legacy—Ria's comment notwithstanding. And Max vaguely recalled a cousin who'd shunned the family altogether and was living on borrowed time, as the people who couldn't afford LifeEx liked to say. But she hadn't been brave enough to reach out to her—because she was probably just as much a hypocrite as anyone in their family.

"Max?"

Max blinked away the memories and refocused on her sister. "What?"

"I said I'll need those files from you, too."

"You can have the one back, even though you and I know I have every right to keep it and that you don't have the rights to the others."

Ria raised an eyebrow. "Is that so?"

"It is. You're interfering with an investigation."

"I was told it was a closed case, just salvagers in the wrong place at the wrong time."

"Maybe. Or it might be worse. I think someone tried to kill my teammate over this, Ria, and I'll be damned if I'm going to let that go. You need to let me look into it."

Ria stared at her for a long moment and Max forced herself to stare back even as the room did a slow whirl around her.

"Fine, but you keep me in the loop. Or I'll tell Mom and Dad you almost fried your brain calling me direct."

"You think I'm scared of them?"

"You should be. Don't think you're safe just because you got what you wanted." Ria's smile was grim and she disconnected, leaving Max staring at the NeoG emblem on her tablet.

Dai—

I found something. My contact at the PeaceKeepers scoured the video footage for the handful of faces I passed on and found footage of not only one of your salvagers, but our dead guy from the Thames in the same frame. See the attached.

I'm glad you're okay. Com when you have a chance.

—Luis

Max—

Check out what Luis sent me from his contact at the LPK. I recognize Shaw and the date's from before we snagged him at the belt and his untimely demise. Does that third guy standing in the background look familiar?

—J

Max—

I've gotten wind of a smuggling ring that's operating out of a warehouse here on Trappist-1e that might be connected to this strange case. The Trappist PeaceKeepers have been watching this place for a while. We're planning on checking it out as soon as I can get approval pushed through.

There's a freighter that left here this morning, though, and its manifest reported having picked up cargo from that warehouse. I don't have to tell you how strange that is. Trappist isn't self-sufficient, there's very little in the way of product being sent back to Earth. They're probably already through Jupiter Control and on their way to Earth, but if you can convince Hoboins to reopen the case you'll be able to go after them.

Good luck, you and Jenks be careful.

—N

"We got it." Max set her tablet down in front of Rosa with a smile.

"What am I looking at?" Rosa tilted her head at the image. "Or rather, *who* am I looking at?"

"Sebastian Cane, Wilson Shaw, and my admirer from the preliminaries." Max pointed at each of the men in turn. "Mr. Cane boarded *An Ordinary Star* on June 17, 2330, and was reported missing with the rest of the passengers and crew until his body appeared in the Thames a few months ago. Mr. Shaw, as you know, was arrested by Nika and then died aboard the naval transport ship en route to Earth from what we all assumed was an ill-timed accident. This photo was taken off surveillance footage from before you arrested him. We still don't have a name for this man." She tapped the third face.

Max was practically bouncing where she stood and Rosa smiled. "Where'd you get this?"

"Luis. He passed the faces we had on to his friend at LPK. They did a search through the archives around the time Mr. Cane was found in the river. This picture was taken the week before Shaw was arrested by the NeoG."

Rosa studied the image, biting back her second smile when Max shifted into parade rest in an expected display of patience she was becoming rather famous for. Jenks would have been peppering her with a thousand questions. Max thought she had something, she was just waiting for Rosa to give the go-ahead.

The problem was, they still didn't have anything that would justify NeoG reopening a case. Rosa opened her mouth to tell Max sorry, but then she frowned. "What did you mean 'we all assumed was an ill-timed accident'?"

Max leaned down and tapped the tablet, changing the image from the trio of men to a mangled ruin of wires. "Fire suppression system on board the transport." She tapped again. "Jenks's EMU."

"Okay?"

"I had D'Arcy look at the images. He can't be certain without seeing them in person, and unfortunately the suppression system's already been disposed of, but he was pretty certain they were both wired by the same professional."

"He used the word 'professional'?"

Max nodded once.

"How did you know to ask him?"

There was the hesitation. Rosa hadn't seen it on Max's face for this entire conversation until now. "Being a Carmichael is a pain in the ass a great deal of the time, but there are some . . . perks to it—like access to more sensitive information. I like to know who I'm working with. Especially if that someone used to be an explosives expert for a terrorist organization."

"I have a feeling I don't need to tell you it's not common knowledge D'Arcy used to be a Mars separatist."

"You don't," Max replied. "I understand, even if I don't agree, and his past is his to share. But I didn't want to take this to someone I didn't trust. I trust him."

"Did you tell him that?" Rosa fought to hold in her grin when Max nodded, and she was a little sad she'd missed the shock that had likely raced over D'Arcy's face. "So we have something to link the death of our criminals with the attempt on Jenks's life. Good. I'll go talk to Hoboins."

"I've got something else, Commander," Max said as Rosa stood. "Nika sent me the manifest for a freighter—*Bandit's Bane*—that picked up cargo from a warehouse suspected of being involved with a smuggling ring on Trappist-1e. They passed through Jupiter Control at about oh-seven-hundred this morning."

"Did they—" Rosa broke off with a laugh when Max tapped the tablet a final time to reveal an official request from the TPK for the NeoG to board the *Bandit's Bane* and verify that the items on the manifest from Trappist-1e were the only items collected from the warehouse. "Go get everyone moving, and call D'Arcy. Hoboins might want more teams, but I want *Dread* with us at the very least."

"*BANDIT'S BANE*, I REPEAT. THIS IS THE NEOG INTERCEPTOR *Zuma's Ghost*. You are ordered to heave to and prepare to be boarded under the authority of the CHN."

"I'm a duly registered freighter operating from Trappist-1e. You don't have the right to board me."

Jenks snorted and Max shot Rosa a sympathetic smile as the captain of the freighter continued to argue.

"This is not a discussion, *Bandit's Bane*," Rosa said, cutting off the oration. "I have authority to board and inspect via section eighty-nine of CHNC fourteen. You have one more chance to power down your engines."

The captain's reply was garbled and Jenks's snort turned into laughter.

"Oh, this is gonna be a shit show," she said, cracking her neck.

Rosa sighed. "Captain Dale, did you copy all that?"

"Roger, Commander. We'll hit them with the pulse, should put everything down." The captain of the Karman Patrol Cutter was responsible for the pulse weapon that could take ships' engines off-line. The tech was similar to an electromagnetic pulse, but wouldn't cause the containment on the engines to fail, nor would it shut down life support.

"D'Arcy, you ready?"

"As we'll ever be."

"Captain Dale, you have clearance to fire. Hit the airlock, you three. Ma and I will be behind you."

Max nodded and headed off the bridge, Jenks and Tamago at her back.

"Doge, you know the drill," Jenks said, and Max swore the ROVER gave the same grumbling whine he always did.

"I never asked why he can't come on boardings."

Tamago giggled, cutting off when Jenks shot them a glare. "He shot a guy," they said to Max.

"Nearly got melted down for scrap," Jenks muttered as she pulled her sword out of the rack and shoved it onto her back. "I had to promise Hoboins no more boardings, and I had to study for the promotion test, *and* stay out of trouble for six months. Damn dog. The guy deserved it, though, he was gonna stab me."

Max swallowed down the laugh. "Crew of thirty-seven."

"Assume armed," Jenks said, fastening her helmet. "If they're not completely suicidal it'll only be shotguns."

"I'll never understand that," Max replied. "It could still mess up their ship."

"Better protection against pirates," Sapphi chimed in over the com.

"Why do pirates carry swords?" Jenks singsonged.

"Because swords can't walk!"

Max choked as the other three burst into peals of laughter.

"All right, focus time," Rosa said over the com. "Sapphi, what have we got?"

"We're docking in three, on the lower port side of cargo bay three. *Dread* is coming in on the starboard side, same cargo bay. I've got control of their airlocks and the doors on either side, so you don't have to fight your way on board, but they've got someone who knows her shit. It's going to take Garcia and me a minute to box her in."

Zuma's Ghost shuddered as she docked with the freighter and the doors cycled with a hiss.

"Roger that," Max said.

"I do not have visual, so you're going in blind."

"Coming out of the airlock on the far side, Max," D'Arcy said over the com.

"Noted." Max pulled her sword free as she stepped into cargo bay.

The members of *Dread Treasure*, except for Spacer Lupe Garcia, who was still on the ship, appeared across the cargo bay and Max met them in the middle.

"Three levels," Rosa said, joining them with Ma at her side. "Huang, you and Murphy stay here and hold the cargo bay." She pointed at *Dread*'s warrant officer and PO. "Jenks, take Tamago and Akane to the bottom and sweep through." PO Ito Akane nodded and tapped Tamago on the shoulder as she passed.

"Max, Locke, and Ma, sweep the middle. D'Arcy and I are going up to have a chat with the captain."

"Do we have to take helmets with, Commander?" Jenks asked.

"Sapphi?"

"We've gotten into engineering and life support," Sapphi replied. "Good to leave helmets behind. Commander, I could just shut everything down."

There was a moment of silence. Max straightened from setting her helmet on the floor and caught Rosa's look, shaking her head once. Shutting off life support was risky and NeoG didn't need the bad press that could come if they accidentally killed someone—even if the captain of *Bandit's Bane* was resisting a boarding.

"No, Sapphi, we'll handle it. There's—"

A noise echoed in the cargo bay and everyone froze. Max tapped Jenks on the shoulder, gesturing with both hands that they circle around the pallets where the noise had originated. Jenks nodded, pointing at Rosa and mouthing *Keep talking*.

Max felt her heartbeat ratchet up a notch as she crept past the cargo and peeked around the corner. A woman huddled on the floor with a handful of kids, all under the age of ten. Her arms were wrapped around them and her head snapped up when Max cleared her throat.

"Lieutenant Max Carmichael, NeoG. Ms. Perrilin," she said, reading the woman's name off her DD chip handshake and hoping she was pronouncing it right, "I'm going to ask you to stand up carefully for me. Are you armed?"

"N-no. I'm a teacher. We were supposed to do a science lesson today."

"Are you going to arrest us?"

Max caught Jenks's eye from behind the group before looking down at the kid whose handshake read *Manuel Terz, undecided*. "I'm reasonably sure I won't need to," she said with a smile. "But we'd like for you all to be somewhere safer."

"My dads are engineers." Manuel slipped out of his teacher's grasp and Max held up a hand at her gasp.

"Really?" Max ushered the kid toward the others, Jenks herding the rest of the group along after. "This is Petty Officer Aki Murphy, she's also an engineer."

It took them several minutes to get the kids situated as Rosa and D'Arcy peppered August Perrilin with questions. At a wave from Rosa, Max nodded to Locke and they headed for the door to start their sweeps.

"Hey, Sapphi, which direction are the stairs so I can mark Jenks's arm?" She winked at Jenks, who was gaping at her.

"Go right, LT, you'll have a chance to spread out before you run into any crew." Sapphi's voice was thick with suppressed laughter.

Jenks, Tamago, and Akane headed to the left; Max and the others went right, Locke and Ma falling into formation behind Max in the wide corridor. That was the one good thing about freighters: there was more space to work in. But there were also more places to hide.

"CHILDREN." ROSA SHOOK HER HEAD WITH A SIGH AS SHE and D'Arcy headed through the eerily silent ship toward the bridge.

"Not a huge surprise," he replied. "Most of these freighters are long-haul. Easier to get crew if they can bring their families."

"Less that and more about this captain putting them all at risk by smuggling shit with children on board."

"Fair enough."

"Sapphi, are we going to be able to get on the bridge when we get there?"

"I'm working on it, we've almost got this hacker locked down. Give me five minutes."

"You've got two."

"Doesn't work like that, Rosa, and you know it."

"We could just knock," D'Arcy said with a grin as they stopped in front of the door to the bridge.

The captain hadn't responded since his initial refusal to heave to and Rosa doubted a polite knock on the door would garner any different response. "Just wait," she said with a smile, watching the clock ticking in the corner of her vision. At the 120-second mark, the door slid open.

Rosa winked at D'Arcy and slipped through the door. The captain, a burly man with a wild black beard, was already rushing her way. Rosa sidestepped him, driving her elbow into his back on his way by and scanning the room for other targets. There was a redheaded kid who didn't look over fifteen sitting at a console muttering as they furiously tried to regain control of the ship, and the first mate had a sword in her hand but seemed to be hesitating.

"Put it down," Rosa said. "You don't want to do this."

"Janna!" The captain grunted and Rosa glanced quickly over her shoulder to see D'Arcy pulling that same damn sword-stealing move he always did. Only this time he hit the captain in the face with the hilt of the man's own sword.

Janna gripped her sword tighter and Rosa put her free hand up. "I'm serious. You will not win this. Do you know what your captain is carrying?"

"He said it would be good. We'd get paid a lot of feds. We could buy another ship, start a fleet. I could maybe even send Patch to school on Earth."

"Janna, I'm not going to lie to you, this isn't a good situation. But you put that sword down and I'll see what I can do for you."

"Janna, don't you dare!"

"Gun!" D'Arcy shouted.

There was an abrupt squelching sound and Rosa watched as the first mate's eyes went wide and the woman lunged, not toward her but toward the kid. She didn't even have to look around to know D'Arcy had killed the man, and she was hoping she wouldn't have to do the same to the first mate.

"Mama, I'm blocked." The kid at the console finally realized there were other people in the room and froze, staring at Rosa with big blue eyes.

"Put your sword down, Janna, please."

The sword clattered to the deck and Rosa breathed a sigh of relief.

"ALL CREW, THIS IS FIRST MATE JANNA CANTREL. YOU ARE ordered to stand down and comply with the NeoG's orders.

Captain Fitch is dead, I am in command. Lay down your weapons." The order rang over the ship coms and into the air from several speakers.

Max bit down on the curse as she shoved her knee into the woman's back. "Hear that? Stay down."

"Lieutenant, you good?"

Max finished cuffing the woman. "Yeah." Then took the hand Lieutenant Commander Steve Locke from *Dread Treasure* offered and got to her feet, leaning back down to pick up her sword. "What's the situation?"

"Middle deck is cleared. There's a handful of crew who aren't paying attention to the surrender order." His grin was sharp. "D'Arcy said to head down and give Jenks a hand." He waved Aki Murphy over. "Take this one to Commander Montaglione."

The Neo nodded and grabbed for the woman, hauling her to her feet and out the door.

"Hey, Jenks, where are you?"

"Section forty-three" came the reply over the com, followed by a grunt. "Little busy, LT."

Max hit Locke on the shoulder as she headed for the door. "Jenks started the party without us. We'd better hurry." She sprinted out the door and down the corridor, sliding down the stairs with Locke on her heels.

They rounded the corner. Jenks was in a sword fight with a guy who was wielding a crowbar like he knew how to use it. Another crewman was trying to circle around Jenks, and Max tapped him on the shoulder with her sword.

"I wouldn't," she said, and the man froze. "Hands behind your back."

Locke moved in to cuff him. Max waited until he was secure and then stepped around the pair. "Need some help, Jenks?"

"Naw, I got it."

The man snorted. "I'm gonna crush your skull in and then your friend's."

"Then what?" Max asked.

"What?"

"Ship's ours," she said with a shrug. "Your captain surrendered. Where are you going to go?"

He frowned, and Max saw Jenks shift, but she waved her off with her left hand hidden partially behind her leg. "Anywhere's better than here. I won't end up like those poor bastards on Trappist," he said.

"You don't have anywhere to go, and you're not getting two steps before—" Max stopped and smiled. "Do you want to know what's going to happen? The real version, not the crush-our-skulls fantasy. You're going to swing that thing at Jenks here, she's going to catch it. She's stronger than she looks. She's going to reverse it on you and hit you in the throat, but it won't crush your larynx. She's got better control than that.

"But that means you'll lunge forward and I'm going to have to run this sword straight through your heart." She held her sword up and it didn't waver at all. "Seems like a shit way to die."

The crowbar clattered on the grating when he dropped it.

Jenks kicked it away. "Get on the floor." She slapped her sword to her back, cuffed him, and stood up and pointed a finger Max's way. "Two things—you totally stole my fight, but I'm going to let it slide because you just Westley'd that idiot."

"I'm sorry, I what?"

Locke's snicker turned into a full-blown laugh. "Oh my God, Jenks. Max, don't ask her, it just encourages her."

"I need no encouragement." Jenks took her sword back and he shook his head, still laughing at Max's confusion. "It's a classic, LT, we'll watch it when we get back to Jupiter."

"Okay." Max pointed at the door behind them. "That's the cargo bay we want, let's go take a look at what was so important as to start this fight in the first place."

"You two go. I've got this one, and according to the crew list everyone else is accounted for," Locke said. "D'Arcy and

Rosa are headed down. The *McKelvey* just docked and is bringing reinforcements."

Max nodded and followed Jenks to the door. She pulled up the manifest lists as they slipped into the cargo bay. "Supposedly the stuff they picked up on Trappist-1e is over there."

"Do they say what it is?" Jenks scanned the cargo bay as they crossed to the area marked on the grid.

"A shipment of strawberry plants? Really?" Max frowned. "Trappist-1e is still struggling for self-sufficiency. Why would they be shipping live plants *away* from the planet?"

Jenks kicked one of the cargo pods, a round barrel marked LIVE PLANTS, KEEP COOL, and looked at Max. "Can I open it and find out?"

Max nodded and Jenks popped the lid off. There was a whoosh of pressure releasing and both women stared into the barrel at the liquid-filled bags marked with the recognizable LifeEx logo.

"Well," Jenks said finally. "Shit."

"Yeah." Max rubbed a hand over her face.

JENKS LEANED AGAINST THE WALL AS MAX ARGUED WITH her sister over the com. The lieutenant had learned her lesson from the previous incident and was being very careful about not mentioning what was in the forty barrels out of frame.

"I just need to know if there have been any break-ins. Anything that wasn't covered in the press?"

"And I need to know why you need to know, Max." Ria shook her head. "We're on an unsecured channel and you've probably got half a dozen people in the room with you. You know I'm not going to talk about sensitive company issues in such a public setting."

Max's snarl was poorly concealed and Jenks reached a hand out, staying out of the tablet's camera as she put it on Max's arm. It was a fascinating thing to watch, how an interaction with her family messed with her control, but they needed that patience back. It was only a matter of time before Ria found out about the LifeEx in this cargo bay, but they could use all the extra time they could get before she stuck her nose into their investigation again.

"Fine. I'll call you when I have a secure channel." Max shut down the com without waiting for a reply from her sister.

"Take a breath, LT." Jenks waited a beat as Max complied. "They get to you, don't they?"

"Always." Max rubbed at an eye. "It feels like all my patience, all my control, just flies out the airlock. The *company*." She spit the word out and threw her hands up in the air. "It's always the company, the name. The legacy. I hate it so much sometimes."

Max took a deep, shuddering breath. "I'm sorry, I'm sure you don't want to hear me—"

"Hey." Jenks shook her head. "I get it. You don't have to apologize. They care more about something else than they do about you and it hurts. My parents were the same. Only difference is I don't know what it was they loved more than me." She gripped Max's hand tight. "You're a good person and a better Neo. I know I was hard on you when you started, but you're a part of this team. Which means you're our family now."

Max's answering smile wobbled and Jenks shook her head. "Do not get teary on me, LT."

"Hush and go see if Ma needs help." Max gave Jenks a little shove and went to meet Rosa and D'Arcy at the entrance to the cargo bay.

MAX'S HEART STUTTERED WHEN SHE CAUGHT SIGHT OF THE grim look on Rosa's and D'Arcy's faces. "What is it?" She watched as Rosa's gaze flicked to where Jenks stood at Ma's side across the cargo bay and then returned to her. "Rosa, what is it?"

"There's been an explosion."

"Where? On the ship?" Max had a moment to wonder why the alarm system wasn't going wild before Rosa replied.

"No. On Trappist-1e."

"Okay . . ."

"Nika's been hurt."

The air rushed out of Max's lungs at the words. Words that for a single terrifying moment she hadn't been able to hear past the hammering of her heart. Words she'd been sure were going to end with "killed" instead of "hurt."

"What happened?"

"There was an explosion at that warehouse in the Horst district on Trappist-1e the TPK was investigating. We don't have all the details yet, but it looks like there was a lab hidden inside the warehouse. Nika and his team were on-site along with TPK officers serving the search warrant when it blew. We—"

Max squeezed her eyes shut as Rosa broke off and cursed under her breath in Spanish that the Babel either couldn't or wouldn't translate.

"They've got him loaded onto the CHNN carrier *Hamilton Bane,* and she'll be opening a wormhole here in under an hour. Max, he's hurt bad, and Jenks . . ." Rosa blew out a breath. "Jesus preserve us, she's going to melt down."

"What do we need to do?" Max looked at D'Arcy, who lifted his hands.

"Get her back onto *Zuma* without her hurting herself or anyone else. If we're getting Jenks on that CHNN ship, she'll need to be ready—and composed when you hook up with it," he said. "I know that's a lot given the circumstances, but they won't let her on if she's raging."

Max's gut was screaming at her and she put a hand up as Rosa started forward. "Commander, let me do this."

"You?" Rosa shook her head. "Max, she's going to start throwing punches. I'm not even joking when I say she could kill you."

"I know that, but I also think I can do this without her getting violent." The disbelief surging across everyone's faces didn't make the knots in her stomach any easier to deal with, but Max straightened her shoulders and looked Rosa in the eye. "Commander, trust me. Reading people is one of the few things I'm good at."

"I thought you couldn't get a handle on Jenks?"

"Not most of the time. But this? This I think I've got. Do you have details?"

Rosa glanced in Jenks's direction and finally nodded. "I'll send you the file. You get one try. If she loses it, you get your ass out of the way."

"I will." Max took a deep breath and headed across the cargo bay with Rosa trailing behind. D'Arcy whistled a complex tune and the members of *Dread Treasure* converged on them with uniform precision. Just in case they needed to dogpile Jenks.

"Hey, LT, I was just thinking, why would they be smuggling LifeEx to Earth? Wouldn't the other way around make more sense?"

"Petty Officer Khan, come sit down. We need to talk." Max made eye contact with Sapphi and Tamago, who were standing nearby.

"What?" Jenks snorted and laughed, but she complied, boosting herself onto a nearby cargo bin. "You look really serious. What's up?" she asked. "Commander?"

"Lieutenant Carmichael's in charge at the moment, Petty Officer," Rosa replied.

"Look at me." Max gestured until Jenks's eyes tracked back to her. "The clock is ticking, I need you to remember that after I tell you what I'm about to tell you. You're going to have to go back to *Zuma*, get packed, and be ready to go. You don't get to fall apart until I tell you. That's an order, am I understood?"

Jenks's eyes flicked to Rosa as she worked the answer over

in her mouth before allowing it free. "Yes, Lieutenant. You're understood. What is going on?"

"Commander Nika Vagin was severely injured in an explosion at approximately thirteen hundred hours on Trappist-1e. He's on board the CHNN ship *Hamilton Bane* coming through a wormhole to Jupiter and then continuing on to Earth. They'll stop long enough for us to board." Max kept everything phrased in the most precise terms she could find from the file Rosa had sent, the most grounding military procedure that she could hammer past the emotions she knew were rolling around in Jenks's head right now.

Because she'd figured one thing out about Jenks in the last few months, and that was that Jenks would wiggle around rules as long as she thought she could, because the close-knit structure of the Interceptor team encouraged familiarity over rank. But give her a direct order, put her on a mission, and she followed protocol without question.

"Nika's h—"

Max watched as Jenks's hand gripped her sword hilt over her shoulder and raised her voice slightly. "Petty Officer, are you listening to me?"

"I'm listening, Lieutenant." There were tears in her eyes, though, as she got off the crate. Tamago was already crying, a hand pressed against their mouth.

"Good. Let's go then, we've got a ship to meet. Sapphi, go with her. I'll be right behind you both."

"Can I—can I take Doge?"

"Yes."

"Thank you, ma'am," Jenks said mechanically. She headed across the cargo bay with Sapphi at her side.

Max glanced at the people still staring at her. "What?"

"How did you do that?" D'Arcy asked. "Because that was amazing."

"I'm her officer," Max replied. "And that's what she needs right now. We're all hurting, but no one as much as Jenks, and it would tear her apart if I let it. So I didn't let it. You ever no-tice how she switches when she's on a mission?"

"Like hitting a button. To be honest, I always assumed it was because of Nika," Rosa murmured. "I would have ap-proached her as a friend."

"It wouldn't have been wrong," Max said with a soft smile. "Except we don't have the time. You as a friend would have meant she could break down. Me as her lieutenant means there's a job to be done. This way, she's forced to be Petty Of-ficer Khan until I tell her otherwise."

"Go on then, Lieutenant." Rosa gave a sharp nod. "Ma, I want the three of you to stay together. And keep your eyes open."

Max returned the nod. "Yes, Commander. We'll check in after we're on board."

Jenks couldn't say exactly how she got on board the CHNS *Hamilton Bane*, only that Max's hand was on her the whole time, a comforting weight holding her in place.

Part of her wanted to punch the shit out of Max, but a larger part was grateful beyond words for what the lieutenant had done. She'd known, somehow, she'd figured out that following orders would keep Jenks in line. In control.

Sure, there was that screaming little girl in the back of her brain sobbing for her big brother, but all outward appearances had Jenks calm and coherent. The fact that her hand was locked in Doge's collar was just to keep the ROVER from wandering.

"Admiral Hoboins said he was in critical condition but stable," Max said in a low voice as the three Neos walked with shoulders back and game faces on down the bustling corridor of the carrier toward the medical bay. "We're going to go see him and then go back to our quarters and then you can do what you need to do, including throwing a punch at me if it will help."

It hadn't been a direct order, but Jenks murmured an assent because it seemed expected as they crossed over the threshold. Ma touched her back for just a moment as he passed her.

"Lieutenant Maxine Carmichael, Ensign. You have a patient we're here to see—Commander Nika Vagin. Who's his
doctor?"

The woman blinked at them. "Carmichael."

Jenks watched as Max dragged air in through her nose, a
move she already knew the lieutenant did to stay calm. "Yes,
Ensign, I am a Carmichael. Now with that out of the way, who
is the doctor?"

"She wasn't asking about your name, Maxine. She
means me."

Max's hand tightened for just a moment on Jenks's arm
and then that wall slammed down over her expression. "This
is not your ship."

"Correct," Rear Admiral Josiah Carmichael said with a
small chuckle.

Jenks bit her lip, looking between Max and the man she
assumed was her father. They looked nothing alike. The rear
admiral was a stocky bear of a man with dark skin and a
wide face. An odd contrast to Max's slender build and lighter
brown skin, but looking closer, Jenks realized their eyes were
the same.

"I was on Trappist-1e with your mother on leave when the
explosions happened. Your young man here was the worst off
of the survivors. Given what I know of the Trappist facilities
and the abilities of the Near-Earth Orbital Guard medical
staff, I decided to follow him to Earth to make sure he had the
best care." Jenks watched Admiral Carmichael's gaze flick to
Ma and then back to Max.

"He's not my young man," Max bit the reply off. "And before you tell me we're not allowed in here, this is Petty Officer
Altandai Khan, my teammate and his sister."

Max's father studied Jenks with dark eyes that were
strangely emotionless, and she decided she didn't like the man.
His practiced smile was for show. "Petty Officer Khan," he said
at last. "Your brother has been injured, but he is in good care."

The only thing keeping her together was Max's order, so her question was perfectly polite. "May I see him, Admiral?"

"You and Lieutenant Carmichael may visit. Master Chief, if you'll wait here. Five minutes, no more. You'll have to decon. Changing room and scrubs are through there."

"Thank you, Admiral." Max took Jenks by the upper arm and walked away.

"That was your father?" Jenks watched her as Max ushered her into the changing room and started to strip down.

"Yes," Max replied. "Which is good news for Nika. Best doctor in the CHNN overseeing his care is a good thing. He's just not great on the parenting front. Get changed, I won't put it past him to count this time in our five-minute limit."

THANKFULLY JENKS DIDN'T ASK ANY MORE QUESTIONS, JUST stripped down in silence, and less than two minutes later they were standing in front of the decon chamber outside of the ICU. Max could see Nika through the glass, his face peaceful in what was likely a medically induced sleep despite the violent bruising and gash that cut across his lower lip.

The realization that she cared—possibly more than she should—about a man she'd just started getting to know slammed into her with enough force to take her breath away.

Max shoved her interaction with her father out of her mind—she hadn't expected him aboard this ship, and certainly didn't know what to make of their brief chat. His dismissive attitude about the competency of others wasn't the least bit surprising. The closed-off military formality was standard even when she was on the best of terms with her parents, and considering how their last conversation had gone, she was vaguely surprised he hadn't kicked her right out of the medical bay.

He'd barely glanced in Ma's direction and his dismissal had been cold. Max felt a surge of guilt that her actions could have severed their friendship so thoroughly.

What really made her stomach clench was that Nika's right arm, his sword arm, was wrapped so heavily she couldn't tell what was wrong with it. She gripped Jenks's hand as they passed through the decontamination process, then entered the room.

Jenks took a step forward, reaching a hand out, but stopped and looked at Max's father. "Doc, may I touch him?"

Josiah nodded. "Over here. There's a stool."

Max bit her tongue, surprised not only by his unusual kindness but by the jealousy it woke in her as he led Jenks around the bed and sat her at Nika's side, then backed off to join Max once more.

"I'm told he was herding his team and civilians ahead of him. The fact that he made it to the doorway before the explosion is what saved his life. They rescued a lot of people."

"That sounds like Nik."

"You know him well?"

"No, we—" Max thought of all the letters sent back and forth across the light-years, all the calls, the quiet support from a man she'd only just met. "He was on my NeoG team before I arrived."

"There's a lot of internal damage," Josiah said, unsurprisingly choosing work over emotions. "A broken right ankle that will have to be reconstructed once we get to Earth. The worst of it is his right arm. It was crushed at the elbow, the ulnar nerve severed, humerus also broken, though not as badly as his radius and ulna."

Max pressed a hand to her mouth as the tears threatened. "Will he lose it?"

"Most likely. Even I am not that good. The nerve is damaged so badly they'd have to regrow a new one, and that tech is still not reliable. He'll be better off if we amputate, but we're waiting for the swelling from the head trauma to abate. Once he regains consciousness, we'll talk it over with him. It's not a risk to his life at the moment. Though with his sister here,

I'm assuming she would have medical power of attorney. I could—"

"You won't ask PO Khan," Max said, cutting off her father, surprised at how calm she was. "That's too much to put on her right now and she'll tell you to wait for Nika to wake up anyway."

"Proper procedure—"

"She's my subordinate, Admiral." Her voice sharpened as her grip on her temper slipped. "I'll tell her."

"Very well, Lieutenant." Josiah blinked. "Time is up. Do you want to inform the petty officer or should I?"

"I'll tell her." Max crossed the room, laid a hand on Jenks's shoulder. "Petty Officer, it's time to go."

Jenks wiped the tears from her face and stood. As she headed for the door, Max leaned down, pressing her palm to Nika's exposed left hand. "Fight for this," she whispered against his ear. "We're here, don't give up."

"Thank you, Admiral," Jenks said.

"Of course. I'll call you if he wakes. You're both welcome to come by tomorrow. I'll let the staff know."

Max gave her father a nod as she ushered Jenks from the ICU and back to the changing rooms. The other woman was quiet as she pulled on her own uniform and met Ma at the entrance to the medical bay. He shared a look with Max, wrapped an arm around Jenks without a word, and headed down the corridor with her tucked against his side.

"Lieutenant?" Jenks whispered as they crossed into their quarters.

"Yes?"

"Can I melt down now?"

"Give me a moment, Petty Officer." Max scrubbed her hands over her face and then turned around. "There are some ground rules here, okay? No breaking things, no hurting anyone, and if I say it's back on I expect you to stop right then."

Jenks nodded. "Yes, Lieutenant. I understand, Lieutenant."

"Okay." Max smiled. "You have my permission to melt down, Jenks."

Jenks sagged into the nearby chair and Max shared a look with Ma when she didn't say anything at all for several long moments.

"What do you need?" Max asked softly, going to a knee next to Jenks.

"I don't know." The words were hesitant and it broke Max's heart to hear that kind of uncertainty in someone like Jenks. "I don't know what to do, Max." Her voice cracked. "His arm. His sword arm! What are we going—"

Max swore through gritted teeth. "Jenks, I'm sorry. I told my father not to—"

"He didn't say a word. I've got eyes in my fucking head, Max. I saw his arm. You don't do that kind of wrap job unless there's a very good reason. What's wrong with it?"

Max told her, linking her fingers through Jenks's when the woman gasped, and tears started sliding down her face.

"I can't make that choice for him. I won't."

"I know. That's why I told my father it could wait until Nika woke up. His life isn't in danger from it and if things take a turn for the worse, my father will do what needs to be done and we'll deal with it from there." She grabbed Jenks by the back of the neck and pulled her in, pressing their foreheads together. "I want you to get some sleep, okay?"

"Okay. Thanks, LT, for everything. I appreciate it." Jenks stood when Max released her, accepted a hug from Ma, and then wandered into the head without comment. She emerged a few minutes later and crawled into her bed, rolling toward the wall.

Max exchanged a look with Ma and tipped her head at the door. He nodded, following her into the other room. "Is she going to be okay?" she asked.

"I think so," he replied, reaching out and squeezing her by the shoulder. "You did good today, Max. I'm proud of you."

The tears welled and next thing Max knew she was sobbing against his chest. Ma held her, big arms wrapped around her shaking shoulders as he murmured nonsensical words of comfort in her ear.

"Better?"

Max straightened and wiped the tears from her face. "Thank you."

"Of course."

"My father didn't speak to you at all, did he? Beyond that bullshit formality."

Ma smiled. "Don't worry about Josiah, Max. He and I will sort this out. It's not your burden to carry. You concentrate on Jenks and Nika."

"I want to find the bastards who did this, Ma. I'm going to make them pay." Grief spent, Max turned her attention to the fury in her chest. Someone had hurt her friends, her new family, and damned if she would let them get away with it. "When we get to Earth I'm going to go talk to my sister. I think she knows more than she's telling me."

The question Jenks had asked just before Max delivered the news slipped back into her head. Why had the freighter been carrying LifeEx from Trappist *to* Earth? A black market of stolen serum made a hell of a lot of sense, but to take it to the manufacture point—

"Oh god."

"What?"

"Rosa said TPK thought there was a lab in the warehouse." She pressed her hand to her mouth, watching Ma's expression as the implication sank in. "Ma, what if someone is duping the LifeEx? I have to call—" She cut herself off, shoving the impulse away. "If I call Ria about this we'll be back at square one."

Ma shook his head. "You know she'll do the same thing she did when she found out about the maishkin. What do you want to do?"

Admiral Hoboins's warning about what side she was on wasn't necessary, but Max could hear it in her head anyway as she replied. "There's got to be someone back on Jupiter who could analyze the serum we found on the freighter. We don't have a sample of the real LifeEx to compare it to, but I'd be able to look at the major compounds at the very least and spot a difference."

"You sure?" Ma held his hands up when Max glared. "Just checking, kiddo." He cued up the com. "Let's talk to Sapphi, I think she can point us to where we need to be."

Max forced herself back into the composure that had fled when this whole thing started and hitched a hip up onto the desk as Ma sat in the chair and put the com through to Jupiter Station.

"How's Nika? How's Jenks?" Sapphi asked. "Tamago, go get Rosa."

"Jenks is sleeping, she's all right, though." Max tried for a reassuring smile. "Nika is alive. My father's overseeing his care. He's in good hands."

"That's a lot unspoken, Max," Rosa said as she appeared in the frame.

"I know, I'm sorry. We did get to see him. He's not conscious, though." Max couldn't make the words "he's going to lose his sword arm" come out of her mouth.

"It's not good, Rosa," Ma said. "We'll talk about it when he's awake. Right now we need you to do something for us."

"Anything."

"Did you get a sample of that LifeEx off the freighter? And has LifeEx Industries been notified yet?"

The trio looked at each other. "I advised Admiral Hoboins that it would be in the best interests of our case to hold it for a few days. He's in agreement. I certainly didn't order Sapphi to take a sample of a highly controlled and protected substance."

"That's too bad," Ma said, and Max was impressed by the

straight face he kept. "We thought there might be a possibility it's not real, but the only way to check would be to run a sample and let Max here take a look."

"You think the LifeEx isn't real?" Rosa tapped a finger on her lips. "That is too bad, isn't it? Max, couldn't you make a call?"

"I don't think it would be helpful, Commander. You know what happened last time."

"Fair enough." Now Rosa smiled. "Well, why don't we see what we can do around here. You all focus on Nika. We'll talk to you when we get to Earth. We won't be far behind you."

Max laughed and rubbed at the back of her neck when Ma disconnected the com. "That's the most cloak-and-dagger conversation I've had in my life."

"Never a good idea to plan a criminal endeavor on a live com. You never know who's listening."

"I wouldn't know. I've never planned one."

He grinned at her. "Now you have. Welcome to the NeoG."

"Better than letting my sister steal everything out from under us," Max replied. "I know that all this is connected, Ma. I just have to figure out how and what they want." She glanced toward the bedroom. "Is Jenks going to be okay?"

"Nika will be, so will she." Ma nodded. "She'll sleep the shock off and be focused again in the morning. You really did a good job with her, Max. I don't think any of the rest of us could have made this go quite as smoothly."

"You all would have figured it out." Max smiled and rolled a shoulder in discomfort.

"Take the praise," he replied. "I know you're not used to it, but you deserve it. I'm going to see if I can't get in touch with Stephan again. If we want to know what these people are up to he's the one who can help with that. We need to get ahead of them before someone gets killed."

Max swallowed and nodded. "I'm going to change and go to the gym. I'll be back in an hour."

"Hey, Max?" She stopped and turned when Ma called after her. "Watch yourself."

She nodded once. The cold reality that they couldn't be quite sure of who to trust even here on a Navy ship settled into her bones and stayed with her like a nightmare that she couldn't quite shake.

Rosa sat back and rubbed both hands over her face. Nika wasn't part of her team anymore, but that was like saying that just because she was away from Angela they weren't family. "I should have been there," she murmured. "Should have done something more about this."

"There wasn't anything you could do, you know."

Rosa dropped her hands and looked at Sapphi. "You think? I didn't take it to Hoboins the first time Max and Jenks brought me the information they had."

"You didn't tell them to stop looking, either. Besides, we all knew there wasn't enough for a report." The ensign was watching her, a sad smile on her face. "LT did good there, huh?"

"She did."

"And even Jenks respects her. It just took her a while to warm up. I'm glad she's here. Though I feel like we sent Nik off to get hurt."

"I know, but didn't you just get done saying there wasn't anything we could have done to stop it?"

"Fair enough." Sapphi's sweet face hardened into something hungry. "We couldn't stop it, but we can sure as hell finish it. What are we going to do about this?"

"Well, you're certainly not going to get working on that sample of LifeEx I know you didn't take."

Sapphi grinned. "I'll also not be asking around to my contacts for any news."

Rosa rolled her eyes. "We're not on the com, Sapphi."

"Hey, you started it, and someone is always listening."

"I'm going to go talk with Admiral Hoboins and get clearance to take the ship back to Earth to pick up our crew." Rosa pushed to her feet. "Tamago, get started on laying everything out. I want us to go over every piece of information we have on the system jumper, the dead, and what we know so far. It'll give us a place to start from when we get to Earth."

Her console buzzed and Rosa crossed the room to answer it. "Martín here."

"Call for you, Commander. Commander Yevchenko."

"Put him through."

"Rosa." Stephan's face appeared on the screen. He looked tired, with bluish-purple circles under his eyes, and his hair was in disarray. "Sorry I didn't call earlier—we've been trying to facilitate things between here and Trappist-1e since the explosion."

"It's all right. We'd already heard about it."

"I know. Heard about your freighter collar, too. Good work there. Just got off the com with Master Chief Ma; he wouldn't tell me the details beyond the fact that you found something interesting. We're going to meet them as soon as they dock. Nika will have a full escort and detail to the hospital. If whoever is doing this wants to try again, they're going to have to come through all of us."

"I appreciate that." Rosa rubbed at her chest, blinking back the tears with a smile. "Do you have any leads?"

"Nothing yet, which I don't have to tell you pisses me the hell off." Stephan's jaw muscle tightened for a moment as he stared off-camera. "We're working on it, though. Admiral Chen has given me permission to do whatever it takes to find out what's going on."

"We're about to go over what we have here and then *Zuma's Ghost* will be headed for Earth. I'll message you as soon as we have something."

"I've got new encryption for you. Only you, me, and the Admiral will have it."

Rosa raised an eyebrow and Stephan answered it with a tight smile. "You think it's that bad?"

"I don't know what to think right now except that someone has managed to kill people on board a naval vessel and attempt to kill two Neos by getting into facilities that should have been secure. What I do know is I'm done. No one else is getting hurt, not on my watch."

Rosa recognized the venom in Stephan's voice because it was the same anger rolling around in her own head. "Not on my watch," she echoed. "I'll talk to you when we have something or when we're under way, Stephan."

"Sounds good. I'll see you soon."

MAX SAT BY NIKA'S SIDE, THE HUM OF THE MACHINES A COUN-terpoint to the book she was attempting to read out loud to his still form. She hadn't questioned the fact that her father had put her on the list of approved visitors. It was better not to and just take the blessing.

"My favorite line from that is the one about standing in the waves, feeling them try to steal the very ground from beneath your feet. I would not have pegged you for a fan of Alice Schuman, Max Carmichael."

"I'm a woman of many mysteries." She smiled, reaching for Nika's left hand and squeezing it gently. His fingers tangled with hers, held. "I read this a lot growing up. Alice's poetry is a comfort."

"This is a new dream," he murmured, and her heart ached.

Why are you dreaming of me?

"Not a dream." She watched the confusion flicker through his blue eyes.

"Why are you here? Where is here?"

"It's all right, you're on the CHNS *Hamilton Bane*. Do you remember what happened?"

"No." He tried to move, and the frustrated growl when he realized he couldn't was surprising.

Max slid from the stool, setting aside her tablet and touching Nika's face, drawing his attention back to her. "You were in an explosion. You were hurt and need to lie still. Jenks and Ma and I are here."

"How bad?"

"I'll get my fath—your doctor." She started to pull away, stopped when he tightened his grip.

"I need you to tell me. Please."

Max dragged in a breath and leaned against the edge of the bed. "Your right arm is badly damaged. They don't think they can fix it." She knew everything else was secondary to that, so she left the list of his other injuries unsaid.

His hand flexed around hers. "It's still attached? What were they waiting for?"

"You to wake up so you could make a decision. I told your doctor that Jenks wouldn't want to make that call and since you weren't in any danger from it at the moment they could wait."

"I can't feel it," he said.

"They shot you up with a nerve blocker," she replied. "But your ulnar nerve was severed at your elbow when your arm was crushed." It was harder than she thought to get the words out. She watched it filter through his eyes, striking with all the precision of a tactical plasma gun.

"How's Jenks?" The question surprised her and Max blinked at him when a smile curved Nika's mouth.

"She's all right. We managed."

"There's a wealth of meaning in those words, but I'm going to go with the hope that she's not in jail." He turned his head slightly, pressing his lips against her palm, and Max's stomach flopped. "You should probably go get the doctor and Jenks. I don't know if they can take this arm off now, but—"

"Nika."

"No," he said, squeezing her fingers once more before letting her go. "It's coming off, there's no point in fighting it. Only question is when it happens, and I at least get to make that choice."

"Okay. I'll go find the doctor and be back."

"YOU'RE SURE ABOUT THIS?" JENKS HAD MANAGED TO KEEP the tears at bay, but she couldn't stop the quaver in her voice and she knew her brother heard it.

"What's my option, Jenks? A useless arm?" Nika shook his head and smiled. "It's better to get it over with and move forward. Right, Doc?"

The admiral nodded. "I could give you percentages and chances of recovery both with and without your arm, Commander, but it seems like you understand the decision you're making."

"I do." He glanced at Jenks when she couldn't stop her hand from tightening around his.

Admiral Carmichael nodded. "I'll get the surgical team prepped. We should finish up the surgery just about the time we get to Earth."

Jenks leaned down to kiss Nika's cheek. "I love you."

He turned his head and kissed her. "Love you, too. Watch your back."

"Max has it. I trust her." She watched the surprise flicker in his eyes and smiled. "Look at me, growing up and shit."

"I'm proud of you." He squeezed her hand one last time. "You'll be there when I wake up?"

She swallowed at the words she'd always said to him in those early years together, when Nika had promised not to leave her alone. "Always." Jenks nodded to Admiral Carmichael and turned on a heel. Beneath her calm composure her thoughts were whirling, and they carried her through the changing room and back to the shared quarters. Max and Ma looked up when she came in the room, the silent question hanging in the air.

"They're going to amputate," she said. "Dr. Carmichael feels it will be a relatively easy surgery. They should be finished about the time we get to Earth."

"Rosa and the others are meeting us at Earth. Stephan will have a security detail for the ship to keep Nika safe, but you could stay here with him if you want," Max offered, but Jenks was shaking her head before she got halfway through the sentence.

"Just long enough for him to wake up. Then we go." She fisted her hands. "Someone's going to pay for this."

Max shared a look with Ma before she stepped into the other woman's way and slowed her pacing. "What do you think is going to happen here?"

"I'm going to put the hurt on someone."

Max muffled a sigh. "I don't think so, Jenks. You and I both know Nika wouldn't want you getting in trouble for his sake."

"You'll want to stay out of my way on this, Lieutenant." Jenks flexed her hands, the need to hit something a painful shard in her chest. "I don't want to hurt you, but I will."

Max smiled and reached in, catching her by the back of the neck before she could dance away. "You're my team, Jenks. I can't let you go off and get yourself killed, and make no mistake, whoever is behind this will try to kill you. They've tried once before. If you go off on your own now, there won't be anyone to watch your back."

You trust her, Jenks. It's okay. She won't let you down.

Jenks dropped the facade and Max followed her to the floor, holding her as she cried. "They tried to kill Nika, Max. I don't care about myself, but they tried to kill my brother."

"I know. For the record, I care about both of you. As far as I'm concerned you're all my teammates," Max murmured against Jenks's forehead. "And 'tried' is the operative word there. He's still alive, so are you, so are the rest of us. And I'll be goddamned if I'm going to sit here and wait for them to try again."

Jenks hiccupped. "I thought you said—"

"I said no going off on your own." She pulled back and cupped Jenks's face in her hands. "So dry your damn tears, Petty Officer, get on your feet, and let's go to Earth. We'll figure out who's decided they can wage war against the NeoG."

T-MINUS SIXTEEN WEEKS UNTIL
THE BOARDING GAMES

Max rubbed the heels of her hands into her tired eyes with a groan as the words in front of her blurred for the third time. The smell of coffee suddenly floated across the air and she dropped her hands, looking up to see Luis.

"You are a blessing," she said when he handed a steaming cup over. "And also, how does a guy as big as you move so quietly?"

"A lot of practice trying to be invisible as a kid so the other kids didn't start shit with me," he replied, settling into the chair next to her. "You've been at that for a few hours, I figured you could use a break."

"You're not wrong." Max sipped the coffee, grimaced, and shot Luis a sidelong glance when he chuckled.

"I probably should have told you to save your praise until after you tasted it."

"I'd forgotten how bad this is. How is the coffee on Jupiter so much better?"

"Hoboins is a coffee hound. Chen drinks tea." Luis shrugged and drank his own with relish. "I'm surprised you didn't pick up the tea habit as her aide."

"I've never cared for it." She lifted her cup. "I do wonder sometimes if this stuff is so vastly different from the coffee that existed before the Collapse."

"Jenks could tell you, probably." Luis grinned. "She's fascinated with that whole era."

"I have figured that out. Though I still don't know what she's talking about most of the time."

"No one does, beyond a few hundred history buffs and nerds in her online group." Luis took a drink of his own coffee. "I know there are a handful of places that have tried to cultivate original strains of coffee beans instead of the synthetically modded ones. I've never had the cash to give it a try."

"I'm not sure I'd want to develop a taste for something so hard to get. This is coffee." She grimaced again. "Horrible coffee, but still." She put her mug down and stretched. "So you don't share Jenks's interest in the Collapse?"

Luis shrugged a shoulder. "It's over and done, isn't it? We survived, and when I say 'we' I mean humanity and some of the species on Earth. But damned if we didn't do a good job trying to kill everyone and everything on this planet with our greed. As far as I'm concerned that's the lesson to take away; anything else is disaster porn." He smiled. "In Dai's defense, what she loves is the years prior to the Collapse, at the bright and shiny point when humanity was partying before the fall happened."

"I don't blame her for that." Max studied him for a moment before taking a deep breath. They'd been at HQ for almost a week and she'd started to get a handle on the people around her. "Feel free to tell me to piss off if this subject is way too personal, but are things okay with you two?"

His grin was bright. "With Dai it's sometimes hard to tell. I'm working on not rocking the boat, for obvious reasons."

"She cares about you, you know."

"I do, and for right now that's enough." Luis grinned again. "I'm a patient man, Max, and Altandai is something else." He sighed her full name, making Max smile.

"I'm not great at this whole relationship thing, but I know that look." She bumped her shoulder into his. "You're a good man, Luis Armstrong. For what it's worth I'm rooting for you."

"It means a lot, actually. So, what are you going over?"

"A very detailed report from Sapphi about the serum we found on the freighter. It's not LifeEx. I'm not a chemist, but it is impressively close." She'd asked Rosa to let her keep the information between her and Sapphi, trying to preserve as much of her family's intellectual property rights as she could.

"You think that's what they were making in the lab that blew?"

"I do." Max sipped at her coffee. "What I can't figure out is if the lab blew on purpose or accidentally, and why they were shipping it back to Earth."

"Why manufacture it on Trappist in the first place? Seems like a lot of work to get supplies out there."

"They'd have to." Max shook her head. "There're too many eyes on Earth. Trappist actually makes perfect sense. What I can't figure out is *how* they did it." She didn't elaborate, even though she felt Luis's amber gaze on her. The varieties of red algae her great-grandfather had hunted down and rescued from extinction in the tidal pools along the rocky coast of Ireland would go on to form the component maishkin in LifeEx. It was now a closely guarded crop with some of the tightest regulations in the CHN.

But she could see it right there in the makeup of the serum they'd found on *Bandit's Bane*. Or something very much like it. The dupe wasn't perfect.

"You are hard to read, Max, but you're not telling me something."

She laughed. "Family is messy."

"Tell me about it." He grinned. "I suspect yours is a little more so, circumstances being what they are."

"Maybe. They're—" Max broke off.

"You know how dangerous the risk of knockoffs is."

Ria had known.

"Max?"

Coffee sloshed in her cup as she set it down and got up to pace the room. She didn't know how she knew that. Couldn't even articulate it to herself, much less to Luis, who was watching her.

Knockoffs were always a concern for the family, but never a serious one. The control of the ingredients, the secrecy of the formula, all of it was there to safeguard against the possibility of a knockoff. But that had been Ria's first response when they'd talked all those weeks ago.

And she wasn't the least bit surprised when I told her we found traces of maishkin. She just wanted to know where *we found it . . .*

"Where's everyone else?" Max spun back around, her mind going a million miles an hour.

"Rosa and Jenks are at the hospital visiting Nika. I'm not sure where the others are, possibly with Stephan."

She grabbed him by the wrist, bumping her cup and spilling coffee on the counter in the process. "I'll call them on the way. Come on."

"Max, I am really good at my job, but I'm not a mind-reader."

"Right, sorry. We need to go see my sister." She pulled Luis from his chair. "We need a transport to LifeEx headquarters. I'll explain on the way, promise."

ROSA WATCHED THE WAY JENKS'S FINGERS CURLED AROUND Doge's collar and knew that bringing the robot along with them had been a good choice. As silly as some people thought it, the robot was good at grounding all of them when they needed it.

Which didn't stop the strange looks from the medical personnel as they strode down the hallway of General Kyo Hyo-Jin Hospital near the NeoG headquarters.

Those looks didn't concern her, though. What she was keen on was the fact that Jenks seemed to have settled in the last week, and all of Max's reports had confirmed the petty officer was doing as well as could be expected.

"Nika looked good, considering," Rosa said as they passed through the doors into the bright sunshine.

"He looked better than on the ship."

"His adrenaline and cortisol were elevated," Doge chimed in. "Though that's to be expected in the situation. He's also experiencing some phantom pain, but he was doing a good job hiding it from both of you."

Rosa's DD chip pinged and she answered the call from Max. "Lieutenant?"

"Oh good, that must mean you're out of the hospital. Is Jenks with you?"

"She is."

"Meet us at the hospital landing pad, we'll pick you up."

Rosa looked at Jenks, who was watching her expectantly. "Come on."

"What is it?"

"I have no idea, because Max is nearly as bad as you are about telling me what she's going to do before she does it." She grabbed Jenks by the arm and headed across the wide pavilion toward the flashing marker on her map.

"Did she apologize?"

Rosa chuckled and pulled Jenks into a hug as the military transport zoomed through the sky, settling down onto the landing pad several meters ahead of them. "She did not, and to be honest, I'm not sure if that's good news or bad." What she did know was that it was nice to hear Jenks making jokes again.

The ramp lowered and they went up it at a half jog, Max meeting them just inside the door. "They're in, Luis." Rosa spotted Armstrong in the pilot seat of the tiny transport and gave Jenks a little push toward the front of the plane.

Jenks didn't argue, which was also a good sign, and Max patted Doge on their way by.

"Commander," she greeted Rosa.

Rosa smiled when Jenks took Luis's offered hand and leaned in for a kiss. "I'm hoping you didn't steal this, Carmichael."

Max grinned and Luis laughed. "No, Commander, it's Intel's. I borrowed it—with permission," he said over his shoulder.

"We're going to talk to my sister. This seemed the fastest way to get from here to there." Max sat on one of the benches, strapping herself in as she answered. "Did you know that LifeEx bought the system jumper from Off-Earth almost as soon as the Navy turned it over?"

"I did not."

"It was a pretty quiet deal and I didn't even think about it, which was a failure on my part, so I didn't have the ship flagged and didn't follow up on it after like I should have. LifeEx also bought the other ship the Navy picked up last year. Again, very quiet sale, very little press about it."

"How did you find it?" Jenks was strapped into the copilot seat, helping Luis with the flight sequence, but she glanced over her shoulder at them when she asked the question.

"Buying records are public, though I'm probably going to get a call from my sister about it now." She pointed at her head. "Because accessing the files would have also flagged them for her attention."

"Are you going to answer her?"

"Nah." Max shrugged. "We're headed there anyway, it'll spoil the surprise."

"So that's the reason for this trip?" Rosa asked. "Just to ask your sister why LifeEx bought a pair of derelict jumpers?"

"No," Max said with a shake of her head. "It's to ask her why she didn't tell me that she knew about the dupe LifeEx when I talked to her about the autopsy report on those salvagers."

"She knew?" Rosa raised an eyebrow.

"She did. I don't have any proof beyond my gut, but she wasn't the least bit surprised when I asked her if Hobbs had worked for LifeEx. She just jumped straight to talking about how dangerous knockoffs could be for the company. I think she's known all along. Those system jumpers would have been the perfect smuggling vehicle for going from Trappist to Earth, off the radar and mostly unlooked for. The ship came from Trappist-1e, or so its computer said. You picked it up in the belt. They were headed *into* the system."

"We swept the ship," Jenks protested. "So did the Navy."

"I know. And maybe there wasn't any serum on *An Ordinary Star*. Maybe there was something else. Whatever they were moving was so important they did a really good job hiding it, but I think my sister not only knows what it was—she found it on the ship."

"How do we get one of the most powerful women in the universe to tell us what we want to know?" Rosa asked.

"I've got a plan," Max replied with a smile.

MAX WAS AWARE OF THE EYES ON HER AND THE OTHERS IN their NeoG uniforms as they walked through the front door of the main building of LifeEx Industries a little over three hours later. The company took up a large chunk of previously submerged real estate along the New Jersey shore. She had four voice messages from her sister, and fifteen texts, each one increasingly more annoyed.

"Whoa," Luis murmured, and Max muffled a grin.

"Yeah, it's pretty impressive." She squared her shoulders and marched across the sprawling foyer to the front desk. "I want to speak with Ria Carmichael," she said to the man sitting behind it.

"I'm sorry, Ms. Carmichael doesn't see random visitors. Do you have an appointment?" he replied without looking up from his screen.

Max tapped a finger on the screen. "Now."

The man lifted his head, and his eyes widened. "I'm so sorry, I didn't realize—I'll call your sister right away, Lieutenant. Please hang on a moment."

Max tucked her hands behind her back with a nod, resisting the urge to share the grin that she could see on Jenks out of the corner of her eye.

There wasn't any sound coming from the front desk but she could see the man's mouth moving, so he must have turned on the noise filters and she could only imagine the kind of chaos that was now going on up in the top offices of the building.

Finally the man looked up at her and smiled. "Ms. Carmichael's assistant will be down to get you. Your companions will need to stay—"

"They'll come with me." Max's tone brooked no argument. "This is Chief Petty Officer Luis Armstrong with NeoG Intel, and my teammates: Commander Rosa Martín and Petty Officer Altandai Khan. Give them passes."

The man paled, but moments later a pass was tagged to each person's DD chip. Max smiled, thanked him, and gestured for everyone to follow her over to the set of tasteful armchairs just off to the left of the front desk.

"I am super impressed," Jenks murmured out of the side of her mouth. "People don't get to see Maxine Carmichael very often, do they? I'll bet you could get us the best table at the swankest restaurant by snapping your fingers."

"You buying?" Max shot back with a grin.

"Maybe, once we get this all wrapped up." Jenks settled into a chair. "Or, you've got more money, Max, I think I'll let you do it."

Rosa chuckled but didn't sit down. She and Luis both crossed their arms over their chests and surveyed the room.

It was surprising how easy it was to fall into a rhythm here. There was none of the awkwardness she usually felt dealing with people whenever she went home.

Max was about to reply to Jenks, but the elevator nearby dinged and a woman stepped out with a ready smile.

"Lieutenant Carmichael, we've spoken on the com before but haven't met. I'm Suzanna Carol, your sister's assistant."

"It's nice to meet you, Suzanna. This is Commander Martín, Chief Petty Officer Armstrong, and Petty Officer Khan. I realize we've come with no notice, but I need to speak with Ria on a matter of some urgency."

"Yes, she understands. She is in the middle of a meeting, but it should be wrapping up here shortly. I'll take you upstairs in the meantime." Suzanna kept up a stream of easy chatter as they rode the elevator up to the top of the LifeEx building and then she led them down the hall and into Ria's office.

"Can I get you anything?"

"We're fine. Thank you, though."

"I'll be right outside if you change your mind. Ria should be about four minutes out."

"This office is bigger than my apartment," Luis murmured, and Jenks snorted with poorly suppressed laughter.

"You wouldn't trade it to have someone monitoring your schedule down to the minute," she whispered.

Max wandered to the window and Rosa joined her a moment later.

"Is this going to go well, or not?"

"Well—I think—whatever's going on has Ria just as shaken. I don't think it's something the company has done wrong."

"But you don't know for sure and we are standing in the office of one of the most powerful women in the Coalition."

"I feel like I should maybe be insulted at the insinuation that I'd hurt my baby sister, Commander," Ria's voice came from the doorway. "Though I might slap her upside the head for not answering my calls."

Jenks eyed the well-dressed woman who came through the door. She had a perfect smile on her face, the kind that was welcoming only as long as you did what she said when she said it. Someone used to being in charge.

That it was on a face very similar to Max's made her uneasy, because Jenks had never seen that kind of look on her lieutenant.

Rosa hadn't jumped at all at Ria Carmichael's words, but Max had, just a little.

"Commander Rosa Martín Rivas, Ms. Carmichael." Rosa stuck out her hand and Jenks watched Max's sister shake it firmly.

"It's a pleasure to meet you, Commander. I've heard great things. Max." Ria turned and held her arms out to Max. The hug she gave her sister was brief but warm, and it knocked some of the tension out of Jenks's shoulders.

"This is CPO Armstrong and PO Khan."

Jenks put a little more force into her handshake than was probably necessary and saw the slight wince Ria couldn't—or didn't try to—hide.

"It's a pleasure to meet you both," Ria said. "Also, I will never hear the end of it from my children if I don't get your signatures. They enjoyed your fights in the preliminaries very much."

"You were there?" Jenks watched Max's eyes widen in surprise.

Ria laughed. "Oh no, I couldn't get away, but they watched it on the screen at home." She sent Max a smile that was a curious mix of apology and amusement. "I have been hounded daily for tickets to the Games, which I think is at least partially your fault."

"The time off might do you some good," Max said. "You look tired, Ria."

"It's been busy as always around here." Ria's heels made no noise as she walked across the swank carpet and leaned against her desk. "Have a seat. I know you're not here just to talk about your niblings."

"We'd like to take a look at the system jumpers you bought from Off-Earth."

Jenks watched the reaction flutter across Ria's face before the shutters came down.

"I'm not sure I know what you're talking about."

Max snorted and crossed her arms over her chest. "Come on, Ria. Your first call to me was less than five minutes after I'd looked at the public sale records. LifeEx bought both system jumpers that were picked up by us and the Navy—why?"

"Max, I'm in charge of a multibillion-fed company here. Why would I know anything about some pre-wormhole ships?"

"Because you're in charge and nothing happens without your say-so. Talk to me, Ria, we need to know what's going on here."

"It's a company matter."

Jenks could practically hear Max's teeth grinding together and shared a quick look with Luis. She called up their chat.

JENKS: It's going to be tricky getting out of here if she decides we don't get to leave.

LUIS: Reasonably sure Max's sister won't try to kill us, whatever's going on.

JENKS: You've got more faith in rich folks than I do.

"For once, just once, I'd like you to think about something more than the company and this damn family," Max finally said. "People have died. My friends are being targeted. Why didn't you tell me about the LifeEx dupe?"

"I said I don't know what you're talking about," Ria replied, but Jenks had seen the flinch and exchanged a smile with Luis.

"God damn it, Ria!"

"Don't you shout at me, Max!"

The sisters were now nose to nose. Jenks slid out of her chair as Suzanna came back into the room.

"Enough, both of you." Rosa put up a hand. "Ms. Carmichael. While I can sympathize with your position on what you clearly feel is an internal matter, we're here pursuing a recognized investigation for the Near-Earth Orbital Guard."

"Ms. Carmichael, are you all right?"

"Everything's fine, Suzanna." Ria straightened her teal-blue jacket and waved a hand at her assistant, who left them alone. "You can't look at the ships. They've been destroyed. Broken down and sold for scrap."

"Because you found what you were looking for," Max said, voice cool. "Was the dupe in the pods? I know it wouldn't have been just lying out in plain sight or we'd have found it, but there must have been a hidden compartment retrofitted in there for smuggling."

"I don't have the answers you're looking for. LifeEx is the only life-extending serum available."

Jenks snorted and Ria's gaze flicked to her.

"Something to say, Petty Officer—Khan, was it?"

"You think your sister is stupid? Or that the rest of us are?" She crossed to Max's side.

"I hardly think you're the person to lecture me about family," Ria replied.

"Watch yourself, Ria." Max's warning had no heat but it rang through the air like a pair of swords crashing together.

"Thanks for the backup, Max," Ria said.

Max shrugged. "She's my teammate."

There was a beat and Jenks watched as Ria processed Max's simple declaration, almost feeling sorry for the woman. *You all had your shot,* she thought. *Max is ours now.*

"Let me tell you about family. My brother almost died in an explosion, Ms. Carmichael." Jenks may have wanted to put her fist into Ria's perfect nose, but she could play this game as well as the next person, and what Ria didn't realize was that she was completely outnumbered. "One caused by a lab on Trappist that was manufacturing a dupe of your serum. Someone tried to kill me, too. Someone could try to kill your sister."

"That's not the best part, though, Ria," Max said, her shoulder brushing Jenks's as she shifted.

"I don't have time for this." Ria threw her hands in the air and started for the door.

"I think you have time for this: We've got a freighter packed full of bags with the LifeEx logo on them. Only the serum inside? Isn't LifeEx." Max crossed her arms over her chest. "You want to lie to me again, or you want to tell me what in the hell is going on so we can help you?"

MAX KNEW RIA WAS GOING TO FOLD EVEN BEFORE HER SIS-ter's shoulders sagged. She hid her pleased smile as she took a step forward. Their plan had worked better than she'd hoped. This problem was bigger than Ria could handle on her own.

"You said people are dying. You're right." Ria swept a hand through the air and it filled with images of corpses.

"Fuck me," Max said.

"Watch your language," Ria reprimanded her, but it was a halfhearted attempt. "I shouldn't even be telling you this. It's a violation of company policy." Ria sighed. "But we need help, and you're right, someone appears to be taking this fight to the Near-Earth Orbital Guard as well. Whoever is behind this has been shipping small batches of the dupe to Earth using the system jumpers or short-range craft they bring in via wormhole, and then slipping the knockoff into normal distribution channels."

Max's stomach twisted at her sister's next words.

"They've managed to get the dupe into shipments of four separate batches of product over the last year."

"What is going on?" Max asked, and Jenks leaned in to study the photos. "What happened to these people?"

"The duplicate formula is incompatible with ours."

"Because it's not a true dupe," Max said. "It's close, but it's not LifeEx."

Ria dragged in a breath. "I'm going to pretend I didn't hear you say that, because I certainly don't need to know that you've looked at the breakdown on either of the serums."

"So what does 'incompatible' mean?" Jenks grinned at Ria's raised eyebrow and Max had to muffle a sigh. She knew Jenks was poking at her sister just because she could, and part of her didn't feel like stepping in to stop it.

"Our cells fail. It's what eventually kills us in the end, or rather, causes any of the myriad natural things that kill us. But it all starts in our cells. Impairments and failures. The DNA repair processes mutate. I don't think you need the scientific details to understand. We can't stop it, we're hardwired to die. LifeEx delays that cell response. Buys us some extra time. But it also filters out of our systems after a while—hence the need for a booster." She took a deep breath and met Max's eyes. "This dupe blocks the booster's effectiveness and, even worse, in one case out of twenty it causes *rapid* aging."

"You think they did this on purpose? It wasn't just a failure of the product?" Max could see the wheels turning in Jenks's head, but her own thoughts had gone in the same direction.

"The first jumper we snagged didn't have anything on it but traces," Ria replied. "But the one the NeoG picked up? It was coming to Earth and it was packed with product. We've been studying it for about five months now. The defect isn't a defect, it's intentional."

"They're trying to undermine LifeEx." Luis's murmur dropped into the air like a stone. "We'd be seeing a lot more deaths if they were pushing it wholesale, but they want it to look like LifeEx has the flaw."

Jenks cleared her throat and he blinked, looking away from the images with a grim smile.

"I ran a few drug cases with the PKs last year," he said. "This is how a few small-scale territory wars went down. One group slipped a few bad batches into their enemy's supply chain. People started dying. They stopped buying from regular suppliers, and the other gang was right there to offer new, 'clean' product. I suspect our mysterious adversaries are planning to do it on a much larger scale."

"That's what we're afraid of," Ria said. "We didn't even make the connection to LifeEx at first; the dead were too random. But when we did, we started looking for possible sources and the missing system jumpers would have been perfectly untraceable. We've backtracked from this family here. They're the most recent." She waved her hand again and a smiling trio appeared, then vanished to be replaced by a trio of bodies. "And found more than a dozen individuals who were possibly killed by the dupe."

"Who's in charge of the investigation here?" Max knew full

well what the answer was going to be and that she wasn't going to like it, but there was a hope that Jeanie Bosco, head of LifeEx security, somehow wasn't leading things.

"Bosco is," Ria replied, smiling at Max's aggravated sigh. "I know your history with her, Max, but she's the best in the business. I'll message her and tell her to contact you."

"Do that," Max replied with a nod. "We should get back to London."

Rosa took the cue and started for the doorway with the others after saying their goodbyes.

"I need the files on all these people, Ria," Max said, stopping just out of earshot of her team and gesturing at the images still hanging in the air. "No arguments. You should have come to us from the get-go. I know you have resources, but we have more. I can bring the full weight of the NeoG to bear on this, and possibly the CHN. If there's someone out there deliberately trying to bring this company down, we have to stop them. It will kill thousands, if not millions of people if LifeEx is compromised. We won't be able to travel in space without the protection. I need your assurance you'll cooperate with us, no matter what."

"Max—"

She lifted her hands and smiled at her sister's protest. "I'm not downplaying the seriousness of it as far as the family goes, just pointing out that there might be something worse coming down the pipe. If we stop these guys, then it not only protects the business, but—more important—saves lives."

Ria sighed. "Fair enough. Look, I'll be honest, I'm happy to have this off my plate. It's been a stress I didn't need. Which sounds cold, I know . . ."

"But you have a business to run." Max folded her sister into a hug, trying not to be disappointed that Ria would choose the business over lives. "I get it, but it does sound a little cold. Jenks almost died, and her brother lost his arm. Those people in those photos are real—they had hopes and dreams."

So do the ones who'll die early because their boosters don't work.

"I know," Ria whispered. "Just, tell me you'll find out who's doing this and take them apart?"

"I promise. I'd like Great-Granddad's journal, too. Not the original, a scan is fine, but I don't want the edited one."

"Why? You've never expressed an interest in the history before."

"Gut feeling." Max felt annoyance surge at Ria's disbelieving look. Her team banked their lives on that instinct. In her family's world it was just one more strange thing about Max that separated her from everyone else. "This feels personal. Maybe I can find something in the journal as to why."

There was a flicker of expression in her sister's dark eyes that was gone before Max could decipher it. "I'll send it right away."

"Good."

"We've had security on high alert since Bosco made the connection between the dead and the dupe. We're trying to figure out a way to test all the batches that went out to see if there are more." Ria shook her head. "We can't do a full recall. That would cause too much panic. I've got scientists working on a way to reverse the damage."

Max nodded. "I love you, Ria. Take care of yourself."

"I'll be fine. You watch your back."

"I've got people for that now," Max replied, hooking her thumb at the trio by the door.

Ria glanced at the doorway. "You trust them?"

"With my life. This was the best decision I've made in a long time."

"Good." Ria leaned in, pressing her cheek to Max's. "You tell them all, though, if you get hurt I'm sending a hit squad after them," she murmured.

"I don't think you want to give Jenks that kind of warning. You might end up down one hit squad." Max laughed, squeezing her sister once more before stepping away. "I'll keep you updated."

She caught up with the others and they rode in silence down to the ground floor. By the time they'd checked out and exited the building, Max had an email from her sister and a message from Bosco.

> Bosco, J: **Hey, kiddo, your sister said you were in town and working on the same thing I am. Care to chat?**

Max sighed and fired back a response.

> Carmichael, M: **Come to London this evening. NeoG HQ. 1800 hours. Otherwise I'll call you.**
>
> **Also, not a kid.**

"So, who's Bosco?" Jenks asked, and Max rolled her eyes.

"My sister's best friend. She's also now the head of, I don't even know what, some super-secret corporate espionage task force for LifeEx. We never got along all that well. Luis, message Stephan to get everyone else together. We'll grab dinner on the way back. I'm buying." She settled onto the bench next to Rosa, who'd fallen into an odd silence while they were at LifeEx, and strapped herself in.

"Will do," Luis replied, and the ship roared into the sky.

T-MINUS THIRTEEN WEEKS UNTIL
THE BOARDING GAMES

"We've got sixteen victims we've found so far who had DNA in the LifeEx system registrations scattered across the globe. None so far in the habitats. All of them basically died of old age, though none visibly looked any older. We're trying to quietly follow up on all those who didn't have the extreme reaction but may have trouble with a booster down the line.

"I also had three other bodies that seemed to fit the cause of death. We couldn't identify them until Lieutenant Carmichael suggested we look at the system jumper lists from the early trial runs in 2330. They matched." Jeanie Bosco pointed to the series of faces hanging in the air behind her.

Rosa and the others were scattered around a conference room at NeoG HQ, where they'd been for weeks now, trying to untangle the mystery of the LifeEx dupe. While Rosa was grateful for the chance to spend some time on God's green earth and see her family every night, she knew the rest of the team was getting restless. And some part of her was in agreement.

She wanted to wrap this up and get back out into the black.

Why did you give us the stars, God, if you didn't want us reaching for them?

"That doesn't include Sebastian Cane. So the total of original travelers headed for Trappist is four at the moment, and that's not even the weird part." Max picked up Bosco's narrative seamlessly. The pair bickered like cats and dogs, but seemed to be working together relatively well. Probably in part because Jenks had punched the older woman in the nose the first time she'd sneered "kiddo" in Max's direction and Luis had had to drag Jenks out of the room.

Rosa, however, had gotten in the security chief's face immediately after and told her that the next time she failed to refer to Max with the respect she was due as a lieutenant of the NeoG, she wouldn't let Luis step in and save her from Jenks. If she didn't handle it herself.

Bosco knew when she'd been beaten, but whatever apology had passed between her and Max had been made out of the earshot of the others. That was three weeks ago, and it seemed as though everyone was now working together.

"Four corpses mysteriously appearing on Earth isn't the weird part?" Jenks demanded.

"Cane died in the river. These three"—Max pointed at the three people on the left—"their bodies were found in an apartment in New York last month."

Rosa sat up in her chair as the images appeared. "That's not possible."

"They look like they've barely aged a decade," Luis said. "They should be closer to a hundred and thirty, right?"

"Right, if we assume they were either not frozen when they left Earth or thawed very shortly after takeoff. We don't have any way to know for sure." Bosco tapped the console and brought up a photo of a smiling couple and another of a young man. "This is Ostin Prech and Robin and Simon Holute, assigned to the system jumper *An Ordinary Star*. They headed for Trappist-1 on June 17, 2330." She tapped the console again. "Ostin was thirty-two. Robin was fifty-four. Simon fifty-seven."

There was a moment of silence. Jenks pointed at the screen. "LifeEx doesn't do that."

"It's not supposed to," Max agreed. "It slows the aging process, doesn't stop it. We still age, children grow up on a normal schedule, the serum kicks in when the cells start having trouble."

"The dupe slows the aging process at a rate that appears to be three times better than the current version of LifeEx. It also is a one-and-done," Bosco said. "No follow-ups, no additional treatments. I'd kind of appreciate if everyone in this room kept that information to themselves. We certainly don't want people seeking out this dupe, and that news is just the sort of thing that might make them."

"Of course," Rosa said for everyone, giving her team a stern look that made it clear they'd answer to her if they violated that agreement. They all nodded back. "Good. We're assuming they started taking the dupe some point shortly after 2330, right?" She got up to pace the room. "Which means that the drug was already in development."

"At least in early stages," Max agreed. "Though how?"

"The components of maishkin are a closely guarded secret," Bosco agreed. "Up until last year when we found the first signs of the dupe no one but family and a few loyal employees had even gotten a look at the compound." The woman shoved her messy black bangs out of her narrow face. "We questioned the employees as soon as we realized what was going on, followed them for months. Backtracked and triple-checked their security clearances. Nothing. Not a hint to indicate that one of them had passed it on to a buyer."

"And family?"

Rosa slid a sideways glance at Max and then returned her gaze to Bosco, who was grinning. "There were some objections initially," Bosco replied. "But I convinced your sister to let me do some digging off the record. Still nothing."

"There was a scandal involving a cousin of Max's a few years ago, wasn't there?" Rosa asked.

The flat stare directed her way froze the room into silence. Bosco blinked once, slowly, and then nodded. "Islen Carmichael is harmless—well, she'd object to that categorization—but she's not involved." The smile wasn't quite natural and Rosa raised an eyebrow.

"Something we need to know?"

"Islen runs a traveling clinic up and down the Congo most of the year. During the rainy season she camps on the south end of Lake Tumba and folks come to her. She's been there since before this started, and though her issues with the family have caused a great deal of tension, she wouldn't do anything to put people's lives at risk."

There was more there, but Rosa was sure Bosco would try to break her nose if she pushed any further, so she filed it away with a nod. She'd talk to Max about it and see what else they could dig up on this other, and it seemed slightly more, renegade member of the Carmichael family, who had some kind of history with the security chief.

Jenks blurted, "Is anyone else bothered by the fact that we have four missing travelers who just appeared out of the goddamned blue?" Rosa shot her a look about the language and the petty officer had the grace to wince. "Sorry, Commander," she said, but continued on. "Or is it just me? I said those ratios were off. Those system jumpers didn't vanish into the black."

"Someone deliberately rerouted them," Tamago said. Rosa looked at them across the room. They were frowning, which was never a good sign, but she picked up on the thread.

"Whoever it was is involved in—or in charge of—this operation," she said. "My assumption is that our mystery boss got their people on the system jumper lists leaving for Trappist, fully intending to make the journey and settle on one of the Trappist planets. And somehow they did that without getting tagged as actually arriving there."

"And once there, they began manufacturing the dupe."

Max rubbed her hands over her face with a groan. "Less regulation would definitely make it easier."

"They'd have to have figured out how to make it first," Bosco said.

"When the wormhole tech was developed, they took the chance to vanish. No oversight and no record of their existence." Ma whistled. "It's an easy way to disappear, but the question is—"

"Why?" Max finished.

"Why disappear?" Jenks echoed. "They could still have worked on the dupe even as registered citizens of the Trappist habitat. It wouldn't have prevented them from doing anything illegal."

"If they were wanted on Earth for something, it would stand to reason they didn't want to be registered," Tamago offered.

"However, some of them had to stay on record. It would be the only way for them to get supplies." Sapphi looked up from her spot in the corner. Rosa knew she'd been listening even as she searched through files on her DD. "At least one of the ships got picked up and taken to Trappist officially. They could have facilitated things from the inside."

"This is a long game," Luis said, and grim looks met his announcement. "Someone's been looking to disrupt or take over LifeEx production for over a hundred years."

"Who?" Rosa asked.

Bosco shook her head at the same time Max did. "I've been looking at way more recent suspects, not someone with a hundred-year-old grudge against the Carmichael family."

"So, weeks of digging on this and we still have nothing?" Jenks dropped her head to the table in front of her with an audible thump.

"Not necessarily," Stephan spoke up from in front of the window. He'd been standing with his back to them, staring out into the dark while Bosco and Max were summing things up. "We've got pieces that are starting to come together. We've got possible motives—namely bringing down the Carmichael hold on the production of LifeEx and/or disrupting the military's ability to travel out in the black."

"Or both," Luis muttered.

"We just don't know who's responsible." Max rubbed at the back of her neck.

"We'll find them," Stephan replied. "I think it's a good idea to call it quits for today, though. We've been working hard between this and keeping up your training for the Games." He glanced at Rosa. "Take the rest of the evening off?"

He was right. They'd dead-ended this for the moment until something else broke.

"Sounds good to me," Bosco agreed. "I'm going to take the company transport back to the Americas, check in with Ria, pack a new bag, say hi to my cats. I'll be back tomorrow afternoon?"

"That works, we'll call you if something comes up."

Bosco tossed a salute and strode out of the room, taking the tension with her.

"I really want to punch her again, Rosa," Jenks murmured, and Max laughed.

"That's a regular occurrence." Then she sighed. "She's a decent person, loyal to my sister. Just abrasive as can be."

"All right." Jenks stood, slapping her hands on the tabletop as she did. "I need a drink. Max is coming. Luis, you in?"

"I don't get a say?" Max asked.

"Wow, I got dropped to second place." The air woofed out of Luis when Jenks elbowed him in the stomach.

"Sapphi, Tamago?"

The pair shook their heads. "I think we're staying in. *Royale*'s premiering tonight and I want to see if it lives up to the hype," Tamago replied.

"My wife is inbound," Rosa said with a smile. "Gloria's staying with my mother for the next two days. Isobelle is with friends."

"I've got work to do," Stephan said.

"Ma?"

"One beer," he replied. "Then I'm coming back to sleep."

"Spoilsport." Jenks grinned at him and the others chuckled.

AND THAT WAS HOW MAX FOUND HERSELF PACKED INTO A corner booth in a dimly lit bar where Luis apparently knew half the patrons. She watched as he exchanged handshakes and hugs, kisses in a few cases, and then settled into the booth next to her.

"Do you do that with everyone?"

"Do what?"

"Somehow make them feel really at ease."

"I've got one of those faces." Luis chuckled. "It helps that I grew up here, dinky little apartment just around the corner. My mum worked in a synth-flower shop below. It was next door to the grocer's where my other mum worked. They met there."

"That's sweet."

"MM, that's Mom Monica, sold the grocer's about ten years ago. They still own part of the flower shop, though, and live in the apartment above it."

"He'll talk about his moms all night if you let him," Jenks said, setting the glasses on the tabletop and sliding into the booth next to Max, leaving the open space next to Luis for Ma. "One water for the lieutenant, one nasty synth-whiskey for Armstrong."

"Hey, no judging the drink choice."

"Your mom judges it all the time."

Max choked down the mouthful of water she'd just taken as Luis laughed. "I feel like I should maybe move seats."

"You're fine." Jenks put a hand on her arm as she took her beer from Ma with a grin.

"I'm telling them you said that," Luis replied.

"Do it, Gina thinks I'm hilarious."

"When did you start calling my mom Gina?"

It was Ma's turn to choke back a laugh. Max watched in amazement as the blush spread over Jenks's brown skin.

"I may have had lunch with her yesterday," she muttered into her beer. "We're not talking about this here."

"We should," Luis said. "You won't take a swing at me with Max in the middle of us. She won't let you."

"Depends on if I think it's justified." The words slipped out and Max clamped her mouth shut in shock, but Jenks laughed and the others joined her.

"You're not going to have any sympathy there," Ma said. "They've been thick as thieves since Max saved Jenks's ass."

"I never did thank you for that," Luis said.

"Don't bring the mood down." There wasn't any heat in Jenks's order.

Max settled into the booth, letting the conversation flow around her. The subject jumped from music to the Games to a heated discussion about the ending of a show Jenks and Luis had very different opinions on.

"That's my beer, I'm out." Ma pushed out of his seat and tapped a knuckle on the table.

"I should—" Max cut off when Jenks clamped a hand on her leg and sent her a pleading look. "Get some more water. Have a good night, Ma."

"Don't let these two cause any trouble." He smiled and headed for the door. Max slid out from the booth and made her way to the bar.

"Lieutenant." The bartender nodded at her.

"Just water, please." She passed over her glass and took the refill with a smile. "I really like your eyeliner."

He batted his lashes, revealing more of the gold-flecked glitter. "Thanks. I'm trying something new."

"It looks good. I can't seem to manage it."

"You have beautiful eyes, don't stress about it." He leaned on the bar, motioning her closer, and Max had a moment of panic that her compliment had somehow taken her into territory she was clueless about. "Ask Luis if he knows those three guys in the farthest corner from you. Reggie said they were asking about you all."

Max kept her smile in place. "I will, thanks for the tip."

"I take care of my Neos." He tapped his cheek. "Plant one there to keep up the facade, though it was lovely to chat with you. You can, of course, refuse, and my pout will be only partially for show."

But Max laughed and leaned in, giving him a dramatic kiss. She grabbed her water and headed back to the table.

Her return broke whatever staring contest was going on between Luis and Jenks, the former sliding out of his spot so she could get back into the booth.

"Luis, the bartender asked if you knew the men in the far corner from us. Jenks has a line of sight on them."

"Which bartender?"

"With the glitter eyeliner."

"Ah, Clair. He likes looking out for us." Luis smiled and reached up. "You've got glitter on your face."

"He was pretending to flirt so he could tell me about those guys."

Jenks chuckled. "Oh, honey, Clair doesn't pretend to flirt with anyone. He must like you."

"Oh. Shit."

"You're fine." Jenks waved off Max's panic before it could set in. "He doesn't expect anything in return, it's just his nature. But you flirted back, apparently, which is new for you." She looped an arm over Max's shoulders and squeezed. "You don't have to change unless you want to, Max. We like you just the way you are."

"Yeah, I don't know those guys," Luis said. "And I'd bet a few feds their public identities aren't real."

"Should we get out of here?" Max asked.

"No, not yet. Drink your water and tell me a story about your childhood," Jenks replied.

Max frowned, but she complied and launched into a story about the time she and her older sister Pax had ditched their classes to play hide-and-seek in the garden on board the Navy carrier their parents were stationed on.

Jenks lifted her beer and took a sip, eyes wandering toward the trio across the bar. They were all well built, wide shoulders and big arms hidden behind plain black jackets. Luis was right, the handshakes from their DD chips were pristine and the names as forgettable as any mediocre white man's.

She zeroed in on their mouths, waiting a beat for the conversation to fall into line in her brain.

"Gerard said to watch only, not to engage."

"It's definitely the one we pulled off of Shaw's DD before he died. She's been locked in the NeoG HQ since she's been here on Earth, or with someone. If we get her alone, we can probably take her."

"That seems like a bad idea—have you watched the video from the preliminaries?"

"Pfft. Cage matches aren't the same as real fights. She'd last two seconds."

"I'll let you go first."

Jenks snorted. "Keep talking, LT," she said when Max trailed off.

"You're not listening."

"I am and it looks less suspicious for me to be staring at these guys across the bar if you're talking."

"And why are you staring?" Max kept her eyes pinned on Jenks even though she desperately wanted to look in the same direction her teammate was.

"Did I mention I can read lips?"

"No, but your brother did—oh."

"Yeah." Jenks grinned and took another drink. "Now keep telling me about your awful childhood. It must have been rough to sleep in a bed every night."

"Jenks thinks she's cool because she's got street cred." Luis snorted. "We don't have the heart to tell her she's just a big nerd."

"So are you." Jenks stuck her tongue out at him. "Anyway, they're talking about how they think they can take me in a street fight." She grinned. "But they're apparently under orders not to engage us. Which makes me really want to do this."

Ignoring Luis's protest, she got up from their table and fake-staggered her way across the bar toward the trio.

With a wink at Clair, who sighed and crossed himself, Jenks grabbed a regular at the bar and kissed her. She was going to have to apologize to Tessa later for it, but it seemed the fastest way to start a fight.

"Hey!" Her date, predictably, objected and threw a punch at Jenks. It took all day to connect with her jaw, but she let it. She tripped to the side, overcorrecting and throwing herself at the table, catching the man nearest her with an elbow to his temple that laid him out immediately. Her other hand swept out, ostensibly to catch herself but somehow managing to upend all the glasses on the table instead.

The two remaining men jumped to their feet with cries of outrage.

"Hi, shit, sorry!" she slurred amid their exclamations. She could hear Luis and Max scrambling to intervene, but they were too far behind her.

"You—" One of the remaining men got to his feet, a wet stain from the spilled beer spreading over his shirt and pants.

Jenks ducked his punch, put her shoulder into his middle, and lifted him off his feet as she drove him into the wall. His breath rushed out in a wheeze and he slid to the floor when she dropped him.

Her final opponent was more wary. Jenks caught the chair he kicked in her direction without taking her eyes off him. Only when she spotted the gun in his shoulder holster did she pick the chair up and fling it back at him. He went down in a shower of broken wood.

The man she'd slammed into the wall was trying to get to his feet, hand groping for what she could only assume was an identical gun. She kicked him in the face, her boot making a satisfying crunching noise.

"Jenks," Luis said, grabbing her by the shoulders. She shook him off and bent to pull the gun from the man's holster.

"Guns." She tossed it Max's direction, pleased when the LT didn't bobble it. "Luis, call HQ. I'm sure Clair or someone has called the local constables, but I don't want these guys going to local. They'll just end up dead again, and I want a chance to have a conversation."

She stripped the others of their weapons and grabbed chair guy by the collar, lifting him onto his feet and pinning him to the wall with one hand. He blinked groggily at her.

"What the hell?"

"You know the important difference between a cage match and here?" she asked with a smile.

"What?"

"I generally like the people I fight with in the cage." She punched him in the stomach, dropping him and jumping back before he threw up all over her boots.

"IF I HAD KNOWN THAT LETTING YOU ALL GO FOR A DRINK would result in me having to cut my night with my wife short, I would have confined you to the base." Rosa rubbed at her face to block out Jenks's unrepentant grin.

"To be fair," Max said, "they were following us, and they were armed."

"And now we have them in custody," Jenks said, a bit too eager.

"*You* are not questioning them." Rosa pointed a finger at her. "At the moment all we have is your testimony that they were talking about you. Then we have a dozen witnesses who saw you start a fight."

"You did, technically." Max nodded and Jenks deflated some.

"Commander, they were following us. They were talking about abducting me—or trying to." Jenks snorted. "They've all clearly got fake IDs."

"At the moment that's all we can hold them on," Luis said as he came into the room. "That and the fact that Clair's got folks telling the investigators they started the fight with Jenks." He made a face. "That won't stand up if they push for surveillance footage, but I suspect they won't."

"Are we going to be able to leverage anything into information?"

Luis ran his tongue over his teeth as he considered Rosa's question. "No, we don't have enough. Stephan's going to let them go."

"*Excuse* me?"

He held his hands up at Jenks's protest. "Don't. This is my job, Dai, let me handle it."

Rosa watched in amazement as Jenks actually backed down, though she crossed her arms over her chest and glared in Luis's direction for a long moment. "Can I ask why at least?"

"So you can follow them." It was Max who answered, and Luis nodded.

"They're not going to talk, and as much as I hate to admit

it, we need to back off." He shook his head and Rosa's heart sank. "It's a different caliber from the crew running the system jumper. More professional. The longer we keep them here, the less chance we have of finding the person in charge. If the pattern follows, they'll just make an attempt to take these guys out—which could cost us lives and would certainly kill our only lead."

"If you let them go, then what?" Jenks asked.

"They go back to the nest and we follow. They've all got trackers on them that will likely be found, but I put an extra one on the first guy Jenks took out. They might miss it because it's off until I activate it."

Rosa shared a glance with Max, the younger woman nodding once before she looked back at Luis. "Tell Stephan to do it. How long do you think until we have something?"

Luis shrugged. "Depends on how long they decide to wait to report in. I can put a tail on them, they'd be expecting it anyway, so I'd say a day or two at the very least. Probably longer." He smiled. "Go on back to bed, Commander. We'll call you if there's anything else."

"You two get some sleep," she said. "We'll most likely head back to Jupiter tomorrow if Stephan thinks pulling back is the best way to go."

"We will." Max gave Jenks a little shove toward the door before she could protest again. "Good night, Rosa."

"It's morning already," Rosa grumbled, but she smiled at their retreating backs and headed out the other door toward her room. It was still dark in there, Angela asleep. Rosa stripped and slid back into bed, wrapping her arms around her wife and pressing a kiss to her back.

"Sorted?" Angela asked sleepily.

"For the moment." Rosa inhaled. "When are the kids scheduled for a LifeEx booster?"

"Not until next year for Isobelle, and Gloria has three more. Why?"

"What about you?"

"Couple of months." Angela was awake now and she rolled over, cupping Rosa's face in her hands. "What's going on?"

"I can't tell you." She felt the way her wife's fingers tensed on her face. "I know. Just do me a favor and check with me again before you go?"

"Okay." There was a wealth of trust in that word.

"Thank you. We've got a few hours and then I'll have to head back to Jupiter."

"Well, if we've only got a few hours . . ."

Rosa slid her hands over Angela's skin and found her mouth in the dark, sinking into the kiss with a sigh that contained a multitude of *I love you*'s.

"BACK TO WORK LIKE NOTHING HAPPENED." JENKS SLUMPED in her chair in their quarters on Jupiter Station with a grumble. "This makes no sense."

Max looked away from the journal entry she was reading and smiled. "Stephan and Luis know what they're doing. If this really is a plan a hundred years in the making, we're not going to solve it overnight. I know your solution is charging in and pummeling things into submission, but that's not going to work here."

"Why not?"

Max swallowed down the sigh that threatened and shut the file on her DD so she could focus on Jenks. "Tell me something. How did you get food when you were living on the streets?"

"Stole it." Jenks shrugged. "Or bought it with money I scrounged. Some guys hunted rats and bigger things. I couldn't do it." She reached down and patted Doge's head unconsciously.

"When you stole it, you didn't just walk in and take whatever and walk back out, yeah?"

Jenks frowned at her. "That's the fastest way to end up

with the PKs on your ass, Carmichael. You wouldn't last a day out on the streets. No, you pick a shop, watch, and wait for the busy times. Then you slip in when they're distracted. Even better if you can find someone to cause a scene."

Max gave Jenks a flat look, waiting patiently for the woman to realize what she'd just said. It took a minute, but Jenks wasn't impulsive by nature so much as by choice.

"Oh," she said. "I get it. We're watching and waiting."

"Precisely. We're letting Intel do their jobs while we do ours."

"You want to go spar?"

"No. I'm reading. Go find Locke and beat on him for a while."

Jenks heaved a dramatic sigh but got up and headed out of the quarters. Max chuckled. She knew Jenks understood what they were trying to do here and that at least some of her impatience was for show. But she was restless. They all were. Going back to Jupiter had been the best move, but it meant they'd left the investigation largely in the hands of Intel, and Max knew it was making them all feel out of the loop.

Max reopened the scan of her great-grandfather's journal that Ria had sent her. So much of Alexander's journals dealt with the post-Collapse world and his thoughts on the reconstruction efforts, which were well under way by the time he'd started writing with any regularity. She'd never read them all the way through, only the pieces that had been assigned in school.

She found the famous entry where he'd first come up with the idea of the life extender—which was etched onto the wall in the entrance of the LifeEx headquarters. The one that contained the oft-quoted line "We shall go into the stars and live forever."

Max flipped to the next page, one of the many that hadn't made it into the public scans that were available of her great-grandfather's thoughts.

Talked to G. He had thoughts about my plans. For once they
were good thoughts. He believes that with a few tweaks we could
have a workable model by the summer. I am doubtful, but since
I've confided in him anyway I should follow this through and see
where it goes.

"Who's G?" Max frowned and ran a search for the capital
letter, coming up with more than a thousand hits. She refined
the search, removing the first word of sentences unless it was
the single letter, and set her chip to compile the results by date.

Over eight hundred hits spread among close to five hundred entries.

With a muttered curse, Max got up and wandered over to
the coffee, pouring out the cold dregs and fixing a new pot. As
it brewed she started reading.

Two and a half hours later, Max had drunk more coffee
than was good for her and had a head swirling with a one-sided
tale of a mysterious friend who'd helped her great-grandfather
develop LifeEx and then tried to steal it from him.

It was a story she'd never heard so much as a whisper
about, not even from her family.

Max checked the time and then shot Ria a message.

Carmichael, M: **We need to talk, call me as soon as you can.**

Her tablet rang a few minutes later and Max got up to pace
the empty quarters with it in her hand. "Ria."

"Max, what's up?"

"Who's G? And why is this the first I'm hearing about a
friend of Great-Granddaddy's being involved in the development of the serum?"

"Thomas Gerard died in an accident before the serum was
released. And this is the first time you're hearing about it because it's not worth talking about."

But that wasn't true—at least, not anymore. The men in

the bar had been talking about reporting to a Gerard, and Max wasn't about to chalk it up to a strange coincidence. "But he was responsible for the formula, and then they had a falling-out? The journal entries around that period look like pieces are missing."

"Great-Granddaddy ripped parts out of his journal and destroyed them. No one knows what he was thinking during that time. The best I've been able to piece together is that Thomas wanted to go a different direction, one Alex didn't agree with." Ria lifted her hands. "I'm sorry, Max, I don't know what else to tell you."

"So it's a dead end?" Max rubbed at the bridge of her nose, wishing she trusted her sister more. "Did Thomas have any family? Someone who'd want to get back at us for what Alex did?"

"Alex didn't do anything, Max, except create a serum that allowed us all to travel into the stars and live longer, healthier lives. Thomas died. Alex owned the formula. Whatever input Thomas may have had into it, it belonged to Great-Granddaddy. I'm sorry, I wish I could help you more with it, but this line of thinking isn't going to take you anywhere. Bosco is currently running through all past employees with your Intel folks."

"Yeah, that's going to take a while," Max muttered. "All right, well thanks for clearing up that mystery at least."

"Hey, no problem. It's always good to check things off the list, right?" Ria smiled. "I've got to go, but I'll email you later."

Max nodded and disconnected with a sigh. "Damn it."

Ria wasn't telling her the truth, she knew that from the far-too-easy explanation her sister had ready about Thomas Gerard, but there wasn't anything Max could push her with to get a confession.

There's no way I can get my hands on the actual journal, especially if Ria's hiding something.

The question was: What was Ria trying to hide from her?

Nika—

You know that feeling you get when you're staring at something for so long that everything blurs together and becomes a big mess? I feel that way about this whole case. The journal idea ended up being a bust. I was able to confirm there was a man who helped Alex Carmichael develop the LifeEx serum in some capacity, but he died before anything became of it.

Or so my sister claims. I'm not sure I trust her, but I have no access to the physical copy of the journal, and even if I did I don't know if I'd find anything different from what I've seen here. It's so frustrating. All I do know is that the men in the bar who were watching us said they reported to a Gerard and the name can't be a coincidence.

We're going back out on regular patrol in the morning and part of me is glad for a return to routine. I know the Games are a big deal and we have a lot riding on our performance. The training has kicked up a notch and I don't mind it at all. But I also just want to be able to focus on the job.

How are you?

—M

Max—

I do know that feeling and I wish I had a good answer for you. The journal was worth checking out, even if nothing came of it. Though I agree the name match is odd. I know Stephan had some leads he's following up on, might be worth it to shoot him an email or give him a com and see if there's anything else you can take a look at.

I'm doing okay. This is both harder and easier than . . . well, I can't say I imagined it happening. That's always in the back of our minds, though, right? The fact that we could get injured or killed on the job. And yet, I never seriously considered it would be me because I spent all my time worrying about keeping Jenks safe.

It's been quiet since you left. I'm grateful Stephan and Luis visit as much as they do, though I know they have work of their own to focus on. I'm supposed to focus on getting better, whatever that means. This ankle is proving to be a bigger pain in the ass than my missing arm. I'm tired of not being able to walk.

Sorry, I probably should have waited until I was in a slightly better mood before I emailed you back. I hope you're well, take care of yourself out there.

—N

T-MINUS TEN WEEKS UNTIL THE BOARDING GAMES

"We go through this door, I'm going low left with Akane right behind me. Jenks and Max are sweeping to the right—low, high." D'Arcy pointed at them in turn, grinning at Jenks's noise of protest. "You're always low, Jenks, deal with it."

"Discrimination," she muttered. "We'll come around that corner, yeah? There's no cover."

"Right. You'll have to make some."

"I'm putting yogurt in your coffee tomorrow," Jenks said, and D'Arcy raised an eyebrow at her.

"The warning actually makes me nervous. We're going on three. Ready?"

"I've got an idea," Jenks said, and Max's half groan, half laugh echoed above her. "No seriously, you trust me?"

"Of course I do."

"Okay, we're ready."

The door hissed open and Jenks scrambled through, Max above her. "Stay." She scanned for a target, found one, and sprinted the short distance. The first man went down with a sword strike to the back and then Jenks hit the unsuspecting

Neo next to him hard enough to knock the air from his lungs. "Hey, Piper, how are you?"

"Gonna need my lungs realigned, Jenks, you asshole. What are you doing?" Petty Officer Piper demanded when she picked him up.

"Come on, LT. Got our cover." The presence of guns on ships was rare, a deadly decision that could cost everyone on board their lives, but it didn't mean that the Neos didn't need to train against them, and their occasional appearance in the Boarding Action was proof enough of that.

"I hate you so much," Piper said, jerking involuntarily as the shots from his teammates slammed into his suit. "Your PO is a menace, Carmichael."

Jenks felt Max reach past her shoulder to pat Piper. "I know, but she's our menace. Hold for a moment, Jenks."

Jenks stopped moving and Max fired off six shots in quick succession. The silence that followed was quickly filled with cursing.

"Time!" Rosa's voice came over the channel. "Nice shooting there, Carmichael."

"Didn't even leave any cleanup for us," D'Arcy said, laughter thick in his voice. "Jenks, did you use Piper as a human shield?"

Jenks set Piper down as the lights came up, holding on to him so he didn't fall over. "I dislike not having cover, D'Arcy. You know that."

There was more laughter as the members of *Orbital Jam* came out from their cover.

"Good shooting there," Captain Haltz said to Max as she stuck out a hand. "You're all going to kick some serious ass at the Games if you keep that up."

"Thanks, Captain."

MAX SAT DOWN NEXT TO JENKS, THE WARMTH OF THE BIO-recycler wrapping around her. "Brought you a beer."

"Thanks."

"Can we talk?"

"Sure."

"About Nika." Jenks's face was a blank slate and nerves made the words pour out of Max's mouth. "I'm not—it's not like that."

"Then what is it? I like you, Max, but you break his heart and I'll be legally obligated to put my fist in your face."

"I don't know what it is. I don't even know what I want it to be." Max shoved both hands in her hair, the miserable feeling sloshing in her stomach. "I just don't want it to interfere with our friendship. We are friends, right?"

Jenks chuckled, bumping her shoulder into Max's. "We are, LT. Whatever gods are out there help your poor soul." She sobered quickly and gave Max a serious look. "My brother is a good person and so are you. This world kinda sucks, all we've really got is each other. I can't tell you what to do here. I wouldn't. If you like him, that's all that matters."

"I like him, but I'm not good at this. I never have been. It helps to have a name for it and to know why, but it doesn't change the fact that I worry all the damn time over every word that comes out of my mouth." She waved her arms helplessly. "I like his brain." She sighed and put her face in her hands. "That sounds weird, doesn't it?"

"To me, yeah," Jenks said, and put her hand on Max's back. "But we come at this from two different directions. Butts, brains, whatever works, right? You really should be having this conversation with him, though, you know."

"I know." The words were a groan between her fingers. "I've been kinda busy."

"Yeah, hunting mysterious drug lords. Training for the Games. Whatever. I know excuses when I see them." Jenks snorted. "But look, everyone's fumbling their way around this damn thing. I am shit at relationships. They're too much work, too fucking dangerous. I'm a selfish bitch."

"You are not."

Jenks took a drink of her beer and stared at the surface of Jupiter swirling in the massive window. "You remember the prelims when I knocked out Pashol?"

"Yeah?"

"Right before that Luis told me he loved me."

Max sat up and blinked. "Wait, let me get this straight. Luis told you he loved you, so you punched out Commander Pashol?"

"I said I'm no good at this, Max."

"Yeah, me either."

They sat in silence for a long moment, Max finally reaching out and tapping a short nail on the bottle in Jenks's hand. "You asked me why I don't drink. It feels like a lifetime ago, but it wasn't all that long, was it?" She laughed, the sound bitter even to her ears.

"You don't have to tell me—"

"No, it's fine. Nothing all that explosive, really. My folks drank a lot when I was growing up, and they fought even more. All very carefully out of the public eye because—Carmichael." She waved her hands in the air, blinking back the tears. "God, I hate that it still gets to me. It's stupid, but I sometimes think I would have totally taken a life on the streets instead of what I had to deal with."

"Max." Jenks turned her head to stare at her. "Did they—"

"Nah." Max shook her head, surprised by the muscle ticking away in Jenks's arm as she gripped her beer. Warmth wrapped itself around her heart, easing the hurt, and she reached out to put her hand on Jenks's forearm. "They wouldn't have dared to hit us. I don't even think that's fair to say because I don't think it occurred to them to hit us. But they took their fucking fury out on each other and us with words and that still hurt.

"My mother had done her duty, and while there's at least some affection between them, I never doubted that my father married her because she was a Carmichael. He took her name without the slightest hesitation because he knew what it would give him. They don't love each other. The thought of a life like that makes me sick." She spread her hands. "So I don't drink. I spent enough of my childhood without any control over my life and I don't want to end up like them."

"Holy fuck, Max."

Max shrugged. "Eh, it wasn't a completely terrible childhood. Like you said, I got to sleep in a bed every night and had three squares a day."

"Naw, that was a dick thing to say. I'm sorry."

"Don't be. Sometimes I even got a snack."

"Let me apologize, for fuck's sake." Jenks cleared her throat when Max stared at her. "Yeah, my childhood sucked. But then I met *Babulya* and even though the time I got to spend with her was too short, I got Nika out of the deal. And I never once asked myself if they truly loved me for me, you know? So I'm sorry for giving you so much shit, LT, you didn't deserve it."

Max leaned her shoulder into Jenks's. "Thanks."

"Your family sucks."

"Tell me about it."

"Sooo." Jenks drew the word out. "I have a proposition for you, and I hope you know how painful this is for me to even suggest, but I promise I'll talk to Luis if you talk to my brother."

Max felt her chest constrict. "Is there a time limit on this?"

Jenks drained the last of her beer and then rolled the bottle between her palms. "Call it a week because I am a coward but if I dodge Luis's coms for much longer he's going to fly out here himself to corner me. I don't care what he says about being patient, no one is that patient."

Max was reasonably sure Luis was that patient, but she swallowed down her laughter. "Deal," she said, patting Jenks on the back as she stood. "I've got some paperwork to tackle anyway, maybe I'll see if Nika has a moment to talk."

"Overachiever."

Max laughed and waved a hand, heading for the exit. Anxiety took the place of her amusement as she stepped into the low-g tube and dropped toward the passage for the quarters.

"Hey, Max." Lieutenant Amalie Dubois from the *Impossible Star* waved at her, stepping back as Max grabbed for the bar. "We're headed to the gym for a game of no-g dodgeball, you wanna come?"

"I've got some work to catch up on, but thank you." It surprised her to realize she kind of wanted to go, and not just to put off the impending com with Nika. "Also, watch out for Hudson's sidearm throw. I had a welt the color of a nebula for a week when we played last."

Amalie laughed. "Duly noted. Have a good night, Max." She waved and jumped backward off into the tube.

Sapphi and Tamago were curled up on Sapphi's bunk when Max came into the quarters. "Hey, LT. We're just starting *Last Stand at the Houndstooth Saloon* if you want to watch."

"Thanks, but I'm going to use the com and then finish up some reports."

"Sure thing." Sapphi grinned and flipped her VR visor shut.

Max dug through the chest at the end of her bunk, the one she'd moved into after they'd returned from the preliminaries, and grabbed for her tablet. The office was empty and a check of the team calendar told her Ma was off to dinner with some friends and Rosa was practicing in the gym.

"All right, Max, just suck it up and send him a message." She tapped out the email and hit send before she could stop herself, and then dove headfirst into the mission briefings for the next week until her DD chip pinged with a message from Coms.

"Hey, Sully."

Sullivan smiled at her. "Hey, Max, got a call for you from Commander Vagin."

"Thanks."

"I'll put it through to your tablet."

"Shut up, you brat."

They grinned again and Max resisted the sudden urge to smooth her hair before Nika's image appeared on her tablet.

"Max, what's up?" He looked better. The pain that had been etched onto his face was gone and his hair had grown out some during his medical leave. He was dressed in a plain white T-shirt and an unzipped gray hoodie. She could see the pinned-up sleeve, despite how he'd angled his right side away from the camera. He'd started doing that, and she wondered if it was a conscious choice or not.

"How are you? You look good."

He smiled, a slow, knowing smile that made her feel at home. "I am good, or better, at least. Getting fitted for my prosthetic tomorrow. Stephan seems to think that once I get used to it the muscle memory for sword fighting will be easy to refresh." This time his smile was tighter and Max felt an ache for everything he'd lost.

"I'm sure he's right."

"Anyway. Your dad called me."

That she hadn't been expecting, and Max blinked at him for several seconds, trying to process both the words and the grin Nika was aiming at her. "Why?"

"To check up on me. You know most of that ship ride to Earth was a haze of pain meds, right? I wasn't all that focused on what was going on outside of my arm and you all. Was there a point where you were going to tell me my doctor was your father?"

Max looked at the ceiling instead of meeting Nika's curious gaze. "I figured you'd get the news sooner or later."

"To be honest, every time someone said 'Carmichael' I just thought of you." Nika shoved his left hand into his hair, peeking at her past his arm. "He—"

"If he said something about me, I don't want to hear it." Max squeezed her eyes shut until the threat of tears subsided, and when she opened them again, Nika was staring at her with a concerned frown pulling at his mouth.

"He didn't, Max, and—shit—" He blew out a breath. "I know he's your dad, but all this is fucking cold of him. You're an adult and damn good at your job, and he should at least be proud of you for that. Look, I had my own shit father. He drank himself to death when I was twelve, left my mother and me at the mercy of some pretty nasty individuals. I almost—sorry. I just wanted to tell you that I understand, at least a little of it. If my father were still alive I wouldn't want anything to do with him, either."

"Thank you."

"I'm sorry, Max. That's probably not why you wanted to talk." Nika tipped his head to the side and studied her. "So, what's up?"

She wanted this, Max realized. Wanted to see where this path in her new life would take her. She was done living scared. She'd walked away from the life her family wanted for her, but in some ways had still been living in that shadow. It was time to let go of all of it.

"I know I don't have a lot of experience with this." Her heart was hammering in her chest. "And I don't want to make something out of nothing, so it's easier to just ask you straight out. What are we?" She winced. But he smiled that smile again, rubbing at his chin with his hand.

"Ah. To be honest, I don't know, Max. What do you want us to be?"

"I don't know," she choked out, suddenly miserable. "Jenks said—"

"You've been talking to my sister? Max." Nika's laugh was half-amused, half-frustrated. "I love Jenks, but she is not the person to talk to about emotions. Half the time she doesn't know what she's feeling and the other half she's trying to convince herself that she's not feeling it. If you want to wait to have this conversation, I'm okay with that."

"No, it's not that. We were talking and the subject came up and she said I really should be talking to you about everything." Max rubbed at her face and attempted a smile. "Only, I don't know where to start?"

"How about with what you said to her?"

"I like your brain. Oh my god." Max buried her face in her hands. "I'm hanging up, right now, and going to space myself."

"Max, don't hang up." Nika was laughing so hard he could barely get the words out, but it was warm and delighted, smoothing away Max's embarrassment with an ease that stole her breath. "For what it's worth, I like your brain, too."

"I'm never going to live this down, am I?"

Nika's grin morphed into a smile that was much softer. "I'm hoping I'll get to tease you about it for a good many years, Max. Right now I'm good with us being friends. You don't have to push it into anything you're not comfortable with."

"What if I want to?"

"I'm totally okay with that, too."

"Oh." The flutters were back, but Max managed a smile through them. "Well, all right."

"We good?"

"I think so."

He rested his chin on his hand. "So, tell me what kind of trouble you all have been getting into since I talked to you last."

T-MINUS ONE WEEK UNTIL
THE BOARDING GAMES

"Welcome to the Games, *Zuma's Ghost,* you're cleared to proceed to dock ninety. A representative will meet you to take you to your quarters in the village."

"Thanks much, Games Control," Rosa replied, and clicked off the com. She leaned back in her seat as Ma brought the Interceptor around in a wide arc toward the flashing lights of their assigned dock. She spotted *Dread Treasure* coming in for their landing in the dock next to them.

The Boarding Games facility was a collection of buildings covering thirty square kilometers on the western edge of what was once the ruins of a major American city, but was now a sprawling and thriving community built almost exclusively around the annual event of the Games.

"Everyone on the bridge," Rosa announced over the team channel, and the scrambling of feet answered her. Sapphi and Tamago were wearing identical grins. Jenks was practically vibrating with excitement, while Max looked as though she was going to pass out. "Breathe," Rosa said with a smile.

"Trying to, Commander." Max winced when Jenks slapped her on the back.

"Everyone except for Max knows the ground rules, but we'll go over them anyway. For the next week I expect you all to eat regular meals. Easy on the drinking. Get your fucking sleep. You've got a week to get used to being on Earth, so take advantage of the downtime. We'll meet in the main gym for practice unless otherwise noted on your calendar." She put her hand out, palm up. "I want you all to know how proud of you I am, no matter what happens here. You're a great team, I couldn't ask for better."

Jenks slapped her hand down on Rosa's, the others piling on top. "Motherfucking NeoG is here to kick some ass."

Rosa laughed. "Too right, Jenks. I'll see you all later. Stay out of trouble."

The group scattered, leaving Rosa and Ma alone in the ship. Rosa watched Jenks grab Max by the hand as they left and suppressed a sigh of relief. They'd all jelled better than she could have hoped for. Whatever happened with these Games, she'd meant what she said. This Interceptor team was one of the best she'd built.

"You good?" Ma asked, patting her shoulder as he passed.

"Beyond the normal nerves?" She pulled him into an impulsive hug. "Yeah, I am."

"Good to hear."

"Permission to come aboard?" The high, clear voice of her younger daughter echoed through the ship and Ma laughed.

"Granted." Rosa slipped out of the embrace and came down the stairs to meet Gloria and scoop her up into a hug, but her daughter sidestepped her.

"Can I go to the bridge?"

Rosa blinked, recovered, and nodded her head toward the stairs. "Ma's up there, go on. Where's Isobelle?"

"Out front with Jenks and Max." Angela's reply, and her smile, were strained. "Gloria waited longer than I thought she would."

"It's fine." Rosa took her wife's outstretched hand and

pulled her against her. "Means I get to do this," she said, and dropped her mouth to Angela's, letting the taste of her wife smooth away the worry.

"I missed you," Angela whispered against her mouth before sinking into the kiss. "How long do you think we can get away with leaving Gloria on the bridge?"

Rosa pressed her forehead to Angela's for a moment before kissing her again. "Seems like she'd be fine there indefinitely, but I have to go check us in. Is she okay?" She felt her wife tense under her hands and frowned. "What is it?"

Angela forced a smile. "It's fine, don't worry about it."

"I'm surprised Mom didn't come with you."

Angela's smile faded. "She said she'd come up for the Games but didn't feel up to the whole thing."

Worry spiked and Rosa frowned again. "Is she okay?"

"She's fine."

Rosa knew that look and cupped her wife's face. "What is it?"

"I don't want to bother you with it. You've got enough on your plate."

"Ange, come on. I am capable of multitasking, you know." That sparked a small smile and Rosa pressed. "I'll worry more if you don't tell me, not to mention make up some awful scenario that involves you leaving me."

Angela laughed. "Never in a million years." She took a deep breath. "Okay, your mom is a little—'frustrated' is probably the best word—with Gloria. Or me, it's hard to tell at the moment." She worried at her lower lip, looking past Rosa as an array of emotions scrolled through her eyes.

Rosa kept her questions in her mouth. She'd learned over the years that Angela needed the space to find the right words. Her darling mechanical engineer wife, so serious and precise. So unwilling to give things over to emotion and faith.

Finally she said, "Gloria doesn't want to go to church anymore."

"Ah." Rosa breathed the word, surprised by the hurt blooming in her chest. She held it down with the firmest hand she could. *My faith is mine. It is not to push on anyone, not even my own daughter.*

"She's skipped church two weeks in a row now. The first time she claimed a stomachache, so obviously I let her stay home. But the second week I knew she was fine and just didn't want to go. Rosa, you know I have been as supportive of this as I can be, but—" Angela shoved her hands into her hair. "Your mother. It's worse than when Isobelle stopped going. She was already at our house the second weekend when Gloria said her stomach hurt and she didn't want to go."

Rosa sighed and rubbed a hand over her face. "I can guess how that went."

"Your mother tried to drag her out the door. Gloria had a meltdown, complete incoherent screaming, and I—" Angela's hands were shaking and Rosa spotted the tears in her eyes before she turned her back. "I lost my temper, love, and I am so sorry."

"Hey, don't do that." Rosa crossed to her, wrapping her arms around Angela from the back and pressing their cheeks together. "You have done so much work, Ange, so much parenting all alone while I've been gone. I've got your back on this."

"Are you still going to say that when you hear what I said?"

"Yes."

Angela laughed, the sound bitter and sharp. "Rosa, I told her Gloria didn't want to go to church anymore. That she doesn't want confirmation right now and she doesn't know what she believes. She accused me of poisoning our daughter against God, and—" Angela choked on the words and Rosa tightened her grip.

"I know my mother, I can guess. And she's wrong. Look at me." She turned her wife around, cupping her tearstained face. "Gloria's our daughter and we agreed, didn't we, that our children would get to make that decision and when they made it we would support it?"

The relief on Angela's face almost undid Rosa's own fractured composure. "We did, but—"

"No. We agreed. I'm not going back on that. She's old enough to make the decision. Gloria's life is hers—not ours, certainly not my mother's. I won't lie and say it doesn't sadden me a little that she doesn't want to be part of my faith, but it's my burden to carry. I'm not putting it on her."

"She's terrified you won't want to be her mother anymore."

"What?" Rosa gasped in shock, hands falling at her sides as Angela's whispered, broken words slammed into her and her daughter's sudden avoidance made sense. "Is that why she was so standoffish? Why would she—please tell me my mother didn't say that to her."

"Not in so many words, but it's what Gloria took away from the shouting match."

"How dare she!" Rosa spun, stalking for the console, a red haze of fury coating her vision and clogging the breath in her lungs.

"Rosa, no." Angela grabbed her by the arm, holding out her other hand. "I won't lie, part of me wants to listen to you tear into your mother. But I know you, you'll say something you'll regret later."

Rosa dragged in a breath and then another until the rage settled into a dull roar in the back of her head. She took a step toward Angela, burying her face against her wife's shoulder. "I hate it when you're right."

Angela chuckled. "I know. I love you. I'm sorry."

"It's not your fault. You've been living your truth. I would never begrudge you that. I couldn't."

"Everything okay?" Ma asked.

"Yeah," Rosa mumbled, reluctantly pulling away from Angela. She turned and spotted Gloria, hiding half behind Ma's leg, and the fear in her daughter's eyes cut her to the bone. Dropping to a knee, she held her arms out. "Gloria, you are my heart. Whatever you choose to believe in, I will love you forever."

Gloria rushed her, and Rosa wrapped her arms around her daughter. It was a struggle to stay with the pain and not let the anger at her mother's carelessness take over as her daughter's shoulders shook with sobs.

"Gramma hates me."

"Oh, my love." She smoothed Gloria's hair back and wiped away the tears. "Gramma doesn't hate you."

"She does. She hates me and Mommy and Iso and you're going to hate me too because God will hate me for not believing."

Rosa heard Ma's quiet intake of breath, followed by Angela's murmuring explanation. Then she pushed it aside to look Gloria in the eyes. "Do you remember the talk we had about how people sometimes say things that they don't mean when they're angry?"

Gloria's lip trembled. "Yes. I called you stupid, but I didn't mean it."

"Right, and I forgave you for it." Rosa smiled and pressed a kiss to Gloria's forehead. "I'll talk to Gramma, my love. But you listen to me: Your mom and I love you. We always have and we always will."

"Even if I don't go to church?"

"Even if you don't go to church," Rosa repeated, pulling her daughter into a hug and pressing her cheek to her hair. "What's the rule?"

"No cookies in my pillowcase."

Rosa blinked and Angela's laughter burst into the air. "That's the newest rule," she managed between fits of giggles. "Baby, I think Mama's looking for the big rule."

"Live your truth. Whatever it is."

Rosa squeezed her eyes shut at the tears and hugged Gloria tighter. "Live your truth, my love. Whatever it is."

MAX LOOKED AROUND THE ROOM THAT WOULD BE HOME FOR the next two weeks with a happy sigh. Their spacious apartment had four bedrooms, two baths, a massive dining and living room area, and a decent kitchen. Across the hall from them was a similar apartment where Rosa and her family would be staying. Ma and Nika would also be in that apartment, Ma's daughters renting a house on the other side of town with their spouses and children.

"Luis is here," Tamago said, sticking their head into Max's room. "Come watch Jenks pretend like she's not ecstatic to see him."

Max laughed and left her half-unpacked suitcase on her bed, following Tamago into the living room. Her amusement vanished, though, when she spotted Nika in a wheelchair.

"Oh, yeah, Nika's here, too," Tamago whispered.

"I may kill you," Max murmured at Tamago, who answered her with a delighted laugh.

Nika looked better than the last time she'd seen him, but she could see the strain of recovery in the new lines on his face. His color was back though and he was dressed in civilian clothes, which was a new sight, but it was his smile that dug itself right into the pit of her stomach and stayed there.

"After the Games anything is fair!" Tamago sang, kissing Nika on the cheek on their way by.

"Hey." Max waved a hand, trying not to notice how the room had suddenly emptied of everyone but her and Nika. "Wasn't expecting you to be out here so early."

"Hospital gave me a temporary pass, though Captain Merlo was extremely reluctant about it until I said you all needed me to be your good luck charm." He smiled and held a hand out to her. "Then Luis asked if I wanted to catch a ride with him. You up for a hug?"

"Yes." She crossed the room and took his hand. "It's really good to see you," she said, leaning in and hugging him with one arm. "I am trying very hard not to make this weird."

He chuckled. "You're doing fine."

"You've been here for all of a minute. Give me time."

The chuckle turned into a full laugh that Max couldn't help joining. "I'm stealing you for lunch, if that's okay?"

Max swallowed down her automatic thoughts of the unpacking she had to do or leaving her teammates or any of the dozen excuses her brain wanted to push into the air. "I would really like that," she said instead.

"Good." He released her with a smile and tipped his head at the door. "I know just the place."

Jenks and Luis had already disappeared into Jenks's bedroom, and after a quick round of goodbyes with Tamago and Sapphi, who assured her they were fine and headed out for food in a few minutes, Max found herself pushing Nika down the sidewalk in the late-fall sunshine. She hadn't missed the way he'd only held out his left hand to her instead of the prosthetic on the right and agonized for a moment before she asked the question.

"Feel free to tell me to not talk about it, but how's the new arm?"

"It's . . . strange," Nika replied, with a deep breath between the words. He held his prosthetic hand up, rubbing his thumb and fingers together before offering her a smile over his shoulder. "Doc says we'll do skin calibration once he's sure my body won't reject the hardware and that it'll feel less like—more like a part of me. Right now I can feel things with it but it's a bit like I've got the whole thing shoved in a sealed bag, if that makes any sense."

"It does." She had more questions but stowed them away.

324 K. B. WAGERS

She'd seen the flash of uncertainty on his face and didn't want to push. Something told her Nika would answer them regardless of his personal feelings, and she didn't want to cause him more pain. "So where are we going?"

"Just up the street." Nika pointed. "There's a great little shop that makes some of the best knishes I've had since my grandmother passed away."

Max followed the line of his finger, but what she saw wasn't the shop. It was the too-familiar face of her brother coming down the sidewalk toward them.

"We could duck—"

"He saw me already." Max pasted a smile on and, despite wanting to hang on to Nika for dear life, let go of his wheelchair and stepped up to his side.

Captain Alexander Scott Carmichael III, only son and second oldest of the Carmichael children, was a handful of centimeters taller than Max with a build that seemed slightly more put-together than her own awkward limbs.

Named for his great-grandfather and grandfather, he'd gotten their mother's grace and good looks. But he had their father's brain, and skin darker than any of his siblings'. As well as a sense of duty Max had been measured against her entire childhood.

My entire life, really.

Once she'd adored him, followed him everywhere she could. Her big brother. They'd had such grand plans for their lives.

And then he abandoned them. Abandoned her.

Oh god. I am not prepared for this.

"Maxine." Scott came to a stop, eyes flicking to Nika. "Commander Vagin. I heard about your injury. I'm sorry. I'll miss competing against you."

Nika smiled slowly. "You'll have your hands full with Rosa, Carmichael, but I'll see you again. You can count on it."

"I look forward to it." Scott dipped his head in acknowledgment. "Mind if I speak with my sister in private?"

Nika looked in her direction, the question clear in his blue eyes, and Max gave a smile she hoped was reassuring. "Can you go ahead? I won't be long."

"I'll just go over there." He pointed up the street. "Captain."

"Commander." Scott watched Nika wheel past him before returning his dark gaze to Max. "So, you two—"

"You have two minutes, Scott." She wasn't about to have that conversation with him of all people. "What do you want?"

"I—" He seemed stunned by her flat response and fumbled. She watched something flicker behind that oh-so-familiar Carmichael mask they'd all perfected. "Wanted to wish you good luck in the Games. I thought maybe we could talk after?"

"We're doing that right now. Thanks for the good luck, we don't need it." She crossed her arms over her chest and stared at him.

"That's impressively arrogant." Scott crossed his own arms, his mouth pulling into a thin line of disapproval that made him look amazingly like their mother.

"Well, that's what you're looking at." Max dropped her arms and shrugged. "I have spent the better part of my life not fitting into the Carmichael name. I've found a new family and I think everyone will be glad to see the back of me. You especially."

"How could you think—you're my sister, Maxine." Was that actual hurt in his eyes?

"Am I? Where were you, then?" she demanded, taking a step forward, and she was surprised when Scott retreated. "Were you there to defend me when Mom and Dad dumped me here on Earth without another word for wanting to join NeoG instead of the Navy?"

"They wh—"

Max brushed his words aside and continued. "Were you there for my graduations? Any of them? Any letters? Any calls?"

The tears threatened and people walking by were starting to pay the pair of them far too much attention. A woman with a long blond braid gave her a concerned look as she passed and Max forced a reassuring smile in her direction. The woman nodded and continued down the sidewalk.

Max cleared her throat, struggling to get her emotions back under control, and gripped her fingers together for a moment before releasing them. Scott seemed stricken, but she didn't have the time or the energy to do anything to smooth the concern off his face.

"I've known the people of my team for almost nine months," she said softly. "And in that time have gotten more understanding, more support, more love from them than I've had my entire life from all of you." She stepped around him and continued down the sidewalk. "We're not family, Scott. I'm not sure we ever really were."

"Max—"

"Time's up, Scott." She didn't look back.

"WHY ARE WE OUT HERE AGAIN?"

"Tradition," Jenks replied, slinging an arm around Max's waist and steering her toward the corner tables where D'Arcy and Ito Akane were already sitting. "This is the bar for the Games, and rules are you stake your seats the first day and no one messes with them."

"So, if you want the good seats you have to get here early," Sapphi said from Jenks's other side.

"Bingo." Jenks pointed at Sapphi with a grin. "Go get a seat. Tamago and I will get drinks after a spin through the dance floor."

The music was thumping, winding its way into her blood, and Jenks grabbed Tamago's hand, pulling them with her. She exchanged hugs and kisses about every four steps as she passed friends and old lovers. The stress and worry of the last few months melted away under the onslaught.

Jenks loved her job. Loved it with a ferocity that was rivaled only by the love she had for the few people she'd let into her heart. But the Games were always like coming home. This perfect blend of competition, family, and just enough rivalry to make it interesting.

These two weeks gave her life and she would enjoy every second of them.

She caught Tamago's eye and tipped her head to her left. The other PO nodded and they wove their way through the steadily growing crowd toward the bar that dominated one long wall of Drinking Games' lower level. There was a second bar upstairs, but Jenks rarely went up there unless she wanted to start a fight.

The tradition over seats went further than just teams staking out a spot. NeoG and the Air Force held court in the lower section near the dance floor. Army and Navy stared warily at each other over the bar that sectioned off the upper level. And the Marine teams floated from year to year, settling wherever they felt like.

Jenks spotted a few Marines, and exchanged a wave across the crowded floor before she boosted herself up on the bar. "Casper!"

The bartender and owner of Drinking Games broke into a wide smile that lifted the pair of silver rings in his right eyebrow and made his severe face a little less murderous. "Leeroy Jenkins!"

Jenks laughed and leaned forward so he could kiss her. "The one and only. How's business?"

"About to go through the roof. You ready to kick some ass? I'm hearing rumors that Navy is looking to knock you off your throne."

"Never happen. Can I get a water, two beers, and whatever Tamago wants?"

"Hello, my darling," Casper said, holding out a hand that Tamago took and squeezed.

"How's your boys?"

"Amazing as always. Usual for you?"

Jenks grinned as Casper wiggled the bottle of ouzo he'd grabbed at Tamago. The man had a mind like a steel trap and it still impressed her he could remember their drinks from year to year.

"Beers for you and Sapphi—I got something new from a synth-brewer up in the Rockies I think you'll both like. Is the water for your new lieutenant?"

"Look who's been reading up on us," Jenks murmured.

Casper grinned again. "More like watching the news. You all have been familiar faces lately. How's Nika?"

"He's all right." Jenks smiled. "Yes to the lieutenant. Max doesn't drink."

"Duly noted. Send her to me if she gets tired of water and

I'll make her something nonalcoholic." At Jenks's second nod, Casper turned his attention to the drinks.

"Oh look, it's the NeoG," said a familiar voice from behind them.

"Could be worse," Jenks replied with a smile as she turned and leaned her elbows on the bar. "We could have been called the Space Force. How's your nose, Chad? Looks like it healed straight."

Sergeant Chad Chikowski stared down at her for a long moment before he broke into laughter and scooped her into a hug, lifting her off her feet. "Marry me, Jenks."

"You kidding? I know what you get paid." But Jenks gave him a smacking kiss as he set her back down and turned to the wide-eyed woman standing just behind the Air Force sergeant. "Petty Officer Altandai Khan. Everyone calls me Jenks."

"Senior Aero Tali Jaya." She wasn't much taller than Jenks, with a pretty, heart-shaped face and stunning green eyes. She stuck her hand out. "It's really great to meet you."

"Tali's a big fan," Chiko said, one arm slung over Tamago's shoulders.

"And you didn't tell her you knew me, did you? Just came over here looking like you're gonna start shit and give her a heart attack." Jenks elbowed him before reaching out to shake Tali's hand. "Nice to meet you, too. You competing or watching?"

"She's fighting," Chiko said. "You'll see her in the cage, hopefully."

"Oh, that's cruel." Jenks grinned and winked at Tali. "Let me buy you a drink then and tell you about the time I broke Chiko's nose."

"Cold, Jenks, that's so cold."

"You need me to buy your drink, too, princess?" she asked him with a grin, and dodged his answering swing.

"You owe me a drink for the nose."

"You all got your seats already?" she asked after passing

their orders to Casper and pressing her hand to the paypad he held out to her.

"Taken care of," Chiko replied.

She grabbed her beer and Max's water as the others picked up theirs and Tamago took Sapphi's beer along with their drink before all of them wound their way through the press of people back to the tables.

"Hey," she said when she spotted Luis, tipping her face up for a kiss without thinking. "I didn't think you were coming until later. Where's Nika?"

"He was tired and told me to go on without him, so I wrapped up early." Luis smiled and kissed her. "I'll get my own beer. Hey, Chiko."

"That's a new development," Chad said with a grin at Jenks. "We being public about our affections now?"

"Shut up." She dropped into her seat and passed Max her water. "Lieutenant Max Carmichael, I am sorry to introduce you, but it will happen one way or another. Sergeant Chad Chikowski: smartmouth, decent fighter, but overall pain in my ass. This, however, is Senior Aero Tali Jaya. She seems like a much better sort. I'm assuming she's just stuck with him because they're on the same team. Tali, have a seat."

"Nice to meet you, Max." Chad threw a salute and then clapped Luis on the shoulder. "I'll escort Armstrong to the bar so I can get all the good gossip."

Max surprised her and introduced Tali around to the table, so Jenks sat back and drank her beer, cataloging all the people who wandered into her line of sight. An hour passed, Tali and Chiko retreating to their own space as more NeoG fans and fellow Neos joined them in the corner. Max was deep in a serious-looking discussion with D'Arcy. Tamago was on the dance floor, enjoying themselves with eyes closed and body swaying.

Jenks was three beers in, leaning comfortably against

Luis's shoulder and moving her head to the music, when Sapphi came around the table to sit next to her.

"Navy is strangely absent tonight," Sapphi murmured in Jenks's ear. "Though I spotted Chau and Willington staking out tables when I went upstairs earlier."

"You went upstairs alone?"

"What do you think I am, a newbie? I did warn Max about that, by the way. Naw, D'Arcy went with me. Good thing about having a man with a mysterious rap sheet longer than I am tall on our team." Sapphi grinned. "Nobody came near us. We think Max is famous? They *all* know who he is."

"You haven't found out anything about who they got to replace Holden, have you?"

"Locked down tight," Sapphi confirmed with a nod. She made a little face. "There are rumors swirling like mad they've got some ringer who's going to beat your pants off."

"Ha!" Jenks took a drink of her beer. "Unlikely, but whatever. Let me know if you find something out."

"Oh, you know I will. They're messing with my projections and it is pissing me off. Hey, speaking of assholes." She raised her voice as a trio of naval personnel approached. "Chau, you figure out how to hack a level-one passcode yet?"

"Fuck you, Zika."

"Your mama maybe. You? Not in a million years, sweet cheeks."

Jenks reached for her beer, eyeing the trio over the top of the glass. "Rude to turn off your handshakes, Chau. I know Willington there." She pointed at the slender pilot on his left. "Who's your friend? My new toy?"

"Maybe," Chau replied, but there was something about his smirk that told Jenks they were just playing with her. Still, she was never one to underestimate an opponent, so she eyed the brawny ginger for a long moment before taking another drink.

"Well, if you're not going to be polite and introduce them, run along. You're ruining the music with your face."

Chau flipped her off and turned on his heel, the others following him across the dance floor.

"Wow, are we going to make it through the first night without a fight?" Luis said.

"Nope," Jenks said. She was up and out of her chair as Willington shoulder-checked Tamago with enough force to send the petty officer flying into the crowd. Jenks launched herself at him and tackled the spacer from behind, knocking him into a crowd of people on the other side of the dance floor.

Jenks got in two good punches before someone pulled her off, and the only reason she checked her punch was because there was a good chance it was Luis.

It was not.

The blow to her jaw was hard enough to ring her bell and sent her staggering back into the arms of an onlooker. "Kick his ass, Jenks!" they shouted, setting her upright and pushing her forward toward the unknown ginger. Before she could do much more than make eye contact with him, Max hit the guy like a ship coming out of a wormhole.

They crashed into another table, the occupants of that one able to scramble out of the way before they were tangled up in the fight.

Willington was still down, but Jenks spotted Chau and gestured. "Don't start none," she said with a grin just before Luis and Ito intervened.

"Break it up. Get your men and get out." Luis pointed at Willington as he groaned on the floor.

"They assaulted us!"

Jenks took a step forward, but Luis put a hand on her upper chest. Behind Chau she could see D'Arcy trying to wrangle Max as she spit curses at the unconscious man on the floor and unsuccessfully swallowed a laugh.

"Everyone saw Willington hit Tamago," Luis replied calmly.

"But if you really want to call the cops and go through the procedure, we can. I hear the brig here is pretty nice."

"Or we could take this outside," Jenks said. "Come on, big guy. You wanna fight me? I'll break you in half."

"You're going to pay for this, Jenks!" Chau swore even as the crowd started to close between them, ushering him and his companions away.

"Die mad about it!" Jenks shouted from over Luis's shoulder as he lifted her up and carried her back to the table. They were greeted by cheers when he set her down and Jenks laughed at the sigh only she could hear.

"You are a horrible influence, Dai," he murmured with a chuckle.

"I am the best sort of influence."

People were clustered around Max, laughing and slapping her on the back. Jenks caught her eye, smiled, and tapped her fist twice to her heart before holding it up. Max echoed the gesture with a grin.

Commander Martín/Rosa—

I regret to inform you that we lost the tail on the men from the bar. They vanished somewhere near Cairo despite our best efforts. It was a risk, but I don't know how else we could have held them without some kind of charge (and we all know the bar fight was wholly Jenks's fault).

However, we're having luck elsewhere. I've been informed that PeaceKeeper forces on Trappist-1e have located two more laboratories suspected of producing the LifeEx dupe. They're serving warrants and raiding the places as I write this.

Our forces have locked down on traffic into and out of Trappist. So far no more ships containing the dupe serum have been apprehended. I don't think we're entirely in the clear, but I think we're getting there.

V/R

—Commander Yevchenko/Stephan

Stephan—

Thanks for the update. Will pass it along.

—Rosa

T-MINUS THREE DAYS UNTIL
THE BOARDING GAMES

"Nervous?"

"A little," Max admitted, glancing over her shoulder at D'Arcy and then back at the growing crowd.

"Don't sweat it too much. The press will mostly focus on Jenks. She doesn't mind it."

As if to prove his words, the crowd suddenly erupted into cheers and Jenks lifted her arms into the air as she came through the door. There was a broad grin on her face and her spiked hair was done up in alternating stripes of blue and green. A rush of reporters surrounded her, shouting questions, and she shouted answers back, clearly enjoying herself.

"Lieutenant Carmichael!"

Max jerked as a reporter called her name.

"You don't have to talk to them, if you don't want to," D'Arcy murmured as the man headed their way. "I like to just glare until they go away."

"Somehow I don't think I'm imposing enough for that." Max pasted that practiced smile from her childhood onto her face instead.

Please don't let me say anything wrong.

"Lieutenant Carmichael, I'm Anatol Grace with Military Sports Network. This is your very first Boarding Games, how are you feeling?"

"We're ready to go, it should be a good competition."

"I'm sure you're familiar with the Orbital Guard's epic failure in last year's Games?"

D'Arcy stiffened at her side, but Max kept her smile in place. "I'm not sure I'd call coming in second place among such a difficult crop of competitors an 'epic failure,' Anatol, but yes, I'm aware of last year's performance."

"Your older brother, Scott, is on the CHNN's returning championship team. How do you feel about going up against him?"

Max froze, but thankfully D'Arcy came to her rescue, leaning forward with a smile.

"Max here is in the hand-to-hand competition, whereas her brother is a sword guy. So she'll likely see him in the Boarding Action, but other than that all she's got to worry about is Jenks over there."

"Lieutenant!"

Max looked to see Rosa waving at her and then glanced back at the newscaster. "Sorry, have to go." She turned and headed for Rosa, D'Arcy following beside her.

"Thanks."

"No problem, kiddo. You'll want to start prepping some answers about your competition, though. Those questions come hard and fast during the Games. Especially during the formal interviews, tomorrow. And even I can't get out of those."

"I'll be all right."

"I know." D'Arcy chuckled. "As long as I don't have to peel you off a reporter it's fine by me." He dodged her swing with a laugh and headed across the mats to where Locke sat.

Max blew out a breath. She'd done the prep with Sapphi already and been to all the meetings so far about their competitors, but apparently questions about her family were still going to throw her for a loop.

That's what she needed to get over and fast, because she could almost guarantee someone would ask her tomorrow.

The gymnasium where the bulk of the Games would take place was currently a riot of noise and people. Workers on the far end were putting the final cages together, while on the other end she spotted the blue-on-black uniforms of the Navy team congregated around one of the sword arenas.

"You holding up?" Jenks asked, tapping Max on the arm. "You've got that wide-eyed, 'what have I done' look on your face."

"Feeling it a bit," she admitted. "How do you do so well with all these reporters?"

"Practice, mostly?" Jenks replied with a shrug. "It's just part of the show. But I like being in the spotlight and I know you don't. Don't sweat it, LT. You can totally be the mysterious one if you want. Even in the formal interviews, just give the bare-minimum answers."

"Won't that make me—" Max saw the movement out of the corner of her eye and reacted on instinct alone, catching the blur rushing at Jenks with an arm across their chest. She stepped into the move, putting her hip into theirs and dropping them to the floor.

The silence was broken by laughter. First Jenks and then the person Max had just body-slammed.

"Holy shit, Jenks, did you hire a bodyguard?" They were laughing so hard they could barely get the words out.

"Sorry." Max felt her face heat and stepped back, hands up.

Jenks put a hand on her shoulder, still wheezing with laughter. "Candy's fine, Max. Well, they're a Marine, so that's a variable." She reached past Max and stuck out a hand with a grin. "Haven't you heard? People are trying to kill me."

"Trying and failing," Max corrected.

The slender person in front of her bounced from one foot to the other after Jenks pulled them into a hug and grinned. "We've been on the outer rim doing mining patrols for a month. The *Boondock Saints* were with us so we could practice, and they didn't bother sending us back until yesterday."

"Figures." Jenks shot Max a look. "Marines don't care much about the Games. Candy, this is my teammate Lieutenant Max Carmichael. Max, meet Corporal Flynn Candance."

"Nice to meet you, Lieutenant," Flynn said. They rubbed a hand over their shaved head, which was decorated with what Max thought were brightly colored pieces of candy. "Don't get us wrong. The Games are fun and all. We've just got better things to do out there."

Jenks punched them in the shoulder. "So you think. I know better. You're all playing pranks on each other and bitching about your lives."

"Hey, Jenks," Nika said, coming up on Max's right side. He was out of the wheelchair, but moving slowly with a pair of crutches under his arms. "Rosa wanted to see you."

Jenks nodded and took off across the gym floor.

Max saw Flynn's eyes snap wide at the sight of Nika and the emotions rolling across their face before they forced out a smile. "I was just about to ask Jenks how you were, man."

"Been better, been worse," Nika replied, holding out his left arm as Flynn stepped forward and folded him into a hug.

"It's utter bullshit, man," Max heard Flynn whisper before they kissed Nika on the cheek. "I'm glad you're alive, though."

"Me too." Nika scruffed Flynn's head before he stepped back.

"Lieutenant, it was nice to meet you. I'll see you in the cage, God help me."

Max smiled and waved, watching the corporal lope off before she met Nika's curious gaze. "I may have body-slammed them. Hush. They were running up on Jenks, I didn't know what to expect."

"Still twitchy about the other night?" Nika chuckled. "You are getting more like Jenks with every day that passes, which, I will not lie, is a terrifying prospect. Next thing I know I'm going to have to help Luis carry you two out of bar fights."

Max laughed. "I doubt it."

"You're probably right." His grin was delighted as he teased her. "If only because if we let you and Jenks loose in a bar again there's not going to be anyone standing."

"I'm never going to live that down, am I?"

"It's looking unlikely."

"WHAT'S UP?" JENKS ASKED ROSA.

"Finally got a roster sheet for the Navy team, and . . . over there." She pointed.

"Holy shit, would you look at that," Jenks murmured, tracking the massive man who'd appeared across the room.

"Lieutenant Parsikov, demolitions expert. That's your competition, Jenks." Rosa patted her on the back.

A slow grin spread across her face. "Oh, this is going to be fun. No wonder they've kept him a secret. They think they've got a ringer. Sapphi?"

"They must," Sapphi replied, "if all the effort they went to hiding him is any indication. I am already on it. Lieutenant Tivo Parsikov. Two years out of the Naval Academy, but only been in the SEALs for a year. Dominated the ring in the boxing circuit for the academy, though. There's video."

"Look at the range on him," Max murmured as she and Nika joined the group. "His legs are almost as long as I am tall."

"His hands are the size of your head, Jenks." Tamago's comment was a little breathless and Jenks snorted in amusement even though the sight of the man had her own heart racing a little.

"If I thought they'd let you within ten meters of him I'd say go break his heart, Tamago."

Tamago grinned. "I've got my ways past whatever blockade they try to put up. Might try it anyway."

Jenks chewed on her knuckle while watching the Navy team move across the floor. The excitement that always accompanied the Games had just ratcheted itself up a notch. There were some obvious challenges with this new Navy fighter—specifically, his reach and height meant she was going to have to move in close to land punches, and she was pretty sure she didn't want him grabbing her and choking her out with those hands of his.

JENKS: Hey, Luis. Can you pull anything you can find on a Lieutenant Tivo Parsikov? I'll owe you.

LUIS: Navy's fighter finally appeared?

JENKS: Yup. He's . . . large. *grins*

LUIS: *groans* Give me a little bit, I'll see what I can find out.

"Hey, Commander, feel like taking a walk?" She smiled at Rosa's curious look.

"Sure. Max, come with us."

"Where?"

Rosa pointed across the arena. "I've got a sudden burning desire to check out the sword rings. Hey, D'Arcy, you want to see the sword rings?"

"You know I do," he replied with a wicked grin.

"Rest of you stay here." Rosa started across the mats, Jenks catching up with a hop and a skipping step. "Do I need to remind you two that this isn't a bar?" Rosa asked, and Max groaned while Jenks chuckled.

"Naw, we're good." She kept the swagger in her walk as they rounded the sword ring and Rosa fell into a detailed discussion with D'Arcy about the specs.

Jenks pulled on Max's hand and the pair leaned on the ropes, both women staring across the space at the gathered Navy team until several of them, Parsikov included, turned to look.

"Damn," Jenks breathed. He *was* large. Not solid like Luis but more rangy with those long arms and legs. Shaggy black hair and a pair of blue-gray eyes that were surprisingly friendly. She watched as Chau said something and Parsikov responded, shaking his head and holding up a hand.

"And he's coming over," Max whispered as the man ducked through the ropes of the sword ring and crossed to them.

"Ladies," he said, dropping into a crouch in front of them and holding his hand out to Max first. "Tivo Parsikov. Lieutenant Carmichael, it's nice to meet you."

"Likewise," Max said, taking his hand.

"Jenks." Those storm-cloud eyes turned on her and she couldn't stop the grin that spread over her face.

"We're at 'Jenks' already?" she asked, taking the offered hand. Tamago had been right, it was the size of her damn head, but it was that smile on his face that was making her stomach do all sorts of interesting dance moves. "I haven't kicked your ass yet."

Tivo laughed, the sound booming out into the open air, and Jenks knew more than a few eyes were locked onto them. "I guess I'll be calling you Petty Officer Altandai Khan for a while, then."

"You think?"

"I've heard a lot about you."

"I should hope so—I'm a legend. Meanwhile, we've been left in the dark about you. It's a shame, isn't it, Max?"

"A tragedy, even." Max was grinning.

He still had a hold of Jenks's hand, and was running his

thumb over the backs of her knuckles. "Looking forward to this, Petty Officer Khan," he said, finally releasing her and pushing to his feet and walking away.

"Back at you, Lieutenant Parsikov," she replied, reluctantly pulling her gaze away from his ass so that she could blow a kiss in Chau's direction. The commander's grin faded, and Jenks had to suppress a laugh as she looped her arm through Max's, waved to Rosa and D'Arcy, and headed back across to their team.

"Holy shit, Max," she whispered when they were more than halfway across the floor. "I was expecting evil jerk guy, but instead—" She fanned herself.

"Even I could hear the sizzling between the two of you, but I want no part of it," Max replied.

"I'm still gonna kick his ass, though."

"Well, I should hope so."

Jenks heard D'Arcy laugh from behind them.

"GOOD EVENING, FOLKS! I'M PACE MCCLELLAN, AND HERE with me as always is Barnes Overton for TSN—The Sports Network. I hope you're all ready for the beginning of the hundred and first iteration of the Boarding Games! We're excited to be here. There are five amazing teams about to go head-to-head for the championship trophy and a year's worth of bragging rights. A lot of familiar faces, but also some newbies we are very curious to watch."

"I'm especially excited to see what Lieutenant Maxine Carmichael is going to bring to the arena, Pace. We had the opportunity to watch her compete in the preliminaries. Obviously Petty Officer Khan still rules the cage for the moment, but Carmichael is one to watch in the Boarding Action."

"Absolutely, Barnes. Many of you were with us last year when the NeoG team—composed of Interceptor squads *Zuma's Ghost* and *Honorable Intent*—suffered a devastating loss by only three points to the Navy team. I'm sure they're wanting to avenge that loss, but it'll be interesting to see if they can. Not only does *Zuma's Ghost* have a new player, but they lost their best swordsman."

"Too right, Pace. And a shout-out to Commander Nika Vagin, who was grievously injured in an attack on Trappist-1e a few months ago. We'll miss seeing him compete."

"I'm already hearing rumors that he's going to be back in the sword ring, Barnes. Something tells me we haven't seen the last of Vagin. *Zuma*'s not competing alone, though; they've got a new squad with them—*Dread Treasure*. In charge there is Commander D'Arcy Montaglione, and if this guy's background doesn't make the competition a little nervous, I don't know what will."

"What we do know, Pace, is that this is going to be a heck of a ride!"

BOARDING GAMES—DAY ONE

"Don't mess with it," Rosa said, batting Jenks's hand away from her uniform. "It's even."

"This is the worst part of the Games. Why do we have to dress up in these things?"

Rosa chuckled as she moved on to Tamago.

"Because it's as much for show as the rest of it," Max answered, and Rosa didn't have to turn around to know she'd also knocked Jenks's hand away from her collar.

"It itches."

"The more you fuss with it, the more it will itch."

In some fashion Rosa was glad for Jenks's annual "why do we have to wear these" gripe session. It gave Max something to do besides fret about the fact that they were about to walk out in front of hundreds of thousands of people in the arena itself and hundreds of millions watching all over the galaxy.

"We good?" Rosa asked D'Arcy, and he nodded, smiling when she reached out to adjust the row of medals on his left breast.

"This is going to be like going through a wormhole, isn't it? We'll blink and be on the other side."

"Yes," she said. "Enjoy it when and as you can. It passes as quick as spark to flame."

"Poetry from you?"

She smiled again, brushing an imaginary piece of lint from his shoulder. "Scripture, if you can believe it."

"I'd hug you, but we'll mess up our uniforms." He winked.

Rosa dragged in a breath, exhaling all at once and holding the emptiness for a moment before she inhaled again. "Thank you for being here, D'Arcy. There is no one else I would rather have at my back than you and your team," she murmured, and then turned to the others before he could reply. "Circle up, Neos."

They all circled around her and Rosa felt her heart shake for a moment when she met Ma's eyes. He reached out and put his hand on hers. "We go out into the black," he said.

"To protect the lost," Sapphi continued.

"And weary travelers far from home," Locke and Garcia said together and shared a grin.

"We go out into the black." D'Arcy's rumbling bass was in Rosa's ear as he reached past her, putting his other hand on her back.

"Without thought of return." Akane's clear soprano rang through the tunnel and Rosa knew the other teams were watching them.

"Because it is our duty to stand between." Tamago filled in the gap on Rosa's other side.

"Those who need us," Huang said.

"And all the things on silent wings." Murphy's eyes were shining with unshed tears.

"That come to steal their lives away." Jenks met Rosa's gaze and then Max put her hand on the top of the pile.

"We are the sentinels, always ready to defend the pale light that shines in the black."

"We are the NeoG," Rosa looked around, nodded once, and dropped her hand. "Let's go win this thing."

They lined up. Their hovering handler had thankfully been unwilling to interrupt, but now they escorted the NeoG team up the walkway. Rosa took another deep breath, shared a smile with D'Arcy, and headed out into the roar that filled the arena.

MAX SHOOK HER ARMS OUT AS SHE WALKED IN A CIRCLE. The excitement of the opening ceremonies yesterday was still spiking through her and it looked as though it was going to carry her through this fight.

The early-morning crowd was thin; a few spectators wandered around the stands, most of them clustered around the cage end of the arena as they waited for the first matches to start.

Ma's fight was later in the day, so he was watching *Dread*'s pilot, Huang, and Lieutenant Commander Locke during their race. The hacking competition didn't start until tomorrow, which meant Sapphi and Garcia had the day off. They were hanging by the team area, heads pressed together while they studied something on a shared screen only they could see.

Nika and Luis were nearby, having a quiet conversation over cups of coffee. The smell of it was driving her a shade mad.

"Hey." Jenks waved a hand in Max's face. "You focused?"

"Yeah." Max gave a sharp nod, eyes straying to the cage as the official in charge walked around it checking the walls.

"Hands." Jenks shook out the first wrap and began winding it around Max's left hand with quick, precise movements. She moved on to Max's right, wrapping it in the same bright green fabric. "Give me the rundown on Montauk."

Max pulled her gaze back to Jenks. "She's fast, watch for the spinning back kick. She'll take my head off with it if I drop my guard."

"Guard up." Jenks's hand flashed out and Max blocked it, bringing her right hand over to catch the follow-up punch. A glow of pleasure filled her chest when Jenks grunted in approval. "So much better. You've come a long way, LT. You've got this fight. You're smarter than she is. Use that creepy pre-science of yours and hit her first. Make it count, ring her bell, and get her off-kilter. Never let up." She patted Max's butt as Rosa came over.

"You ready?"

"Let's do this," Max said, and headed for the cage.

There was music over the speakers and Max was dimly aware of the announcers saying her name as she took the trio of steps up into the cage.

"Lieutenant Carmichael, I'm Travis Vance, your official for the fight."

"Nice to meet you." She smiled and shook his hand, turning as her opponent came up the steps.

Spacer Emery Montauk wasn't fresh out of basic training, but she looked it with a round baby face and deep green eyes. She was Max's height with the same long arms and legs, and even worse, she moved like she was comfortable in her bones. She shook the ref's hand, and then held her hand out to Max for a quick, impersonal greeting.

"You've both signed off on the rules," Travis said. "I expect a good, clean fight. Good contact. Back off when I say hold. We've got three rounds or until someone goes down for good. Tap and to your sides."

Max tapped her fists to Montauk's and then deliberately turned her back on the woman, sauntering back to the NeoG side of the cage with an insouciance she did not actually feel.

It did what she expected, though, and the crowd, small as it was, burst into laughter and applause. Jenks was grinning. Rosa shook her head with a laugh.

Max turned and lifted a hand to the audience. They re-acted with a second round of impressively loud cheers.

"Play to the spectators, Max." Something Jenks had told her months ago rang in her head. *"They can't award you more points, but their support can make the difference when you're on your knees about to lose."*

The whistle blew and Max brought her hands to her face, slipping her mouthguard in and meeting Montauk in the middle of the cage. She already had the woman off-balance. Her opponent expected a hesitant, nervous fighter based on her performance at the preliminaries, but Jenks was right. She'd come a long way since then.

"BARNES, I DON'T THINK ANYONE EXPECTED THAT TO START off this fight. Carmichael turned her back on Montauk and then came out of the gate with a punch that further threw the Navy fighter off her game."

"I think *I* felt that punch. We all know Jenks is a heavy hitter, but it appears Lieutenant Carmichael is no slouch in the force department when she decides to be. That was one of the best first rounds to start the Games in I don't know how long. I'm almost not mad you made me get up at such an ungodly hour, Pace."

"Hey, I warned you this was going to be a fighter to watch. For anyone just tuning in, you are in luck. We've still got two rounds to go here in the cage match between Lieutenant Maxine Carmichael of NeoG and Spacer Emery Montauk with the SEALs. Our referee, back for his tenth year, is Travis Vance. He's signaling the start of the second round."

"Montauk is a good fighter, Pace. She made it to the third round last year before Master Chief Ma laid into her with an uppercut that knocked her out, but she can't seem to get a handle on Carmichael's moves."

"The fighters in the prelims had the same issue, Barnes. Montauk with a nice spin kick there that Carmichael couldn't quite get out of the way of fast enough. The glancing blow to her right thigh is going to be a point for Navy. The fighters have backed off for a minute to catch their breaths, much to the disappointment of the crowd."

"Sorry folks, if you're looking for no-holds-barred fighting you'll have to wait and tune in to Jenks's fights later. Carmichael is clearly a deliberate fighter. She's weighing the options of moving in again, and it seems Montauk isn't going to rush against this unorthodox style."

"Too right, Barnes. That shot knocked Carmichael's lead down to two points and I'm sure she's calculating in her head just how to maintain that lead for the next round."

"Looks like Montauk's not going to be content to let Carmichael run the show here. She's moving in, Pace . . . but Carmichael avoids her and drops Montauk with a sweep that bounces her head off the mat!"

"That woman is a ghost. Montauk is struggling to get back to her feet. Parsikov and Tole are watching the clock a little nervously, hoping the time will run out before Carmichael can finish her off or the ref waves it over."

"This is where you see Carmichael's inexperience, Pace. She should be pressing her opponent. You can see Jenks shouting at her to do just that. But it's too little too late because there's the buzzer for the end of the second round."

"Saved by the bell. Carmichael's still ahead on points. That sweep put her up by five, Barnes, and from the way she's been moving I don't think Montauk is going to be able to make up that lost ground in the last round of this fight."

"I agree. Unless a miracle happens this is going to be a NeoG victory. While we wait for the rest period to wrap up, Pace, let's talk a little bit about Lieutenant Carmichael."

"The name says it all, doesn't it?"

"You'd think, but she's the first Carmichael who's gone into the Near-Earth Orbital Guard. We all know the story about how everyone in the family is expected to serve the CHN or LifeEx Industries in some capacity, but with few exceptions, the Navy has been the home for the Carmichael family."

"I've heard some rumors her parents weren't particularly happy about her choice, Barnes, but from what we've seen so far I think the NeoG is counting themselves lucky."

"Commander Rosa Martín sure is. She's got a reputation for training up some of the best and brightest in the NeoG. If you're going to make a joke about that not saying much I'd advise you to do it well out of earshot of any fans at the Boarding Games. All right, looks like Travis is signaling the fight crews to get on back out of the cage and Jenks is, of course, jawing at Parsikov."

"It's no secret that the SEALs brought him in to unseat Jenks from her undefeated throne, but she doesn't seem the least bit intimidated by him."

"Pace, I'm reasonably sure Jenks isn't afraid of anything, but I am sure looking forward to that fight if it happens. For now, though, we're about to start round three in this fight between Montauk and Carmichael. If you've just joined, Carmichael is up by five points and has been easily avoiding most of Montauk's attacks. As expected, Montauk is coming off the buzzer on the attack. She's moving in on Carmichael, who's easily defending against these punches."

"Oh—Carmichael drops an elbow there and that's going to leave a bruise on Montauk's left arm that'll last for a while. You can put a bet down on Montauk catching up here, but Barnes and I would both advise against it."

"Carmichael's going to go up against the winner of the fight between Captain Ramos of the Army team and Lance Corporal Patterson of the Marines. Which should be an interesting matchup no matter which way it goes—"

"Watch out! Carmichael narrowly avoided that punch. It would have shaken her brain a bit. But she *did* dodge, and that seems to be her calling card. Still, while Montauk is going to lose this, she's not going to make it easy for the NeoG lieutenant. The crowd is on their feet chanting Carmichael's name as the clock is ticking down."

"Three, two, one . . . and Pace, that's the end of it! Jenks is taunting the SEALs across the cage as the buzzer goes."

"Of course she is. Yet the winner, Carmichael, is just taking it in stride."

"Can't wait to see what she does next match."

"Me neither! But if you're just tuning in, the replay for *this* match will be this afternoon on The Sports Network, check your local schedule. Spoiler alert: the fight went the full three rounds but Carmichael won easily on points."

"Here's hoping Montauk does better in her pilot competition—though she'll have to go up against Ma and Carmichael in that at some point. I'm not sure she's going to fare any better there, either!" Barnes's laughter was wrapped around his words. "Carmichael was much more hesitant in the cage during the prelims, Pace. It looks like the past few months of training have seen Jenks's notorious attitude rubbing off on her teammate."

"Attitude or not, the skill has certainly jumped up a notch, and these Games—particularly the hand-to-hand fights—are going to be ones for the books, that's for sure!"

THE LIVING ROOM OF THE APARTMENT WAS FILLED WITH laughter, the remains of dinner evident on the scattered plates, and satisfied Neos sprawled on the floor and the various bits of furniture. Jenks sat on a bar stool half listening to Sapphi and Garcia talk about their strategy against the Air Force hacking team for their bout tomorrow and half watching the rest of the room.

The officers were glued to the screen on the far wall, watching the coverage of the Big Game. Army, thanks in part to their last-place finish in last year's Games, had drawn the first-day slot.

"How're you doing?" Luis murmured in her ear, and Jenks leaned back against him with a sigh and a smile.

"Looking forward to tomorrow. It was weird not to have

any fights today. I had to sit around and watch everyone else kick ass."

Luis's laugh rumbled against her back. "You looked good doing it."

"Everyone who had a match today dominated." She leaned up briefly to grab her beer before settling back against him.

"Makes you nervous, doesn't it?"

"A bit." She grumbled at the amusement in his voice. "You know me too well."

"You weren't complaining last night," he murmured, and she didn't bother to keep the smile from spreading across her face. "You have a chance to look at that info on Parsikov I sent you?"

"I did, you're the best." She turned her head to kiss his cheek.

"You're thinking of climbing that one like a tree, aren't you?"

Jenks laughed and then took a drink of her beer, the reply spilling out without much thought. "Maybe after I whomp him." She paused and turned to look at him. "Not until we have a chance to talk about it, though."

"We can do it later," he agreed. "I don't think you want to have that conversation right here."

"True," she agreed. "Bad enough with Nika in the room. That one is pretending like she's not listening, but she is." She pointed at Sapphi, who grinned. "And we might set Garcia's ears on fire having a poly conversation where her sheltered self can hear."

Sapphi snickered. Garcia proved Jenks right by flushing a deep red.

The chat window popped up in the corner of her vision.

LUIS: for the record, nothing's changed with my admission of love to you. You're free to do who (or what) you want. You don't need my permission.

JENKS: is that so?

LUIS: hey, I love you. That includes whatever makes you happy.

JENKS: you make me happy.

LUIS: you trying to make me cry in front of your friends?

Jenks chuckled.

"Besides," he whispered in her ear too low for anyone else to catch, "from what I dug up, Parsikov might be interested in both of us."

"Now that is something we haven't done in a while, isn't it?"

And Jenks hummed a contented sigh as she drank the last of her beer.

"THAT WASN'T A BAD FINISH," ROSA SAID AS THE OFFICIAL for the Big Game announced the Army team's completion of their mission.

"They were sloppy clearing the bottom level," Max said, waving a hand at the screen. She was on the floor, leaning shoulder to shoulder with Nika against the bottom of the couch, a half-eaten bowl of spaghetti between her knees. "It cost them eighteen points."

"How would you have done it?" D'Arcy's question was more curious than combative, and Rosa watched Max stare at the screen for a moment before she answered him.

"I would have split us and cleared both sides of the lower level before going upstairs."

"Cost you in time," Locke said with a shake of his head.

"True," Max replied. "However, the time spent would cost far less points than leaving three targets behind and getting one of your people shot in the back. In the real world the time isn't the issue. Keeping your people alive and uninjured is."

"She's not wrong."

Rosa smiled at D'Arcy's agreement.

"Army came at it like a game. I mean, it is," Max said, waving a hand at the screen again. "But their concern was the time and getting to the objective. Sloppy."

"Fair point," Locke conceded, rubbing his chin. "So you think we're better off moving slow than risking leaving enemies behind us?"

Rosa shared a look with D'Arcy as Max leaned forward. Her eyes were full of excitement and she'd started doing that talking-with-her-hands thing that only came out when she was really comfortable with people.

"Not slow. We just move like we would if we were clearing a ship, yeah? Or anything else. Look, the Boarding Games were practically designed with NeoG in mind. The other branches, they've got their infiltration teams, but the Interceptors do this for a living. All day, every day."

Jenks cheered from across the room and Rosa lifted her own beer in response. "Max is right. Let's huddle up, folks, and then it's time for bed." She grinned at the groans. "You all know the drill. It's another early start tomorrow and a long day for everyone. But right now, we'll take a moment to toast the fact that every single person who competed today won. Well done!"

"To the NeoG!"

BOARDING GAMES—DAY TWO

The preliminaries were one thing, but as Max headed through the streets toward the docking bay for the piloting competition, she got a better sense of just how massive the Boarding Games were.

It was late morning, and a scrolling tally of results was already in the corner of her vision. The Marine and Army teams had just wrapped their Boarding Action, with a last-ditch effort by Army to take the win, surprising a lot of people. Tamago and D'Arcy had both won their sword fights, but Huang had taken the Neos' first loss of the Games—falling to Commander Chau's steady assault in the sword arena. Chau was good; even Nika admitted he was going to be a challenge, but he seemed firm in his opinion that Rosa could beat him.

Sapphi and Garcia were set to take on the Air Force team in half an hour for their first round of the hacking competition, and there'd been more cage matches than Max could keep up with.

"Lieutenant." The guard at the door gave her a smile and a nod as he scanned her badge. "Good fight yesterday. You ready for Captain Ramos?"

"Of course." It was still so strange to have people she didn't know asking her about the fight, but it was getting easier to fake the confidence with every question that was tossed her way.

"Head straight back. Master Chief Ma is already at the ship. I'll call ahead and tell them you're on your way."

"Thank you."

"Anytime. Good luck this afternoon."

Max said her goodbyes and headed down the corridor into the hangar.

"Carmichael."

Max turned at the voice and found herself eye to eye with Chau. "Commander. Congrats on your win today. I hope you keep winning."

He hadn't expected the civility and it threw him. Max smiled. "At least until you run into Rosa."

Chau's startled laugh was genuine, as was the grin that crinkled the corners of his dark eyes, and Max found herself grinning back. Though she sobered quickly as the memory of his teammate knocking Tamago across the dance floor popped back into her head.

"You need something?" she asked.

Chau cleared his throat, smile fading. "Your brother's a good friend of mine, Max, and I—"

"Probably need to think about minding your own business," she said before he could finish.

"Normally I would, but I've watched him wrestle with his little sister not wanting anything to do with him from day one of our friendship. Whether he's admitted it to you or not, it hurts."

"You want to talk about how much he hurts?" Max shoved her hands into her pockets before she could curl them into fists. "Really? *That's* the route you're going, huh?"

"Max, he—"

"You okay, Max?"

She had never been so happy to hear Nika's voice, and

the solid warmth of his hand on her back pulled some of the tension from her shoulders. "Fine."

"Chau," Nika said, leaning on his crutches with a nod to the SEAL.

"Vagin." His eyes flicked to Nika's prosthetic arm. "Tough break there."

"I could still beat you with my left hand, Chau," Nika said with a smile that didn't waver. "We should get going, Max, Ma's waiting for you."

Max nodded and let Nika lead her across the hangar toward the ship.

"You sure you're all right?"

"Yeah."

"What did he want?"

"I don't know." Max took another look over her shoulder. Chau was still standing there, shoulders hunched and a frustrated expression on his face. They wove through the crowd and Max was surprised by the number of people who called her name or waved a greeting at her.

"Look who's popular," Ma teased, folding her into a hug.

"We'll see if it lasts."

"Nerves kicking in?"

"They've been kicking for quite some time." She shrugged. "But it's not worth being concerned about, though I'm glad for all the other things to do. That keeps me from having too much time to worry."

Ma smiled and patted her face. "You don't need to worry anyway, though I know that's like telling you not to breathe, kiddo. I'm super proud of you."

The sob was unexpected and Max threw herself into his arms again, hugging him tight as the loudspeaker cut in with an announcement for the pilots to go to their ships.

"Go rock the course," Nika said with a quick hug.

Max followed Ma to the ship, trying to get her rolling emotions under control. More than anyone, Ma had been a father to her, and the note of pride in his voice had struck her right in the heart.

She spotted Willington boarding his ship and gave the man a slow smile before she grabbed the railing and bounced up the stairs.

She could hear Nika laughing from behind her as the door closed.

JENKS RUBBED ABSENTLY AT THE BRUISE ON HER JAW AS Max unlocked the door and the pair entered the quiet apartment. "I forgot how fucking hard Vi hits," she said. "If he could only get a little control he'd be a way better fighter."

"Do you even realize you do that?" Max asked with a laugh.

"Do what?"

"Coach every single person who comes into your orbit."

Jenks pursed her lips and shrugged. "Not really. It's just habit."

"It'd be a good career for you after all this." Max smiled when Jenks blinked at her. "Sorry, that's my thing, remember?"

"Planning ten thousand steps in advance, yeah." Jenks laughed. "How's that working for you, LT?" To her surprise a shadow crossed Max's face. "What's up?"

Max looked away. "Nothing. It's nothing."

"Don't bullshit me, Max." Jenks leaned on the doorframe of her room. "We've got time for this. Rosa won't start screaming over the com for another ten minutes at least."

"I didn't think it would hurt this much." She forced the words out. "To see Scott."

Jenks raised an eyebrow but didn't say anything and Max took a deep breath before continuing.

"We used to be close. Well, it was a long time ago, so I don't know if it even counts. He's ten years older than me, I'm sure that sounds silly. How could a child have any meaningful connection with anyone?"

Jenks was pretty sure those were Max's parents' words coming out of her mouth. "Hey, you're babbling a bit, LT." The rebuke wasn't mean-spirited, just a simple statement meant to yank Max out of her spiral, and she marveled at how well it worked.

"When Scott was nearing graduation, he started talking about NeoG." Both Jenks's eyebrows went up at that and Max laughed. "I know, right? I barely remember it beyond being really excited and promising him I'd grow up and join, too. It was our thing." Max shoved both hands into her hair and looked at the ceiling. "Ma had just retired from the Navy and gone straight to NeoG. I remember Dad being less than pleased but Scott and I thought it was the coolest thing.

"Except one day out of the blue, Scott told me he was going to the Naval Academy. Said he'd changed his mind, that there was no future with a bunch of washed-out vets and baby cops. I was sad, but I still loved him." She dropped her hands, surprised by the ball of heat in her stomach the memories had set fire to. "He went away to the academy. Had promised to write me every day, but nothing. Mom said he was too busy and then when he came home after school, he was so different."

Max looked at Jenks and managed a rueful smile. "To be fair, I was different, too, and I'm not sure I'd have talked to him even if he'd tried. I was so mad about being abandoned."

"You had every right to be." Jenks looked down at her own hands and then up again with a smile. "I'd probably punch my own mother for ditching me if I ever saw her again."

"Yeah, you're not known for your self-restraint."

Jenks laughed. "True enough. But still, Max. I'm not gonna tell you what to do about your family, but I think they're a bunch of jerks."

"I'm inclined to agree with you." Max crossed her arms over her chest and leaned against the wall next to Jenks. "I know I probably shouldn't let it bother me. Chau was going on about how much Scott was hurting and I—I don't know what to even make of that, Jenks."

"Hey, whatever happens," Jenks said, tapping her fist over her heart, "I got your back."

Max smiled, completing the handshake and touching her forehead to Jenks's. "I got yours, too."

"And for what it's worth?" Jenks kept her eyes locked on Max's as she said the words that scared her. "I wouldn't mind having you for a sister."

"Me either, Jenks."

"REMEMBER TO WATCH HIS FEET," ROSA SAID TO TAMAGO, NOT taking her eyes away from Captain Carmichael's fight. He'd just swept Captain Mpho Bailey to the ground, and the Air Force officer rolled away, barely getting to his feet in time to block Scott's swing.

"He's really good, isn't he?" Tamago replied, chin in their hand, braced on the low wall they were standing behind. "I'm kicking myself a bit for all the times I didn't pay good enough attention, Commander."

"Don't worry about it." Rosa put her arm around their shoulders. "We all depended on Nika just a little too much."

"Here's hoping it doesn't bite us in the ass. Hey, there's your mom and Gloria." Tamago crouched and held their arms out, spinning Gloria in a circle before setting her down again. "Inez," they said with a smile. "I'm going to take Gloria down into the pit."

"Mama." Rosa leaned down and kissed her mother on the cheek.

"You're always busy at these Games," her mother said. "Seems worse this year."

No, I've just been avoiding you. Rosa chose a noncommittal noise instead of the truth and looked back at the fight.

"I know you're under a lot of pressure to win this thing,

so I don't want to bother you, but I would like to speak to you about Gloria afterward."

Rosa swallowed back the sigh. God love her mother, but the woman didn't know when to let things go. "There's nothing to speak about, Mama."

"I see Angela already got to you."

"Of course we talked about it, Mama—she's my *wife*. We do speak." Rosa was not grateful for the ref's whistle signaling the end of the match. Bailey had given him a fight, but Carmichael had won on points. She took a deep breath and looked at her mother. "I love you, but we've had this conversation once already. The raising of our daughters is up to Angela and myself. Not to you."

"I see."

Oh, the disapproval her mother could pack into those two words. Rosa glanced around, relief flooding her that no one in the area was paying them the least bit of attention.

"Mama—"

"No, it's fine." Inez held up a hand. "It's not like I've spent the last several years helping raise your daughters while you've been off God's green earth."

The words and the feelings behind them shocked Rosa into silence for a long moment before she could find the words and make them come out of her mouth. "Now is not the time or the place to rehash that argument, Mama. We are thankful, have always been thankful, for your help, but it was not demanded. It was given freely, I assumed, because you loved your granddaughters.

"And your granddaughters are free to find their way to God rather than to be forced into it." Rosa smoothed shaking hands down the sides of her legs. "If that's not something you think you can support, there's nothing else for us to discuss."

She didn't wait for her mother's reply, but turned on her heel and headed for the changing room, grateful for the emptiness that echoed the sudden hollow space in her chest. With a shaking exhale, Rosa sank down onto a bench, buried her face in her hands, and cried.

"Rosa?"

She jerked at the sound of D'Arcy's voice and his hand on her back.

"What happened?"

The story spilled out of her. D'Arcy listened without comment and then pulled her into a hug as she wound down. "Seems to be the day for family drama," he murmured. "Carmichael apparently had a run-in with Chau about her brother this morning."

"A run-in? Is she okay?"

"Yeah, not like that." D'Arcy shook his head in amusement when Rosa pulled back. "She's fine, and we're talking about you right now. Though damned if I'm not glad for not having a family right this moment."

"You do have a family, you jerk."

D'Arcy's grin was quick and sharp. "True, and it's sometimes as messy as anything. But we're talking about your mom here, not my startling lack of a past." He cupped her face. "You're doing the right thing, in case you need to hear that. It's not the easy thing, but it is the right one."

Rosa swallowed. His words eased some of the hurt in her chest. "It does help. Thanks."

"Anytime." He smiled.

BOARDING GAMES—DAY THREE

It was a delight to watch someone fight who was the same caliber as she was. That was the first thought that Jenks had as she watched the cage match between Parsikov and Lieutenant Commander Locke.

The second was that Locke was *not* the same caliber.

Jenks muffled a curse. "Locke, move your feet before he takes your fool head off!"

"Too late," Max murmured next to her and half a second later Parsikov's kick slammed into the right side of Locke's head. The lieutenant commander bounced off the cage wall and slumped to the ground.

"Hold!" the referee shouted.

"Get up, Locke!" Jenks shouted. He shook his head, managed to get to his feet, and then the ref blew the whistle. She scrambled around for the door, slipping through as soon as the ref had it opened and catching Locke before he face-planted.

"Fuck."

"You're telling me. When did you get so heavy?" she muttered as Max grabbed his other arm and helped him down onto the stool she'd brought into the cage.

He grinned at them both. "Jenks, you're going to have to watch out for this guy. He's good."

"We'll worry about me later." She snapped her fingers in front of his face. "Focus for me. You're not allowed to let him knock you out, is that understood? You've got one more round to go, Locke. That means you've got to stop letting him kick you in the fucking head."

"Any ideas for how to make that happen?" He coughed at the smelling salts Max held under his nose, recoiling and almost falling off the stool.

Jenks caught him, shared a look with Max, and then sighed. She knew how she would avoid those wicked fast legs Parsikov had, but how to translate that into something Locke could manage?

"Fighters, you have one minute."

"Move in on him," Max said, and Locke's eyes opened wider than they had with the smelling salts. Jenks shot her a look and Max shrugged. "Staying out of range is begging for him to move in on you just enough to kick you. Move in, take that away. You're going to have to grapple for five minutes, but you're a wiggly little shit, Locke, you can keep him from pinning you." She smiled. "Plus every hit you land on him gets us points."

He looked back at Jenks and she lifted her hands. "It's a better option than letting him knock you out. I'd do it, but it's your ass out there."

He took a deep breath and stood as the ref called for all crew to leave the cage. Jenks gave him a pat on the chest and followed Max to the door. On her way across the mat she felt Parsikov's eyes on her, so she stopped in the doorway and looked at him.

The wink was slow, deliberate, and followed by a lift of her chin, and she saw the grin that split his face before she turned and bounced out of the cage, whistling her favorite old song.

"All right, fighters! Five more minutes. Keep it clean." The ref blew his whistle and the fight started again.

There wasn't anything else she could do for Locke as he moved in, disrupting Parsikov's space. The move startled him enough that Locke landed several good body shots before Parsikov recovered and caught one of Locke's arms. The lieutenant commander slithered free, ducking under a surprisingly wild swing from the Navy fighter and punching him hard enough in the kidney that Jenks saw his right knee buckle.

"See where you need to be?" Max murmured.

"Yeah." The outcome of the fight was a foregone conclusion, they'd all known it, but Jenks was still startled by the cold-bloodedness of Max suggesting they throw Locke to the wolf just so Jenks could get a sense of how Parsikov fought when presented with an opponent up close.

It was a risk. Locke could have gotten caught, but he somehow managed to stay out of Parsikov's massive hands for the whole final round, and when the ref blew the whistle both men were exhausted.

Jenks let Max slide an arm around Locke's waist as he left the cage, tucking her hands behind her back as Parsikov came down the stairs. His black hair was plastered to his forehead and he sent it into further disarray when he scrubbed at his face with a towel.

"Good fight," she said. The cameras were on them, jockeying for position in the air.

"You think? I let him get in a few too many shots there in the last round."

"You should watch out for those close-range fighters. They slip inside your guard, cause all sorts of problems."

Parsikov took a step closer, putting Jenks eye to—well, sternum, really—with him. She tipped her head back to glare at him. His lips twitched as he looked down at her. "Do I need to find you a ladder to stand on?"

Jenks bared her teeth in a grin, but before she could say anything Rosa and Scott both stepped between them. "Save it for the match," Rosa said, and then added in a lower voice filled with laughter, "If someone lit a match between you two the whole place would go up in flames."

"Believe me, Commander, I know." Jenks waited until they were out of sight of the cameras to fan herself. "I do love the Games," she said with a happy sigh.

Rosa laughed and pulled her into a one-armed hug. "Come on, you menace, it's time for your fight with Ma."

"THEN WE JUST SLID INSIDE LIKE—WHOOSH." SAPPHI SLICED her hand through the air as Garcia giggled. "They were so stunned that Garcia moved in on their stuff and had their files wiped before either of them reacted. It was awesome!"

Max smiled as the two women exchanged a fist bump and the others scattered around the living room lifted various glasses in acknowledgment. The hacking duo's victory over the Navy team had been a breathless show that Max only partially understood.

Rosa, Ma, and Nika had retired early but some of *Dread Treasure*—including a worn-looking Locke—were still in their apartment. Max and Tamago moved around the small open kitchen doing prep work as D'Arcy cooked up something that was making her stomach rumble and her eyes burn.

"Sapphi, what do projections look like?" she asked. The hacker pointed at the wall, where a mass of scribbles and arrows and other assorted marks that made no sense to Max resided. Max gave her a flat look and the ensign grinned.

"We're in the lead. Not by much. But Rosa's win today against Lieutenant Commander Niochi and our victories in the piloting and hacking rounds were enough to offset the beast that is Parsikov."

"He is a beast," Tamago said, poking their tongue out when D'Arcy snorted. "Did you see the video of him and Jenks after Locke's fight?" They pointed over the counter at Jenks, who was sprawled on the couch with her head in Luis's lap. "You two impregnated half the galaxy with that little stunt."

"All we were doing was shit-talking. Hush, you." Jenks elbowed Luis when the man snorted with laughter and rolled to her feet. "But Tamago." She dragged their name out with a grin. "He's fire."

"I know, and you still have to focus on kicking his ass. But I'm free," Tamago countered.

Max leaned in to press her head to theirs even as Jenks reached over the bar divider. "You fought good. Don't stress about it. Captain Carmichael's a hell of a sword handler. You managed to slow him down, that's what matters."

"What she said," Jenks agreed, releasing Tamago's hand when the door buzzer went off. "That might be Candy. They said they would stop by if they could get away."

"You really did well," Max murmured, going back to work on the carrots in front of her.

"I know." Tamago sighed, forced a smile. "Losing sucks."

"You've got some fucking nerve."

Max looked up at the tone of Jenks's voice and stopped chopping the veggies, setting the knife carefully to the side.

Luis was already on his feet, crossing to the door, but he stopped when Max stepped in front of him. Her brother stood in the doorway, facing down a very angry Jenks, who was all but vibrating with the need to put her fist in his face.

"Jenks," Max said softly, and had to repeat her name a second time before it filtered through to the woman. "I've got it. Go on." She pushed Jenks toward Luis, smiling when her teammate retreated with a poorly concealed snarl in Scott's direction. Max stepped out into the hallway and closed the door behind her.

Scott swallowed under the scrutiny, but Max was content to cross her arms over her chest and stare at him until he found the words he wanted.

"Chau told me he tried to talk to you. I wanted you to know I didn't ask him to do it."

"Okay." Max nodded and turned for the door.

"Max—" Scott grabbed her by the shoulder, and then pulled his hand away at her sharp look. She glared at him, surprised by how miserable he seemed. His next words were a whisper. "We used to be—Max, what did I do?"

"What did you *do*?" She surprised herself now with the venom of her hissed reply. "You left me! You promised you wouldn't and then you went to the Naval Academy just like they wanted and never looked back!" All the old hurt she'd buried came to the surface in a rush.

"I wrote you!"

"You didn't. Don't lie to me!"

"I wrote you." His agonized words hit her like a punch. "Every day until you told me to stop, I—"

"How could I tell you to stop when I never got a single message?"

The door across the hall opened and Rosa stuck her head out, Ma in the background behind her. Curiosity turned to cool anger as her eyes flicked from Max's face to Scott. "What's going on here?"

Max squeezed her eyes shut, feeling her cheeks burn with embarrassment. "We're fine, Commander. Captain Carmichael was just leaving."

"Come in here, both of you." It was Ma, not Rosa, who issued the order, and Max snapped her eyes open to stare at him. He waved a hand. "Come on. There's something you both need to hear."

Max dared a look in Scott's direction, but he was as confused as she was. Rosa stepped out of the doorway and Max followed her brother into the other apartment. Nika came out of his bedroom, arms crossed and a frown on his face that didn't vanish with Max's attempt at a reassuring smile.

Angela was on the couch and she stood with a sympathetic smile, whispering something in Rosa's ear before she retreated to the other bedroom.

"You know, I promised myself I wouldn't get more involved in this than I already had," Ma said, rubbing his hands together as he paced the living room. "But I've had my mouth shut for almost two decades now and I'm done seeing you two hurt because I put your parents' feelings before yours."

Max blinked. "Ma—"

She cut off when he raised his hand.

"You've asked me before what I fought with your father about. What we stopped speaking over," he said. "It was about you two. It's always been about you two. Your brother wanted to go into the NeoG, Max, because of me. Your parents objected. They threatened to disown him, and when that wasn't enough, they threatened the one thing they knew would get him back in line."

"Ma, don't do this." Scott's protest was choked with desperation.

"She needs to know, Scott. She deserves to know what they did. I'll tell her if you won't."

Max frowned, looking between Ma and Scott. There were tears in both men's eyes. Scott's jaw was flexing in a way that was all too familiar to her.

"What?"

"You, Max." Scott's voice was raw. "They threatened to disown you."

"I was eight. They wouldn't have." Max could do little more than stare at her brother and then at Ma. Even as she said the words, she knew they were untrue. Her parents very much would have done it to her. They'd left her on Earth after that fight in the restaurant, after all.

She thought about how that fight would have gone if there'd been anyone younger than her, a sibling who needed protection, and her heart suddenly ached for her brother.

"They did, Max." Ma's reply was gentle. "He went into the Navy because the alternative was unthinkable."

Memories of whispered conversations about the NeoG, plans to be the best in the service, came slamming back into her head. What had Scott given up for her? *Because of* her. "I can't breathe."

She heard Nika's cursing through the rush of blood in her ears, felt Rosa's hand on her arm lowering her into a chair, but couldn't make the words make sense in her head.

"Max." Scott dropped to a knee in front of her, cupping her face in his hands. "I am so sorry. I was trying to keep you safe. I swear to you, I wrote you every damn day."

"Nothing," she said. "I didn't get a single message. I thought you'd abandoned me. Mom said you were busy and didn't have time for me. That I needed to grow up and let it go."

"Your parents didn't let any of those messages through, Max," Ma said, and Max whipped her gaze up to him. The older man shook his head, a grim look on his face. "I'm sorry about that. If I had known sooner, I would have—I don't know, done something. Ai and I would have gladly taken you in. I would have done everything I could to keep you and Scott together. But I didn't find out about it all until you started pushing about the NeoG yourself. I'd always thought Scott had just changed his mind. Your father slipped one day when he was ranting and I threatened to beat the story out of him. Still clocked him pretty good when he finally did tell me the truth." Ma's laugh was devoid of humor. "Scott, I know you got at least one message you thought was from Max. It wasn't."

There was anguish on Scott's face and Max threw herself into his arms, knowing her face mirrored his. "I'm sorry. All these years. I'm sorry I didn't reach out, didn't try harder. I'm sorry I believed anything they told me!"

"Shh, it's all right, Max. It wasn't your fault, none of this was. I'm sorry I let them keep us apart. I should have been stronger." His arms tightened around her. "I love you, kiddo. I've missed you so much."

"I love you, too."

Max heard the commotion at the door but didn't move until she heard Jenks's disappointed question. "Does this mean I don't get to punch him?"

Max laughed and turned her head on Scott's shoulder. "Not right now, Jenks."

"Not ever," Scott muttered. "I saw that video of the preliminaries."

Max leaned away with a second soft laugh and pressed her forehead to her brother's. "We have a lot of things to talk about, don't we?"

"Yeah." He nodded and then stood, pulling her to her feet and into a hug. "After the Games, I guess."

"After we kick your ass?" Her hands were shaking, but she still managed the grin.

Scott started to answer, then looked around at the room full of Neos. "Jesus, I'm outnumbered," he said, and Max laughed.

"You'd better get out of here before Chau comes looking for you with the rest of your squad." Max walked him to the door.

"Good luck tomorrow, Max. I mean that."

"You too." She gave him one last hug and then closed the door, pressing her head to the surface for a moment before she turned to face the eyes watching her. "I—" The tears started before she could control them. Tamago was the closest and wrapped her into a hug.

Max stood there for a long moment, lifting her head to meet Ma's eyes. "I want to know everything," she said.

He nodded. "I'll tell you what I can."

BOARDING GAMES—DAY FOUR

Murphy came sprinting over to Jenks, her face split by a wide smile. "She won, Jenks! Commander Martín beat Chau!"

Jenks looked up from where she was tending to Max in the cage. "Hear that, LT?"

Max nodded, winced, and rubbed at her chest. "This guy's kicks feel like getting shot at close range by a rail gun, Jenks."

"So stop letting him kick you."

"I can't wait to throw that back at you."

"If you kick his ass here, we won't have to worry about that, will we?" Jenks grinned. She patted Max's cheek and helped her to her feet as the ref shouted out the time. "You've got one more round and you've kept him close. I know you're tired and you're hurting, but give me five more minutes of Max being a goddamned ghost."

"Okay." Max took a deep breath, rolled her shoulders, and held her fists out. "Let's do this."

Jenks tapped her fists to Max's. "Kick his ass, LT." She headed out of the cage without a second look, knowing that Parsikov was expecting it at this point and anything she could do to unsettle him was worth it.

She couldn't get over how fast he was. Every fight, every opening move seemed to come out of nowhere, and Jenks fisted her hands in the pocket of her hoodie as Max only barely avoided a punch just moments after the whistle blew.

Stepping inside his guard was going to take away so much of his power, Jenks knew it, but the trick was going to be keeping him from taking her to the mat. She did not want an extended grappling session with him.

Not in the cage, anyway.

Her laugh burst out into the air. Parsikov looked in her direction and Max's kick caught him right in the chest, an answering shot for his rib-bruising kick on her in the second round. He staggered back, hands down.

"Move in on him, Max!" Jenks shouted as the tide of the fight shifted so unexpectedly that the crowd went silent.

Max moved, dropping into a sweep that Parsikov managed to avoid at the last second, though he stumbled, his footing unsure. The noise from the crowd swelled, drowning out everything else, even Jenks's own cheers. Max kept her momentum from the sweep, spinning in with a backfist that glanced off Parsikov's block.

He was already moving, throwing a punch with his right fist. Jenks cursed.

Max saw the punch. She just couldn't block it in time. Jenks could tell by the way she dropped her chin to take the blow.

It connected and Jenks could do nothing but watch Max go boneless and fall to the mat.

The cheers of the crowd vanished into silence, broken only by Travis's shouted "Hold!"

Jenks was already moving, scrambling for the cage door as Travis bent by Max's side. "She's out! That's match." He crossed to where Parsikov was pacing on the other side of the cage as the medics came through the door with Jenks behind them.

She heard the crowd cheering, knew without looking away from Max that Travis was lifting Parsikov's arm and declaring him the winner.

"We can roll her," the medic next to her said. "No neck or back injury on the scan."

Max groaned, eyes fluttering open when Jenks slipped a hand under her head. "Fuck me, what happened?"

Her second laugh bubbled up and out into the air before Jenks could stop it. "You got dropped like a bad habit, Max, and I think Parsikov knocked loose your objection to cursing in the process."

"I don't object, I just don't do it much." Max blinked a few times. "Damn it, I knew that punch was trouble. I couldn't—"

"You're fine." Jenks patted her on the shoulder.

"Is she all right?"

Jenks looked up at Scott as he dropped to a knee next to Max, and swallowed back the first answer that came to her mouth. Instead it seemed safer to gesture to the medic, who answered for her.

"She'll be all right. Think you can stand, Lieutenant?"

"I got her," Jenks said when Scott moved to help. "Tell Parsikov I'll see him in the cage tomorrow."

Scott, surprisingly, nodded once and moved off as Jenks and the medics helped a woozy Max out of the cage to the cheers of the crowd. D'Arcy met them just outside the door and followed them to the changing room.

"Rosa's on her way, I've got to get to my match." He reached out and touched Max's face lightly. "Good fight, kiddo."

"Kick his ass, D," Jenks said, sticking her fist out.

He tapped it with a grin and took off across the arena.

ROSA MADE HER WAY INTO THE CHANGING ROOM WITH GLO-ria still clinging to her hand.

"She's okay," Jenks said with a smile. "Hey, Gloria, did your mom kick Chau's—" She broke off with a grin at Angela's look and Isobelle's laughter. "Did she win her fight?"

"She did! You should have seen her."

"I know. I was watching Max fight, though."

Rosa crouched down next to Max as Jenks led Gloria away under Angela's watchful eyes. Her mom had gone home yesterday. Rosa wasn't going to pretend it didn't hurt, but she was also not going to let it distract her. They'd all worked so hard for this and there wasn't anything she could do to change her mother's mind.

"Hey there," she said to Max. The lieutenant was sprawled on the bench, an arm over her bruised face.

"Hey, Commander." She cracked an eye open. "I think I wanna switch to the sword."

Rosa chuckled and patted Max's shoulder. "You're all right. Rest up, we've got a match this evening. We'll have someone take you back to the village and you can sleep until your flight with Ma."

Max didn't protest, so Rosa patted her again and got to her feet. She wanted to shower and change, then get back out into the arena to watch D'Arcy's fight. The championship pilot match was in three hours, and while she was reasonably certain Ma would beat Staff Sergeant Rig for the third year in a row even with Max being a little loopy, she wanted to be there to watch it.

Navy would be running their shot through the Big Game at the same time, and then in the evening the major entertainment was NeoG's final Boarding Action match against Navy.

She checked Sapphi's stats as she headed for the showers. They were still up, but not by much. One wrong step here, one missed point or lost match there would make all the difference.

Meanwhile, the reports from Stephan were still filtering in. The Trappist PeaceKeepers had locked down yet another facility on the far side of the planet, and the NeoG crews around Trappist had snapped up one more shipment trying to make its way to Earth.

"There you go again."

Rosa looked over her shoulder at her wife. "I what?"

"You had that 'this is super serious' look on your face." Angela grinned, crossing her arms over her chest as she leaned in the doorway of the shower.

"You know there are rules about ogling people while they're showering."

Angela laughed. "I married your ass, I'll ogle it all I want."

Rosa rinsed her hair out, sticking her face under the running water with a sigh. "I was actually thinking about this case we've been involved in," she said, wiping the water away from her face with a hand.

"Towel's on your left." Rosa felt Angela's fingers brush hers as she took the towel. "The one you can't talk about?"

"Yeah." Rosa pressed the towel to her face for a moment before meeting her wife's eyes. "I didn't ever tell you thank you the other day for trusting me."

"I know you. If I'd really needed the reason why, you'd have given it to me. This isn't all about the case, though, right? I know how much these Games weigh on you."

"We were this close last year and it all fell apart. I don't want that to happen again."

"It's not all under your control, love." Angela held out another towel as Rosa turned off the water and gestured for her to turn around so she could dry her hair. "What were you thinking of when you were fighting the lieutenant commander?"

"I was, uh . . . nothing, really?" Rosa frowned.

"It showed. You were focused." Angela took her by the shoulders and turned her with a smile. "You doubt yourself so much, my love, but you are so amazing. Believe that for me, in this last fight. No matter who you go up against. Fight like your life, or ours, depends on it."

Max's words from earlier in the week filtered back into Rosa's head. *The Interceptors do this for a living. All day, every day.*

Now it was time to show them all just how true that was.

BOARDING GAMES—DAY FIVE

"Rosa, are you listening?"

Rosa dragged her eyes away from where Scott paced the opposite side of the ring to focus on Max. Her lieutenant was none the worse for wear after yesterday's fight, though she sported an impressive-looking bruise and partial black eye on the left side of her face. "I'm listening." She took a deep breath.

"He'll lead with his sword, but the dangerous part is always his feet," Nika said. "Watch them. The moment he shifts his weight, you reach down and hook his ankle with your sword."

"And if he takes my head off?"

"He'll swing. You duck." Nika smiled. "I have faith that your reflexes are faster."

"You're up by three points," Max said. "He's frustrated. He'll push because of it. Be ready." She pointed and Rosa glanced behind her at where Angela and her daughters stood. Gloria was jumping up and down, cheering as loud as she could. "You're fighting for them, Rosa, for us. Get out there and win this."

Rosa nodded, her eyes still locked on her family. Angela bent down to say something to Isobelle, laughing at the response, and when she came up her eyes locked on Rosa's.

In the moment between one heartbeat and the next, Rosa was twenty-two again, staring into those brown eyes for the very first time, feeling the words tangle themselves together in her mouth.

Then she was twenty-three, getting down on a knee in front of their friends to ask Angela to marry her. Forty-three, struggling through the birth of their first daughter. Fifty-one, watching Angela do the same with Gloria. All the years in between filled with love and laughter and the endless yawning distance of the black between them.

"Fight like your life, or ours, depends on it."

"I DON'T KNOW WHAT PASSED BETWEEN COMMANDER MARtín and her people during the break, Pace, but Captain Carmichael didn't have a chance in that last round of their fight."

"Too right, Barnes. I've watched Martín fight a lot of rounds over the past few years and she's never been as focused as she was when that round started. For those of you just joining us hoping to see the end of the Carmichael-versus-Martín fight, you are too late. Less than fifteen seconds into the round, Commander Rosa Martín landed a blow that Captain Carmichael's suit registered as a mortal wound. It was a stunning sliding strike across his chest and won the match for the NeoG team."

"It was a thing of beauty. If you watch the replay, Martín is gunning for him the moment she turns around and the whistle blows. She wanted this fight over with and did she deliver or what, Pace?"

"Her win puts the NeoG in a significant lead over Navy. However, the NeoG team still has to get through the Big Game, and this evening we've got the fight you've all been waiting for. We thought for a few minutes there that Lieutenant Max Carmichael would steal the spotlight from Lieutenant Tivo Parsikov in the semifinals and leave us with an all-NeoG championship round. But his knockout of the ghostlike Carmichael was a doozy."

"I'm sure her ears are still ringing from that, Pace. Though she held her own yesterday as the navigator for Master Chief Ma's win in the piloting competition."

"Without a doubt, Barnes. Without a doubt. Anyhow, things are heating up on this final day of the Boarding Games. Stay tuned here on TSN to see how it all plays out. Will the NeoG go home with a trophy? Or will they once again fall to the might of the naval team?"

WATCHING A FIGHTER TELLS A LOT, BUT IT'S NEVER THE SAME as being in the fight. Jenks ducked under Parsikov's swing, landed a punch of her own that didn't seem to faze him much, and scrambled out of reach.

"You gonna make me chase you around the cage?"

"It's the only approved way to wear you out in public, right?" she replied, and watched his grin flash.

Everything had vanished. The crowd. The referee. It was only the pair of them, and the first two rounds had gone by in the blink of an eye. They each had a handful of points and more than a handful of bruises.

She'd managed to get a lock on Parsikov's left shoulder and dislocated it briefly in the first round. He'd favored it the rest of that round but his team had popped it back in for him and it didn't seem to be bothering him now.

The biggest problem, Jenks knew, was that she couldn't keep running away. She was burning through her reserves. They'd just started the third round and she was already sucking air into her lungs in big gulps.

She blocked Parsikov's jab, kicked for his knee, and spit a curse into the air when he somehow managed to avoid it at the last second. He was so fucking *fast*.

His answering punch hit her in much the same way he'd tagged Max. Jenks reeled, crashing into the cage wall, and instinct alone kept her moving. She felt the impact of Parsikov's follow-up kick as it rippled through the links, and continued to roll to her right, trying to give her head time to clear.

I am not going to win this.

The thought was painful and more than a little terrifying.

But above all it pissed her off.

The fucking hell I'm not.

She ducked under Parsikov's guard, landed two punches to his gut before his answering roundhouse clocked her right upside the head and sent her flying to the far side of the cage. She hit the wall and went down on a knee.

It had been his left arm. The one she'd dislocated in the first round, and it still hurt him. That was the only reason she was still conscious.

The roar of the crowd was a jumbled mess, except, for just an instant, Jenks heard Max's voice as clear as a bell.

"Left side! Use his left side!"

Jenks wiped the blood from her mouth as she stood. Took a deep breath. Straightened her shoulders. The crowd fell silent, or maybe not, but it was quiet in her head and that was all she needed.

She smiled at Tivo and blew him a kiss.

The frown hadn't finished forming across his handsome face before she was sprinting across the cage at him. Two steps, three, a handful more.

She swerved to the left at the last second, knowing he would follow. Jenks planted her bare foot on the wall of the cage and launched herself into the air, grabbing Parsikov by the throat and jamming her right fist up against his carotid artery, securing it with her other hand. She locked her legs around him, pinning his right arm to his body, leaving his weakened left arm free.

She couldn't keep him in this hold for more than five seconds per tournament rules, and the clock in her head seemed to tick down with agonizing slowness.

Five . . . four . . .

Jenks grunted as Parsikov desperately slammed her back

against the wall, the pain rocking through her with each blow, but she held on.

Three . . . two . . .

Come on, you bastard, pass out on me.

She felt him go slack, and let go as he toppled forward, pushing off his back and landing on the mat as he hit the ground hard.

Travis dropped to the mat next to Parsikov, checked him, and then slapped his palm down. "He's out! That's match!"

There was a heartbeat of stunned silence and then the crowd erupted into wild celebration. Jenks bent over, dragging in air even though every breath hurt. She straightened, found Max's eyes through the cage wall, and tapped her fist against her heart before thrusting it into the air.

"Still undefeated, Jenks," Travis said, grabbing her other wrist and hoisting upward. "Winner, Petty Officer Altandai Khan!"

MAX FOLLOWED TAMAGO ONTO THE PODIUM, THE CHEERS OF the crowd filling the air. "Good job, Lieutenant," Rosa said, taking the medal from the man behind her and putting it around Max's neck.

"You too, Commander." She stepped to the side as Rosa repeated the action with everyone else on the team. She felt Tamago slip their arm around her waist and leaned into them for just a moment, her vision going misty.

"Spectators! I give you the winners of the hundred and first Boarding Games—the Near-Earth Orbital Guard!"

Max caught Scott's eye and barely managed to keep her mouth closed when her brother snapped into a salute, the rest of the Navy team following. She nodded in her brother's direction before she slung an arm around Jenks's shoulder and pulled her close.

"To family, Max." Jenks hugged her back.

"To family."

ONE WEEK POST-GAMES

Max woke in the unfamiliar room at HQ and lay for a moment in the dark, listening to the quiet breathing of Sapphi and Tamago. Rosa was with her family, Ma with his. Jenks had spent the night at Luis's apartment.

Life had settled back into something of a routine after their victory at the Games, though Max was surprised by the order from Admiral Chen to head for London rather than go back to Jupiter Station. Despite losing the tail of the men from the bar, Stephan had dug up a new lead on their mysterious Gerard and that was enough to bring *Zuma's Ghost* back for the hunt.

She slipped from her bed and grabbed for her gym clothes, making her way in the dark to the bathroom and closing the door behind her before turning on the light. She kept her eyes half-closed against the bright assault and flipped it off again as soon as she was dressed.

The officers' gym nearby would be open, but hopefully not all that occupied, and she needed to go for a run.

Just her luck—the gym was empty. Max headed for a treadmill in the corner, hopped on, and started flipping through files as she ran.

Yet try as she might, she couldn't leave the journal alone

and kept coming back to Thomas Gerard. Dead or not, there was something tying him to her family and to LifeEx. Stephan had found mention of Gerard buried deep within the darker parts of the 'net, whispers of a revolution that would save humanity.

What Max couldn't figure out was what that had to do with Alex.

"What were you up to, Great-Granddaddy?"

Spurred by a sudden thought, Max ran another search through the journal.

Can hardly believe he's dead. What a waste. I thought I knew him better. It was horrifying how casual he was about the danger. "Built-in population control," he called it. The risks are too great, even for an extended life span beyond what the safer option provides us. We're so close to the edge already, I couldn't take the chance that his drug would slaughter one person in twenty. He wouldn't listen to reason. I had to tell the authorities.

"'Built-in population control'? What's he talking about?" Max whispered. Alex had to be referring to the dangers of the dupe here, Max's gut was certain of it. She was also still reasonably sure Ria knew more than she was telling her. It shouldn't surprise her that her sister would lie to her, but it did sting.

The question was, if Gerard had died, who'd taken over his legacy and his name?

The movement out of the corner of her eye dragged her attention back to her surroundings and Max jolted involuntarily at the person on her right.

"Sorry, was trying not to startle you." The blonde smiled and waved a hand, her handshake reading *Lieutenant Sammi Alexander, she/her.* "Good morning."

"Morning."

"I don't usually see anyone else here this early."

"Trying to clear my head." Max stopped the treadmill and hopped off as she scrubbed at the sweat before it could drip in her eyes.

"Lieutenant Sammi Alexander. Like it says on the handshake." The woman extended her hand. "Are you new here?"

Max shook her hand for real this time, feeling the solid pressure of Sammi's grip. The woman looked oddly familiar, but she couldn't quite place where she'd seen her. "Lieutenant Max Carmichael. I'm not stationed here. Just visiting. I'm with the Interceptors."

"Oh! You're on *Zuma's Ghost*. That's why you look familiar. I watched your fights." The woman laughed and gave an awkward little wave. "Big fan."

Max smiled, relief at being recognized for something other than her name flooding her. "It's nice to meet you. You work here at HQ?"

"I'm an instructor's assistant at the academy, marine biology. Plants, mostly—I focus on resurrection of extinct species."

"Interesting." Max's thoughts immediately went to the algae used in LifeEx. The tightly controlled, otherwise extinct algae.

I wonder if it could be grown on the planets in the Trappist system? That would explain the lab and the shipments back to Earth. If someone else involved with the serum agreed with Gerard and took samples . . .

Almost lost back in her own thoughts, Max remembered to say, "It was really nice to meet you," as she headed for the door. "Ow!" She looked down at the spot of blood welling up on her upper arm and then up to a pair of cold green eyes.

"Your security is too good," Sammi said, her voice smooth. "But everyone slips up eventually."

Max kicked Sammi in the chest and ran for the door, activating the panic button on her DD before her legs stopped working and she dropped like an Interceptor ship coming in for the kill. Two men, recognizable as the ones from the bar, came through the door of the gym and hauled her to her feet.

"Oh, Max." Sammi was rubbing at her chest, wheezing a little from the force of Max's kick. "I wish you hadn't done that. You really want me in a good mood. Have a nap, we'll chat in a bit."

"Fuck you," Max managed as she saw the fist. There was answering pain and then the world went black.

"GONE? WHAT DOES HE MEAN 'GONE'?"

"Jenks." Rosa's reprimand was quiet and almost not enough, but she watched as Jenks wrestled her anger under control and backed out of the face of the hapless Neo who was standing at attention at the door of the officers' gym. Luis was behind her, his jaw tight and his eyes worried.

"He means someone tailed Max to the gym, broke in, drugged her, and kidnapped her before we could respond," Stephan said, waving at the trio. "Get in here."

"The others are right behind us," Rosa said, her stomach twisting at the blood on the mat just inside the door.

"It's Max's," Stephan said quietly once Jenks was out of earshot. "Enough for maybe a broken nose. I've already talked to Ria, she's on a transport with Bosco headed this way."

"What?" Rosa rubbed both hands over her face. Her head was pounding from the residuals of the alarm attached to Max's DD that had gone off in her head. "Let's back up. What was Max doing here?"

"Running," Jenks said. "It helps her think."

"Most likely. The surveillance footage is scrambled." Stephan scrubbed a hand over his short brown hair. "We fucking dropped the ball on this, Commander. I am so sorry. I don't know why they came after Max."

Jenks bounced up from her crouch. "I do. She's a Carmichael. These people are producing a dupe. It makes sense for them to go after a family member."

"They may want to use Max to blackmail Ria about the

drug," Luis said, "since we've been pursuing them on Trappist and LifeEx has eliminated all the dupe serum that made its way into production. This could have pushed them to do something reckless."

"We've got a face. Camera down the street caught the attackers as they were coming around the corner. Also got a name—Sammi Alexander."

Jenks snorted as Ma, Sapphi, and Tamago spilled into the gym. "That's not a real name. Those dinguses at the bar had fake handshakes; ten feds says she did, too," Jenks said.

"What's going on?" Ma said.

Luis filled them all in.

"Do we have a trace on Max's DD?" Rosa asked.

"Yes and no," Stephan said. "Hitting the panic button started an instantaneous tracking beacon. We were able to follow it about halfway across the Atlantic and then it vanished."

"They took her off-planet?" Jenks muttered a curse.

Rosa shook her head. "It would have tracked even off-planet. If it just vanished they figured out some way to stop her beacon."

"How?" Stephan frowned. "Those are supposed to be tamperproof, except—"

"Don't." Jenks held up her hand. "Don't you say it, Stephan. We already established they wanted her alive."

"All right," Rosa said with a nod at Luis. "You stay here and get what you can from Max's sister. We're going to the spot of the last transmission from her tracker to see what we can find from there. Send me the coordinates."

"Gear's in the ship," Ma said.

"Go. Jenks and I will meet you in the hangar."

Ma nodded and took off with Sapphi and Tamago on his heels.

"Have we pieced together anything more?" Rosa asked as she watched them leave.

"We hit another dead end with the stuff from the 'net, but

if Jenks is right, then Max was maybe trying to sort something out in her head." Stephan frowned. "I shouldn't let you go after them," he said. "Not if we don't know what we're dealing with."

"We're the same rank, so you can't really stop me," Rosa replied, mouth twitching into a wry grin. "More important, though, she's our teammate, Stephan. I'm not sitting around waiting to see what they do to her."

"I wouldn't expect you to. Just be careful." He pulled her into a hug. "I'll take Angela to your mom's and leave a detail on them just in case."

"Thanks." As she pulled away she spotted Luis with his forehead pressed to Jenks's.

"Of course. Bring her home, Rosa."

She nodded tersely. "Call me if anything changes. Jenks, we're moving."

THE DULL TASTE OF BLOOD WAS IN HER MOUTH AS MAX REgained consciousness in little bits and pieces. She kept her eyes closed as the events that put her here filtered to the front of her throbbing brain. Once things were in some sort of order she took a quick inventory.

Arms cuffed together. Legs too. It's zip ties, though, not metal cuffs.

Still have my shoes on. Good decision on going for a run, Max.

DD chip is—inactive? She frowned. *No, it's still working . . . sort of.* She could flip through her internal files, but there didn't seem to be any signals going or coming. Wherever she was being held was shielded.

My face hurts. She wiggled her nose and the burst of pain that accompanied it confirmed the readout in the corner of her vision warning of a broken nose.

Max let the sounds of the room sink into her. It was silent, mostly, but the same familiar humming as on Jupiter Station had her heart dropping in her chest.

Did I get taken off-planet?

She cracked an eye. The room was dim, shadows from the single overhead light thrown about the corners like Jenks's scattered clothing on her bunk.

A door opened on her right, the person silhouetted against the light. "You awake, Max?" It was Sammi. "I brought you some water."

"My hands are sort of occupied."

Sammi stepped into the room and rattled the cup in her hand, the metal straw clinking on the side. "I planned ahead." She held the cup up to Max's mouth. "Go on, it's clean. I want you awake and aware."

Max debated the merits of trusting this woman for a moment before deciding she didn't know how long she'd been without water and getting the copper taste from her mouth was too appealing to pass up.

The water had a cold, familiar recycled taste and the surety that she'd been taken off-planet settled in once again. "Who are you? Where are we?"

"My name is Sammi Gerard. Thomas Gerard was my great-grandfather."

"Thomas Gerard didn't have any family."

"And yet, here I am." Sammi spread her hands wide. "As for where we are, you know I can't tell you." She smiled, pulling the cup away. "Even with the DD chip blocker active, it'd be silly of me to give you coordinates."

A flash of hope that she wasn't going to get killed sprang to life in Max's chest. "I've seen you—at the Boarding Games. I was talking to Scott on the street."

"Good job, Max."

The condescending tone reminded her so much of her mother that Max had to choke down the snarl before she could speak. "What do you want?"

"Not here." Sammi's pert nose wrinkled. "It's dismal, don't you think?"

"You are not going to want to let me out of these." Max lifted her legs.

Sammi laughed and rubbed her free hand over her chest. "Yes, I learned that the hard way. Sorry about the broken nose, by the way. Watching you compete and experiencing it firsthand are two very different things. Plus, I rather like you, Max, and I don't want to have to kill you. Which is what I'll do if you come after me again." She snapped her fingers and the door opened. "This is terribly undignified, I'm sorry." Sammi shrugged as one of the goons from the bar came in and hoisted Max over his shoulder.

"Thomas was a genius. So was Alexander, from what I've heard. Even exiled and forced into hiding so far from home, my great-grandfather always spoke of yours with a certain amount of respect. I want you to know this, because it's important for how the story goes."

"You're responsible for the fake LifeEx," Max said as Sammi walked beside them. The goon's shoulder was shoved into her stomach, and with her hands locked behind her back there was no way for her to reach the knife at his belt.

"I am a cog in a very complex machine," Sammi replied. "No more or less important than anyone else who's joined our cause."

"Are we alone here?" Max jerked her head at the goon. "I mean, besides this guy. Hi there, asshole. Jenks is going to kick your ass again when she gets here."

Sammi laughed. "Oh no. My people are here working."

"Where is here? And working on what?"

"You're persistent about that. Okay, we'll swing through the atrium. It will answer your question, though not to your satisfaction, I suspect."

There was a long moment of silence as she went left and continued down the hallway, coming to a sealed doorway.

Sammi stepped around them and pressed her hand to the panel. The door slid open and Max gaped in shock as the goon carried her farther into the room.

The atrium was dominated by a single curving window and beyond—the endless black of the ocean rather than the stars Max had been expecting.

"We're underwater?"

"A proper hero's hideout," Sammi replied with a self-deprecating smirk. "When things started to go sour between my great-grandfather and yours, he told Alex that this place flooded. It had been a minor lab, dedicated to attempts to grow the seaweed, which had already been accomplished by that point. So who cared?" She shrugged. "I guess no one ever double-checked to verify it really had flooded. Now I use it as a good base for Earth. It's cool and quiet and, best of all, unknown."

"You're not growing the algae here now, though. Your operation is off-planet, isn't it? It has to be. You couldn't risk the authorities discovering it was being produced." Max muttered a curse. There was a slight whoosh behind her as the door closed. "That's why we found the dirt from Trappist, isn't it?"

"Very good. You're smart, Max. I like it. Trappist-1e was wild enough we were able to hide our production facilities on the opposite side of the planet. In the early days we could blend in with the others in the habitats and have access to supplies and shipments from Earth. But lately we've had to accommodate the spread of humanity across the surface. Trappist-1e has water at the right salinity levels, though just a smidge higher than Earth's seawater. There've been some payoffs for having more people there. It was trickier initially, but now there's so much traffic no one knows who's coming from where. And IDs are easily hacked."

It was more than a little terrifying how she said that with such light dismissal. IDs should not be easily hacked, and the things Sammi was telling her spoke of an organization with a far greater reach than she'd thought. To have hidden this on Trappist . . . Shaw had been right.

We had no idea who we were messing with.

A second door opened on the far side of the atrium into something that looked like a small mess hall. It was as deserted as the rest of what Max had seen, and the goon carried her over to a table, dropping her on her feet and then pushing her down before she could even contemplate rushing him. Sammi took a seat at a different table, crossing one leg over the other in a pose of careful nonchalance, and waved a hand at the goon in dismissal.

"So," Max said. "Want to tell me Thomas's side of the story?" She wasn't about to admit to Sammi that she didn't know the details of what had happened to cause a grudge that had lasted past her great-grandfather's death.

"They were partners, Max, at least until Alex decided he wasn't going to listen to Thomas anymore. And the reality is, Alex wouldn't have gotten very far without my great-grandfather. He's the reason they had a breakthrough with the seaweeds. He's the reason why the serum works so well to protect against radiation. Your great-grandfather balked when it came time to make the hard decisions. He wanted to make an inferior product because the 'risks' of going all in were beyond him. Even though Thomas had developed a way to hide the odds from the government."

"You mean the fact that one in twenty people would have died from it?"

Sammi stared at her for a long moment, a muscle ticking at the side of her jaw. "It's a necessary flaw in the design, if you even want to call it that. Thomas knew that it was the only way to make the treatment work for longer and not require followups. But the newly formed Coalition government never would have gone for something in the early days that would have put people at risk like that. So he told Alex they needed to hide the results."

"Alex refused." *Sorry, Great-Granddaddy, I underestimated you.* "He was doing the right thing."

"Don't act like Alex was some saint. He chose to sell it. He chose to put a leash around humanity for all time in the name of making a legacy for himself. Endless boosters and still less effective than what we've developed." Sammi fisted her hands. "He betrayed my great-grandfather! He was going to turn him over to the Coalition government, testify against him on charges of attempted mass murder and danger to the survival of humanity!"

Max lifted an eyebrow.

Danger to the survival of humanity wasn't a charge the CHN threw around without reason, but she could see it being applicable in this case. The images of the dead people in her sister's office flashed through her mind and Max picked her next words with a great deal of care.

"So what happened?" she asked. "At the risk of getting you mad at me, this is the first I've heard of any of this. There's no record of your great-grandfather in any of the history books."

"Thomas knew the authorities were closing in on him, so he paid a man to do a DNA sheet and then blew up his car with the man in it. Everyone was so relieved to think that he was dead, they just erased him from the narrative and didn't bother to look any deeper."

Max swallowed down the horror as Sammi so casually talked about her great-grandfather murdering a man so he could run instead of facing the consequences of his choices. "So he hid here on Earth?"

Sammi smiled. "He had samples of his drug, enough for him and those few he still trusted after your great-grandfather turned everyone against him. He developed a plan to get off-planet as soon as the habitats on Trappist were finished, and the ships started leaving."

"The missing system jumper ships."

"Some of them. There were only two from the first group.

The others had far more recruits, especially the later waves. We needed the ships and the people to work in the labs. All those unregistered would stay off the radar, made it easier to move about." Sammi stood and spread her hands wide. "Plus, everyone thought he was dead."

"Is your great-grandfather still alive?"

"No." Sammi shook her head. "As good as the first serum he developed was, it won't keep a person alive forever. But my grandfather and my father made it off this planet. I was born on Trappist and it's far more my home than Earth will ever be."

"So, the big question," Max said. "What do you want with me? Hostage? Ransom?"

"Oh, no. We're working on something even better than what my great-grandfather created, Max." Sammi leaned against the table, bending over to look at Max, and the fanatical flame in her eyes was terrifying. "I want you to join us. I know you don't like your family. Help me destroy them and you'll live for a thousand years."

"Sector fifty-seven is clear," Jenks said with a sigh. She leaned back in her seat and rubbed at her burning eyes.

"Swap out with Sapphi," Rosa replied, and Jenks stood, gratefully handing over the tedious search to her teammate.

"I'm going to go give Nika a call, get him caught up."

Rosa nodded without looking away from her screen. Jenks left the bridge and hauled herself up the stairs to the common room, collapsing into the worn couch in the corner. Ma was sleeping. Tamago was flying the ship over the endless black water of the Atlantic. The lost signal was about as much help as trying to find a flag on a buoy you'd planted an hour previously. They had a general idea of where to look, but that was it.

She'd sent Nik a message just before they'd taken off, a short and to-the-point note about what had happened, but it had done next to nothing to keep him from trying to figure out more. The newest message from Luis said that Nika had shown up at HQ with a very beleaguered nurse in tow.

Jenks took a deep breath. "HQ Control, this is Petty Officer Khan with Interceptor Zz5, can you put me through to Commander Nika Vagin?"

"Can do, Petty Officer. Please stand by."

The screen in front of her went black and then Nika appeared. His hair was disheveled and his face even paler than normal. His left arm was covered by the dark blue hoodie he was wearing, but the right sleeve was pinned up and Jenks had to tear her gaze away from it before the pain swallowed her whole.

"Jenks." His eyes narrowed. "You look like shit."

"Pot and kettle," she replied. "Shouldn't you be at the re-hab facility?" She wondered why he didn't have his prosthetic on but couldn't bring herself to ask the question.

"Thank you!" came someone's voice from off-camera and Nika's grin flashed bright for just a second.

"Captain Merlo agrees with you. But I got discharged from the hospital for good just after the Games, so he's only around because I'm letting him annoy me."

A handsome man with a neatly trimmed beard poked his head into the frame. "Enrique. Hi, Jenks. 'Discharged' doesn't mean running around at all hours of the night. Maybe you can talk some sense into your brother."

"Don't count on it," Jenks replied. "His head's as hard as a rock."

"Are you two finished?"

"Not hardly." But the captain smiled at her and mouthed *He's all right* before he pulled his head back out of the frame.

"I don't have any good news for you," Jenks said, rubbing at her face. "We're going over the area where Max's signal was last seen but it's a lot to cover."

"That's all right, you'll find her." Nika smiled, then winced as he shifted. "We've got some stuff here. Hey, Enrique, go get Luis, will you?"

"Don't fall out of your chair again while I'm gone."

"Again?"

"He's joking." Nika shook his head. "I'm fine."

"You're not. Damn it, Nika. You should be in bed. What's going on?"

"My body didn't like the fake arm, or the stress caused a

reaction. I'm fine," he repeated, his blue eyes filled with a familiar annoyance. "If you think I'm going to lie in bed while Max is in danger you've been kicked in the head one too many times."

Jenks blinked at the fury in his voice and her next words were softer. "Nik, you know she'd be the first one to tell you the same thing."

"I know." He sighed. "But she's a Neo, which makes her family." He smiled softly. "I can't sit here and do nothing, any more than I could if it were you out there."

His answer wrapped around her heart and Jenks closed her eyes for a moment at the surprising tears that threatened. "I know you would. Where do you think I learned that kind of loyalty from?"

Luis appeared in the frame, settling into a chair next to Nika. "Hey, Dai."

"What've you got?"

"Slowly piecing things together here. Bosco and Ria seem to have decided to grudgingly cooperate now that a Carmichael's life is actually on the line."

Jenks raised an eyebrow at the bitterness in his voice but didn't comment.

"Your target is Sammi Gerard. I'm sending you a file on her, but the important detail is that she's apparently the great-granddaughter of Thomas Gerard, who was a partner of Alexander Carmichael's. We don't know if she's in charge of the dupe LifeEx operation, but it seems likely. Ria thinks she's been brainwashed by stories of how Carmichael somehow cheated Gerard out of a stake in the company." He shrugged a shoulder and glanced off-camera with a frown.

"We're just finding this out now?"

"I know." Nika shook his head. "Pretty sure that's not the only secret they've kept from us."

"Great—a fight between rich people."

"The story I'm getting from Ria, with a great deal of push-back considering her sister's in danger, is that Alex wanted to use the less risky version while Gerard wanted to lie to the CHN about the dangers of the original serum. He was apparently something of a Populationist."

Jenks winced. Populationists were hard-liners. People who believed that the unchecked spread of humanity had caused the Collapse and that the only way to prevent a second disaster was draconian population control. They'd lost favor and ground in the centuries since the Collapse, but there were still some cells left who hadn't bred themselves out of existence.

"Alexander turned him in to the Coalition government, there was a fugitive hunt, and he died when his vehicle exploded."

"There are some massive holes in that story," Jenks replied.

"Starting with the fact that he had no family. So where did his great-granddaughter come from?" Luis rubbed a hand over the back of his neck. "I'm leaning on Ria as much as I can, but it's difficult with Bosco running interference and Stephan reminding me that she's not a suspect." He gave Jenks a rueful smile. "Not gonna lie, I kind of wish you were here instead of looking at a whole lot of water."

"Tell me about it." Jenks made a face. "Though experience tells me that would just end in me getting demoted again."

Nika chuckled. "We'll handle it. I'm about to go in and play up the wounded Neo bit, see what we can't shake loose."

"You don't have to do all that much playing," Jenks replied. "Luis, if he's not back in the rehab facility after he gets done with Ria I'm holding you personally responsible."

"Understood."

"Really?" Nika looked at Luis, who shrugged.

"Sorry, Commander. I'm way more scared of her than I am of you. Plus, I've got Captain Merlo on my side."

"He does!"

Jenks chuckled at Enrique's interjection and waved good-bye before she closed out the connection.

"How's Nika?" Rosa asked as she came up the stairs.

"He looks awful, and he's at HQ."

"What?" Rosa stopped on her way toward the kitchen.

"I know, maybe you can call back and yell at him. There's a nurse with him, though, and I just threatened Luis with bodily harm if he didn't take Nika back to the rehab facility right after Nik talks with Ria. Who's not being particularly cooperative, by the way." Jenks pushed to her feet.

"I need coffee and for you to start at the beginning," Rosa said, and continued to the kitchen.

ROSA STARTED A FRESH POT OF COFFEE, GRATEFUL THAT Jenks got the hint and was quiet for as long as it took to brew and for Rosa to pour herself a cup.

"Luis said Ria isn't being as forthcoming as he'd expect her to be given that Max is in danger. Bosco is also—" Jenks paused as she rolled a few word choices around in her mouth before she picked something surprisingly diplomatic and brought Rosa up to speed.

"Ria knew this whole time just who could be responsible for the dupe." Rosa sipped at her drink, swallowing down her bitter curse along with the coffee.

"The more I learn about her family, Commander, the more I dislike them."

"I'm in agreement with you. I trust Nika and Luis to get what they can from her. That's all we can do for now. We'll—"

"Commander, get on the bridge!" Sapphi's call echoed up from downstairs even as it came through the com channel, and Rosa muttered a curse that would have earned her a slap from her mother.

"Pick one or the other, Ensign!" she hollered back, grabbing her coffee and rushing down the stairs with Jenks on her heels.

"Sorry, Commander. I got excited. Look, I was tired of staring at nothing at all, so I decided to play with the filters some to see if anything unusual would pop up on the scans." Sapphi tapped at the console as rapidly as she spoke. "Ultraviolet filters, extra CO_2 output, any variation in the heat would have even helped, but nothing. So instead I started pok—"

"Sapphi, I need you to focus," Rosa said, "and just tell me what you found."

She blinked. "Right, sorry again. I found that." She pointed at the screen.

"And what is that?"

"An underground lab that used to belong to LifeEx Industries."

"Why the f—" Rosa cleared her throat. "Why didn't we know about this from the outset?"

"It's not on the list of properties owned by the company," Tamago replied before Sapphi could. "Saph and I were talking about how rich folks never put all their things on paper and we got to wondering if there would be something up here. You know, because of the seaweed."

"And again. How did you find the *location*?"

There was a moment of silence. Then Sapphi smiled a smile Rosa knew all too well. "I'm not saying I did, but I may have hacked into LifeEx's archives for the location."

Rosa closed her eyes and took a deep breath.

"It was just the archives. Their security is good, but I'm better, and I figured—"

"Sapphi, it's fine," Rosa said. "I think we'll come up with some other reason for finding it, though. If you can stand not to brag about it."

The ensign mimed locking her mouth shut and tossing the key over her shoulder.

"So, do we think she's in there?" Jenks asked.

"We're going to find out. Go wake Ma up and get prepped. Sapphi, get us a reading for the water so we can sync our gear. I'm going to put in a call to HQ." Rosa headed for the side console as the others scrambled to follow orders.

"Hey, Rosa." Nika was sitting shoulder to shoulder with Luis when he answered the com. "What's up?"

"I'm told you'll be going back to the rehab facility when you're finished there."

"That's the rumor." Nika grinned. "Mom."

"Commander Mom," she corrected absently. "And good. We found an underwater lab."

"What? How?" Nika asked, Luis's words tumbling over the top of his.

"Sapphi. I'm sending you the coordinates and the specs. What I need is for you to get someone at the NeoG station off the coast of Scotland to give us permission to go in. You've got ten minutes until we get to the site."

"They're going to want to send their own people in, Commander."

Rosa glanced at Luis. "I know, but forward them on to me if you need to. We're here. It's my crew in the water. We're going in, with or without permission."

"I'm scrambling two more Neo teams from here. I want you to have backup. There's no way of knowing what you'll be facing down there," Luis said.

"I'm not going to wait, Luis." She watched the expression race across his face before he shook his head.

"You should, Commander."

"You're sure Max is in there?" Nika asked.

"It's the only thing even remotely close to where her signal vanished," Rosa replied. "And I'm not letting her be someone's prisoner one second longer than I have to."

"Okay," Nika said with a nod. "We'll make it happen. Got it. I'll call you in ten."

Rosa tapped a fist to her chest. "You got my back."

"You've got mine," Nika replied. She saw his hesitation as he tapped his own chest with his left hand, but he leaned forward to touch his forehead to the screen.

Rosa nodded once and the screen went dark.

The best thing about the Interceptor ships was that despite their primary use in space, whoever had designed them had decided to stay as close to their Coast Guard roots as was possible and made the ships multipurpose. They could run in space, in atmo, or underwater.

"We're on the surface, nose in the water. Beginning propulsion swap." Ma nodded to Tamago and the petty officer hit the switch.

"Captain Russo, Commander Uli, we are beginning descent," Rosa said to the other two Interceptor boats from HQ who'd pinged them just moments ago.

"Roger that. We are about half an hour behind you, Commander Martín. Save some for us."

"No promises."

Jenks couldn't remember the last time they'd taken *Zuma* underwater and so she had to struggle to keep her foot still and not rapidly tap it on the floor as the propeller section on the back of the ship slid out. The impulse engines kicked over, shutting down their outside ports as the propellers rose. Their energy would feed into the propellers instead, pushing the ship silently through the water.

"Propeller section locked."

Jenks exhaled. "That's one," she muttered, ignoring Rosa's amused look.

The next test was the pressure. Interceptors had a design depth of fifteen hundred meters in the waters of Earth and various ratings for the atmospheres of Jupiter and Venus. Jenks wasn't even going to apologize for being nervous about taking *Zuma* out of her normal element and into the dark waters that were lapping against the main window. It wasn't the water that bothered her; it was that everything failed eventually.

"Go on, Ma," Rosa said.

Zuma's Ghost slipped into the ocean without a sound. "Lights on."

"They can't see us coming, right?"

"Shouldn't be able to," Rosa replied just behind her shoulder, and Jenks looked up. "We're shielded, running silent."

Ma piloted them along the ocean floor.

"And it's just a laboratory anyway."

"It's an evil lair," Jenks shot back at Sapphi. "If I was in there I'd be keeping an eye out for someone coming to rescue the person I'd kidnapped from NeoG headquarters."

Rosa put a hand on her shoulder and squeezed lightly before releasing her. "Then we're all glad you're in here with us."

"Yeah, me too." She rubbed her tongue over her teeth and glared out at the darkness on the other side of the window. "I'll be better when Max is safe, though."

"Right there?" Ma pointed off to his right and Sapphi looked up from her console.

"Yes. Schematics say there's an airlock just fifteen meters away. The wreckage over there will help hide us."

"Wow," Jenks breathed into the air as the hulking remains of an ocean vessel loomed up out of the darkness. "Do we know what ship that is?"

Sapphi tapped on her console. "There's a few in this area from the early days of the Collapse wars—could be HMS *Queen Elizabeth*, guessing from the size."

Jenks swallowed down the impulsive question about going to look for the name. Her teammates wouldn't think she didn't care about Max; they knew better, and her random fascinations were hard enough to manage without something as amazing as an actual relic of the early Collapse wars. But the other two Interceptor teams Luis had scrambled were also on the line as they flew in and she didn't know them at all.

"Someone make a mental note to plan some kind of diving trip for Jenks the next time we're on leave," Rosa said, and Jenks grinned as the others chuckled.

"All right, we're down. Doge, you're in charge until we get back." Ma grinned at Sapphi's look. "I'm kidding. Doge, the ensign is in charge."

"Roger that, Master Chief," Doge replied over the team channel. "Ensign Zika is in command."

Jenks patted Doge on the head as she stood. "Behave yourself, pup. We'll bring the lieutenant back."

Doge bumped his head into her leg, same as he did before any mission, and then took up a spot next to Sapphi's chair.

"Let's go," Rosa said with a nod. Jenks echoed it and followed her to the airlock. Ma and Tamago got in behind them and they slipped their helmets on, the soothing sound of checks and double checks filling Jenks's ears before Rosa gave a thumbs-up. Jenks gave her own and the commander turned back to the panel.

"Cycling the airlock now, Sapphi. Brace, everyone."

Jenks grabbed for the bar behind her as the water started bubbling up from the vents in the floor. Within moments the airlock was filled with seawater.

"Opening the outside door."

"Roger that, Commander. We'll keep the lights on here for you," Sapphi replied.

Jenks hooked one hand around the strap of the pack on her back, reaching for the opened doorway with her other and flipping on her helmet lights as she followed Rosa into the blackness.

They headed through the dark, weaving their way across the wreckage-strewn ocean floor, following the map Sapphi had synced to their DD chips.

"You almost into the system, Sapphi?" Rosa asked. "We'll need someone to open the door for us and I don't think that the current occupants will be all that helpful about it."

"I'm in. Trying to figure out how to isolate that airlock so it doesn't show on the internals. But here, watch a show while you're waiting."

Jenks blinked as the security camera feed came online in front of her eyes and immediately zeroed in on Max, zip-tied at wrists and ankles. There was blood on her shirt and her nose looked broken, again, but otherwise she was unharmed. A slender blonde whom Jenks assumed was Sammi Gerard was talking animatedly to her while perched on a nearby table. "Saph, do we have more channels?"

"You've got the whole package, just flip through."

"Lot more people than I thought. Is this a working facility?" Jenks said.

"Looks like it. Tamago, give me a rundown on security," Rosa replied.

"I'm seeing four in what looks like a security booth on the north end. Three more in a room sixteen meters from our current location. And three sets of two on patrol throughout the facility. One group headed toward Max, the other two groups are in the east and west corridors. They're all armed, swords and what I really hope are stun guns rather than real ones because that would not be smart."

"Confirmed," Ma said.

"Here's a map of the facility—I can update locations on it but they won't be in real time so you're going to have to pay close attention to those patrolling goons," Sapphi said. "I'm cycling the airlock now, Commander. Be prepared; if my ruse didn't work you're going to have about thirty seconds to get in and get to stomping heads."

"Sapphi, what's the closest room to the airlock?"

"To your right, first door you hit on the right. There's . . . one occupant. Scientist, I'm assuming from the lab coat. Unarmed. I'm starting a loop for the security feed now."

"Is the door locked?"

Sapphi whistled. "No, but I'll open it for you when you get there. I'm trying to get control of the whole system. It's just going to take me a little bit to do it without being noticed."

"Jenks, once we're in the airlock give Max's suit to Ma. You take point. I want you to subdue that person in the room before I clear the doorway."

Jenks blew out a breath as the answers came across the channel and rolled her shoulders, preparing herself for what was coming. "Am I killing, Commander?"

"Not unless you have no other choice."

Rosa's voice was reassuring. Jenks didn't like the thought of it, but she'd do it if necessary. As much as she loved to fight, people so often assumed she didn't mind the killing, and she had killed people already in the name of the NeoG and the CHN.

But it took a little piece of her to do it, and she wondered sometimes if she'd end up empty at the end of it all.

The outside door opened and they moved inside, Jenks shrugging out of the pack that held Max's suit and passing it over to Ma. The water level started to drop as Sapphi cycled the lock again.

"We are still clear as far as I can tell," she said.

"No movement from the goons?" Tamago asked.

"Just normal."

"We're keeping helmets open but on, everyone. I want to be able to grab Max and bolt if necessary. We're outnumbered and in unfamiliar terrain here."

Jenks shifted past Rosa, pulling her sword free and moving into the corridor. The hallways were quiet and empty. She reached the door on the right and it slid silently open.

"Haskins, please tell me you brought lunch with you. I'm—" The words died on the man's lips and he went cross-eyed staring at the blade Jenks pointed in his face.

"Hi there," she said.

"I KNOW YOU DON'T LIKE YOUR FAMILY. HELP ME DESTROY them and you'll live for a thousand years."

"If I say no, are you going to kill me?" Max asked.

Sammi laughed. "Well, not today, though I admit I won't be able to let you go right away, either."

"Believe me when I say I'm not looking for you to change your mind on this, but why wouldn't you?"

"Max, it's a wide universe out there with a lot of places to hide. You have no idea."

"I work out there, you know; I kind of do have an idea." Max tapped a finger on the arm of the chair. "But I get it, you'll vanish. We won't be able to find you. What do you want from me?"

"I want your help, Max. I can't get someone inside LifeEx Industries, believe me, I've tried. Your sister's security is too good. But you? You could go anywhere, access anything."

"To do what? I'm not part of the company. I don't have access to anything in the building unless my sister gives me permission. Your operation on Trappist is on the ropes, and even if it wasn't, it's not like you can take over LifeEx Industries. That's not how this works."

Sammi's smile was cold. "Max, you misunderstand me. I don't want to take over LifeEx. I want to burn it to the ground." She reached in her pocket and pulled out a syringe. "You have access to your family, to their private stores of the serum. There's enough in here to contaminate the whole batch. They use it and poof!"

Max's stomach twisted in horror. "You're talking about killing my family."

"Well, yes. See, Thomas figured out how to isolate that risk factor that accelerates the aging. He couldn't remove it from the serum, but he could increase its effectiveness." She wiggled the syringe with a smile. "The early version was a very effective way of dealing with traitors."

"Robin and Simon Holute. Ostin Prech. You killed them."

"They objected to our plan. Got cold feet at the thought of slipping the dupe into the mainstream LifeEx distribution and the deaths it would cause. Necessary deaths, you understand. Humanity is already expanding past what we should."

A second horrible realization crawled up Max's spine. "You're a Populationist."

"Of course I am." Sammi shook her head. "We forget all too easily. It's only been a few hundred years since the Collapse, but now it's nothing but the arena of historians and fodder for entertainment. LifeEx has made it worse, giving people longer lives. We were going to use the dupe for the first culling. But now we'll have to resort to more drastic measures."

Think, Max. You've got to figure out a way to get out of here and warn someone.

"How much of that do you have?" Max asked, tipping her head at the syringe.

"Not enough, but we're ramping up production at the facilities we have left. NeoG has been putting everything in jeopardy with their poking around. I had to change my timetable up some. When it's ready we'll proceed. This one is contagious." She smiled. "As I said, the early version was effective on everyone. Only those who are using our serum will be safe from this. What do you say, Max? You in?"

"You are . . ." Max grappled for a word to use. "No. I'm not in. This is genocide."

"This is justice. You hate your family."

"I don't want them dead!" Max pushed to her feet. "You

don't get it. This isn't just about my family. It's about the oath I swore. I won't turn my back on that and leave people to die. Not on my watch."

THE TECH'S NAME WAS HAN WANG LEI AND HE PROVED TO BE a helpful source of information once Rosa was able to get him to stop babbling about not wanting to die.

It was, of course, all bad news. The lab they were in was being used for research into the dupe and development of the particular defect that sped up the aging process.

"Fucking Populationists," Jenks muttered from her spot next to Han, who gave her a nervous look.

"We can't have a repeat of the Collapse . . ." He trailed off when Rosa snapped her fingers at him.

"Your boss kidnapped a member of the Near-Earth Orbital Guard, Han. Which makes you an accessory, never mind the charges that are going to happen when things settle from this shit storm." Rosa gestured around them. "At this point a second Collapse is the least of your worries."

"Commander, I've got the other two Interceptors on approach. Captain Russo is wanting to speak with you."

"Put him through, Sapphi," Rosa replied, moving away from their captive and closer to the door. "Captain."

"Commander, what's your status?" Captain Yuri Russo was a stocky, dark-skinned man.

"We're in a lab just off the south airlock. Sapphi can send you a breakdown on the hostiles. Lieutenant Carmichael is in enemy hands on the far side of the base. We're currently figuring out the best way to reach her without alerting anyone to our presence."

"Hey, Rosa."

"Josie." Rosa smiled. "Wasn't expecting to hear your voice."

"Heard you needed some help," Commander Josie Uli replied. "I'm seeing three airlocks in total, is that correct?"

"It is. We've got one locked down. Sapphi's working on the rest of the system."

"I'm almost in, Commander."

The door opened on the heels of Sapphi's announcement and for a split second it was a toss-up who was more surprised, Rosa or the guard standing in the doorway with a lunch tray.

Rosa recovered first, years of training moving her sword arm up in a sweeping arc. The razor-sharp blade cut through metal, clothing, and skin. She saw the guard's mouth open but the shout of alarm died in a choked gurgle as the woman crumpled to the floor.

Han's terrified scream cut off with a thumping noise and Rosa turned as Jenks lowered the man to the floor. "He's fine," she said. "I mean, concussion probably, but better off than her." She gestured at the dead guard and the rapidly spreading pool of blood.

"Rosa, what's going on down there?" Josie demanded.

"Little surprise, we're all fine here," she replied. "Get moving, you two. Sapphi, where should they come in?"

"Wipe your face," Ma said, tossing a spare lab coat in Rosa's direction. "We're going to need to move. I'd bet they've got some kind of biometrics on their guards."

An alarm rang through the air.

"I've got control of the airlocks, Commander," Sapphi said. "Might be best for backup to come in through the south one and make for the bay. There's two ships in there right now. We'll want to make sure no one slips out that direction."

"We'll park the ships outside," Captain Russo said. "Just to deter anyone from getting any ideas."

"Keep people alive if you can," Rosa replied. "I want someone to question when this is all over. This thing is bigger than just Max's kidnapping."

"Sounds like a plan. You go retrieve your wayward lieutenant, we'll hold things down around here."

"Hey, Rosa, about Max?"

"What, Sapphi?"

"She's on the run, headed your direction."

MAX FELT ODDLY CALM AS SHE STARED SAMMI DOWN. SHE was going to die here, that much was certain, but far better to do it standing up for what was right. What she'd fought to have her whole life.

"Max, you are making a terrible mistake."

The door to her left opened. "Sammi, you need to come look at this," the man in the doorway said, and Sammi huffed a little sigh before she got to her feet and followed him from the room.

Door at the far side, Max, move!

She bent over even as the voice in her head shouted the order and brought her bound hands down sharply against her back. The zip tie snapped on the second try, the edges cutting into her wrists.

Whispering a prayer of thanks to her kindergarten bodyguard, Max dropped on a knee, fumbling at the heel of her sneaker for the razor blade she'd kept hidden in the sole of every pair of shoes since Hoa had shown her the trick.

"You never know when you may need it, my darling."

She sliced through the zip tie at her ankles just as Sammi came back in the room. Max vaulted over the table and sprinted for the door. It slid open as if expecting her and she slipped through it, hearing Sammi's shouts as it shut behind her.

Max didn't stop to investigate the impact noise or the sudden grinding as the door shuddered closed, dodging around the white-coated lab techs who appeared in the corridor. They were milling about in confusion over the sudden alarm blaring through the air.

"Get down!" shouted an unfamiliar voice, and the lab techs complied. Max vaulted over one man, grabbing for the corner and skidding around it in a sharp left turn. The sizzling sound of an illegal pulse rifle cut through the air, the electrical shot slamming into the bulkhead behind her, leaving a burn mark the size of her torso. Now she knew what that noise had been and she did not want to get shot by that gun.

I have nothing, no map, no fucking exit. Think, Max!

There had to be a ship bay in this place.

She grabbed a tech who emerged from their room, jerking the wide-eyed person close. "Where's the transport?"

"What?"

"The fucking transport!"

"That way, I—"

Max barely let them go in time. They went down twitching as the next shot hit them square in the back.

"That's enough, Max," Sammi said from down the hall. "I will have Carmine shoot you. It won't kill you but it'll hurt."

Max took one step back from the unconscious tech toward the hallway behind her and then another before Carmine snarled at her and the pulse rifle made a threatening whine.

"I'm not going to help you." She was calculating the odds of being able to dive to the dubious safety of the hallway before Carmine shot her when Jenks skidded around the corner out of sight and Max had to bite back a sob of relief.

"Yes, you will." Sammi shook her head. "Oh, Max, one way or another you're going to help us."

JENKS CREPT CLOSER TO THE EDGE OF THE WALL. SHE COULD see Max with her hands in the air, had seen Max's involuntary jerk when she spotted her.

"Max, how many are there?" Jenks hissed.

Max curled down all but two fingers on her left hand for just a moment. "Look, I don't want to be shot with that pulse rifle any more than you want to shoot me with it." She tipped her head slightly to the right.

Jenks felt a little swell of pride. "Commander, found our

girl. We've got two hostiles. One on the right has a pulse rifle trained on Lieutenant Carmichael," she reported over the com.

"I see you, Jenks. Confirm that. The man on the right is Pat Carmine. Busted for smuggling in 2431. Dishonorably discharged from the CHN Marines in 2432 after his trial."

"Why is it always the big fuckers?" Jenks muttered when his profile came up in her vision. "Sapphi, give me something. I can't charge him, he'll shoot me with that rifle and I am not in the mood."

"Hang on. I've got the lights. Can't turn off a section, I'll have to do the whole base. Commander, you copy?"

"Got you, Sapphi. Everyone prepare to switch to night vision on Sapphi's mark."

"LT," Jenks whispered. "Sapphi's going to cut the lights in three. I want you to drop." She watched Max's chin lower in the barest of acknowledgments. "On my three, Saphs. One, two, three."

"Mark it."

The lights went, dropping them all into blackness. Jenks flipped on her night vision, staying low, her hand trailing over Max's back as she kept herself pressed to the wall. The idiot discharged his pulse rifle into the dark just like she'd hoped he would. Three times and then it went silent.

"Empty!" Max shouted, and Jenks sprinted for the pair. She tackled Carmine head-on, heard him grunt as the air was knocked from his lungs, and punched him twice before sliding out of his grip. She already had him on the ground and this wasn't a cage match. Jenks grabbed him by the head, twisted, and felt the fragile bones in his neck snap under the pressure.

"No!"

Jenks saw Sammi lash out at her. Something snagged on her suit as she leaned out of the way. Then there was a rush of air and a thud as Max crashed into Sammi.

Max, whose DD chip was down and who couldn't see in the dark.

"Sapphi, give me the damn lights back!" Jenks shouted, squeezing her eyes shut and turning off her night vision.

The lights came up and she saw Max scrambling to her feet. Sammi lay on her back, a syringe sticking out of her chest. Sammi screamed and Jenks watched in horrified shock as the woman began to age rapidly before their eyes. Soon there was nothing left but a pile of unrecognizable flesh and goo.

"Oh god," Max gasped. "She was telling the truth." She grabbed Jenks's arm. "Run!"

They took off down the hallway, Jenks refusing to look back.

"Jenks, tell Sapphi to shut this sector down. Get all our people out. Shut it down, the filtration, too!"

Jenks relayed the message.

"Jenks, what is it?"

"I don't know! Max said run, I'm not arguing." The pair sprinted down the hallway in the opposite direction.

"You're the only two still in that section, Jenks. I can't close the doors—"

"Close the goddamned doors, Sapphi!" She saw the bulkhead starting to lower at the end of the corridor and pushed Max ahead of her. "Slide! Slide!" she shouted, and Max dropped, sliding under the rapidly dropping bulkhead. Jenks rolled after her, crashing into the LT's side.

"Everything's locked down. Jenks, you want to tell us what the hell is going on?" Sapphi demanded as Rosa and the others came running down the hall.

"Swear to god those things always move slower in the movies," Jenks murmured.

Max laughed weakly.

As the other Interceptors secured the facility, Sapphi flew *Zuma's Ghost* into the transport bay and the team loaded on to fly back to London. Rosa sat in the copilot seat as they left the base.

"We're both fine, Nika." Jenks's voice floated up from the common room. "You, however, are not going to be if you don't get your ass back to rehab."

"Don't look at me," Max said after Nika's garbled reply. "I'll help her. We're headed back to Jupiter as soon as we're done, anyway. We'll see you soon."

Ma chuckled. "He's outnumbered."

"And those two are thick as thieves now," Rosa murmured. "What kind of nightmare have we created, Ma?"

"Not a nightmare. A dream team." He grinned at her.

"I'm going to remind you of that the next time we have to retrieve them from a bar fight." Rosa pressed suddenly shaking fingers to her eyes and felt Ma's hand on her shoulder.

"They're all right, Rosa. We rescued Max. It's all good."

"I know." She took a deep breath and blew it out.

Back at HQ there was a tearful reunion with Max's sister, on Ria's side anyway, though the tears dissipated as fast as they'd formed. The LifeEx president smiled her practiced smile and thanked Rosa for a job well done.

Rosa didn't miss the hard look Jenks threw at the woman's back as she left.

"Sammi said that her serum would protect her from the defect," Max said as Stephan patiently walked her through her official statement.

"I don't think any amount of immunity could stand up to having a syringeful of it injected straight into her chest," he replied.

"I suppose you're right."

"What happened after you tackled her?"

"She was on the ground. The syringe was sticking out of her chest. It was empty. It must have gotten depressed when I landed on her. She screamed, and then . . ."

"Gooshed?" Jenks supplied.

Rosa closed her eyes but didn't say anything. She knew Jenks was as rattled as Max was; humor was just her way of dealing with it. They'd all watched the security feed as Sammi Gerard had dissolved into a pile next to Carmine's dead body. The closed-off section now extended on either side until the CHN Disease Center could arrive and figure out what they were dealing with.

"All this over revenge," Max murmured.

"Pfft." Jenks rubbed at the back of her head. "Some of the best feuds in history were over revenge. I'm not surprised this isn't any different. Hatfields and McCoys. MacGregors and Campbells. Purple and Green Drazi—"

"Jenks." Rosa shook her head.

"I'm just saying."

Stephan chuckled. Max was smiling, though Rosa could see the strain around her eyes.

"You did good," she said. "Both of you."

"We done here, Commander?" Jenks asked Stephan.

He looked to Rosa and she shrugged. "You know where to find us if you have more questions."

"It's going to be a while sorting through those techs and the muscle Sammi hired. I suspect I'll have a visit from the CHN suits before sunrise anyway and they'll claim jurisdiction on all this. To be honest, I'm okay with that." He shook his head with a grim look. "This is a mess, and one that's looking more and more like it's over my pay grade."

"Tell me about it," Jenks said, and Max laughed.

"Get on out of here," Stephan replied, extending a hand with a smile. "I appreciate all the help, Rosa. Good luck keeping these two in line."

Rosa took his hand with a smile of her own. "I'll see you in the sword ring, Stephan."

"HEY, RIA, WE'RE HEADED OUT ON A RUN. WHAT'S UP?" MAX held her tablet up out of the way as Tamago ducked past her with a bag thrown over their shoulder.

"Just wanted to let you know the Disease Center is turning over all the compounds found at the Atlantic lab and another they raided yesterday on Trappist-1e to LifeEx. I've ordered all of it destroyed except for samples of the newest dupe and the contagion so our scientists can—"

"Max, we're headed down."

She waved a hand at Jenks. "I'll be right behind you. Tell Rosa I'm talking to Ria about the dupe." Max looked back at Ria. "Sorry, go ahead."

"So our scientists will be studying it to see if we can't find a cure for the contagion they've created."

Max nodded. "Just tell them to be careful with it. I don't even want to think about what would happen if someone else got their hands on it."

"We will. I promise."

"Great. Was there something else?" Max prompted when her sister didn't continue. "I need to go."

"You're mad at me. Max, I wanted to—"

"You knew. You knew about Sammi the whole time and you didn't tell us." Max met her sister's gaze with a level look.

"I have a business to—"

"I don't want to hear a single word about the business or the legacy. People died, Ria. I could have died. If nothing else matters—that should. Next time you lie to me about a case I'm working on I'll bring you up on charges."

Ria gaped at her. "You really would, wouldn't you?"

"I'd recommend not testing me."

"I'll keep that in mind." Ria stopped in the act of reaching for the disconnect on her tablet and tilted her head. "My baby sister, all grown up. Max, are you happy there?"

"I've never been happier."

"Good." Ria nodded, a pleased smile pulling at her perfectly made-up mouth.

"Do you want me to say thank you?" Max tried, and failed, not to grin at the way Ria blinked at her. As mad as she was at her older sister it was nice to be the one dropping the surprise for a change.

"How long have you known?"

Max shook her head. "For certain? Not until right now. But I suspected back when we met you in your office. You pretended not to know Jenks, but then made a comment about her family—or lack thereof. I already knew there was something strange about me ending up on the best NeoG team out there, I just never thought my own sister would have done something like this."

"You deserved to be with the best. Are you mad at me for it?"

"No, but I would like to know why."

"Because I do love you. Whatever you may think of me right now." Ria smiled. "And I know this family sucks at saying that.

I stood by and watched what our parents did to Scott. I stood by and watched while they did it to you. I couldn't undo either of those things. So I did the only thing I know how to do. I made a deal, got you where you wanted to be." There were tears in her eyes. "But you did the work, little sister. Don't ever let anyone tell you otherwise. You belong there. I just made sure you ended up with people who could keep you safe while not crushing the life out of you."

The emotions surged up in Max's throat and she had to swallow hard to keep them down. "I appreciate you looking out for me. Don't do it again."

"Max, you're my sister."

"I know, but I'm also their family now." She gestured around the room. "If you want to do something for me, lean on the CHN about getting us better equipment, more recruits, a larger budget to do our jobs. We're doing important work out here with barely enough to keep the lights on. These people deserve better. The people we're saving and protecting deserve better."

"Okay, okay." Ria held up her hands with a laugh. "I can't promise anything, but I'll see what I can do. Meanwhile, you take care of yourself out there."

"I will," Max promised. "Love you."

"Love you, too." Ria waved and then disconnected.

Max slipped the tablet into the bag on her bunk and headed across the empty room, tapping a hand against the shining, spiraled Boarding Games trophy as she made her way out of the quarters and toward *Zuma's Ghost*.

ACKNOWLEDGMENTS

I don't want these acknowledgments to ever feel rote or repetitive. The past few years have been a whirlwind and you'd think for the sixth book going to press I'd be old hat at writing these. However, it's the same mad, tearful scramble to remember who helped me during the writing of which book and worry that I'm going to forget to thank someone.

deep breath

All the thanks and love go to my partner, Don, for answering my question of "Should I add to my already overworked schedule?" with "How can I help you?," and for being there to follow through on that offer. I love you more than Jenks loves punching people.

My family and friends mean the world to me; if you're in that group you already know it, and I hope I say it enough. Life is too short not to love each other. Thanks for helping me normalize saying "I love you" to the people we really care about.

To my CP Lisa Didio, who is forever my sister and always so ready to say "What the hell are you doing?" when I stray too far from the plot.

To my agent, Andy Zack, as always, for keeping an eye out for me and for never failing to tell me the truth. Your support and input are invaluable.

To David Pomerico for answering my "Why me?" question in our first phone call with a glowing endorsement that still sometimes gets me emotional. Thanks for putting your trust in me with this idea. It takes a great deal of courage to hand something over to someone else and let them run with it.

Thanks to Laura Cherkas for your amazing copyedits—you are the catcher of repeated words and the asker of the tough questions. And to the rest of the team at Harper Voyager, for all your work to bring this wild bunch to life.

Special thanks to Vadim Sadovski for the simply stunning cover art. It's beyond anything I could have dreamed of and such a stunning representation of this world.

To Mike Headley for reading an early draft of this and immediately throwing his lot in with Jenks. I appreciate all the feedback and the plot help in the zero hour. You're a steely-eyed missile man with a fashion sense the Doctor would be proud of.

Shout-out to my Patreon crew, my social media folks, and everyone who's ever sent me a little note to tell me how much the worlds I've created mean to you. Thank you, from the bottom of my heart and the depths of my soul, for your kindness and your support and your love.

To all the folks on Twitter who threw out a metric ton of names when I was desperately trying to put together competition brackets and realized what I'd gotten myself into. Some of these suggestions made it into the story, others just made it into the brackets. I think I've gotten everyone so I'm desperately sorry if I forgot you. Thanks go out to: @veg-ragabash, @just_hebah, @invisibleinkie, @Rustymarble, @leydhen, @majkia, @synGMW, @jessicaelwood, @iagofromtheash, @SeanMLocke (who offered up his own name and earned a special spot among *Dread Treasure* for it), @saintburns, @ryder_kendra, @MxMaxine, and @Narina_Vhey.

I owe Walk the Moon a debt of gratitude for their song "One Foot." I listened to that thing on repeat through so many of these scenes and there is no better song that exemplifies the love and devotion that the members of *Zuma's Ghost* feel for each other. And Daughtry's song "Undefeated," which was playing in the car on my way to work when I saw how the fight between Jenks and Parsikov was going to go down and I ended up screaming "YES!" in my car at six o'clock in the morning. Keep making music, y'all. We need it.

To Dr. Katie Mack, whose poem "Disorientation" is responsible for the name of the ship that started it all. It can be found at astrokatie.com/disorientation.

To all you new readers, thanks for coming along for the ride; buckle up and watch your hands and feet.

Finally, to my readers who love Hail and Co. so very much. I hope you love this new world and these new characters. Your support has gotten me here in the first place. I am eternally grateful for you.

ABOUT THE AUTHOR

K. B. Wagers is the author of Orbit Books' Indranan War trilogy (the first of which, *Behind the Throne,* has been optioned for film and television by legendary UK film producer David Barron) and Farian War trilogy, which feature the life and trials of former gunrunner/now empress Hail Bristol. *A Pale Light in the Black* is their first book in the NeoG series with Harper Voyager. They are represented by Andrew Zack of The Zack Company.

Having grown up on a farm in northeastern Colorado, K. B. graduated from the University of Colorado with a bachelor's degree in Russian studies. They now live in the shadow of Pikes Peak with their husband and a crew of poorly behaved cats. They are especially proud of their second-degree black belt in Shaolin Kung Fu and three Tough Mudder completions, even if they can't run like that anymore. There's never really a moment when they're not writing, bullet journaling, or hand-lettering, but they do enjoy photography and a good whiskey.

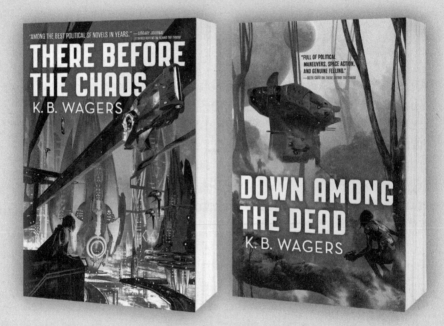